Within Arm's Reach

ANN NAPOLITANO

Within

Arm's Reach

A NOVEL

Shaye Areheart Books
NEW YORK

Published by Shaye Areheart Books, New York, New York.
Member of the Crown Publishing Group, a division of Random House, Inc.
www.crownpublishing.com

SHAYE AREHEART BOOKS and colophon are trademarks of Random House, Inc.

Printed in the United States of America

Design by Lynne Amft

Library of Congress Cataloging-in-Publication Data
Napolitano, Ann.
    Within arm's reach : a novel / Ann Napolitano.—1st ed.
        p. cm.
    1. Irish American families—Fiction. 2. Conflict of generations—Fiction.
3. Pregnant women—Fiction. 4. Catholic women—Fiction. 5. New
Jersey—Fiction. I. Title.
    PS3614.A66W58 2004
    813'.6—dc22

                                                              2003021525

ISBN 1-4000-5188-6

10 9 8 7 6 5 4 3 2 1

First Edition

This book is dedicated to my parents,

CATHARINE MCNAMARA NAPOLITANO *and* JAMES ROMEO NAPOLITANO,

for giving me every opportunity.

Acknowledgments

Helen Ellis and Hannah Tinti have read nearly every word I've written for the last eight years. Thanks isn't a strong enough word, but it will have to do.

For their constant support I'd like to thank: Stacey Bosworth, Lauren Strobeck, Michael Napolitano, Leah Napolitano Ortiz, Peggy Kesslar, Kristen Fair, Suzanne Klotz, Dan Levine, Mrs. Ronning, Dr. and Mrs. Nap, Carol Fishbone and Toby Hilgendorff, Dina Pimentel, Jen Efferen, Chelsea BaileyShea, Joshan Martin, Theresa Lowrey, and the Sumner family.

Thanks to my editor, Shaye Areheart, and my agent, Elaine Koster, for loving this book and giving it life.

For inspiration and instruction I thank my teachers: David Boorstin, Blanche McCrary Boyd, Paule Marshall, and Dani Shapiro.

My love and gratitude to Dan Wilde, who holds my hand.

And I thank the McNamaras for their stories—both the ones they reluctantly told and the ones I made up.

Part One

GRACIE

My grandmother gave birth often, which I suppose increased her odds for tragedy. Her firstborn, a sweet, chatty daughter, died when she was three years old from dehydration and the flu. My mother had become the oldest McLaughlin child by default, and three more of my five aunts and uncles were already walking or crawling, climbing over furniture, and driving my grandfather, whose heart had broken with the death of his first baby, crazy when my grandmother became pregnant with twins.

Today twins are considered a high-risk pregnancy. I'm sure they were then, too, but my grandmother had four kids under the age of six to clean, dress, feed, and teach manners to with the help of Willie, the live-in black maid. My grandfather was a lawyer and on the weekends he played golf and in the evenings he drank scotch. This was long before the days of coparenting, long before it was even a word.

My grandmother had to get my mother and Pat into neatly pressed uniforms and off to single-sex Catholic schools every morning. She had to keep the two youngest home with her while she and Willie split the cleaning, laundry, and cooking. She had to write letters to her mother and her husband's mother each week, updating them on the family's life. On Sundays, out of respect for the Lord, she met the challenge of keeping all of the children quiet and prayerful in their bedrooms without toys or any books other than the Bible.

Pregnancy, even of twins, did not get in the way of the daily routines. It couldn't, really, since my grandmother was, for the first eleven

years of her marriage, more often pregnant than not. So she picked up
toys and assigned the children chores and shushed them around their
father and kept an eagle eye on their manners at the dinner table and
supervised prayers before bedtime as her five-foot-two, petite body
swelled. She occasionally allowed herself a small nap while she sat
upright at the kitchen table, a bowl of peas waiting to be shelled under
her fingertips. But that was it. Birthing children, making a big family,
raising it up right was her main job. She ignored all sharp pains, any
warning signs that something might be wrong. She was never one to
complain. Even now, at the age of seventy-eight, she refuses novocaine
at the dentist's office. She lies perfectly still, hands folded on her waist,
while the dentist, shaking his head in amazement, drills into her teeth.

My grandmother went into labor very suddenly one night after she
and Willie had finished serving the evening meal. She set down a bowl
of broccoli and pressed the heels of her hands hard against the edge of
the table. "Children," she said. "Meggy, elbows off the table. Your
father and I will be eating later tonight. Kelly"—her sharp blue eyes on
my mother, the oldest now that the true oldest was gone—"you're in
charge here, understood?"

She walked carefully out of the dining room, aware of the children's eyes on her, turned the corner, and collapsed. The doctor didn't
make it in time. Willie boiled water and carried a stack of clean towels
to the bedroom and wept while my grandfather, scared and therefore
annoyed, stood by the head of my grandmother's single bed and told
her to keep it down. He cursed the doctor for his slowness. He cursed
Willie for moaning under her breath at the sight of blood. He cursed
his pipe for not lighting on the first try. He cursed the children in the
other room for their existence. He cursed his first child, his sweet baby
girl, for dying on him and leaving him here like this. Shipwrecked and
lonely. Useless.

The doctor, his pockets filled with lollipops for the McLaughlin
children, showed up just as the twins were born. Stillborn. My grandmother must have felt it. After the long last shudder of labor she turned
her head to the wall, shut her eyes, and began to wail. My grandfather
and the doctor were shaken by the noise. The doctor bent over the

babies, one boy and one girl, making sure that there was nothing he could do. There was nothing he could do.

My grandmother's cries got louder.

"Now, Catharine," my grandfather said, looking from the still, purplish babies to this woman whose contorted face he did not know.

The doctor gathered the infants in his arms. "Get them out of here," he said to my grandfather. "She can't take the sight of them."

My grandfather grabbed the babies and, glad to have something to do, an answer to the misery in that room, an order to follow, rushed through the house. He stumbled two steps at a time down the stairs. He strode through the living room, where Kelly, Pat, Meggy, and Theresa sat on the couch and on the floor where Willie had told them to Keep Quiet and Pray. The children watched, frozen in their places as their father moved past them, blood covering his crisp white work shirt, two purple babies held against his shoulder. He was in their sight for only a few seconds, but that was long enough.

Then my grandfather was in the kitchen, where Willie had gone to hide after the doctor arrived. He yanked open the door to the garage and rounded the corner to where the huge metal garbage cans were kept. He lifted off one of the metal lids, and dropped the babies inside. They fell one after the other onto a cushion of broken eggshells and milk gone bad and a few potatoes that had sprouted knobs and spuds too unsightly to just cut off and ignore.

THE STORY of the twins' birth is a strange comfort to me. I recognize myself in the story; I recognize the people I come from and am surrounded by. It proves that even when the worst thing imaginable happens, the individuals involved still survive. The McLaughlins were able to limp away from the death of those babies. They remained a family. Daily routines, petty arguments, and relationships continued. I run this story over and over in my head because I need the convincing right now. I need to know that my world is not about to explode, in spite of any surprise or botched plan I throw at it.

The twins' stillbirth is just one of the refracted images that have

made their way down through the communal memory of my family,
breaking over each of us like a wave. My mother witnessed that day
with her own eyes, and then twenty years later those same eyes saw my
birth. She never spoke of the twins—because my mother, like her own
mother, never speaks of anything important. But still, I was aware of
what she had seen from her seat on my grandparents' living-room floor
long before I was able to put words to it.

That has become my obsession, and sometimes livelihood, putting
words to sensations, inklings, feelings. Looking for the back-story. I
write a weekly advice column for the *Bergen Record*. I used to date the
editor of the paper, and Grayson both came up with the perfect job for
me and let me keep it after we broke up. He is probably my favorite
ex-boyfriend. I love to come up with the right phrase, and to pinpoint
the stories that have made people who they are. I enjoy working out
other people's problems. I like to come up with the final word, the
right answer, and to see that printed indelibly in black and white.

No one in my mother's family ever talks about anything that can
be categorized as unpleasant or having to do with emotions, and, as a
result, they no longer have anything to say. My mother has no idea how
to carry on a normal conversation; my aunt Meggy never stops talking
and yet never says anything constructive; and getting more than four
words out of my uncle Pat is a major feat. For them it's not a matter of
keeping secrets; it's a matter of being polite, mannerly, and tough. The
McLaughlins couldn't spill their woes or ask for help even if they
wanted to, because they don't have the vocabulary. They are stranded
within themselves, convinced that the only way is to silently persevere.

My last name is Leary, but I have a lot of McLaughlin in me. It's
like looking at a reflection in a broken mirror; I can see the sharp corners and growing cracks of my family. I see pride fix my thin lips shut.
I see the irony of my profession, where I ask everyone to come to me
with their heart on their sleeves, while not allowing anyone a good
look at who I am. I spend my nights at the Green Trolley, laughing,
drinking, making eye contact with some man I've never met before and
feeling that lightness spread through me, but I know this is not—was

not ever—a step toward revealing myself. I tell lies in that bar. I sometimes give a false name. I tell men whatever I think they want to hear, and once the words are out of my mouth, I half-believe them. I never tell anything close to a whole truth, to anyone.

Unfortunately, I now have a secret that I won't be able to hide for much longer. There's no lie, fib, or narrative that will keep people from knowing this truth. Everyone will take one glance in my direction and know my story. My belly will give me away. Twenty-nine-year-old woman, not enough steady income, no husband, pregnant.

Tonight I picture my dead grandfather hugging his dead infants to his shoulder, ruining his fine white shirt forever. Breathing steadily, in and out, aware of the muscles in his calves as he pumps down the stairs, aware of the throbbing at his temples, the dryness in the back of his throat, which means he will have a drink at the first chance he gets. He clutches the babies and feels all these things and thinks, At least *I* am alive. Then he thinks it as a question, as he rushes past the living children sitting tight as balls on the floor and on the couch.

Am I alive? Is this my life?

CATHARINE

I stop the car because everyone I have ever lost is standing in the middle of the road.

They are lined up across my lane of traffic in front of the Municipal Building. I see them from a distance but don't immediately recognize their faces. They look like a family on their way to visit the Municipal Building to log a complaint, or to have their day in court. Their body language and slightly formal clothing make them appear serious and purposeful. There is an elderly couple, and behind them a middle-aged man holding an infant, his free hand stretching back to a three-year-old girl with white-blond hair. I wonder where the mother of the little girl and the baby is. Why is the middle-aged man alone with two children? The elderly couple is clearly too old, and too dependent on each other, to be of much help—the man's hand is under the woman's elbow, their heads are cocked toward each other as if afraid to miss one word.

I have to remind myself that times have changed. There are single-parent households now, and wives leave husbands, whereas in the past the man nearly always left the woman. There is no telling what might be possible these days. I am, in fact, thinking about what might be possible as I drive along North Central Avenue toward the Municipal Building. Specifically, I am thinking about my granddaughter Gracie. I am on my way home from a visit with her.

I hadn't seen Gracie or Lila for two weeks, while I was getting over a bad cold. But I noticed the change in Gracie as soon as she walked into the kitchen. There was a heaviness to the way she moved, and a shine to her face. There was more to her than there had been. I didn't say anything, of course. I told myself that I couldn't be right. Gracie's not married. And my instincts are not as trustworthy as they once were. There is no way this young boy-crazy girl—she is still a girl to me—could be with child. I must be losing my mind.

"What's with that face?" Gracie had asked, her hand on the teakettle.

"There's nothing wrong with my face," I heard myself say. "Your grammar is atrocious. Do you even listen to yourself speak? You should pay more attention to language, Gracie. You and your sister don't speak proper English. Your cousins are even worse, I'm sorry to say. Maybe if you'd spent more time in church, listening to the fathers preach . . . Everything's been diluted in you." I had to shake my head to make myself be quiet.

"I know, Gram." Gracie smiled and rolled her eyes at me. I could tell she was trying to help calm me down. "All my problems would disappear if I went to Mass regularly."

"It couldn't hurt," I said. My head ached. "It couldn't have hurt."

I stopped talking then, but I felt no better, no more in control. I couldn't stop my thoughts from careening after this impossible idea about the girl standing before me making my tea the way I like it, with no sugar and a drop of milk. Leaning against the rickety kitchen table in the house Gracie rents from her father, I saw myself, my past, in her. That period in my life when I was endlessly making, carrying, delivering babies. After all, when I was Gracie's age I was halfway through making my family. At twenty-nine I was carrying Meggy, or perhaps Johnny. I had lost my daughter, but not yet the twins.

I am thinking about my babies as I drive closer to the people strung like a chain across the street. I have always had the ability to identify a pregnant woman before she has even begun to show. I wasn't expecting motherhood in Gracie, which is why I wasn't sure right away. But now, my hands wrapped around the unwieldy steering wheel of my car, I know it is the truth. I just don't know how I should feel about it.

I'm nearly on top of the family before I recognize them. It is just a feeling at first, a seizing in the pit of my stomach, and that's when I begin to slow down. My foot presses down on the brake seemingly without my control. The car bucks beneath me. I recognize the individuals, one by one. Mother. Father. Patrick. My eldest daughter. And, cupped against Patrick's chest, is not one infant, but two.

I stop the car. Except for the twins, who are busy yawning and fussing against Patrick's suit jacket, my family looks in my direction with little expression. Patrick doesn't seem to see me at all; he is busy with the children. Mother and Father are leaning toward each other. My daughter is bent over pulling up her knee socks. I give an extra-long moment to gazing at the twins. I have never had the chance to lay eyes on them before. They are so very beautiful, and so very mine that my old shriveled breasts ache, hoping for milk.

When I can think again, I think, My God, I must be dead.

My mother speaks. *No, Catharine, you're not.*

My mother is smiling, and it is a smile I had seen many times before, during my childhood. It is the smile I'd always dreaded because it meant lies and craziness. I had hated to see my mother turn her eyes away from me to look at people she only imagined were there. But now she was pointing that loony smile straight at me. And she had said that I was alive. And somehow I knew my mother had engineered this moment. She had brought me my family.

I scan their faces. Patrick is bouncing slightly on the balls of his feet, trying to quiet the baby boy. The infant and his father look so similar I feel a catch in my throat. Each has a frustrated, balled-up expression on his face. The three-year-old girl, my daughter, tugs on Patrick's suit jacket, wanting his attention. Patrick's face pinkens. I can tell he wants a drink. I can tell he is about to explode. I have seen that look before. I want to warn the children, to get them out of the way, but I can't move.

I told your father you would be able to see us, my mother says.

Please help the babies, I say.

My parents are not listening to me. They are sharing a look. They have forgotten me and mine. Patrick now has our little girl by the arm and he is shaking her, trying to make her quiet. At first she fights him and then she stops fighting and she moves like a rag doll under his touch. The twins, both crushed against Patrick's chest, are shrieking at the top of their lungs. I feel my own breath leave me. Their screams are deafening. Their tiny faces turn purple.

I think, Oh Jesus, it is happening all over again.

And then everything gets louder, worse. The nasal roar of car horns and tires screeching overwhelms the cries of my babies, and then my car door flies open. I think, Oh thank goodness, I can go to them now. I can save them.

But the road in front of me has emptied. My family has disappeared and Kelly's husband, Louis, of all people, is leaning over me, unbuckling my seat belt, taking me by the elbow, half-lifting me out of the car into the clear white light of midday. He is talking to me. His words dance over my head like stars. My son-in-law tells me that I must hold myself together, that my children need me, that my influence is greater than I know, and that before I even think about disappearing—in any way—I need to make things right with them.

LOUIS DRIVES me to the hospital against my will. I want to go home. I want to sit calmly in my room, among my things. I want to be alone, so I can figure out what is happening.

But instead I am put in a wheelchair when I am perfectly capable of walking on my own, and wheeled into an exam room, where a young doctor with a bushy mustache and hair growing out of his ears pokes and prods me and sticks a needle into my forehead and asks stupid questions. When he leaves without even saying *It was nice to meet you*, or *Good-bye*, the nurse tells us to wait and then we are left alone.

I give Louis a good glare now and ask, "What are we waiting *for*?"

"They didn't say," he replies.

This non-answer doesn't surprise me. I have always liked my son-in-law, but he tends to be weak.

There is a clatter out in the hall, and then Lila is standing in the doorway of the exam room. She is wearing a white coat like everyone else in this godforsaken place, but she has the clipped stride and stressed face of my second oldest grandchild. She is in her third year of medical school and she is a natural worrier. It's clear that finding me here in her hospital as a patient has upset her hard-won sense of balance. I blame her father for this, too.

She looks to him first. "Daddy, what's going on?"

"Sweetheart, hi. There was a little accident across the street from my meeting. I just happened to be there."

"I'm fine, Lila, don't worry," I say. "I had a fender bender, that's all. I wouldn't have even come here, but your father insisted. This is an obvious waste of time and money."

Louis clears his throat. "I told you I would cover any costs, Catharine."

"But the waste of time," I say, and am surprised by how upset I sound.

Lila moves to the side of the bed and takes my hand. She is checking my temperature, and to see if my skin is clammy or dry. Lila is my own personal health watch team. Every time I see her she takes my pulse and asks a few specific questions about how I'm feeling. Anger and fright struggle across her round face as she presses her fingers into mine. "How many stitches did they give you?" she asks. "What happened?"

I wave my free hand toward her father. "Louis, why don't you go and track down that woman who said she would check me out. Lila will keep me company."

Louis seems relieved to be freed into motion. "Right," he says. "I'll see if I can't speed things up a little."

We are not a touchy-feely family, and I can tell Lila is as aware as I am that my hand is still in hers. I pull away slowly. I say, "Don't you look professional, in your white coat."

Lila puffs up with pride. "My coat is shorter than the doctor's," she says. "That's how people distinguish the students from the real thing. But I did get to put in stitches yesterday morning. It was kind of an honor, being allowed to do that."

I nod, but I am only half-listening. It has occurred to me that I should take advantage of this time with Lila. If I am going crazy I should make something positive come out of it. I need to talk about my family to my family.

"Gram," Lila says. She still looks shaken. "Do you think it's possible for people to change?"

I am already on my own track; I don't know what she means, and I can't stop to think about it. I say, "I want to get the entire family together for Easter."

Lila squints. "Easter is in a few weeks. Everyone? Even Uncle Pat?"

"Everyone. And I want to have the party at your and Gracie's house."

Lila takes a step away. She has her doctor-in-training expression back on. She thinks I've become disoriented, that I don't know what I'm saying. "You mean Gracie's house, don't you, Gram? I'm just staying there for a few days while I sort out my medical school housing. You know that."

"I don't want you to leave her. I want you to live with her for good."

Lila gives a short laugh that doesn't sound at all amused. "What are you talking about? Gracie and I haven't lived together since we were kids, and there are good reasons for that. Besides, you know that I need to live alone."

"Nobody needs to live alone. You're just more comfortable that way. A little discomfort might do you good."

Lila is squinting so hard her brown eyes have almost disappeared.

"Look, dear." I try to make my voice softer, more charming. I know how stubborn my granddaughter is. By pushing her I am just pushing her away. "Your sister needs your level head. You've always had more common sense. Besides," I say, "it must be financially difficult for you to afford your own apartment. Living with your sister makes sense on so many levels."

"I need my own space, Gram, whether you believe it or not. It's not that easy around here and I need a place to go where I can lock the door and be alone."

I lean forward. I want my grandchildren, and everyone I love, to be strong and tough. Sometimes that requires my giving them a little shove. "Who ever said becoming a doctor was going to be easy? Life is not supposed to be easy, Lila. Easy is a cop-out."

Lila has darker hair and more freckles than her sister. Gracie is pale of skin, hair, and eyes. Gracie often looks washed out, but when she's happy, she is lit by an inner light. Lila always looks strong and vibrant and, at the moment, angry. She is a spotlight to her sister's candle.

I don't look away from her gaze. If Lila wants a staring contest, I will win. She should know that much by now. I say, "So we'll all gather at your house then, for Easter. I can't fit everyone into my room at the home, and your mother gets too stressed out when she has to host these kinds of gatherings. You and your sister will help me, won't you?"

Lila opens her mouth to speak, but the nurse comes in then, a clipboard in her arms, announcing in a bullhorn voice that she is here to check me out. Louis is one step behind her. I'm not concerned that our conversation is cut short. If Lila has something else to say, I'm sure she'll track me down and let me hear it.

WHEN I lay my hand on the doorknob of my room at the Christian Home for the Elderly, I am suddenly so weak I have a hard time turning it. I didn't realize how shaken the accident had left me until then. But I feel better with each step inside. My room reminds me of the hotel suites where I grew up. I am safe in this place, which reduces my whole life to one room. In old-age homes, as in hotels, personal taste and unique touches are necessary to distinguish your space from that of your neighbor next door. It is your possessions—your favorite chair, your grandfather clock, your large black-and-white photograph of every single one of your children smiling at the same moment—that make it home, not a mortgage or a backyard or a husband or a view. This is how my parents lived their entire lives, and this is how I am able to feel close to them now. I prefer feeling their presence in this room to confronting their dead selves in the middle of the road in the middle of the town that I have lived in for most of my adult life.

We lived in three different hotel suites while I was growing up, in three different cities. One in Atlantic City, one in New York City, and the last in St. Louis. It was in that hotel suite that Patrick courted me, and it was in that hotel suite that I left my parents behind when I headed east as a new wife.

I met my husband when I was twenty-three years old, and already an old maid. My two sisters had long since married. I lived with my mother and father in the hotel my father ran. I had graduated from college the year before, and upon my return, the few friends I had left from the area called me a snob within my hearing and ignored me when I spoke to them directly. I didn't care. I was proud of my degree, a Bachelor of the Arts in Nutrition. I was content to live a life that consisted of going to church each morning with Mother and eating dinner with her and my father each night. I was never one who needed much company.

My parents were both from Ireland, but my father seemed to have become American the minute his feet hit Massachusetts soil. He was tall and he stood up straight. He always wore a three-piece suit, rarely drank, and had a firm handshake. He was a successful man who managed four-star hotels in major cities. He had met Franklin Delano Roosevelt and played golf with Babe Ruth. He was a wonderful father.

My mother, on the other hand, had only seemed to grow more Irish, and more eccentric, with each year in the States. Her brogue became so strong that only our family could understand her. During thunderstorms, she hid in the coat closet and prayed at the top of her lungs. She carried a rosary in every pocket; most days she had two or three on her at a time. She would nervously touch the front pocket of her dress, and then her handbag, and then her closed right palm, checking on, reaching for, the ever-present beads. Seated at the breakfast table in our hotel suite, she would often address the empty chair by the window as if it were filled by whomever she was missing most from Ireland just then. Her mother, or her sister Nancy, or her girlhood friend Diandra. "Look, girls," she would say, "see the smile your aunt Nancy has on her face? She always did love my tea best. Say good morning to her, girls. Mind your manners, won't you."

My father would play along. If he'd just walked into the room, he would act pleased to have the chance to chat with Nancy. He behaved as though my mother had done him a favor by delivering her to our hotel suite. "How's the weather in old potato land?" he would say to the empty chair by the window. "Can't say that I miss the gray skies, but I do miss your lovely face, Nancy lass. And I can't tell you how much Lorna longs for your company."

I knew my father did not really believe that my aunt was sitting there under the ray of sunlight, the way my mother did. And as much as I loved him, I could never understand why he pretended to share her delusions. Why did he appear to love my mother *more* for providing him with her silly games and fantasies? Why did he encourage her? It made no sense. When my mother insisted that I address Aunt Nancy, or Diandra, or some other person I had never even laid eyes on, much less spoken to, all I could do was smile stiffly at the empty chair. I was never rude, but I refused to play along.

On my thirteenth birthday, when my father had taken me out alone for an ice cream, I asked him why he didn't lay down the law with Mother and tell her she was acting crazy.

"You're not doing her any favors, Papa." I sat up straight on the counter stool, so pleased that I was finally an adult, and could finally have this discussion with my father. We could speak openly, as one grown-up who had put up with my mother for many years to another. "She thinks it's acceptable to act the way she does because you don't tell her otherwise. If you told her to stop it, she would. Then we could be a normal family. We could talk about normal things. We wouldn't be forced to offer tea and dinner rolls to her, to her"—I struggled for the right word—"her ghosts."

My father put his elbows on the counter, then folded his hands under his chin. His movements were measured and calm. "Another root beer when you have a moment please, ma'am," he said to the waitress. "Catharine, your mother simply brings more life to the room. She is not crazy. She's Irish in a way you and I are not. You must treat her with respect."

I gasped. I was never reprimanded. I never did anything wrong. I couldn't bear for him to think I did. "I love Mother," I said. "I *do* respect her."

But the second part was a lie, and I never got over feeling badly about that. I tried to make up for the lack of respect by loving her even more. I concentrated on how to love her better. I showed her my love every day by running errands, by buying a single yellow daisy to sit in a cup on the windowsill. I gave orders to and fielded complaints from the hotel maids, because I knew Mother hated to look at or talk to black people. I kept her company while my father was downstairs in the offices. I stayed home long after my sisters had married and left. It seemed clear that I would have to give up my entire life in order to prove I respected my mother. And I was prepared to do that.

But then Patrick appeared, and he offered me a way out.

I met Patrick McLaughlin in the dining room of the hotel. I knew my father had engineered the meeting. Patrick was a young lawyer from New Jersey, in town on business. He met my father's qualifications for a son-in-law: He was Irish and he could support me. His parents were poor immigrants who ran a grocery store in Paterson and had sacrificed everything to put their sons through school. But there was no Paterson and no grocery store in Patrick McLaughlin's walk. He was cocky. He carried himself like he thought he was the President, the cat's meow, and the next in line for the throne all rolled into one. I didn't think much of him, until I saw him with my mother.

The first evening he visited our hotel suite, my mother told a story about her home (a story she started reciting before I was born, and which seemed to go on for as long as she was alive, without end) and in the middle Patrick joined in. He spoke about Ireland, too, even though he had never been there. He said his mother was from County Wicklow, and my mother beamed. She leaned forward, her hands

folded over her heart, and told him she had spoken to her old next-
door neighbor Diandra that morning over tea. Diandra had sat right
there—and my mother pointed at that damned empty chair I wished
every day someone would take a match to. Patrick nodded; his eyes lit
up. I gave him a sharp look and saw that he understood that Diandra
had not really been here. Like my father, he was playing along, not
missing a beat. Patrick told me later that at that moment he had felt like
he was home.

I never saw Patrick drink during his stay in St. Louis, so it was only
in his interaction with my mother that I noticed his Irishness. I thought
of what my father had told me ten years earlier, and knew that Patrick
was crazy Irish in the same way my mother was. Yet he was smart, too,
a lawyer, and sensible. He had a down payment on a house in a town
called Ridgewood in New Jersey. He was thirty years old. He was ready
to marry. I couldn't get over the fact that he was equally comfortable
talking money with Father and leprechauns with Mother. He presented
a package in which I could accept the traits he shared with my mother.
I realized, the first evening he sat in our suite, his hat on his knee, that
the answer I had never even imagined existed lay in Patrick
McLaughlin. I would be able to love, and, most importantly, respect my
mother through him.

We married three months later, in front of thirteen guests, at St.
Paul's Church, two blocks from the hotel. Patrick wore white gloves
and a morning suit. I wore a floor-length dress with tiny buttons running from the nape of my neck down to the hem. We left for New
Jersey the next morning in the middle of a thunderstorm. My father
drove us to the train station, and as we pulled away from the hotel I
waved out the back window of the car in the direction of the suite's
windows, even though I knew my mother would be nowhere near the
window in this kind of weather. She would be deep in the closet with
the door shut, her face buried in my father's overcoat, her rosary beads
clutched to her chest. My mother's prayers and violent claps of thun-
der swept me out of St. Louis.

I planned to go back for a visit that Christmas, but by then I was too far along with the baby to travel. And then came Kelly and Patrick Jr. and life became so that I was rarely able to leave the house for a few hours, much less cross the country for a few days. Father came to visit when my first child died, but Mother didn't make the trip. I never saw her again.

LOUIS

I have just walked out of a pointless meeting with the mayor, Vince Carrelli, and the town council when the accident happens. I am standing on the steps of the Municipal Building, trying to decide if it's worth going back in to have another word with Vince, who is acting like an idiot because I caught him drinking again last week, when I recognize Catharine's gray Lincoln heading down the street.

The license plate reads MAC 6. Every Lincoln Town Car Patrick McLaughlin bought had that same license plate, the only difference being which number car it was. When he died, MAC 5 had been parked in the garage. I prepare to wave to my mother-in-law as soon as she is close enough. I figure she's on her way home from Ryan's. Her youngest son lives just over the railroad tracks, in a run-down building across from Finch Park.

As the car draws close enough for me to see Catharine's gray curls and her silver-rimmed glasses, I think she has caught sight of me as well, because she's slowing down. But almost immediately I realize she's slowing down too rapidly. She's driving down the center of a busy road where cars regularly exceed the speed limit. A minivan is gaining on her from behind; I can't tell if the driver has noticed the Lincoln's deceleration. And then, unbelievably, Catharine comes to a stop. She parks the car right where it is.

It's all over in a second. I watch Catharine take her hands off the wheel as if she has decided she is done driving, and then the minivan is on top of her. The driver tries to swerve at the last moment, but he isn't able to clear her completely, he clips the fender of the Lincoln.

I am running across the street before the minivan makes contact, afraid Catharine is going to step out of the car into the traffic that is now passing the Lincoln on either side. I put up my hands, palms out, to signal the other drivers to stop. I pull the car door open and lean in. Catharine is sitting neatly in front of the steering wheel, as tiny as a child, her purse gathered on her lap. There is blood trickling down her forehead.

"Louis," she says. "What in the world are you doing here?"

I DRIVE FAST, but paying close attention to the road, while glancing over to make sure Catharine is still conscious, is not enough to distract me from where we're headed. The last time I was at Valley Hospital was two months earlier, and on that occasion I arrived in an ambulance with a young man who was already dead. It is not a place or a memory I want to revisit, and unfortunately I am now speeding toward both.

When we turn into the hospital's parking lot, I pull over to let an ambulance wail past, red lights flashing. I help Catharine into the emergency room and immediately see the orderly, a chubby red-haired boy, who helped carry Eddie into the hospital. I notice the round scuffed clock above the reception desk that seemed to be stuck at three-thirty that afternoon.

When Eddie was carried into the ER, doctors and nurses surrounded us. People shouted into my ear, across the body. His wife was there, too, in her white uniform, standing on the edge of the fray, although I didn't know until later that it was his wife. That she was a nurse at the hospital who was on duty and had heard the call about the accident, and the name of the victim.

Today I have to stand at the reception desk for ten minutes before I can get anyone to even speak to me. Catharine and I then have to sit on the orange plastic chairs they allot to people who aren't bleeding copiously or in some other way being obvious about dying. Catharine's forehead has a rudimentary bandage on it now and the cut has stopped bleeding, which makes me feel a little better about the situation. She selects a magazine and holds it in her lap. I look down and count the floor tiles. There are sixty-eight tiles in the half of the room we are sitting in.

"You're walking slower than me," Catharine says once they direct us to an exam room.

I look down at her. Despite her resistance, the nurse insisted she be pushed to the room in a wheelchair. "You're not walking," I say.

"You know what I mean," she says. "You're moving like an old man. And why are you screwing your head around like that? Are you looking for someone?"

I almost say, *I am an old man,* but this would just provoke her to argue and there's no point in that. She's annoyed at me for bringing her here, so she's looking for a fight. I stay out of her way by wandering in and out of the exam room until Lila shows up and Catharine kicks me out for good.

I leave the room feeling stronger for the sight of my daughter in her white coat. My beautiful daughter, the future doctor. She makes the hospital look safer to me, more manageable. I feel well enough now to wander the halls. I stop an orderly and ask for directions, trying to ignore the fact that my heart jumps a little every time a nurse turns toward me. I blur my vision as I walk, not looking at faces. What would I do, what would I say, if I ran into Eddie's wife? Maybe if I had known I would end up here this afternoon I would have prepared something, but as it stands now I am not prepared. All I am prepared to do right now is to find the goddamn chapel. I move through the halls—a left, a right, and two more lefts—quickly, trying to look purposeful and collected.

But any composure I have shatters when I turn into the chapel and see the oversized wooden crucifix hung over the tiny altar. I have spent my lifetime attending church, and every crucifix looks different. On some, Jesus has the look of a sweet boy; on others, he is an emaciated man in his sixties. In the church I attended growing up, Jesus had a face as jolly as Santa Claus. The crucifix in the hospital chapel is one I haven't seen before. In this one Jesus has the facial expression and the posture of Eddie Ortiz on the last day of his life.

Right there on the wall is the figure of Eddie lying in a patch of tall grass, curled up on his side as if he has gone to sleep. His flannel shirt tucked into his jeans. His tool belt still fastened around his waist. His dark hair cut short. I can see part of his young man's face. His expression is relaxed. He clearly has no idea what he just lost. On the contrary, his face appears wide open, bared toward a bright future.

My crew had been replacing a roof on a medium-sized Colonial. It was a simple, straightforward job. A couple weeks in duration, tops. Three men on the roof, me checking in a few times a day from the ground. The work was going according to schedule, with no significant hold-ups. Eddie Ortiz had been working for me for six months. He was really good with his hands, and smart, too, a rare combination in a construction worker. He was only Gracie's age, but he had a wife and two little kids, and I knew he had ambitions to move up and gain more responsibility. I'd decided that when this job was finished, I'd give him a raise and he could help me do some supervising. There was too much work for just me to handle by then; Eddie had come along at the perfect time.

But on that cloudless, dry Wednesday afternoon I decided to climb up on the roof to check the men's work. Eddie was showing me a small flaw in the roof's structure when he took a step toward the edge and lost his footing. It happened so quickly that none of us even had a chance to throw an arm out, or yell for help. I will never get over how fast it happened. One minute I was sitting on my heels eating a sandwich and listening to Eddie. The next minute I was standing on the edge of the roof, looking down at the young man lying in a patch of tall grass. His voice still rang in the air.

I am on my knees in one of the pews, but I have not yet uttered a prayer. Eddie is dead on the cross in front of me, Catharine is hurt down the hall. I don't know why I continue to try to fix things. There's no point, but I can't seem to get that through my thick head. It was because I tried to help Vince that the foolish man sabotaged the town council meeting this afternoon and made everyone in the room uncomfortable. I guess you could call Vince and me friends, but it's the kind of friendship that grows out of shared history rather than mutual respect. I've been keeping an eye out for him this past year, since his wife, Cynthia, passed away. Several times, in a wine-induced fog, he has yelled at me about the fact that I am buying up all the land in sight and trying to take this town of Ramsey away from him. After each blowup Vince is embarrassed, and we go through a few awkward weeks, like this one. He probably ran right from the meeting to his barbershop on Main Street, where he will sit with the down-and-out group of guys who are his regulars and who firmly believe the mayor can do no wrong, even if that means him drinking himself into oblivion.

I can't entirely blame Vince for his behavior. I don't know how I would react, or what kind of life I would lead, if I lost Kelly. And yet the truth is that I am in danger of finding out. My wife is barely speaking to me, and I can't blame her. She tried to help me after Eddie's funeral, but I pushed her away. I've continued to push her away. Lately, I have taken to sleeping on the couch in the den, though neither one of us has mentioned that fact out loud. I feel safer there, in the small dark room with the flickering light of television, than I do in our master bedroom. I don't fit well on the couch, but I am able to sleep L-shaped with my legs on the coffee table. It's actually fairly comfortable. I keep the news on all night, the volume low. With the muffled noise in my ears I seem to dream less often and fall asleep more easily. The television keeps me from making up pictures in my head. From hearing voices I don't want to hear. From replaying over and over the afternoon Eddie died.

There is a light pressure on my shoulder, and I jump. I am on my feet and face-to-face with the person before I recognize the nurse who checked Catharine in.

"Is she okay?" I ask. I wonder how long I've been in here. Ten minutes? An hour?

"Mrs. McLaughlin's been checked out. You can both go."

I follow the nurse down the hall. She is a large woman, rectangular-shaped. A white hat perches on her curls like a boat trying to hold on amid treacherous waves. I pose a question to her back. "Do you know if Nurse Ortiz is on duty?"

She doesn't turn around. "No nurse by that name in this hospital."

"Are you sure? I know she works here."

"Not under that name. Is she married?"

"She was." The words are lodged deep in my throat. It takes a cough to get them out. "She was married."

"Maybe she works under her maiden name. Know that?"

I know where she lives. I know that she is bringing up two small children on her own. I know that she appears to be doing all right, from what I've been able to see. "No."

The nurse shrugs with her entire upper body, but the hat still stays in place and I realize I am done following her. I am in the room with Catharine and my daughter, who looks as pale and tired as I feel.

ON THE WAY home from the hospital, I say, in as casual a tone as I can muster, "How are we going to deal with this? Will you make an appointment with a specialist, or should I?"

"There's nothing to deal with, Louis. The doctor said I'm fine. I have a bump on my head, that's all."

I like my mother-in-law, and for over thirty years I've made it a policy not to argue with her. But today seems like as good a day as any to break that rule. I say, "Lila saw your chart. She said the doctor thinks you might have had a tiny stroke."

A minute goes by with me looking at the road and Catharine looking out the window.

"Might have," she says finally. "I've never set any stock by 'might haves.' I might have become a nun. You might have grown up someplace else and never met my daughter. There's no point to that kind of talk."

I glance over at her. "Well, I think you should go back for tests, just to be on the safe side."

"I'll see my doctor."

"O'Malley? That old coot? For God's sake, Catharine, the man's practically blind and deaf. I know Kelly has a doctor she likes. We'll make you an appointment with her. What's important is that we take care of this."

Catharine's voice slams down. "No, Louis. *I* will take care of this. I don't want to discuss it. Tell Kelly what you must, but whatever happens from here on in will be my decision. Now, believe it or not, I have a headache. I'd like to ride in silence."

Her face as expressionless as a slab of Sheetrock, Catharine refuses to say another word.

MY MOTHER-IN-LAW scared the hell out of me the first time I met her. I learned that day that there was no influencing her, and little point in arguing with her.

Kelly had invited me to her parents' house for a Sunday lunch, but it seemed more like she had invited me into a train station. Young adults scattered with a few teenagers seemed to be everywhere at once. Pat and Johnny clapped me on the back and looked me up and down. Meggy came into the living room with a short skirt on, and her father sent her back to her room to change. Ryan and Theresa, the shy ones, each shook my hand and offered me a soda or lemonade. Kelly was shy in those days, too, though less retiring. She stayed close to my side while she made introductions; I could feel how physically anxious she was for them to like me. We were having an early lunch so Patrick could head out to the golf course. Everyone except me had just come from Mass.

"Louis, did you attend church this morning?" Kelly's mother asked. She was a small woman, amazingly trim for having given birth to so many children. I looked at her with some measure of awe. My own mother had given birth only once. She was always talking about how painful that experience had been and what havoc it had wreaked on her body. "Look what you did," she would say, and point to her plump stomach.

Everyone at the table turned polite faces toward me. This was clearly an important question. "I went to five o'clock Mass last night," I said.

"Do you go to Mass every week?"

"Yes, ma'am. With my parents."

Catharine had nodded, and I had been relieved. I planned to ask Kelly to marry me, and I knew that as a suitor I did not have Patrick McLaughlin's approval. Kelly had warned me that he'd written me off because I didn't come from money and though I did have Irish in me, I wasn't one hundred percent. Clearly, I couldn't make up for these lacks, but I was determined to succeed. I'd met Kelly at Bloomingdale's, where she was working at the time, and since then I hadn't been able to think of anything but her. She was so sweet, she laughed at all my jokes, and I suddenly wanted nothing more in life than to take the sadness out of her blue eyes. It seemed clear that she was meant to be my wife. So I thought that if my cause could get some support from Kelly's mother, perhaps she could reason with her husband and I would have a chance. If I only had the opportunity, I was confident I could run with it.

Kelly held my hand under the table during the meal, and that helped me survive the strange, uncomfortable experience. Since Patrick was in charge of leading the conversation from the head of the table, and my presence had rendered him silent above his plate of sliced turkey and his glass of scotch, everyone had to stay quiet. He was a very stubborn man, and even though I believe he grew to like me, it would be nearly a year before he spoke directly to me.

However, there was a wordless current that traveled above and below the table. I was aware of Kelly's legs swinging, kicking at Johnny, who was on her right. There was a shuffling of feet over by Meggy, too, and at one point somebody took a shot that brushed the hem of my pants. Meggy was making eyes at me, her aim more to annoy Kelly than to flirt with me, as far as I could tell. I didn't know who to look at, or whether it was more appropriate to smile or appear expressionless. I felt like I had walked in on a high-level card game for which no one had told me the rules. In many ways, I was to realize as the years went by, I had been right. The McLaughlin family has their own means of communication, secret ways of attack, and fierce allegiances that are unreadable to outsiders. And I have always remained an outsider.

What I did not realize then was that by that point it was fairly rare for all of the McLaughlins to be under one roof at one time. It was school break time—Johnny was only a few weeks from dropping out of high school to enlist in the army, Meggy was home from her Catholic boarding school, and Pat from graduate school. Kelly, Theresa, and Ryan still lived in the stately house in Ridgewood. When the McLaughlins were all together, Catharine was on guard, her eyes moving from her husband to her children's faces and back again. The children, Kelly included, were a bundle of nervous energy, crackling from time to time in a sharp comment, a kick under the table, a pass at a visiting boyfriend. Ryan laughed hopefully at anything even resembling a joke. Theresa pet the small dog under her chair. She had just found the mutt on the street, and it would be promptly evicted by Patrick after lunch. Kelly held on to my hand as if she were a kite in danger of taking off and I was the sturdy post she happened to grab hold of at the last minute.

My own family rarely ate together. My father, who was going to die of a swift, severe attack of pneumonia in two months' time, always ate at his office. My mother, a flighty woman who a few years after my father's death descended into the murky grasp of Alzheimer's disease, served me dinner each night and hovered while I ate, asking if I needed any extra salt, pepper, or ketchup. It didn't matter what I was eating—she always eagerly offered those same condiments. I never saw her sit down and eat a proper meal. She liked to pick at food, she said, and she picked all day long in the kitchen.

In any case, due to my unfamiliarity with the experience of a family meal—much less with a family this big and uneasy—and my unpopular aspiration to take Kelly away from this family to live a different, happier life at my side, I was relieved when Patrick pushed back his chair and the meal officially ended. I stayed at the table with Johnny, Pat, and Ryan while the women cleared the dishes. We fiddled with the silverware until it was taken away, and awkwardly chatted about Jack Kennedy and the Dodgers. Then Catharine called me into the kitchen.

This summons seemed fortuitous, since I had been hoping to have a private word with her. The first thing that struck me as I walked through the swinging door was how clean the kitchen was. We had finished eating a big meal no more than ten minutes earlier, and the counters, the floor, the stove, everything was spotless. All the McLaughlin girls had disappeared.

"Thank you for the delicious meal, Mrs. McLaughlin," I said. "I really enjoyed it."

Catharine held up her hand. "I realize that you have serious intentions toward my daughter, Mr. Leary. I know about your engineering degree, and your position with the architectural firm. I know that you can provide for my daughter. But I saw you looking to me for approval or assistance during the meal, and I wanted to address that. You need to know that my husband makes the decisions for this family. He cannot be gotten at through Kelly or through me. I will not be able to help you."

My breath was gone. I realized that the whole house was silent. I imagined all the McLaughlins pressed up against the door behind me, listening. I now understood why Kelly jokingly called her mother "the iron glove." All I could manage to say was, "I see."

"Good. Now, are you certain you've had enough to eat?"

It took me two more months and a shot of whiskey before I had the nerve to ask Patrick McLaughlin for his daughter's hand. Patrick didn't turn off the golf game on the television set while I asked, or while he answered. He kept his eyes on the small white ball the entire time. He said I had his permission to marry his twenty-six-year-old daughter, but only because Kelly was already an old maid and not that good-looking. I was thrilled with Patrick's response—he had said yes!—until I turned around and saw Kelly standing in the doorway. Until I saw the look her father had put on her face.

BY THE time I drop Catharine off at the assisted-living center and fill the head nurse in on what happened, the day is shot. I sit in my truck in the parking lot for a long minute, arguing with myself. What I should do is drive straight home and tell Kelly what happened. What I want to do is drive to Wyckoff, the next town over. I want to drive into the maze of residential streets and pass the rows of nice, but small, homes, and pull up in front of the house with the yellow shutters. Eddie's house.

Earlier this week I called in a favor from a competitor of mine and had him stop by and offer to do some fixing-up work for a ridiculously low fee. I had wanted him to clean out the gutters, which I could tell were clogged, and check the roof and the basic structure. Obviously I would have offered to do it myself, or sent one of my guys, but I suspected that Eddie's widow wouldn't accept a handout from her late husband's crew. I'd been pleased when my competitor called and said Mrs. Ortiz had accepted his offer. I want badly to stop by now and check on his work. To check if the lawn needs cutting. To check if the kids are playing outside, and if they look happy.

In my several drives by his house since the funeral, I've only seen Mrs. Ortiz and her children once. They had just arrived home and were unloading groceries from Eddie's old white Cadillac. Eddie's wife was wearing her nurse's uniform. There was a boy, who must have been about seven years old, and a slightly older girl. The kids were both dark-haired and hyperactive, bouncing around the car and then chasing each other into the house. Mrs. Ortiz had long hair, so dark it was nearly black, but her skin was several shades paler than her husband and children's. She looked to be in her mid-thirties. I watched her duck in and out of the car, adjusting the bags. It was clear from the slope of Mrs. Ortiz's shoulders that she was tired, but she held her thin frame upright. She gathered an impossible number of brown grocery bags into her arms, shut the car door with her foot, and then made her way into the house. As she passed the shrubs beside the front door, I noticed they needed trimming. When she climbed the front steps, I thought I saw the railing wobble slightly under her hand.

I restart the engine of the truck and drive out of the parking lot, the ache in the back of my head telling me that I am not going to allow myself any relief today. I am going to do what I should do. But, as a small rebellion, I take the long route home, which passes all the pieces of land I own in Ramsey. The route grows longer all the time. I have done a lot of buying lately. Eddie's death soured me on construction. I still do it—the business makes me too much money to stop—but I prefer to buy and sell or rent out land. It's a cleaner business. There are no faulty plans, rusty nails, loose boards, bad weather, incompetent workers. No one is going to lose life or limb over a real-estate deal. You stand only to gain.

I drive the route slowly. I pass the bank on Main Street, the Green Trolley, the vacant lot beside the fire station, the apartment building on Dogwood Terrace, the two houses on Lancaster Avenue, and the house on Holly Court, where Gracie lives. As always, when I pass by her house I consider stopping in, but don't. I think it's important to give Gracie and Lila their space. Most of my friends' kids have flung themselves across the world in an attempt to put as many miles as possible between themselves and their parents. I don't know why my girls have stayed in Ramsey, but I'm glad they have. I don't want to chance making any mistakes that might drive them away.

After I pass Holly Court I turn left, a tactical decision that adds an extra three minutes to my trip. This final detour is different from the others—it is about avoiding a piece of land as opposed to seeking it out. I want to stay far away from the construction site on Birchwood Lane where Eddie died. I do my best these days to steer clear of that part of town.

KELLY IS sitting at her computer in the living room when I get home.

"Have a good day at the office?" I ask after kissing her cheek. This is my usual question, which I use to gauge her mood.

"Decent," she says. "No major crises. Sarah and Giles actually did some work, miracle of miracles. It was a nice change to have a little help."

"Great," I say over my shoulder as I head into the kitchen for a beer. "Have you heard from your mother, or Lila?"

Kelly looks up from the screen. "No. Why?"

"Your mother had a small car accident in front of the Municipal Building. She's fine, though. I happened to be there, so I drove her to the hospital."

I have apparently decided not to tell my wife about the possibility of the stroke. I will give Catharine the benefit of the doubt this time. If she thinks she can fix this on her own, I will give her the space to try.

"Dear God." Kelly turns sideways in her chair, a sudden movement that focuses all her attention on me. "When did this happen?"

"Around two o'clock, I guess."

"And no one called me? Louis, why didn't you call me? You're sure she's fine? What did the doctors say? My God, I should have been there."

"I knew you were busy, and everything happened pretty fast. Lila was working at Valley, so we spent a few minutes with her. There didn't seem to be any reason to disrupt anyone else's workday."

"Louis." Kelly shakes her head, and her frosted hair shakes, too. "She's *my* mother. You have no right to make those kinds of decisions."

"For God's sake, Kelly, doesn't thirty years of marriage make me . . ." I trail off, knowing I've made a mistake. I shouldn't have pointed out our marriage. We never mention our marriage anymore.

Kelly sits perfectly still. "You barely have time to speak to me anymore. I don't know where you are half the time. How are you in any position to be sanctimonious?"

She is right. Kelly is a woman I have to work to love well. She is constantly changing, a fact that has kept me on my toes for over three decades. I have always liked that about her, and about us, even at the moments when I've failed to chart her changes properly. I enjoy the challenge. But I don't deserve her right now. I am unable to step up to the plate and do the work. I wish it were late at night so I could close myself in the den and turn on the television, sound low.

"I'm sorry," I say, and shrug.

"I don't like what is happening here," Kelly says, and for a moment she looks like Lila as a little girl, about to have one of her temper tantrums. "You're not trying! You're not even making an effort."

She throws this at me as if it is the greatest of crimes, and I know that to her it is. But there is something inside me that keeps me from reaching out, keeps my wheels from turning in the direction they should. That something is rock solid and unmovable, and it sits on my chest. It makes me sink down on the couch, sink down in the grass beside Eddie's still body, sink down under the heaviness of the air in this room.

"Don't you have anything to say for yourself?" There is a note of disgust in Kelly's voice.

I don't have anything to say. I wish I did.

"Fine." She stands up, her thin body a collection of sharp angles. "I need to call my mother, then, and Lila, to find out what's really going on."

GRACIE

I know I have to tell Joel. I have to.
(A) He's the father, and (B) even if I broke up with him right now, he lives in Ramsey. He's a local volunteer firefighter. He would find out two minutes after I started showing. There is no town gossip that gets past firemen. You'd be surprised to hear those big burly men talk dirt. And Weber, Joel's best friend on the force, who swears he's psychic, has been giving me weird looks lately. I've actually started keeping the fat slob's favorite brand of beer in our refrigerator so that when he stops by the house with Joel, he's happy and distracted.

In any case, I know I don't have much time. I try to tell Joel when he spends the night, but I end up feeding him instead. I hand him a Heineken when he walks through the door, because I know he likes to have a few bottles at the end of the day. Over the past two weeks, I have made two meat lasagnas, a key lime pie, a roasted chicken, seafood risotto, and turkey sausage chili. I realize, as I cook, that I am making my favorite foods, not his. We haven't been together long enough for me to know his favorites. Or maybe most women know their boyfriends' tastes by the four-month point. Maybe I should have asked.

When I serve him the seafood risotto at eleven o'clock one night, I study his face to see if he likes it. He seems to like everything. Joel is very agreeable. He is very nice. He is someone I was probably a few weeks from breaking up with, before this whole pregnancy thing happened. He's not in love with me, which is fine, but he is in love with someone else. He is not even close to being over his last girlfriend, a loudmouthed redhead named Margaret. He's actively terrified of her. When he and I are out in public, Joel is always looking over his shoulder, checking to make sure she's not in sight. I wonder if she used to hit him. He denies it, but she must have done something pretty terrible to make him this nervous. Sometimes, while we're having sex—and the sex is pretty damn good, which is probably the best explanation for why we've stayed together for four months—I catch him glancing over at the bedroom door with that same look of fear on his face, as if he fully expects her to walk through any minute.

It may be that the spying Joel does in his other job has helped make him paranoid. He is the assistant to Ramsey's mayor, Vince Carrelli, which sounds impressive, but Joel got the job because his dad is on the town council. He took the position because it gives him the flexibility to devote most of his time to the fire department. What he does for Mayor Carrelli is check up on activities around town. Joel drives by the local parks and keeps an eye on the high school (which is conveniently right across the street from the fire department), the alley behind the 7-Eleven where most of the small-town drug deals take place, and various construction sites. He runs into my father frequently on his rounds, as many of the construction sites in town are my father's. Mayor Carrelli also owns and works part-time in the barbershop on Main Street, so between the gossip in the barbershop and the information Joel comes up with, the mayor is able to maintain a nearly complete knowledge of what goes on in Ramsey.

Clearly, if I want Joel to hear the news from me, it's imperative that I tell him about the baby soon. I'm lucky he doesn't know already.

On the afternoon following the second meat lasagna, when I am driving down Main Street with the ingredients for a key lime pie in a grocery bag in the backseat, I stop at a red light and Weber opens the passenger-side door of my Honda. He climbs in and slams the door behind him.

"Jesus Christ, Weber." I press my palm against my collarbone. "You can't do that to a person! Are you trying to give me a heart attack?"

Weber smiles. His crew cut looks freshly mowed. He is wearing a black T-shirt covered with Jon Bon Jovi's smiling face. "Can you give me a ride to the fire department, please, milady? My truck's in the shop."

"Fine." Now that the fright has passed, I am annoyed. I have enough to worry about without car doors flying open when I'm not expecting it.

I haven't driven ten feet before he opens his big mouth. "How about you let me read your tarot cards?"

"My what?"

"Your tarot cards. Let me read your cards. Your aura has been really screwed up lately, and the cards will let us know what's going on."

I stare over at him. "You're a crazy bastard."

"I'm betting the deception card will come up big time."

I look for an opening in the traffic, so I can pull over and kick him out, but I am blocked in on all sides. I have no choice but to drive forward.

He leans against the passenger-side window, his eyes half-closed as he studies me. I hate the feel of his eyes on my skin.

He says, "Are you cheating on Joel?"

I try to stay calm because of the baby. "Get out of my car."

"Answer the question first. It's not like you haven't done it before. I know you cheated on Douglas."

His words, so unbelievable in the middle of the afternoon in my car on the way home from the supermarket, hang in the air between us. I shake my head. If this could happen, then anything is possible. My life officially makes no sense.

Then I actually think, Wait a minute, maybe there's an opportunity here. Maybe I should tell him I did cheat, and then he will tell Joel and we'll break up, and when Joel hears later that I'm pregnant, he'll think it was from the other guy. And then because there was no other guy I'll be like the virgin Mary. It would be an Immaculate Conception. I would have conceived this baby with a night of sex that had never happened. I would be redeemed.

The idea seems brilliant, providential. I have found the answer and, in some way, the truth. My grandmother would look at me with love *and* approval in her eyes for the first time. I'd be above reproach. My mother wouldn't be able to touch me with her sarcasm. I would have achieved purity. My child and I would bask in God's light. We would be blessed.

Then the car behind me honks, and I come to my senses.

I shout at Weber, "No, I did not cheat," and shove him out of the car at the next light.

I DIDN'T lie to Weber. I never cheat on my boyfriends, but I do sometimes hasten the end of a relationship so I can go back to having fun. The boyfriend-girlfriend scenario feels good at first. It is a comfort to know that someone is looking forward to seeing me at the end of the day, to know that I have a hand to hold, to know that someone likes me and has strung that feeling across a series of days, weeks, even months. But eventually the structure of the relationship and the sameness of the boyfriend makes me antsy. I start to think about going out at night, dream about it, and at that point the relationship is as good as over.

I always go back to wanting the same thing: to visit the Green Trolley and sit next to some strange man at the bar. I want to sip beer and flip my hair and feel my eyes come alive under his gaze. I know who I am in those moments. I recognize my reflection in the eyes of men who are interested in me. They have to be strangers, and it only lasts the first night, but it is the most wonderful night. I love every part of that night. I walk through the door of the Green Trolley, a bubble of anticipation lodged in my chest. I am usually wearing my favorite jeans, which hug my hips in just the right way, and a tight T-shirt. I glance over the room, separating the people I know from those I don't. I walk slowly to the bar, take my favorite seat at the end and order a Corona Light with a lime from Charlie, if it's a weeknight, and Leonard if it's the weekend. And then it's as simple as finding someone new to talk to. I start a conversation. I introduce myself with any or all of the following information: name, age, occupation, where I live, political party, religious orientation. I have had some stimulating conversations about God at that bar, and about the meaning of life. Sometimes I make up my answers, sometimes I tell the truth. It really doesn't make a difference. Either way, the information is brand new. It has the crisp authoritative sound of fall leaves crackling under footsteps as it comes out of my mouth.

And then, in the middle of one of my sentences, or at the end of a fully realized thought, expected and yet unexpected, there is a kiss. A delicious first kiss. When I pull away, the man looks at me as if I'm beautiful and amazing and the best thing he's ever seen. And in that moment I am all of those things. I am flush with self-confidence. I am who I want to be. And then it just gets better. I am tipsy and my eyes close, and the way home is paved with soft laughter and more kisses. And then there is darkness and his hands and soft, wet, back-arching kisses sinking into nothingness. There are miles of skin to run fingertips over. There are corners and curves and sharp turns to explore. There is the sense of always pushing forward, always reaching for the next moment, always waiting, the back of my mouth dry, for everything I am to explode.

I HAVE a meeting scheduled with Grayson at the office on Tuesday to talk about my column. On Monday morning I call him during the regularly scheduled senior writers meeting so I can leave a message on his voice mail. I can't deal with talking to Grayson right now, and I certainly can't deal with seeing him. I need to sort out Joel, and get myself a little more under control, before I face him.

Grayson was my longest relationship; we were together for nearly a year. I broke up with him and quit my job in one message on his answering machine. I know that's pathetic, but I'm not good with confrontation. I am not brave. Grayson didn't call me back, but later that week I received a new batch of Dear Abby letters in the mail with a Post-it that read, *I'm not letting you quit—Grayson.* And that was it. I went back to work without a fuss. I loved my job and had only quit to save Grayson the trouble of firing the girl who had just dumped him.

But Grayson and I had become friends during the year we spent together, as well as lovers. (Actually, I think we had become friends in part to compensate for the sex, which was uninspiring.) He never asked me why I broke up with him. We simply went back to being boss and employee. But there is no denying that there is always something a little too intense between us. The terrain can turn rocky if I'm not feeling entirely confident.

"Happy Monday, Grayson," I say into his machine. "Sorry, but something's come up and I have to cancel our meeting tomorrow. Don't worry, though, my column is going really well this week and it will be on time." I hesitate, feeling like there is something more I should say. "Cross my heart and hope to die."

Then I hear myself launch into a nervous laugh, and I hang up the phone before I have a chance to completely fall apart on my ex-boyfriend/boss's answering machine.

I BELIEVE that you can learn from history. Pay attention to the mistakes that were made before you, and don't repeat them.

My uncle Pat, who alternately tried to run away from, please, and horrify my grandfather right up until his death, teaches me that I need to come to terms with my mother. I do not want her to own my life *in any way*. I am still working on that.

My uncle Johnny is a prime example of how you need to hold on to the essence of who you are. He was mischievous and wild as a boy. He spent a portion of nearly every afternoon seated at the dining-room table with his hands folded in front of him and his feet flat on the floor thinking about what he'd done this time under Gram's watchful eye. But he didn't like school and found it hard to concentrate, so when the Vietnam war started, without telling anyone, Johnny joined the army. In the pictures taken of him the day he left, he is a skinny eighteen-year-old boy with a wickedly charming grin. By the time he came back home, the fire was completely stamped out of him. He is among the most serious, unhappy adults I have ever met.

But Meggy has the lesson I need to learn from now. She married Uncle Travis when she was twenty because she got pregnant. I don't think they were ever in love. They are united in resentment, and eternally disgusted with each other for not standing up and demanding better.

It is Meggy I am thinking about when I finally tell Joel. We are in bed with the lights out. We have just had sex because we always do when he sleeps over. Otherwise, what is the point of him staying the night?

I cup my hands over my abdomen. When I press down on the center I feel a solid area the size of my palm. I say exactly what I have said to different men so many times in the past. "I don't think we should see each other anymore."

I listen to Joel's breath catch, and then grow shallow. In my experience, men hate to be broken up with. They're usually not upset about breaking up, but about being on the receiving end of the decision. He says, "What do you mean? I thought we were having fun."

"The sex is good," I admit.

"It's better than good."

I smile in the darkness. I am sure that for all her scary qualities, Margaret, with her no-nonsense demeanor and helmet of red hair, is not a great lover. Then I remember what I am doing, and why this breakup is different.

I take a breath and say it. "I'm pregnant."

This is the first time I've said the words out loud. The news has lived only in my head for weeks. It sounds massive in the air, and irrevocable. I immediately want to take it back. That's all I can think: I want to take it back.

I don't like the sound of the words. They are momentous and stupid and clichéd. "I'm pregnant" is a line right out of every soap opera and sappy movie. And that's not me, I don't want to be the girl who has just said that and now waits for the boy's reaction. I want to explain myself and my situation better. But what else can I say? The language is inadequate. I am trapped by the words, and by this moment. I am that girl, and I am me. And my life has just changed.

Joel says, in a very cautious voice, "Are you sure?"

I nod in the darkness. I can't speak.

"Are you one hundred percent certain? I mean, did you take one of those over-the-counter tests, or did you go to the doctor? Because those home tests aren't reliable."

"I went to the doctor. I'm almost three months."

Joel is lying on his back beside me. He has not moved. Still, his voice seems to come from farther away than the next pillow. "Are you sure it's mine?"

"There's no need to be unkind," I say. "I don't want you to be involved. I really don't. I just thought you should hear the news from me."

"You're going to keep it?"

I shift my weight. I raise myself up onto my elbows, so he is already behind me. This is the only answer I have been sure of, from the moment I watched the line on the first pregnancy test turn pink. It seemed, surprisingly, like the only possible choice. "Yes."

"Yes. Okay . . . yes." He says the word as if he is trying it out, trying to locate its meaning. "I'm sorry about this," he says. "I am. But I have to go now. I'll call you in the morning."

"You don't have to call," I say.

Joel is now sitting on the side of the bed. I am looking at his back.

"You knew, Gracie, didn't you, that this wasn't a serious relationship for me? I was trying to get over Margaret. And you never have serious relationships. Everybody knows that."

"What do you mean, everybody knows that?"

There is fear in Joel's eyes. He is standing, naked, his shoes in one hand and his socks in the other. His mind is on Margaret. He is wondering what she will say. I wonder if any of the men I have been with have ever given me that much thought, that much power. Probably Grayson did, but he gives everything a lot of thought, so that doesn't count.

Joel is looking down at the shoes he is holding. He says, in a dazed voice, "I don't know how this could have happened. I was so careful."

I want him to leave. I am sitting up in bed, the sheet pulled to my chin so all of my bare skin is covered. That time is over. "*We,* Joel. *We.* And we weren't always careful."

But I only half-believe those words as I say them. I know, in the deepest part of me, that this event involved Joel in only the most minimal way. This began in me, and it will come from me. This baby is mine. It's my path, not his. So I am not surprised that he has chosen to argue the point.

"I don't mean to hurt your feelings, Gracie. I really don't. I never wanted to have anything to do with your feelings. But this just doesn't feel like it's true. I don't feel like it's mine. It's not mine." His pants are on. He is in the middle of the last sentence and in the middle of pulling his shirt over his head when he leaves the bedroom.

Downstairs I hear the breezy noise of the refrigerator door opening, then the clink of beer bottles before Joel leaves and the house grows dark and empty. Only then do I feel a glimmer of the sweet relief that always comes after a breakup, when I am left blissfully alone. But this time it is only a glimmer, and I am no longer truly alone.

I MAKE my way into the kitchen the next morning with only one thing on my mind: coffee. French roast with three spoonfuls of whole milk. I haven't had a cup in eight and a half weeks, since I found out I was pregnant. But I need one now, this instant, as soon as possible.

I walk straight to the coffeemaker. When I notice Lila bent over the kitchen table it throws me. I forget that she is staying here. My roommate is usually a stranger whose name I get off the roommates' Web site at the *Bergen Record*. I choose a girl who only needs a place for a few months, someone I won't have to get to know well. One of those girls moved out right before Lila's housing fell through. It's been years since I've seen my sister in her pajamas. In our normal routine we used to meet for lunch or a movie; we only saw each other fully awake and out of choice. Running into my sister in my own home at odd hours of the day and night is new and strange.

"Come look at these pictures," she says. "Gram must have left them the other day. They were in an envelope with our names on it under one of the magnets on the refrigerator. Did you see them there?"

Only when the coffeemaker is warm under my fingertips and the hot liquid is beginning to splash into the empty pot do I join her at the table to see what she is talking about. Lined up in front of the sugar bowl are three photographs of Lila and me as little girls. I was probably seven, Lila five, but we were close to the same size and weight. The three pictures appeared to be taken in the course of one afternoon. We were on a hillside wearing winter coats. There was no snow, only waving grass.

The first picture shows us posed, standing back to back, arms crossed over our chests, our hair whipping past each other's faces. We were clearly under orders to smile, and had ended up with awkward half-mouthed grimaces. If you looked closely, past the puffiness of our parkas, you could see our elbows digging into each other's sides. We were each trying to bring the other down either by calling uncle first, or by getting yelled at by Mom for ruining the picture.

The other two photos show us playing. I was running, fists and body clenched, uphill, while Lila ran past me downhill, her arms stretched out like airplane wings, her mouth a wide O. In the third photo we played dead. We lay on our backs, arms and legs splayed, eyes squeezed shut.

"I can't remember that day," Lila says. "Do you?"

"No."

Lila is still bent over at the waist, studying the photographs as if looking for hidden clues. "I can't stand it when I can't remember something. What good is a photographic memory if I can't remember days from my own life?"

Our parents had submitted us to a battery of psychological tests when we were in grade school: IQ, personality tests, aptitude exams, etc. They had never told us the results of the tests, which was good, because Lila and I were fiercely competitive and cruel to each other up until I left for college. We might not have survived the knowledge of who had a greater IQ. The only thing our parents did tell us after the testing had concluded was that I had an aptitude for reading and writing, and that Lila had a photographic memory. Lila and I have both been struggling under the weight of these ordinary gifts ever since. I think we both wondered if they were true, or whether we had forced them to be true simply because of how we labeled ink blots and matched vocabulary words in some mustached psychologist's rec room when we were nine and eleven years old.

Lila picks up the photographs and puts them back in the envelope. "Did Mom call here last night?"

"No. Why would she?"

"Gram was in a car accident yesterday afternoon."

I hear her, but the words don't make sense, so I push them away with questions. "What do you mean? Is she okay? She's fine, right?"

"I don't actually know the details. She got into a fender bender in front of the Municipal Building and Dad brought her in. She needed a few stitches, and the doctor thought she might have had a tiny stroke while driving, which would have caused the accident. But there's no way to prove that, and she was perfectly clear-headed with me. She's fine."

"You're sure?"

"I saw her."

"Thank God."

I picture Gram behind the wheel of a car careening out of control. I see her eyes widen with fear, and my own fill with tears. I don't want to cry. My sister is not someone you want to cry in front of. I'm not sure she has ever cried, herself. She must have when we were little, but not that I can remember. I pull at the belt on my bathrobe. If I keep talking maybe I will be able to get rid of this picture of Gram hurt. I say, "Are you going to get mad at me if I tell you something?"

"What kind of something."

"I want to tell you this one thing."

"I won't listen to your boy problems."

"I'm pregnant. I told Joel last night."

Lila turns her head and looks back at me, still with her searching squint. "You're pregnant *again?*"

I try not to sound defensive. The tears are sitting behind my eyes, waiting for any opportunity to pour out. "Yes. I'm keeping the baby this time."

"I should have told them to tie your tubes when I took you to that clinic. Why are you telling me this? You know I don't want to hear things like this!"

I breathe slowly, in order to calm us both down. I don't have the energy to deal with her anger. Lila has inherited a tsunami-like rage from our mother, who inherited it from her father. Lila is aware of the trait, and its path down our family tree, and it infuriates her. She concentrates on remaining very calm. Over time she has created a clinical, cool personality that harnesses all emotions underneath. But her demeanor is not a completely successful roadblock. When she is surprised, as I have surprised her just now, her control can blow away as easily as a thin piece of paper on a windowsill.

When Lila becomes angry, all logic, rationality, kindness, and volume control are lost. I have never been so hurt as I have been beneath the hard-driving, pointed, obliterating sleet of my mother's and sister's words. My father and I have tiptoed around them from day one, careful not to offend, or provoke, or, in Lila's case, surprise. I have misstepped this morning. I should have put some thought into how I would tell her.

But Lila catches herself in time. Her slow breathing matches mine. We face each other. Lila is two inches taller than me, so I gaze slightly up, she looks slightly down. I can see the corollaries running through her mind: I'm not married, I'm not in love with Joel, I'll have to tell Mom, Dad, and Gram, I don't make enough money, I have a problem with commitment.

"Does Gram know?" Lila asks.

This almost makes me laugh. How could she think I'd be anywhere near ready, or able, to tell Gram that I am pregnant with an out-of-wedlock baby?

"Of course not."

"Have you lost your mind?" My sister sounds curious.

The smell of the coffee, steaming, waiting for me across the room, makes my eyes fill with tears. I want it so bad.

I had an abortion five boyfriends and two and a half years ago. Three-quarters of the women my age that I know have had at least one. The trip to the abortion clinic (preferably one several towns away from where you live) is a massive silent rite of passage among white, well-educated girls of my generation. It is a careful, deeply held secret even the bigmouthed among us don't discuss. Of the hundreds of Dear Abby letters I've received, only a handful have touched on the topic of abortion, and none have asked my advice on how to recover from one. This is a godsend, as I do not know the answer. My physical recovery was fine; the emotional recovery was a different matter. I was left with an emptiness inside me, and a very Catholic ache that told me I had sinned.

Maybe Lila and Joel are right to be upset with me. Maybe I'm self-destructive. Maybe I wanted this. Maybe on some level I had, despite a semi-consistent regimen of Ortho-Novum pills and Trojan ribbed condoms, tried to get pregnant. Maybe my body knew that this was my only path to redemption and decided, without consulting my brain, to go for it. I believe in my decision to keep this baby, but that doesn't mean I think it's necessarily the right decision, or that I recognize the girl who made it.

My sister raises her eyebrows. She has no use for ambiguity, vagueness, or long pauses. When something confuses her, she wants an answer. She is waiting; wanting to understand why I would veer so sharply off my life's path. She wants to match up the sister in her memory—the one she's known from early childhood to this Sunday morning—with the girl who stands before her now with the big, unwelcome news.

I wish I could help her. I always want to help Lila, although usually it ends up working the other way around. "Maybe I have lost my mind," I say, as calmly as possible.

Then I turn my back to her and putter around the kitchen, trying to compose myself, trying to stay away from the coffee, trying to figure out where I am going to find the strength to stand behind this decision for another ten minutes, then for the remainder of this day, then for the rest of my life.

LILA

Two days after Gracie tells me she's pregnant I catch her sneaking some guy out of her bed and out the back door. It is five in the morning. I'm barely conscious, huddled over a cup of coffee in the kitchen. I'm scheduled to be at the hospital by six.

I haven't turned any lights on because I find it's best to ease myself into the day. I am not a morning person. I feel I have been deeply wronged every time I have to wake up before seven A.M. It is probably for this reason—because I am already on the defensive—that at first the noise in the center of the house scares me. I straighten up and take a step toward the steak knives. I think: Burglar, rapist, six o'clock news, please don't hurt me.

But then the noise draws out and separates into two sets of footsteps. I don't bother to reach for the knives. I realize what is going on. No one is breaking in. Someone is breaking out.

I hear Gracie whisper, "The third step." But he doesn't hear her in time, and the third step gives a sharp whine. They both freeze for a moment, are silent, and then start again. She leads him not through the kitchen, which is directly under the bedroom I'm staying in, but through the dining room to the back door. My sister is good at this. At the door I catch a glimpse of him while they kiss good-bye. I've never seen him before. He's a black guy, really skinny, holding his sneakers in his hand. Then the door is carefully, silently opened, and he is gone.

This pisses me off. It's five fucking A.M., and all I wanted was a little peace and quiet with my coffee. But Gracie can't help herself. Even when she isn't trying, she's throwing her life in my face, trying to make me share it with her. And the truth is, as she very well knows, I'm not interested. We used to understand each other, before I moved in here. We had a nice balance. We respected each other's differences and we didn't push too far. But when I moved in with Gracie, all balance was lost.

I think, If only I hadn't lost my housing and been forced to stay here.

If only Gracie had kept her mouth shut. And her legs.

If only I could have slept until a civilized hour this morning. If only there wasn't so much I had to do.

Gracie walks back through the kitchen and sees me holding my cup of coffee in the shadows. We give each other a good once-over. I see that she's still half-asleep. Her face has that mushy look it gets after she's been laid.

"Please lay off the self-righteous stare, Lila. I don't need that."

"I don't think you can read my expression, Gracie. We're standing in the dark."

There is a sharp clack as Gracie flicks the switch and the room explodes in light. I cover my eyes with my free hand.

"I was just trying to feel good," she says. "I wanted to have a little fun. Just a little. Is that so awful?"

I am so tired the skin on my face hurts. When was the last time I felt good? Or had fun? "Why don't you run out to the corner," I say, "I'm sure there's still a wino or two hanging around that you can bring home and fuck. That would be fun."

Something in Gracie's face flattens out and grows hard, like a frozen pond in the dead of winter. She hesitates, but then shoots back. "At least I'm not some kind of half-assed virgin who refuses to even *attempt* to experience life."

There's not much to say on either side after that.

We end this fight like we did when we were little girls, with a staring match. Editor Boy, one of Gracie's boyfriends who actually hung around for a while, used to say that both Gracie and I were experts in giving silent deadly looks, but that our styles were different. Gracie's look says that she knows more than you do, but she'll keep her vast superiority to herself because to do otherwise would be rude. I, on the other hand, specialize in the fuck-off, if-looks-could-kill approach.

My sister and I stare each other down in the bright light of the kitchen. The window over the sink shows a black sky and not another soul awake or a bulb lit anywhere in Ramsey. We are alone in this room, in this house, in this new day. Blue and brown eyes locked.

You don't know anything about anything.

Fuck you. You don't know me.

I break first, because I have to leave for work. I have responsibilities. I dump the cold coffee in the sink, grab my bag, and slam out the back door without a word.

I SPEND most of my morning at the hospital looking to regain my rhythm. I go through the motions of being a cool, competent doctor-in-training. I phone in lab requests, swab up blood, hold back pieces of skin and tissue so the attending physician can look inside the patient and determine the extent of the damage. In the middle of the morning my attending has to step away, so he allows me to stitch up a minor arm wound without supervision. The patient, a balding, pudgy man who is on the verge of tears, asks for a local anesthetic.

"An injection of lidocaine will hurt more than the stitches," I tell him. "Just let me sew the cut up quickly, and you'll see that you don't need the shot."

"I don't believe you." This grown man is actually pouting. "I want the shot."

"Fine. It's your arm." I pick up the syringe, making no attempt to keep it low and hidden the way the doctors tell you to. Let this jerk see exactly what he's getting.

"Shit, you're not going to just stab that thing into me, are you? Hold on now, maybe I want the real doctor to come back."

Someone leans in behind me; there is a familiar, breathy voice in my ear. "Let me help, sir." Pushy, perfect Belinda offers her toothy smile to the patient. "You shouldn't let yourself get so anxious. There doesn't need to be any pain."

I wonder how Belinda's hair can smell like strawberries during her eighteenth consecutive hour in the hospital. The man smiles back at Belinda. His eyes glaze over. He is apparently wooed by her smell and her dyed blond hair and her one-size-too-small white jacket. "Please," he says. "I want her to do it. Not you."

I shake my head and hand over the needle. Belinda has turned this moment into another battle in the long war between us, and I'm in no mood to fight. During the first two years of medical school I was consistently ranked number one in the class, while she was number two. She senses that the title is now up for grabs and moves in for the kill every chance she gets. I have to admire her tenacity.

"How's your grandmother?" she asks over her shoulder.

"She's fine," I say, and leave the room. Of course, it was Belinda who had been sent to find me with the news that Gram was in the ER. I hadn't believed her at first. I thought she'd taken a left turn toward really twisted and had made up a lie about my grandmother to try to steal away the patient I was working on. When I realized she was telling the truth, that Gram had been in an accident, I'd gotten upset, and I still can't stand that Belinda saw me that way. I can't stand to hear her mention Gram out loud now. I want to keep the rivalry between us all business, all about school.

The first two years of medical school took place in the classroom, which meant a lot of straight memorization. I aced every exam. I barely had to study. I went home while everyone else flocked to the library. My teachers held me up in class as an example. I enjoyed my special status to the hilt. I accepted that being number one meant being a loner. I kept the door to my dorm room closed to chatty people walking down the hall. I gave other students smug looks when I walked out of exams twenty minutes early. I lapped up every last bit of my professors' praise. I consciously enjoyed each moment in the classroom, each semester that I was on top of my game and in my element.

But those days are over. We're in the second half of medical school now and this part is termed "hands-on" experience. There are no more classes, no more books, and few exams. My days of easy excellence have ended. I am in the middle of my medicine rotation. My classmates walk around the hospital with circles under their eyes, complaining about how tired they are, how overworked they are, how overwhelmed they are. We are on call every third night, which means we have to spend the night at the hospital. The students are supposed to sleep on the rickety bunk beds tucked into various corners of the hospital, but no one ever actually sleeps. We make rounds with our assigned attending doctor, seeing every patient that comes into the hospital who isn't clearly a surgical or neurological case. As part of a medical team, we assess each patient, take a history, diagnose, and give a prognosis.

This rotation is a lot of hours, but that's not what bothers me. I don't mind missing sleep. I like seeing how far I can push my body and mind. After three days of little rest, my personal worries go away, and there is nothing but the work at hand. But what does bother me, and what I do mind, are the people.

The hospital is teeming with them. Everywhere you turn there are doctors, medical students, nurses, nurses' aides, nurse practitioners, anesthesiologists, specialists. Everyone has their specific job and they get in one another's way despite the rigid hierarchy that has to be followed. The hospital system is based on education and seniority, so that even if you have the skills and the knowledge, you can't apply either until you've spent a few years following some middle-aged attending around kissing butt. You have to say the right things, and act deferential to the right people. You can't even find peace with the nurses, who think they know much more than the lowly medical students, and who, when the workload slows, want to chat and bond and talk about their lives and my life until I want to throw myself out of the nearest window.

The patients I can tolerate, because with them at least I can use my mind. I check their symptoms against what I have memorized. I consider the possible illness, the possible treatments, the possible complications. But still, there is no purity in the work because I am not allowed to do much, and because far too often the doctor sends me out of the sickroom to speak to the patient's family. This is the worst possible assignment, because with few exceptions the families are a mess. It doesn't matter if they are in the hospital because their ten-year-old is having his tonsils out or because their father is having an emergency triple bypass. The hysteria is always there. I see it in their eyes and hear it in their voices. People know that while they are at the hospital someone in the rooms around them is bound to die, and they seem to believe that if they speak loudly and often and shed tears, there will be a better chance of their loved one being spared.

I suppose I always knew on some level that I wasn't crazy about people. I never had many friends, and I avoided crowded situations like bars and parties. I chose to live in student housing among people who didn't like me because I was left alone. But still, I never consciously thought about the idea that I might be a misanthrope. It's not the kind of personality trait one wants to attribute to oneself. And I had never come face-to-face with that possibility until forty hours after my fight with Gracie, when I had spent two straight days in the hospital without ever having one moment alone.

I am on my way to the bathroom, mostly so I can lock the door to the stall and sit down on the toilet and close my eyes. But someone follows me. It is a woman I have just spent twenty minutes calming down, whose son suffered a concussion and broke his leg skateboarding.

"Miss," the mother says. "He doesn't recognize me. He's not talking. Are you sure he's going to be okay?"

"Your son is asleep," I say. "He doesn't recognize you and he's not talking because he's asleep. We gave him pain medication and it made him drowsy, as I told you before. Can you understand that?" I speak slowly, because I want her to hear me this time. She seems a little slow.

"He just doesn't seem right," she says.

I am at the door to the bathroom. I have to get rid of this woman.

I say, "Your son was drunk when he fell off his skateboard onto his head. He wasn't wearing a helmet. It was an idiotic thing to do. So you're correct. He's not right."

The woman puts her hand over her mouth. I put my hand on the door to the bathroom, but something stops me from walking in. I glance around and see my attending, Dr. Lewis, on the opposite side of the hall. He is staring at me as if I've just admitted to snorting cocaine during my lunch break.

He rushes over, puts his arm around the woman's shoulders, and leads her away. I go into the bathroom. When I come out, he is waiting. He is a bald man, my height. He has deep lines across his forehead.

He comes right out with it. "You don't want to be a doctor, do you, Miss Leary?"

"I was tired," I say. "I had already spent an adequate amount of time with the woman and her son's injuries aren't serious. . . ."

"Serious," he repeats.

I wonder if there is something in the drinking water at the hospital this afternoon that has knocked a few digits off everyone's IQ. "Yes," I say, "serious."

"I wonder if you are serious, Miss Leary."

I remain silent, because he is clearly going somewhere with this and there's no point in my getting in his way.

"I've been watching you." He nods for emphasis. "You have plenty of promise, as you obviously know. You have a sharp mind. But there's no kindness in you, and that's a problem. You're doing well enough now because you've been able to coast on the reputation you earned during your class work. But it takes more than intelligence to make it from this day forward. You'll do well to remember that." He thumps his fist against his chest and then walks away.

DR. LEWIS's reprimand sticks with me. I play it over and over in my head. Am I the person he described? Do I not want to be a doctor?

He was definitely right about one thing. At the hospital, in my work, I am on very thin ice. Every time I meet a new doctor, he or she is excited to work with me, having heard about my accomplishments, my grades, my memory. But that excitement lasts only so long, as I inevitably lose my patience in front of them. I know Dr. Lewis, for one, has requested not to work with me. There may be others who have done the same. This is a worrying situation that seems to have little chance of improving. Even with my stellar reputation, I am using up any second chances.

When I leave the hospital at the end of the day, I call the Realtor from my cell phone and tell him I will meet him the next morning. I would do almost anything for Gram, but not this. I need to be able to seal myself off more effectively. I need my own bathtub to soak in, my own answering machine to leave on at all times, my own curtains to draw closed.

When I get to Gracie's house, she is sitting at the kitchen table, Dear Abby letters spread out before her.

The minute I walk in, she says, "Lila, I'm so sorry about the other morning. Please don't be mad at me."

I listen to her beg me, for what must be the hundredth time in our lives, to tell her that no matter how questionable her behavior, she's a good person, and everything will be all right. I lean into the refrigerator pretending to look for something to eat.

I choose an apple and turn back around. "How are the losers doing this week?"

"They're not losers, Lila."

When she started this job, Gracie used to make fun of the letters with me. After all, the premise is ridiculous. Scores of people, mostly women, send their heartfelt questions and painful secrets to a complete stranger. They actually want, wait for, and take this stranger's advice. And what are the stranger's qualifications to play God? Don't even get me started. For my sister, it was sleeping with the editor of the newspaper. So now women all across northern New Jersey are leaving their husbands, making up with their teenage children, and signing up for college courses because my sister, the good lay, the pregnant, unmarried twenty-nine-year-old, thought it sounded like the best solution.

"It's the letters from the young girls that get to me," Gracie says. "I have seven letters this week alone from girls whose boyfriends are pressuring them to have sex. They don't know what to do because they don't feel ready, but they also don't want to lose their boyfriends. There are also three letters from girls who want help because they're depressed."

Gracie spreads her hands over the rows of letters. Like mine, her hands are pale, without creases, but her fingers are slender where mine are stubby. She looks as exhausted as I feel. "Who am I to give them advice?"

I can't argue with this, so I concentrate on my apple, which is a little mealy. A picture of Gram in the hospital flashes through my mind: old, bandaged, shaken. I wish suddenly that my sister had been there with me to see Gram. I don't want to be the only grandchild with that image in my head. I wish that my memory was able to let go every once in a while. It has been too noisy in my head lately, too raucous. I miss the silence I used to be able to create locked in my dorm room or in my favorite study carrel at the library.

If I were at the library now, I would reread a chapter in my medicine textbook. Maybe the one on epidemiology, which was always a favorite. I'd review the causes and symptoms for Lyme disease, Chronic Fatigue, Epstein-Barr. I'd read about the suppressed immune system that lets in all germs, infections, and viruses and makes a bad situation worse. I am a fan of these kinds of diseases, which are vague in their symptoms, heavy in fatigue, capable of blurring the edges of the people they strike. These illnesses dull everything—personality, skills, drive, memory. I like to imagine, when I am tired and burnt out, that I have contracted Epstein-Barr, and that I now have the chance to step away from my life, and lose myself.

"Are you going out tonight?" I ask.

Gracie gives a rueful smile. "No. I'm off men for a while."

"Literally and figuratively?"

"Funny."

"Well, I'm going for a walk." I'm surprised to hear this come out of my mouth. I rarely go for walks. I am more a lie-in-front-of-the-television-until-I-fall-asleep kind of girl.

But once I'm outside in the cool night air, I know it was the right decision. I had to get out of that stuffy kitchen, away from my sister, away from the letters full of unanswerable questions and inconsolable grief.

I round the block and approach the Green Trolley with its painted sign of a green train car. I consider going inside. Maybe I need to raise some hell. I haven't been drunk since college. I haven't had sex in, well, a long time.

But my legs take me past the front door of the bar. After all, it is Gracie's place. I stare straight ahead so I won't have to make eye contact with half of my high-school class. But out of the corner of my eye I see Joel and his buddy Weber standing beside some overgrown adolescent who is throwing up in the parking lot. Joel freezes at the sight of me, his hand on the vomiting guy's back. But Weber has no problem talking.

"Hey, Doc," he yells, "we need some medical attention. Hellooo, I'm right over here. . . . Oh shit, are you ignoring me, Leary? Joel, she's ignoring me."

Joel stays frozen. Weber takes two skips in my direction. "I knew your sister had a secret," he says. "Did she tell you that I knew?"

I have heard about Weber's so-called psychic gifts. He can't keep his mouth shut about them. As far as I'm concerned, he's just a fat fireman, and not much of a friend to Joel either, yelling about his business in the parking lot of the town bar.

"I can tell you've got a secret, too," Weber is saying. "That's why you're so goddamned uptight. You need to loosen up! I could help with that—come inside and have a beer with me."

I turn my head and meet his eyes. I can tell that the contact chills him, as I'd known it would. He stops bouncing in place. Even his crew cut seems to wilt.

I think, I must have ice water running through my veins.

I say, "Stay the fuck away from my sister and me," and keep walking.

CATHARINE

I won't tell a soul that it was ghosts that made me stop my car in front of the Municipal Building. Nor does anyone need to know that this kind of thing has been going on for some time now. It would take my children about ten seconds with their heads huddled together to decide that I need one of those fancy new psychological drugs. And there's no point in telling any of this to Dr. O'Malley, who is my age, and who hates to see any signs that I am growing old.

I keep him as my doctor out of habit, I suppose. He delivered all nine of my children. I drove panicked to his office with the head of my firstborn in my lap, her breath labored, her face swollen and flushed. I carried her, a big three-year-old whom I had told only one week earlier that she was too heavy to be picked up anymore, from the car to his office door. I sat in the waiting room, my worry spreading like a spider's web across town because Kelly was home alone. Willie had been due back from an errand any minute, so I had decided to leave the eighteen-month-old in her playpen. I told myself that if I'd brought her she would have slowed me down. I had wondered if I should call Patrick at his office. I hated to bother him, so I didn't until later that afternoon when Dr. O'Malley sent me back home with the news that all I could do was hope that my little girl was a fighter.

The visions I've been having are a gift from Patrick. His parting gift. He had always seen things, his entire life. And now he has given his sight to me. We were married for forty-two years. It is in keeping with his character—although I never would have imagined this—that he would brand me with a piece of himself as he left his life.

When our children were young Patrick would sing Irish songs to them in the evenings. While he sang he would actually see the McNamara band march through the living room—few in number but the best in the land—cymbals clanging. He would watch the leader of the band pause behind Kelly's head, his chest swelled with pride. Patrick swore they locked eyes. Patrick raised his glass of scotch to the leader, and the band moved on. He sang of Miss Kate Finnoir, who left her beau standing in the street below her window, singing his heart out. Sometimes in the middle of a Wednesday afternoon, on his way back to the office after a business lunch, Patrick would see the young man standing on the curb outside a Paterson brownstone, his hands clasped behind his back, his eyes on a window two stories up. Patrick would pause and listen as the young man sang of his undying love for Miss Kate.

Early in our marriage, Patrick used to tell me about these sightings. They didn't worry or embarrass or surprise him at all. They were simply a normal, even pleasurable, part of his life. They were as real to him as the sight of his wife standing beside his chair refilling his glass. I never said a word when he came to me, his eyes lit up, and told me whom he'd seen that day. I nodded and smiled and followed along even though when he was excited and it was late in the evening, that was a challenge. I paid perfect attention until he was finished with the story, and then I returned to mending the hole in Johnny's pants, or straightening up the kitchen, or feeding the baby. Did his stories remind me of my mother and that empty chair beneath the window? Yes, but I couldn't lose sight of the fact that my husband provided well for myself and our children. We didn't want for anything. As far as I was concerned, Patrick could see whatever he liked.

That was the situation for years and years. At some point, I can't recall exactly when, my husband stopped telling me about his visions. I'm not sure why. I knew the visions still existed by the shine he had in his lovely green eyes from time to time. Then, one Tuesday afternoon during Lent, Patrick died on me. I had known the end was coming because he wasn't well enough to golf or drink. The circulation in his right leg was off, and he said his scotch had begun to taste oily and thick in the back of his throat. "God is calling you," I said to him. "Don't argue with me about this, because you know I'm right."

We both smiled over that comment; it was a private joke. Patrick always claimed he married me for two reasons: one, for my father's business connections, and two, because I was so utterly levelheaded that I was always right.

He died in his sleep of a massive heart attack. I found him when I went in to wake him from his nap. I sat beside his bed for several minutes, praying, before I made any calls. I could tell that my husband's soul had not yet left the room, and I have come to believe that that is when Patrick gave me his gift. In that viscous, tenuous time between life and death, anything can happen. A forty-two-year-old marriage suddenly ended; I earned the new and unwanted title of "widow," and a chill ran through a room in which every window was shut tight against drafts.

THIS AFTERNOON after lunch I'm sitting at the small table I have set up beneath the one window in my room, when the scenery outside the glass suddenly shifts. I'm watching a group of small speckled birds attack the bird feeder hung from the massive tree in the center of the lawn. Beneath the tree there is a bench where the same two men sit each afternoon with their newspapers, their canes propped against their thighs. I am enjoying this familiar sight. It's a beautiful spring day. I'm thinking about how nice it will be to see my entire family for Easter, and how it won't be too long now before the sun rises on that sacred morning.

First I notice that the birds are gone. I hadn't seen them fly away, so I put my glasses on to check if the bird feeder has suddenly become empty. But the bird feeder is gone, too. That's when I feel that tiny cringe deep inside, and I have to fight the desire to squeeze my eyes shut. Instead, I lean forward and take in what I am supposed to. The two older men and the bench, the newspapers and the canes have also disappeared.

In their place beneath the massive oak tree is a gaggle of young children. There are at least ten of them, and they range in age from nine years old to a baby who is crawling in the dirt, stopping occasionally to pull on a piece of grass. The children are laughing and chasing one another, hopping over the baby. The nine-year-old, a bright-faced girl, picks up a toddler and swings him around in circles. *I'm flying,* the toddler calls out, choking on giggles. The children are familiar; they are freckled and pale and Irish, and at first glance I think they are mine. There is a set of twins, just like I had, and the oldest is a girl. I lean closer to the windowpane, and my breath catches in my throat with disappointment. No, no, no. The twins are both boys, and none of these children have come from me. So, then, who are they? Why have I been stuck with them?

I notice now that the children are a mess. Some of their pants are ripped in the knee. The toddler is wearing a hand-me-down jumper a few sizes too big. The baby begins to cry, and the tightness to the sound means she is hungry. They are wearing the same style of clothes my children wore when they were young. None are wearing shoes. They are clearly all of the same family. Jumbled among them are a few common traits: reddish hair, overly large ears, a wide grin. I have seen them before. I look more closely, scanning for another clue. The children climb and tumble and hug and tussle one another without ever straying more than five feet from the fat oak's trunk. But the close proximity is not out of choice. The oldest girl tries to tug away occasionally. She skips a distance and then stops each time at the same exact point, turns, and walks back to her siblings.

She is tied to the tree. All the children are tied to the tree. They have white sashes around their waists that lead back to a fat white loop around the tree trunk.

These are the Ballen children. They lived in Paterson near where Patrick grew up. As a child, Patrick was friends with the children's mother. The father was a drunk, usually gone. Patrick, the children, and I stopped by their house once, on our way home from a visit with Patrick's parents. We were dropping off some kind of food, perhaps a

casserole, or a pie, from Patrick's mother. I was never comfortable in
that neighborhood. It was so different from where I had grown up. The
tiny cramped grocery store Patrick's mother ran. The two cramped
rooms upstairs where Patrick and his brothers and parents had lived.
The tiny, poorly constructed houses that ran up and down the surrounding streets, filled with Irish. The Ballens' house was no more than
a shack. We pulled up in our shiny Ford that afternoon, and the children piled out before I could stop them. Kelly, Pat, Meggy, Theresa,
Johnny, Ryan. I had wanted this to be a quick drop-off and drive away.
I followed reluctantly, not wanting to be rude. Mrs. Ballen opened the
door, beads of sweat on her forehead, wiping her hands on a filthy dish
towel. She flushed to the roots of her hair at the sight of us. She took
the casserole, or pie, or whatever it was and said thank you. Johnny said,
"Where are your children?" Mrs. Ballen, looking more and more
uncomfortable, said, "Around back." And we all followed Johnny, not
knowing what else to do. After all, what did I have in common with
this woman? Patrick said something to Mrs. Ballen about his law practice and she nodded. I think he had done some pro bono work for her
at one time. We heard her children—one crying, several laughing, a
few squeals—as we walked around the side of the shack. We rounded
the final corner, and saw them. Tied to the tree in the middle of the
yard like a pack of dogs. Mrs. Ballen, her skin still bright red, said in
apology, "It's the only way I can keep track of them."

I had hated that afternoon. Those twenty excruciating minutes
with Mrs. Ballen and her children. Piling our own children back into
the Ford. Driving out of Paterson, past the waterfall, back to
Ridgewood and our neatly ordered, comfortable home where Willie
had dinner waiting. Why would I see those children now? I hadn't
thought of them in years. I had never seen them, or Mrs. Ballen, again.
I knew she had died young of a heart attack, the poor woman. I had
no idea what had become of her offspring, who would now be in their
forties and fifties, the same age as my own children. And yet here they
are, tied to a tree outside my window.

I don't look away. After all, if God or Patrick thinks this is something I need to see, I will not argue. I can stand to be uncomfortable.

I simply rearrange myself in my chair and watch. The Ballen children are there for nearly an hour. After a while, the older children notice me. The oldest girl and the twins wave their arms in my direction, then point at their waists. They want me to untie them. They want me to set them free. The twins stand up straight, two lovely little boys, and press their palms together in front of their chests. In prayer, in supplication, in hope.

"I'm sorry, I can't, I don't know how," I say, over and over, until the vision ends, until the children disappear, until I am left alone.

AFTER THIS sighting, I pay a visit to my son Ryan. Something about the murkiness, the timelessness of that vision, leads me to him. As it is, I visit him every Tuesday afternoon, rain or shine. That is our schedule. He serves Pepperidge Farm cookies and tea, which I eat and drink with as little motion as possible, hoping the birds overhead won't notice I'm there. He has four or five large yellow birds the size of cats. Their wings are clipped so they can't fly, but they are able to jump from perch to perch. I forget what kind of birds they are. I forget their names. They hop from one corner of the room to the other, squawking and talking and going to the bathroom wherever and whenever they feel the urge. I am, of course, very careful about where I sit.

Ryan asks about his brothers and sisters first thing. He has a very good heart. "How is Kelly, how is Pat, how is Theresa, how is Meggy, how is Johnny?"

Today he pretends not to listen while I run through the answers. I tell him everyone is fine. If I don't have something good to say, I skip the subject. I don't tell him about the accident, as there is no need for him to worry. I also skip over Gracie. But there is plenty else to say, and we never stop talking, between the two of us. Or, if we do stop talking, it doesn't seem like it. The thing with Ryan is that you can't listen to him the way you do to just anyone. You have to listen to what is beneath his words. You have to listen to his concern, his faith, his heart.

I liken the way I choose to approach Ryan to my study of the Bible

as a child. You read stories about Noah, Adam, Solomon, Rachel, and
the stories seemed to be just that, stories. You didn't let yourself get
distracted by the details and the background characters. The biblical
tales were enveloping clouds of fiction, but soon enough you found the
hard, sure stones of truth. Respect your elders, care for your fellow-
man, do not steal, do unto others as you would have them do unto you.
Ryan is very honorable. He is deeply committed to our family, and to
the Lord. As am I.

I say, "Meggy is enrolling Dina in the school in their new neighborhood. Hopefully it will be a good change for her. Meggy coddles
her too much, lets her do whatever she likes."

Even as I speak, I am distracted by the memory of those children
tied to a tree. I haven't been able to shake them yet, but I'm happy to
be talking about my children and grandchildren's better chances. I feel
like something is at stake. I wish I could tell Ryan that I know Gracie
is pregnant, that I have seen her more than once now and there is no
doubt in my mind. But this is not the kind of news I can share with
my youngest son. He doesn't handle surprises well. He would cast the
news in the wrong light. It would upset and disappoint him.

Ryan leans forward in his wheelchair, his pale eyebrows furrowed.
I have caught his attention. "Is it a public school?"

"Hmm? Oh, yes, apparently it's quite a good one."

"Public schools are fascist—doesn't Meggy know that? Stalin went
to a public school. They have rules there that squelch a child's spirit.
They tie them up with so many regulations that they have to sneak into
bathrooms and smoke marijuana and wear black brassieres. Dana is a
sensitive girl. Very sensitive. Meggy might as well put a gun to her head,
don't you think, Mother? The child should be in a Christian school.
I'm going to have to call my sister and have a word with her. I have to
do what I can for my nieces and nephew."

"Yes, well," I say, feeling as if I'm losing ground. "Lila is actually
working in the hospital now. Isn't that nice? She's still in school, of
course, but she learns by helping the doctors attend to real patients. I
worry sometimes that she works too hard. She doesn't pay attention to
anything else."

Ryan thinks about that for a moment. "Doctors make too much money," he says. "That's the problem, don't you see? They get corrupted. Lila will be seduced by the money. Mark my words, she'll forget that she set out to save lives."

"I'm not sure why Lila set out to be a doctor," I say, and then shake my head sharply. I am not myself today. I should have changed the subject or just nodded in agreement. I should not have argued.

Ryan is worked up now. He pats the framed picture of Jesus that he has hung on the side of his wheelchair. "Doctors have not been good to us, Mother. Remember when Daddy pushed Pat by mistake and he fell and Dr. O'Malley wasn't able to set the bone in his arm correctly? And before that he couldn't save my big sister, and I never even got to meet her. And doctors certainly have been no good to me. Trying to put me to sleep like you would a dog or a cat. But don't worry, you guys"—he is talking to the birds now, his eyes upward—"I won't let them touch you. No needles, no pills. No, no. I promise. I'll take care of you."

I am standing up now, my purse in my hand. "I must go, Ryan. Dinner is served early today. I'll see you next Tuesday."

"Tuesday," he says as he wheels after me to the door. "Drive carefully, Mother. I'll pray for you."

And I hear my youngest child pray as I make my way down the front steps of the apartment building. His voice wafts out behind me, making its way through chinks in the walls and the cracks in the windows of the seedy, run-down building he has lived in for nearly twenty years. Ryan has a beautiful voice, the voice of a senator, or a priest. It follows me down the front walk to my car, to the inside of my car, where I shut the door and there is no sound. And still I hear him. I hear every syllable.

Our father who art in heaven, hallowed be thy name. Thy kingdom come thy will be done on earth as it is in heaven. Give us this day our daily bread and forgive us our trespasses as we forgive those who trespass against us. And lead us not into temptation but deliver us from evil.

I look around me for neglected children, examples of injustice, specters from my past. I see only a barking dog a few houses down, a man cutting his lawn, a sprinkler watering an overturned garden. My body begins to unclench. I give a small practice smile, just to make sure I am still able to. My muscles oblige. Slowly I regain my even heartbeat, my balance, my sense of self.

"Amen," I say, and start the car's engine.

KELLY IS waiting for me when I get back to my room, which is a shame, because I don't feel strong enough to fight with my oldest daughter. And it is clear, from the first sight of her, that she is here for a fight. But still, I'm happy to see her. I have been happy, in a new, thankful way, to see each of my children, since my car accident. I have struggled for a way to express my gratitude, to speak to them in a new way, but so far I haven't found a successful method.

"I can't believe you were out driving, Mother. Did you take the main roads?"

I set my purse down on the desk. "As opposed to what, Kelly? Driving on the sidewalks?"

Kelly is sitting in the corner of my room in an armchair. She is tapping her fingernails against the sloping arms. Her tone changes, and suddenly she is apologizing to me, though I can't discern for what.

"Louis should have called me the moment he saw that you were in trouble," she says. "At the very least he should have called when you reached the hospital. I could have been there in ten minutes."

"There was no reason for you to be there," I say. "I'm glad Louis didn't call."

"Well, pardon me for thinking I could have been of some help to my own mother."

I shake my head. I am not interested in talking about the accident. It is behind me. I need to focus on the here and now to make sure I don't drift away again. I want to stay myself. I want to appreciate this moment. And I want to make a confession of my own.

I say, "I think I've always been too focused on the past. I spent too much time dwelling on what I'd lost. I wasn't always available for you and your brothers and sisters."

There is a loud silence at my words. I hadn't realized how extreme they would sound in the air, in this room. I have the sense that my furniture, the curtains, and even the photographs on the wall are surprised at me. I think, Why did I never speak like this before?

With a slight movement, Kelly tucks her body into the far corner of the big chair. "Mother, we really need to talk about your giving up driving."

"Listen to me for one moment. I want to apologize to you—"

Kelly interrupts. Her sentences rush after one another. "You're not making any sense, Mother. This is not the time to talk about *apologies.*" She says the word the way she would say *snakes,* as if it is something unpleasant and distasteful. "We have to pay attention to the subject at hand."

"And what might that be?"

"You just had a car accident, remember?"

She seems to be waiting for me to respond, so I say, "Yes, I remember."

"And just because you're physically fine doesn't mean you weren't traumatized somehow. You aren't safe on the road anymore."

"I want to talk about the way I was with you when you were young." Kelly does not return my gaze. Her eyes are focused somewhere slightly above my head. She scans the wall filled with family photos, documentation of her childhood. She seems to be searching for something familiar, something to rest her gaze on. Something that makes sense to her.

"Louis said you parked your car in the middle of the street. Why would you do that? You could have hurt another driver, or a pedestrian. I've spoken to Meggy and Theresa about this, and they agree that you should stop driving immediately."

I am weary again. I don't want to argue. "Soon."

"Soon? What do you mean, soon?"

"I will stop driving soon. I have one more thing I need to take care of first. Now, if you don't mind, Kelly, you've exhausted me and I'd like to take a nap."

The conversation drags on for another tiresome minute or two while Kelly tries to confiscate the keys to my Lincoln. She apparently isn't prepared to go so far as to snatch the keys out of my purse, so she leaves, but not before giving me her customary kiss on the cheek. I can see that the familiarity of the gesture calms her. It lets her put this disturbing visit back into some kind of order in her head.

I decide not to continue trying this approach with my children. Maybe speaking to them one by one isn't the best way. I should think about Easter, and what I might say to them as a group. Individually, they will each think I am off my rocker. It will not occur to them that I am just being honest. Or maybe Kelly did recognize that and that was what scared her. I'm not sure any child really wants to know their parent, or vice versa. Maybe that knowledge and that truth are too much. I'm not sure. These are new thoughts for me, and I need to find a way through them. I am not accustomed to having new thoughts, and at seventy-nine am not at all thrilled to have to learn.

THE NEXT morning, I drive to early-morning Mass, and then from St. Francis's to the girls' house on Holly Court. I let myself in the back door with my key. I fill the kettle and place it on the stove. I sit in the sturdiest chair at the kitchen table and keep both feet on the floor. I am wearing my good tweed skirt with a pink blouse. I don't mind waiting for Gracie to wake up.

Lila comes downstairs first. She is wearing her work outfit of thin blue pants and a matching top. She smiles to see me. "Feeling better, Gram? How did you get here?"

"I drove. And, as you can see, I'm fine."

"I told Mom you were. But she said you'd decided not to drive anymore."

"That's not quite true. I want to thank you, Lila, for looking in on me in the hospital."

Lila blushes at the very top of her cheeks. "Don't be silly, Gram. I just sat with you for a few minutes. It's not like I did anything."

"Well, I appreciated what you did do. Is your sister here?"

Lila opens and leans into the refrigerator. Her voice travels over her shoulder with the frosty air. "You came over to see Gracie?"

"I want to talk to her, yes."

Lila emerges with an apple and a container of yogurt. "I should tell you that I found an apartment over by St. Francis's. I can't move in for a few weeks, but I signed the lease and it's all set."

I nod my disappointment. "Well, if that makes you happy, Lila, then I'm glad for you."

"It makes me happy," Lila says, looking anything but happy. "I have to go to the hospital now, so I'll see you later, Gram. Have a nice chat with Gracie." In a blur of movement Lila kisses me on the cheek, then is out the back door and I am left alone.

I am struck by the similarity between my conversation with Kelly and this short one with Lila. Both mother and daughter like all conversations to go their way, with their topics, their themes, and their desired results. They are displeased when someone else takes control. I'm not quite sure what Lila was hoping for from me this morning, but it is clear that I didn't provide it.

Still, I'm glad to have a few moments alone with my tea. I need the time to brace myself, because I have found that when I see Gracie now, I cannot help but remember back to when I carried my children, and to remember that time is not pleasant. My pregnancies got harder, and seemingly longer and more enveloping, as I went along. My first pregnancy was perfect. I was filled with energy, overjoyed that I was starting my family and that I had made Patrick so proud. At night I would have vivid dreams about the family I would raise, and about how I would be a more dependable, solid, presentable mother than my own mother was. I was tired when I was carrying Kelly, but still strong.

Pat was a big baby, however, and weighed heavily inside me. I went into labor early with him, during the same week we buried our firstborn. The delivery was long and exhausting. I was unable to focus and it seemed he would never come out. After Pat, the pregnancies were more work. They came one after another in an endless row. Like my labor with my first son, I wondered if they would ever end. The children took over my body. They filled up my small frame, and squeezed me out. I grew quieter, harder.

Although who I was became less noticeable as my children developed their own voices, it was always the case that when I did speak, they heard me loud and clear. I ran a tight ship. And underneath the imposed order, and the personalities my children were developing, and the relentless kicks of new life in my womb, I listened to the silence my first daughter left behind, and, later, to the silence of the twins. One boy and one girl who never drew a breath, never opened their eyes.

I was anxious during my pregnancy with the twins. I was busy taking care of Patrick and the children the entire time, and I slept so soundly at night that I never dreamed. I would wake up every morning with a gasp, flushed with panic. That sense of anxiety stuck with me after the birth. I was a wreck while I was carrying Ryan. Even though I had scorned my own mother for always hiding in a closet during thunderstorms, to my shame more than once during that pregnancy I found myself in the coat closet shaking and praying for *this* baby to be all right.

I never spoke of any of the children I had lost. It was dangerous to mention our little girl in front of my husband, but I wouldn't have even if that weren't the case. When Kelly or Pat or even Ryan asked about their brother or sisters, I pretended not to hear them. I sent them to their room. I told them to recheck their homework, straighten out their drawers, set the table, take out the garbage, dress the baby. I laid my quiet down all around them. Their father told them stories of Ireland and leprechauns and lads and lasses and green clovers and the blue sea, and I told them to speak only when spoken to. When they were disobedient, I punished them. When they were very bad, I threatened to send them to their father. I demanded their respect. I was, for the most part, a solid, dependable, and presentable mother. I did what I had to do, and I did it well.

But the lightness was gone. After the twins I did not lose anyone for decades, not until my parents, and then, later, Patrick. But I found motherhood to be a place where I was constantly poised for disaster, braced for loss. Every flaw and weakness in my children I tried to point out and destroy. I urged them to be strong, and tough, and cautious, and especially to be durable.

And I suppose that I was successful, as they have all reached adulthood. My grandchildren have reached adulthood, too, and with them I was able to refind my lightness. I have loved my oldest granddaughter purely, with no motive, until now. Now everything has changed. My heart groans when Gracie walks into the kitchen reading a letter.

"Good morning," I say.

I spoke softly, but still Gracie jumps. Her hair is pulled back in a messy ponytail, and stacks of letters make the pockets of her bathrobe bulge. "Gram, hi. How are you feeling?"

"I'm fine," I say. Then I let a cloud of silence sit down around us. I want Gracie to know that what is coming is important. Only when I see fear round the corners of her expression do I continue.

"Do you remember how your grandfather would talk to you and your cousins about what it means to be Irish?"

Gracie nods. "Whenever he drank too much."

I glance down at my hands in my lap. Beneath the age spots and the blue veins, they are the same hands I raised my children with. They are the same hands I parked on my hips while I told my children which parts of themselves they needed to cultivate so they would be able to survive in a hard world. Now it's time for me to do that work again.

"As you know, Gracie, I was never much for that kind of talk. But I think that perhaps since Patrick's been gone, you and your sister have forgotten what he was trying to teach you. He wanted to educate you children about who you are, even when he told those silly tales. I've been thinking about a story my mother used to tell about a neighbor in Ireland who she called an Irish dreamer. And when I say a dreamer, I mean a real dreamer, not a drunk. He would walk out his front door every morning and put his finger up in the air to see which way the wind blew. He would turn his finger in every which direction, eyes squinted, pipe clenched tight between his teeth. When he finally thought he'd figured the wind out, he'd be ready to start off to work. There were a few ways he could get to his job—on the back road, down the main avenue, or cutting through the next yard. He would turn his entire body first in one direction, then another. When he thought he had made his choice, he would raise his right knee and lean forward, but he never quite took a step. He would stand there all day long, the children mocking him, the housewives shaking their heads. Of course, he soon had no job to get to, but each morning he went through the same routine. My mother said he died out there one morning, his knee raised up in the air, hoping to make a decision. I'm sure the last part wasn't true. That was the kind of ending my mother liked to give stories. No doubt he had a heart attack or died in his sleep, but the point is the same."

Gracie has her hands on the pockets of her bathrobe. "Gram, why—?"

I give a sharp nod, to shush her. "The point, Gracie, is that some of the Irish are like that, locked in indecision, swinging from one possibility to another. And for people like that, sometimes the most dangerous thing is when they accidentally make a big decision. When they do take that step, it's because someone pushed them, or because they tripped."

I see now, from the look on her face, that Gracie is getting it. "You think I'm like that? I'm like the man who can't get himself to work?"

"You need to make something of your life before life makes something of you."

Gracie just stares at me. When I look back, I realize for the first time that Gracie's pale blue eyes are the exact shade of my mother's eyes, and my firstborn daughter's. The realization jars me—how could I not have noticed that before?—but only for a moment. I push the feeling away.

I cross my legs, right over left. Even with only one foot on the floor, there is no dizziness. That is good, as I have only started to say what I came to say. "Gracie, are you planning to marry Joel?"

Gracie takes a letter out of her pocket and grips it with both hands. "Why would you think— Joel and I broke up."

"You're planning to raise this child by yourself?"

She blinks hard, like a child pushing back tears. I have to remind myself that Gracie's twenty-nine years old. She looks half that. "How did you—"

"I bore nine children myself. I know what a pregnant woman looks like." I am happy with the timber of my voice: confident, steady, clear. I sound like the woman Patrick married because she was nearly always right. I recognize myself, and that feels wonderful. "You must need money. How much should I give you right now? We can work out a schedule of payments for the future."

"Gram, I'm going to figure that out for myself. I have a lot that I need to figure out. I don't expect you to fix this for me." And now Gracie is crying; fat tears run down her cheeks. "I'm sorry, Gram. I know I must be a disappointment to you. You think I'm indecisive. . . . I never wanted . . ."

"Don't go losing your head, Gracie. No tears. What's done is done. I'll write you a check and you and the baby will be able to live comfortably. I'll help you."

Gracie seems to notice the letter in her hands for the first time. She folds it carefully and puts it in her pocket. "I have a system for my letters," she says. "The right pocket of my bathrobe is for trivial letters, the ones with small, easy questions. The left pocket is for the tougher situations, things like depression and bereavement."

"I don't give a fig about the damn letters," I say.

I have always thought that Gracie's job was ludicrous. People should keep their problems to themselves. The very idea of publishing your concerns, much less your family's problems, in the local newspaper is reprehensible. I am embarrassed for those women who in times of need turn to a perfect stranger instead of turning to God. And I am not pleased that Gracie thinks she can help these strangers. It is like volunteering to captain a lifeboat that is stranded with no oars in the middle of the ocean. These women are clearly past help. It is a losing battle and my granddaughter will lose right along with them.

Gracie says in a pleading tone, "You can lecture me if you want, Gram. I don't mind. I know you must think this is very irresponsible of me, even immoral. I just want you to understand."

"What exactly do you want me to understand?"

My granddaughter's cheeks are shining, but the tears have stopped. "Why don't you think I can do this? How can you be so sure?"

I reach into my purse and pull out the checkbook. "Obviously I wish you would have waited until you were married, but I do not believe in ending pregnancies. I am going to take care of you and this child. I am going to help you steer your life in an appropriate direction. I'm not going to sit back and watch you bounce from boyfriend to boyfriend anymore, Gracie. I'm not going to watch you wander through your life without a plan. This baby will be well cared for and loved, and you will be back on your feet, if it is the last thing I do. You will both be safe."

Gracie seems to struggle for a minute for words, then says in a blank voice, "Okay."

"Now, before I leave, I'm sure you have expenses like doctor's visits and vitamins that you need to pay for in the near future. How much shall I write the first check for?"

Gracie, tiny in her bathrobe, shakes her head. "I can't . . . I have no . . ."

"I can't talk to you, Gracie, if you can't even finish a proper sentence. I'll leave you a starting amount of money, and then you let me know how much more is necessary."

When Gracie sees me to the back door and then watches me walk away, I think I hear her saying after me, under her breath, instead of good-bye, *I'm sorry, I'm sorry, I'm sorry, I'm sorry.*

BEHIND THE huge wheel of my Lincoln, I feel a little badly that I took such a hard line with Gracie. But I am not pleased with her, or for her. This pregnancy is wrong, and I can't tell her it isn't just to make her feel better. I wish her parents had made her spend more time in church as a child. One of the problems with her generation is that their collective sense of right and wrong is too flexible, and they just end up confusing themselves with too many options.

However, I can't deny that the news of this baby has made me happy. I had feared I would not live to see a great-grandchild, and having four generations of McLaughlins in the world at one time is a lovely thought. Beyond that, my pleasure is more complicated. The strings are crisscrossed to the point that I can't see the beginning or ending of the knot. Gracie's infant is now inextricably linked to those moments in my car before the accident, reaching for and worrying about my own lost babies. I know, with a pang beneath my ribs, that I will do anything for the first of my great-grandchildren.

I drive home slowly. I am cautious, with Kelly's doubting voice in my ear. I press down on the brake a few blocks before each green light, anticipating it will turn red. I take the turns wide. I put my blinker on well in advance. When I pull into the assisted-living center's parking lot, and into the spot that was assigned to me after its previous owner had a stroke, or a heart attack, or died, I turn off the engine and put the ignition key into my purse for the last time.

I am now, sixty-two years after earning my license, a non-driver.

This is not a depressing moment. I have, after all, always been the one to decide when the next phase of my life will begin. I make my own rules. I live by my own choices. No one tells me what to do. I will not bend on this point until it is absolutely necessary. And now, after twenty-four delusion-free hours, that time of personal surrender is the furthest thing from my mind.

GRACIE

Grayson leans across a desk that is messy with loose stacks of paper, half-empty soda cans, and plastic bags filled with quarters and says, "What gives?"

I purposely wore my vintage pink-lensed glasses to this meeting so Grayson wouldn't be able to study my eyes. He is big on studying eyes, listening to the tone you use, noting whether you fidget or not. He is a newspaperman, and he likes to gather information. For the three years I've known him, he has been gathering information on me, first as a girlfriend, then as an employee. Sometimes I am tempted to ask him what he plans to do with everything he has learned about Gracie Leary. But most of the time I don't want to draw attention to the subject. I consider myself lucky to have successfully withheld one big secret from Grayson for the past two and a half years. To protect that one secret, I am willing to do anything. I almost don't mind the fact that I have to tell him about this pregnancy today, soon, any minute.

"You're the one who scheduled the meeting," I say.

"Why did you cancel last week?"

"Something came up." I sit up straight, trying to look professional. But I have never felt professional and it doesn't help that I was distracted while getting dressed this morning and am therefore wearing sneakers with my pantsuit. "Wasn't my column all right?"

"Actually, no," he says.

I take my glasses off. "I spent hours on it—what are you talking about? It was great this week." Then I feel a twinge of doubt. "Wasn't it?"

"I can tell from the letters you're choosing to answer that something's wrong," he says. "A few months ago you wouldn't go near the depressed teenage girls, now you can't get enough of them. And do you even read the advice you're giving them? You told one heartbroken girl, and I quote, 'to stay in the darkness for a while and to learn from it.' You can't say that to a fifteen-year-old, Gracie—that means suicide! We had to edit the line out before the column printed." Grayson raps a pencil against the stack of papers in front of him. "Just tell me what your problem is. You know that if you don't tell me I'll find out anyway."

I am slightly appalled. I remember writing that line, but it didn't sound that negative and frightening in my head. I had meant it to be comforting. I was suggesting growth and self-awareness to the young girl, not death. But I know better than to argue the point with Grayson. Like Lila, he is very logical. When it comes to the newspaper, he doesn't care about intentions, only about what appears in black and white. And the newspaper is everything to him, if something can mean everything to someone as cool and controlled as Grayson.

Grayson is thirty-three. He wrote for the Local section all through college and then became editor of the section three years after graduation. That was all he had ever dreamed of, careerwise, but then his father, who was editor-in-chief of the paper, suffered a massive heart attack at a Giants football game. Before he died he called a staff meeting in his hospital room and named Grayson to replace him as editor-in-chief. The deal was that Grayson would try the job for six months, and if he didn't work out by consensus of all the editors, he would return to his old position. The six-month trial period came to a close three years ago, and though there have been a few complaints, Grayson has held on to the job.

"I hate it when you rewrite my columns, Grayson. You don't do that to your other writers."

"I edit all of my writers."

"I'm not talking about editing, I'm talking about rewriting." I am stalling. Grayson is the one person who always thinks highly of me. I don't look forward to watching his eyes dim and grow hooded.

Grayson shakes his head. "Don't change the subject. What's wrong?"

"My gram was in a car accident."

"I heard about that. Four stitches but she's fine. Try again."

"My mother is driving me crazy."

This gets a small smile, as it is very old news. But his eyes are distracted behind his glasses; he is thinking. "You also chose several letters over the last few weeks involving the problems of pregnant women. So we have depression and pregnant women."

The pink glasses were a pointless defense. I could wear a sack over my head and Grayson would look to see how my breath moved the material and if my head was bowed and whether he could detect a sigh, or a sob, or a giggle.

When I broke up with Grayson I told him that it was because I didn't want to be in a relationship anymore. That was true, but the larger truth was that I had just found out I was pregnant with his baby. He never knew about it. Lila was the one who took me to the clinic, waited for me, and drove me home. She was the only person I told. I never thought of that pregnancy as having much of anything to do with Grayson. I thought of it only as a mistake. Maybe that is why I have never been comfortable with the idea of losing Grayson entirely. He is my link to that experience. And now that I am pregnant again, I can't help but look at the past in a different way. I don't owe Grayson that truth—I will never tell him about my abortion—but I do owe him something. As my belly grows, I'm afraid all my cards will be laid on the table.

I fiddle with my glasses in my lap. Which time is it? Time to hold my cards, or time to fold and make a run for it? What if all of the truth, not just part of it, comes rushing out?

Grayson meets my eyes, and I squirm. The air in the room is so heavy I feel like I could swim out the door. He sees the truth; I watch his brain click on to the answer.

He says, "You're pregnant?"

There's no reason for me to respond.

He guessed it, but there is still shock in his eyes. "You're keeping the baby?"

"Yes."

"Was this planned?"

My face is burning. "No. Joel and I broke up."

He leans back in his chair. He is a small man with glasses and curly brown hair. He runs in the early mornings, and he has a runner's tight, compact body. "Charlene told me that someone I was close to was pregnant, but I didn't pay attention to her."

Charlene is the gossip columnist for the paper. She is the worst kind of gossip, mean and nosy. I do everything I can to avoid her. "How the hell would Charlene know?"

The answer comes to me almost immediately. Joel must have told Charlene, or maybe it was Weber. That fat jerk. He's probably working his way through the phone book making sure all my ex-boyfriends hear the news, having the time of his life. I say, "I wanted to be the one to tell you."

Grayson's hand is in his hair now, tugging at the curls. I used to tease him that he should break himself of that habit, because there was no way his Jewish hair was going to straighten out. He is staring at me, and I wish he would stop. He says, "Do you want to get married?"

"I told you Joel and I broke up."

"Well, yes." I can see how my news has caught him off balance. He is thinking out loud, something he never does. "But you could marry me."

I shrink back until each rung of the chair digs into my spine. My voice comes out thin. "Do you think that's funny, Grayson? That's your idea of a joke?"

"No."

"I don't need pity. I'm going to be fine."

"How are you going to be fine? You don't make enough money. You'll have to get a higher-paying job, and no one will hire a pregnant woman. Besides, what else are you qualified to do?"

I am close to tears. I can hear Gram in my head: *Calm down, Gracie.* I hear her say: *I will take care of you and the baby.* I say, "Back off, will you?"

"Why do you want to have this baby?"

"Stop it," I say. "Stop interviewing me. I don't have to answer your questions. I don't have to explain anything to you. I'm going to have this baby. We're going to be fine, just the two of us. You'll see."

I stumble on my way through the door. My legs have gone numb while sitting in the chair. I lurch into the hallway, my lower half full of pins and needles.

"You'll need help," Grayson calls after me. "You won't be able to do this alone."

I LEAVE Hackensack by way of Route 17. I pass the huge new mall, then the older smaller mall, and turn off at the exit for Ramsey. I am not headed home. There are only three places Joel goes in the course of a day, and I know all of them. At night he's drinking beer at the Green Trolley. In the late afternoon he's at the firehouse. During the rest of the day he's doing spy work for Mayor Carrelli.

I drive in circles around the Municipal Building, slumped behind the wheel. I don't see anyone I recognize. How dare Joel tell anyone my news? How can I be expected to walk around my own life if I have no idea who knows what? Gram is talking again, telling me to calm down. She calls getting upset "losing your head," and she thinks I lose my head too often. She's right. She must be right.

I drive a little faster now, turning the corners surrounding the Municipal Building so fast my tires screech. I go around six times, until I'm dizzy. I never see Joel. I see my father on the sixth go-round, sitting on the front steps of the building. I hear the bark of the mayor's old Chow. I see a flash of red that could be Margaret's hair. She and Charlene are best friends. She surely knows already. I cannot stop what's already in motion, and I don't want to get in Margaret's way. What if she does hit Joel? She loves him; what would she do to me?

When I am forced to stop at a red light directly in front of the Municipal Building, I slump down further in my seat. A single fat bead of sweat runs from the nape of my neck underneath the hook on my bra, down to the waist of my pants. My back aches, and I keep shifting so the bottom of the steering wheel doesn't push into my abdomen. The light stays red forever.

I hear a noise; there are footsteps beside my car. I look up praying feverishly that I am still alone and that no one has seen me. But I'm not alone. There is a three-year-old girl standing in front of the open car window in a lime green dress. As unbelievable as it sounds, I know immediately that this is my unborn child. I recognize her. She is look-ing at me with her head tipped to the side.

I can see that she is about to ask, *Mommy, why are you hiding?* And I can also see that there is no suitable answer to that question. I am not behaving like a mommy. *Go away,* I hiss at her. *I'm not ready for you yet.*

Beyond her, on the steps of the Municipal Building, my father looks unhappy. I have the sense that he is thinking of me. His face is so sad, tears push at the back of my eyes. I can feel in that moment my child and my father worrying over me. Their worry bores into me like a drill. I am not strong enough. They both see my weakness: I don't know who I am.

The light finally turns green, and I slam my foot on the gas. I need to get away. My head is splitting when I finally nose the car into a straight line. I drive across town and don't stop until I reach Sarachi's Pond. Once there, I pull into the dirt parking lot where the teenagers drink and neck after the sun goes down, and turn off the car's engine. I am alone. There are no other cars. Sarachi's is a pond surrounded by heavy woods. There are picnic tables scattered near the water's edge. On weekend afternoons couples bring their young children here to feed the ducks and geese.

My family came here only once that I can remember. I was thir-teen and Lila was eleven. We came here for a picnic, and it remains the only picnic I've ever been on in my life. We are not big on the out-doors in our family. We don't like bugs or sweating or sitting on the ground. We sunburn easily. This one picnic was an exercise in forced spontaneity. My dad bought fancy sandwiches at the gourmet super-market, and Mom pulled an old blanket from the upstairs closet. Lila was assigned to bring her Frisbee and I had my Monopoly board. Mom and Dad had told us their plan in the middle of the previous week so we wouldn't have a chance to back out. When we asked why we were going on a picnic, they answered that we just were, and that was that. It had seemed like a strange thing to do, and a strange time to do it. Lila and I hated each other at that age. We couldn't have been more different. I had just fallen for boys, and I couldn't think about anything but how to get one, and once I got one, what to do with him. I slept with my hair in curlers and anti-wrinkle cream smeared under my eyes. I spoke with a horrible English accent that I thought made me sound sophisticated.

At eleven, Lila was a friendless, straight-A student who was obsessed with reading the newspaper. She read my parents' copies of the *New York Times,* the *Star Ledger,* and the *Bergen Record* every day and focused on the really bad news. She cut out articles on plane crashes, shootings, abandoned children, and freak fatal accidents. Whenever Mom gave her almost daily plea for someone to please talk about something at the dinner table, Lila would pull one of the articles out of her sock, where she stored them. My sister was a weird kid, and I wanted nothing to do with her.

I can see now that the picnic was an attempt on my parents' part to pull our family together. I'm sure it was my mother's idea. She didn't recognize or particularly like the two daughters who were pulling away from her. She would try to brush my hair and tuck me in at night, and I bristled under her attempts to make me stay a child. Lila and I were more relaxed with Dad. We mystified him, but he still enjoyed our company. Mom would be the one to think a picnic would be a great quick fix.

Of course, it wasn't. It was a humid day, and after we ate our turkey and Brie sandwiches, I complained that my hair was beginning to frizz. I walked over to the water's edge to check my reflection, and while I was leaning over, Lila beaned me in the back of the head with her Frisbee. Caught off balance, I took a step forward and lost my right sneaker in the watery muck of the pond. I was mortified, because there were other kids from my school at Sarachi's Pond who might have seen me get hit in the head, and because my sneakers were brand new. It took ten minutes for Dad to convince me that if I took off my other sneaker I would look fine, and I calmed down enough to return to the blanket.

Our parents sat between Lila and me while we played Monopoly. There were strong and sudden gusts of wind, so we had to tuck our cards under our feet, and clutch the fake money in our fists. Silence fell over us, and the game dragged on and on. I began to think I would turn fourteen still sitting on that blanket. Lila kept pulling her favorite article of the day, about a car wreck in South Jersey, out of her sock and then sliding it back in. At one point, just before I threw down my cards and begged to go home, I grew aware of what we must look like to other families, couples, and children in the park. Unhappy, and ill-suited to one another. I realized, in that moment, that even though we were a family, we did not necessarily belong together. We did not necessarily work.

I LAY my hand on my stomach and watch the ducks flap their wings and quack. I visited Sarachi's Pond often as a teenager and then later during college vacations. I lost my virginity here, to Billy Goodwin, when I was sixteen. Soon after, I became an expert on having sex in cars. I knew how to do it in the front passenger seat, with the guy on the bottom, me sitting facing him, pelvis to pelvis, my legs spread as wide as they'd go. I learned, after a few bad bruises, how to avoid the stick shift.

But sex in the backseat was always the best, my head against one door and my feet propped against the other. That was my locked-in position, where I shimmied and quaked beneath the boys. "Free Fallin'" or "Brown Eyed Girl" or something from Billy Joel's Glass Houses album played on the radio. The inside of the car smelled like an over-ripe mixture of Naugahyde seats, sweaty towels from wrestling or football practice, and a sweet hint of the red Slurpee we'd shared earlier at 7-Eleven. I would bury my face in the plush seat and breathe that smell in. I have to say that having sex in bed is overrated. Sometimes it is better to have less space, less range of motion, fewer options. Cramped spaces lead to greater acts of creativity and a special kind of intensity. I had some very good evenings at Sarachi's Pond.

I slide my hand down and touch myself, through the fabric of my pants. Just a soft pressure to say, I haven't forgotten about you. I miss you. Then I pull my hand away, and cross my arms over my chest. Unborn little girls or insanely jealous redheads could approach my car at any moment. Even alone, I'm not safe.

I suddenly hear Grayson's question, *Why do you want to have a baby?* His voice, in the still car, is inescapable.

I don't try to come up with an answer. I don't have one. I am obviously good at getting pregnant, no one can argue with that. Maybe I have found my gift. Maybe this is what I am meant to do. Maybe I will be like Gram and spend the rest of my premenopausal life bearing children.

The problem is, I am not as uninformed as that reasoning sounds. For my own peace of mind, I wish I were. After all, I have written numerous Dear Abby responses to teenage girls telling them that having a baby is not an answer. When the girls complain of a feeling of emptiness inside, I have told them in no uncertain terms to find another way to fill the void. Join a team. Be the creator of something— an art project, or a play. Write in your journal. Try to have a conversation with your parents. Wait until you have grown up and into yourself.

That is what I would have told my teenage self as she was steaming up Billy Goodwin's mother's Volvo at Sarachi's Pond. But I needn't have bothered. I knew better back then. I was vigilant with birth control. I went on the Pill three days after I lost my virginity, and took it religiously every morning for thirteen years. I also insisted that the guys I was with wear condoms. I relaxed my doubled-up birth-control regimen with Grayson—maybe because we were together for so long— and that's how I got in trouble the first time. And then, even before Joel, I began to grow forgetful. In the middle of the week I'd remember that I had forgotten to take my pill for a few days. I grew tired of reminding guys to put on a condom.

I was ultra-cautious as a teenager because I was terrified by the idea of getting pregnant and having my family find out. That was what would wake me up with night sweats. That's what would make my head hurt while I waited for my period to start each month. I was terrified of the reaction of my mother, grandmother, father, and aunts. Pregnancy without marriage was unthinkable in our family.

I honestly don't know what changed. My family still scares me. Gram knows now, and somehow her knowing and planning for me is more frightening than her not knowing. I wake up in the middle of the night sweating, heart flip-flopping in my chest, thinking, Why did I do this? Why?

I have told my readers again and again that a baby is not an answer to anything. Don't make that mistake. Don't fall into that trap. Keep this in mind: A baby is simply, and decisively, and irreversibly, a baby. To give birth to a child is to take on the responsibility of another human life.

KELLY

My first memory is of the day my sister died.

I know that child psychologists would say this isn't possible, since I was only eighteen months old at the time. They say the brain isn't developed enough to hold on to images until a child is closer to three years of age. But, in my case at least, they are wrong.

I remember every detail of that day, and no one ever told me about it. There is no one I could have gotten my information from. My sister was gone, my brother Pat would not be born for another week. For the only time in my life, for a few short days, for the wrong reasons, I was the only McLaughlin child. During that time no one spoke to me. My parents were so shocked and numb, they were not aware I was in the house with them. Willie shushed my tears. The deaths in my family, as well as the births, were occurrences that carried a warning with them. They all happened in slow motion, steeped in silence and disapproval. There was the sense that this should not be witnessed. And, if witnessed, should never be spoken of again. Birth and death were too common, too raw, for my self-made father and my properly raised mother. They were beneath our family; their messiness cheated us out of perfection. Death was of course the worse of the two, and it put a terrible pressure on those who survived to make up for what should not have happened.

My sister's death marked me, both with a sense of shame that I drew from my parents, and with an indelible memory. When she was a little girl, Lila used to wonder aloud who she might have gotten her memory from. I never spoke up and told her that it was me. I wanted to tell her, but somehow I couldn't. It is a secret I have never shared with anyone, and it is also my curse. I watched with wonder and admiration as Lila grew up touting her memory as a great gift. She used it in school to get top grades. She used it in card games to beat her friends. She used her memory at every step of her life in order to be the best. Until I watched my daughter, it had never even occurred to me to utilize my memory to my own gain. It is something I have always worked to deny, push away, hide, ignore. My memory brings me pain, because everything reminds me of everything. Everything is connected. All it takes is a glimpse, a flash of color, a smell, and I am taken into the past.

A fall day with the colorful leaves turning belly up to a stiff breeze reminds me of going clothes shopping with my mother. The six McLaughlin children would line up in age order (me carrying a list of what each child needed as well as their most recent measurements, Pat in charge of carrying pads of paper and crayons to entertain the smaller children) and we'd follow our mother through the department store until every last pair of pants, skirts, underwear, socks, and shoes had been bought.

A glass of scotch reminds me of my father walking carefully into the dining room, his hands reaching for the walls for balance, starting in on Pat before he has even taken his seat.

The first day of school each year reminds me of dropping Gracie off at kindergarten and her crying silently, tears running down her face, her small head bowed when I refuse to give her another hug good-bye.

Bright blue winter skies remind me of the day I married Louis, and the way my hands shook as I walked down the aisle, dropping petals from my bouquet of white roses.

Horses remind me of a teenaged Lila in competition, her jaw fixed, her face locked in an expression of such intensity that once the event ended, even if she'd won, it took time to relax.

Many things remind me of the day my sister died. A toddler with white-blond hair. My mother's strong hands, folded in her lap now or gripping her purse after years of raising, holding, bathing, carrying children. My brother Pat's pale eyes. Lila bragging about her memory, which makes me think about mine, which leads me to think about my first memory. I have no choice but to remember.

My sister's crying woke me that morning. I watched her through the bars of my crib. She sat bolt upright in her bed a few feet from me, her hands cupping her throat as if she were trying to protect it from something. "Water," she said. My mother appeared in the doorway, tying her robe around what was left of her waist since she was eight months pregnant. "Shush now. Your father is sleeping." Mother looked angry, and my sister hid under her pillow. I went back to sleep. Later, after Father left for work, my sister was curled in a ball on the living-room couch. She whimpered, and my mother sat next to her, her hand on the child's forehead. *Give her water,* I wanted to say, but I wasn't able to speak in sentences yet. My sister looked very hot, and I knew that for some reason she could no longer speak for herself. "I can't," my mother said, as if she had heard my thought. "You have to let a fever burn itself out. No fluids. That's what Dr. O'Malley said."

My mother left us to straighten up the bedrooms and wash the breakfast dishes. While she was gone I watched my sister and her fever burn themselves out. I sat on the floor penned by a square of wooden posts. I ignored my toys. For one minute my close attention paid off— my sister made a face at me. She stuck out her tongue and waggled her hands by her ears and I laughed. This was our own private game, a secret from Mother and Father. Some nights she and I did not go to sleep when we were supposed to. My sister would turn on the light and stand on her bed and make her funny faces while I giggled in my crib.

But after that one face my sister didn't look at me anymore. Her eyes closed and her face swelled up and she began to make a strange cough in the back of her throat. Mother came back into the room, wiping her hands on her apron, saw my sister, and said, "Dear Lord." She ran over to the couch. I had never seen my mother run before, and being as pregnant as she was, it was a worrying sight. She gathered my sister up in her arms, turned toward me, and yelled, "Willie." I had never heard my mother yell before, either. Willie didn't appear, and my mother ran across the room to me, my sister quiet in her arms. With difficulty, Mother leaned over the fence, and I put my arms out to be picked up. My mother hesitated, then said, "Not now, Kelly. Be good for Mother." Then she and my sister left the room, the garage door slammed, and the house roared with silence. I waited, perfectly still, for a monster to come and eat me, because that seemed like a completely viable end to this strange morning.

But instead Willie came back, and when she saw me in my cage all alone, she began to bawl, which made me bawl, too. After Willie fed me lunch, my mother and sister came home, which made me cry again, this time with relief, because I thought they had left me for good. But my sister's skin was bluish now and she was even more swelled up, and when I called her name, she didn't hear me. My mother took her into our bedroom, so I couldn't see what was going on. My father came home in the middle of the day and he ran, too, from the kitchen to the bedroom. Then Dr. O'Malley arrived with his black bag in his hand. No one paid any attention to me. I sat in my cage and banged and rattled my toys until they were taken away.

Late in the afternoon it got dark in the house, but it was a long time before anyone thought to turn on the lights. My parents stopped running. Everything grew still and silent. They must have taken my sister out through the front door, because I never saw her again. My father walked in and sat down in his leather chair. He sobbed loudly while he drank a big glass of a liquid the same color as his tears. I thought that was what he was doing, drinking his own tears. The tears seemed to refill the glass as fast as he could gulp them down, and as hard as he could cry. And nobody told me, not my father with his glass of tears, not my mother with her hand on her swollen stomach, that in that afternoon I had become an only child.

This is my first memory. I have wondered, from time to time, what Lila's first memory is. I wonder how early her remembered life began. It is a comfort to me to know it could not have been anything nearly as unpleasant as mine. My daughters have experienced very little death. They grew up in a happy family, with two stable parents. They had all the clothes and food and money they needed and then some. They did not have to deal with alcoholism or child abuse, or any tragic events. I have managed to give my daughters much more than my parents gave me. And I have spared them a lot, too. Any fights Louis and I had while Gracie and Lila lived at home took place after they were asleep. When the girls fought, I steered them away from each other. When they upset me, I told them so, and then we moved on.

I do not understand why, after this placid and pleasant upbringing, my daughters are angry at me. How can they be so unfair? Do they not recognize everything I've given them? I'm not asking them to thank me, for God's sake. I just want them to be something more than civil. I want to know why I am their enemy and their father is their friend. I want them to be *my* friends, now that I don't have to parent them anymore. Now that they've grown up.

AFTER MY mother's car accident I called Lila and Gracie, but no one answered the phone. I left a message on Gracie's machine. It has been three days now and no one has returned my call. This fact is just one more thing that makes a shitty afternoon at work even worse. A little voice in my head says, Just get out of here. So I do, I leave work early. Sarah asks if I am feeling okay, and Giles just stares. God, it makes me feel good, marching out of there with my briefcase, making my own rules. I am the boss, after all. I don't act like it often enough. I chain myself to my desk because I know I can't trust anyone to do the work as well as I can.

In the parking lot I close my briefcase in the trunk and put the top down on my BMW. It's not quite warm out, but the sky is blue and with the heater on I am fine. I decide to take the long way home, winding aimlessly across Ramsey until it occurs to me to visit my daughters. It's not something I normally do, but I know that my mother used to drop by Gracie's house and even Lila's dorm room whenever she felt like it. Maybe I've been hanging back too much in my relationship with the girls; perhaps it's time for me to be more aggressive. I resist calling ahead. After all, I'm their mother. I can just show up, can't I? The idea makes me smile into the wind.

I turn up the radio. The Beach Boys come on with "California Girls." I know all the words, and sing along. I feel light, carefree, young. It is so rare for my mind to unclench, for the worrying to stop. I am grateful when it does; I appreciate these moments. I don't want the song to end. I pass Ramsey High School, the post office, my gynecologist's office. I pass the road that leads to the Municipal Building, and beyond that, to my brother Ryan's apartment. I sing loudly right up until I pull into Holly Court and into Gracie's driveway. When the Beach Boys' harmony dies away, I turn off the car engine and take off my sunglasses. I look up, and Gracie is standing in front of the car, her arms loose at her sides. She must have just gotten home. She looks beautiful, so grown up.

"Gracie," I say, laughing, "don't squint like that. It makes you look like an old lady."

"What's wrong? Is it Gram?"

I get out of the car with difficulty. I love my BMW, but it is so low to the ground that it's a challenge to get out and still be ladylike. I keep smiling, but I heard the chill in my daughter's voice, and now I have to work at it. "Nothing's wrong. Can't a mother stop by and visit her kids?"

Gracie's face relaxes a little. "Of course. It's just that you never do."

"Well, perhaps I should have called first. God knows I hate it when people just show up at my house." We are standing facing each other.

"Yours and Dad's."

"Pardon me?"

"It's not just your house. It's yours and Dad's."

My shoulders drop. I can't win.

"I'm sorry," Gracie says. "I'm just having this really weird day and then you scared me showing up like that."

I try not to sound affronted. "I certainly didn't mean to scare you."

"Please don't be overdramatic. I'd like to go inside and change. Do you mind?"

I think, I can fix this. I say, "Here's an idea. Why don't you keep that lovely suit on? You could put on nicer shoes and then we could all go out to dinner—you, me, and Lila. What do you think about that idea?" I touch her arm lightly, then bend down. Something has caught my eye. "What is that on your pants? Is that chocolate? What in the world—How did you get melted candy on yourself?" I scrape at the fabric with my thumbnail.

"Mother!" Gracie takes a long step away from me.

I straighten up. "You should soak those pants in cool water and take them to the dry cleaners first thing tomorrow morning. I bought you that suit, you'll remember. You need to take better care of it."

Gracie is hugging her waist. Her jacket bunches in the shoulders. She looks small and pale and, with the chocolate stain on her knee, like a child wearing grown-up's clothes. She shakes her head. "How is Gram? Have you seen her since the accident?"

"I went to visit her the other day. She seems fine. A little quiet, maybe, but I think she was still shaken up. She asked me to pick up Ryan and bring him to Easter. Normally she would have brought him with her. But it's understandable that she would feel less comfortable driving now."

"She said she feels uncomfortable driving?"

"Not in so many words. But I'd be happy to know she was off of the road. She's getting too old, Gracie, and her balance is shaky at best. Her giving up driving is the next logical step."

"Toward what?"

"We'll get her a driver when she needs to go somewhere, and they have a shuttle that runs into town every afternoon at the assisted-living center. It'll be fine. She'll be safe."

"She'll die."

I sigh. "Nobody's talking about dying. Your grandmother will out-live us all."

Something ripples across Gracie's face. I notice again how pale she is. She has such nice skin. Lila had blemishes as a teenager, but Gracie's skin was always smooth.

"I don't feel well, Mom. I think I caught some kind of bug. I need to go inside now. I'm sorry. Thanks for stopping by, though."

"Oh, sweetheart, can I help you? Why didn't you say something sooner?"

But Gracie is out of earshot before all the words are out of my mouth. She is half-jogging across the top of the driveway and then around the side of the house. She doesn't glance back before she disappears. And I am very aware, as I get back into the BMW, that Gracie never, during the course of our conversation, either responded to my dinner invitation or invited me inside.

WHEN I get home, Louis is not there. This is not a surprise. He is rarely home now. He has three shirts and a pair of his khakis hanging in the closet in the den. There are clean, rolled-up socks in the pants pockets. He comes upstairs only to shave and shower in the morning. In some way this situation didn't seem real to me until last week when our housekeeper, Julia, said, "Mrs. Kelly, do you want me to put Mr. Louis's clean shorts in the den, or upstairs in his drawer?"

I was livid. How dare she? I simply pretended I didn't hear her. I turned my back and waited until she left the room. She didn't mention it again, and she put his shorts upstairs. But now I am nervous all the time. What if one of the girls or, God forbid, my mother stops by and Julia says something to them? This is no one's business but mine and Louis's.

I need to do something to make Louis go back to the way he was before. For God's sake, there is no reason he can't sleep beside me in our king-sized bed while he goes through whatever he's going through. All I want right now is some semblance of normal, the keeping up of appearances. The house feels cold and drafty at night, no matter how many blankets I pile on the bed. We continue to leave notes for each other on the kitchen table, but now those are nearly the only words that pass between us. I have not changed, but Louis has, and it is time for him to change back. He's not keeping up his end of our deal, and he's crazy if he thinks I'll let *him* end our marriage. There are divorced women in my women's reading group, and they are angry and bitter. I will not fail like they have. I have no intention of getting a divorce.

It is the thought of my reading group that gives me a great idea.

Since Louis seems unable to engage with me lately, perhaps he needs a friend. He might be more comfortable sharing his feelings with another man, one of his peers. I'm excited when I come up with this; I can't believe it didn't occur to me sooner. I've gotten so much out of talking to the women in my group, but Louis doesn't have that kind of male support system in his life. He has lived his life with his two daughters and me. He's been surrounded by women. Male camaraderie is what's missing from his life. That's probably why he misses that young man so badly. A frank conversation with a friend will shake him out of the state he's in.

I drive to the mayor's barbershop feeling very strong. I have found the answer. Now I just need to get the ball rolling.

"Hi Vince," I say as I walk through the door. "Do you cut women's hair?"

The mayor turns around in a slow circle, as if I've caught him deep in thought and it's taking him a minute to come out of it. He is alone in the shop, cleaning his comb with a white cloth. His old Chow, who I somehow remember is named Chastity, is sleeping in the corner.

"Kelly?" Vince gives a big smile. "How nice to see you! To what do I owe this pleasure?"

I have never been in this shop before, although I've driven by it, even walked by it, countless times. It is a single room with three barber chairs, three mirrors, and wood-paneled walls. There is a counter with an old-fashioned cash register. The entire scene looks dusty and dark, even though it's a beautiful sunny day outside.

"I wanted to talk to you about something," I say. "But I need a trim, too, so I thought if I could do both at once, it would be the most efficient use of both of our time. If you cut women's hair, that is."

I admit, I get a little charge from saying this. I'm making this up as I go along, and that is very unusual for me. I didn't know I was going to ask for the haircut. For fifteen years I have had my hair styled at an upscale salon in Ridgewood by an Asian woman named Linda. And I've prided myself on never talking about what goes on in my family, outside of my family. Yet here I am, asking a barber to cut my hair, wanting to talk to him about my husband. It's true, I tell myself, that desperate times call for desperate measures.

He says, "I cut Cynthia's for thirty years."

I had almost forgotten about Cynthia. She died a year ago of breast cancer, but even when she was alive she was rarely seen. She was a round, short Italian woman who came over from Italy with her parents when she was a teenager. She married Vince when she was nineteen and he was twenty-five. They never had any kids, and she never went out with him in public. Even after he became mayor, she chose to stay at home, cooking and cleaning. I had spoken with Cynthia once or twice, but we had nothing in common and she was so terribly shy that conversation was painful. She liked Louis, though, and would talk to him in Italian, a language he can understand but not speak. He went to visit her in the hospital during her final stay. I didn't go with him. I didn't think it was necessary. The mayor and politics and the land and welfare of Ramsey are Louis's passion, not mine. After Cynthia died nothing seemed to change much. Vince was still out around town stumping and hand-shaking, still at the barbershop cutting hair.

I try to remember Cynthia's hair. It was always up in a bun. I feel Vince's eyes pore over my brown hair, then the angles of my face. "Have a seat," he says.

I sit down in the chair, which is surprisingly comfortable, if a little slippery. He drapes a gown around me, covering my gray suit. "How's Louis?" he asks. "Did he send you here?"

I watch my face color in the mirror. I don't know why. "God, no," I say. "I actually came here to talk to you about Louis."

"Close your eyes," Vince says.

I glance up at him.

"Don't worry," he says. "It's just for a second."

He sprays my hair with water out of a bottle. When I open my eyes I see a fifty-six-year-old woman in the mirror who appears to have been caught in the rain. I wonder whether this was a good idea.

"Louis has been an amazing friend to me. I wish I could say I've been better to him." He smoothes his hand over my wet hair, evening the pieces on either side of my face. "I started drinking in the evenings after Cynthia passed away—Louis must have told you that. He's had to pick me up off the floor several times, literally and figuratively."

"Louis never mentioned it," I say. I don't really know what to make of this. Why would this man share this with me? How am I supposed to respond? "But he hasn't said much to me lately at all. That's partly why I'm here."

"You need my help?" Vince sounds surprised.

I breathe in wet air tinged with hairspray. "Louis is depressed. I thought maybe you could talk to him. Try to cheer him up. Tell him that he needs to pull himself together. He won't listen to me. I thought that as an old friend you might have a better shot."

The dog whimpers loudly in the corner, and we both glance over. "Poor thing is plagued by nightmares," Vince says. He clips at the back of my hair with scissors. I watch the ends fall to the floor. "Louis is still upset about the young man who died?"

"Yes, at least that's what started the depression. God knows he should be over that by now. It's not as if it was his fault."

"It's nice that you're so worried about him." Vince touches my head with his fingertips, smoothing my hair first in one direction, then the other. His fingers are warm against my skin. "Louis's lucky to have such a wonderful wife taking care of him."

I wish I wasn't sitting in front of a mirror during this conversation, watching the lines around my mouth move as I talk, watching myself blush. "You don't have to report back and tell me what he says. The conversation would be between you and Louis."

"What if something is really wrong? You wouldn't want me to tell you?"

"There's nothing really wrong. He's just depressed."

"What if he's having an affair?"

I glare at him in the mirror. My hand fumbles at the back of my neck for the snap to release the cape draped over me. The surreal quality of this situation hits me. Why did I think this would work? Why would I let this man cut my hair?

"Hold on," Vince says. "It was a joke! I'm so sorry. I didn't mean to upset you. I didn't think you would take me seriously. Louis would never have an affair. Never. I've known him my whole life and he's one of the best people I've ever met. Now I've upset you and that's the last thing I wanted to do."

I settle back in to the chair slowly. "That's not my idea of a joke," I say. "I hope you understand that what is going on is a private matter and the utmost discretion—"

"I understand. And of course I'm happy to speak to Louis. No one has done more for me since Cynthia died than your husband." He meets my eyes in the glass. Beside us, around us, my hair continues to fall away. I am getting lighter and lighter.

"Don't tell him I asked you to do this."

"Of course not."

"I appreciate it."

"I've liked talking to you," he says. "You have that same gift Louis has—you make me feel like everything's going to be all right."

My whole body is hot. This feels wrong; it feels like too much. This man is too honest, too present. I forget why I came here, and I need to leave. I pull a twenty-dollar bill out of my purse.

"I don't need a blow-dry," I say, and stand up. I unsnap the cape and push the money into his hand. "It's warm enough outside. Thank you for your help."

"You're welcome," he says, and walks me to the door.

I AM too keyed up when I leave the barbershop to go straight home. I need some time alone to collect myself. I drive toward Route 17 and once there I join the rush of cars, each driver speeding away from his job and his day. I make a U-turn and head in the reverse direction. I pass a stretch of forest, and then the gas station and Houlihan's. I slow down in front of the restaurant and turn into the Fairmount Motel parking lot. I park near the end of the L-shaped motel, directly in front of Room 111. I finger the room key in my purse for a moment before I get out of the car.

The key makes a smooth clicking noise in the lock, and the door is released. I step inside and flip the light switch. The two lamps on either side of the bed light up. The curtains for the room's sole window are already shut to block out the sight of the highway. I set my purse down on the bed and walk straight into the bathroom, where I wash my hands with the fresh bar of Ivory soap I left here last week. I dry my hands on a flowered towel Gracie brought home from college. When I walk back into the room I pull the two pillows I bought at the bedding store off the closet shelf and prop them against the headboard. I remove my tan heels and lie down on top of the bedspread. I am sup-ported in a half-sitting position by the firm pillows. Once comfortable, I am completely still, my hands clasped on my waist. I take a deep breath and allow myself to relax.

Sometimes I watch the news here, on the small television in the corner. Sometimes I read one of the novels I have stacked beside the pillows in the closet. But usually I just lie on the bed. I rarely sleep. I simply savor the fact that I am alone, perfectly alone. I don't have to pretend to be interested or sorry or content or whatever else my fam-ily or my employees might want me to be. Here, and only here, can I explore and expose my true self. I can be Kelly McLaughlin Leary: a strong, independent fifty-six-year-old woman.

When I first came here I had no idea who Kelly Leary was. I still am not completely sure, but at least I'm learning. I'd been working to the point of exhaustion for years and had lost all sight of myself. But last year I joined a women's reading group, mostly so I would have someplace to go one night a week. Louis, after all, is gone four out of five nights a week attending all sorts of meetings. I wanted a change. I wanted something that was my own. I had no idea what to expect from the group, but what I found was a lot of discussion in which these women told one another *everything* about their lives in startling detail. And in between the meetings, we read the same books. At first I was better at the reading than the talking. We chose books about finding our paths and our true selves. I came to realize that I had spent my life trying to be what everyone else wanted me to be: a good daughter, a good wife, a good mother. I had done nothing to feed my soul, nothing to set myself free. I mentioned once or twice in the group how frustrating it was to be trapped in the life I had built up around me, and how I craved my own space. After one of our meetings a woman offered me this room. She is from a wealthy family that owns, among other things, a string of motels in northern New Jersey. The Fairmount Motel was not doing particularly well and was never full, so she lets me rent this room for a low monthly fee.

I have had a lot to learn, and to accept. Most of my life I have just lived a moment and then done my best to throw it away. But in this room I have sifted through those moments, through my childhood and my marriage, through those times that got me here. I am a different person today than I was when Louis and I were married. No one ever tells you, when you are young, that your entire personality can change—will change—as you grow older. The twenty-five-year-old Kelly McLaughlin is a completely different woman from the fifty-six-year-old Kelly Leary. My behavior is different, my needs are different. When I was young I needed someone to take charge of me, to take me a few steps away from my family.

When I graduated from college it was my father who told me that despite my high test scores, a woman could only pursue one of two careers: nursing or teaching. I didn't have the patience for teaching and I couldn't stand the sight of blood, so I got a job as a salesgirl at Bloomingdale's. I was bored all day long at work, and then at home every night I listened while my father abused Pat and ridiculed me. I watched my mother hurry from one task to another, one child to another. She appeared deaf to what was being said. To the damage that was being done.

I met Louis at Bloomingdale's. I helped him pick out a suit for a friend's wedding. I liked how physically large he was—I am five foot nine, but I felt petite beside him. His personality was warm and light. He told a lot of silly jokes and laughed at the punch lines along with me. We went out for coffee, and then dinner, and then suddenly we were an item. I was quiet on our dates, letting him do most of the talking. One night, while driving back to New Jersey from seeing a show in Manhattan, we stopped at a red light and I pointed out a house I liked. This small comment caused Louis to bang the steering wheel with his hand and yelp like a dog. I couldn't understand what he was saying at first because I was so surprised by the clatter of words. "I have been waiting since we got in the car forty-five minutes ago for you to say one word. I promised myself that I wouldn't start this conversation—you were going to have to. It was a little test. But forty-five minutes! Jeez, Kelly. Didn't you have anything you wanted to say about the show, about anything?"

I know that I smiled at him at that moment, amused. I know that I didn't find my voice until after we were married and I had moved one town away from my family and quit my job at Bloomingdale's. When, shortly after the trip home from New York, Louis told me that he knew I was the one for him and that we were meant to be together, I chose to believe him. We were married a few months later and I moved from my father's house to my husband's house. I had Gracie just before our first wedding anniversary.

I never had a place of my own until this room. It has been mine, and mine alone, for six months now. I have told no one about this place: not my husband, not my daughters. I now have somewhere to go when I've had another argument with Louis or when I've had my feelings hurt by one of the girls. Or when my mother calls and asks me, once again, to be the head of the family, to convince my brothers and sisters to do something they don't want to do. To do something I don't want to do, either. I should be used to having my feelings disregarded by now. I don't understand why my mother can't be happy with just me, Gracie, Lila, and Ryan. Why can't we be enough? There is little point in drawing all of my brothers and sisters and their families together. What you get when we are all in the same room is not love. It is a potent combination of our childhood, my father's anger, and my mother's deliberate silence and pointless barbed comments. It is the long, thin, thorny end of the rose.

Sometimes I am bored in the motel room. Sometimes, like today, I can't get comfortable. I stand up, pace, try the rickety armchair in the corner, peek through the curtains at the rush of the highway. I know that this time is important in my journey to know myself, but occasionally it is unpleasant. I remember shaking Vince Carrelli's warm hand as we said good-bye, and how we each seemed to hold on to the handshake for a second too long. I flip from thoughts of my mother to my siblings to my daughters, and I feel as if each turn sends me into another brick wall. And then at some point I run out of things to think about altogether, I run out of anger, and I am left feeling blank and empty. Swallowed up in some vague darkness. This is the point when I put the pillows back in the closet, switch off the lights, and leave.

THAT VERY night I am pressed into my role of family liaison. My mother has asked me to make sure all of my brothers and sisters agree to show up for the Easter party. Meggy calls to say that she doesn't understand why she has to be the one to travel here, when she has less money than any of us. I tell her I would be happy to pay the gas money it would take for her to drive from her house in southern New Jersey to northern New Jersey. My sister-in-law Angel calls to say that Johnny's antidepressant had been changed, and now that his headaches are better, he's happier about seeing everyone. Theresa phones to let me know she is baking three pies for the event, even though I had told her that Lila and Gracie are planning to make cookies. Ryan calls to say he is worried about Mother. He says she seemed to have a cloud over her head when she last visited. I am tempted to ask him how he could see a cloud what with all the fat, dirty birds flying around his apartment, but I restrain myself. Of course, I don't tell Ryan about Mother's accident; there is no point in upsetting him. Pat is the only one of my siblings who doesn't call. I had known he wouldn't, but still I had hoped. But Pat knows the time and the location of the party, and he will show up. He will do his duty, and no more.

Louis comes home while I'm on the phone with Ryan. I take these kinds of calls at the table in the kitchen, where I can pay bills or sort through the mail at the same time. He sits across from me and finishes the leftover Chinese food that was in the refrigerator. While I talk, I eye him to see if he's spoken to Vince yet. I wonder what he will say about my haircut, which is very short in the back and on the sides. I haven't decided yet whether I like it, and I trust Louis's opinion.

When I hang up with Ryan, he says, "I wish you didn't have so much stress over this party."

"I'm fine."

"You don't have to take care of your mother and all of your brothers and sisters. Let them take care of themselves. They won't fall apart if you put yourself first for once. You know, you could skip this Easter party entirely if you wanted to."

I stare at him. Sometimes I envy Louis his family, which started out small and then disappeared. Other times I feel badly for his loss. But it is always clear that he has no idea what having a family really means. The ties that crisscross and bind and trip up my brothers and sisters and my mother and me are invisible pieces of thread to my husband. No matter how closely he looks, even when I push his nose right up against the glass, he does not see it. He does not understand.

I say, "Why are you picking a fight with me? You know I have to go to this party. You're coming with me, right?" This is a question I would never have even thought to ask six months ago. Of course he would be coming with me. He's my husband.

He shrugs. I don't know how it's possible, but his size is always a surprise to me. His shoulders are so wide, they completely block the back of the chair he is sitting on. "Of course I'm going to the party," he says. "I'm sorry. I just had a strange day, and I shouldn't take it out on you."

"Strange how?"

"Vince Carrelli made me rearrange my schedule tonight to see him, and then he tried to tell *me* what my problems are. I swear to God, Kelly, I almost hit him."

"Louis!" To hear him even suggest violence is shocking. It is completely out of character. "I'm sure Vince was just trying to be helpful. What did he say?"

He stands up and carries his plate to the sink. "I've been taking care of this guy since we were in the fourth grade. He was always picked on as a kid, and I stood up for him. I was the one who kept him from getting beaten to a pulp by his asshole cousin. I tutored him in math throughout high school. If I hadn't talked him into buying that house by the town pool, he and Cynthia would have thrown away all their savings on rent. And then when he nearly drank himself out of a job this past year, I stopped the board from taking action against him. Jesus, Vince is a career fuck-up. He's the last person I'd take advice from."

I shake my head. "Well then, who will you take advice from? Who's good enough to give you advice? Because you need some, Louis. You sleep on a coffee table every night. When is that going to change? What if people find out what's going on here?"

He looks very tired, standing on the opposite side of the room. "I don't mean to make you unhappy, Kelly. Everything is fine. This is only temporary. I'll be better soon."

"When is soon? And where do you go every afternoon?" What if he has fallen in love with someone else? What if he is having an affair?

"I never ask you where you go after work or on Saturday afternoons, do I? I trust you. I love you. All I'm asking is that you trust me, too. I'm going through something right now, but it will be fixed soon. Will you just trust me?"

I run my fingers through my new short haircut. It dried naturally in a matter of minutes this afternoon. I think the look will grow on me. It's fine that my husband, who used to annoy me by noticing every little thing about me, didn't notice this big change. He is not himself right now. I will cover for him until he comes back to his senses. I will make this household appear the same as always, our marriage unchanged, our habits untouched. I will stick myself in front of his line of vision every chance I get and remind him that I am still here and I am his wife. I can't say that I trust Louis to pull through this on his own, but I do trust myself to hold everything together. As usual.

LILA

Gram, Gracie, Uncle Ryan, and I have been alone in the kitchen for nearly twenty minutes. Mom and Dad have disappeared somewhere. They're probably fighting. The only one who has spoken—apart from "Will you hand me the sugar?" or "Is the oven at the right temperature?"—is Ryan, and he is not someone you can hold a conversation with. We have been rolling out cookie dough, cutting it into the shapes of eggs and rabbits, and placing it in the oven. I have the most muscle, so I roll the dough. Gram and Ryan sit at the kitchen table wielding cookie cutters. Gracie mans the oven, sliding in and pulling out trays. The room smells of sweetness and holidays and warmth.

Only our silence cuts through that aroma, running from each of us in pointed directions. Gracie hasn't had much to say to me since I told her I was moving out at the end of the week. Gracie also seems to be avoiding Gram, not looking directly at her, not speaking to her. And Gram is keeping to herself, bent over the trays of dough. It is hard to tell if her silence is deliberate or if she's just not in the mood to talk. And, as for me, what's the point of opening my mouth?

I figure it's to my credit that I'm at least aware that I am in a bad mood, and that it's probably best that I keep quiet. I'm exhausted because I was on call last night and got only two hours of sleep. Things are getting worse at the hospital. I can't seem to say the right thing to the patients, no matter how hard I try. And Belinda has been testing what little patience I have left.

Also, I am in no mood for the boredom and the stress of one of these gatherings. The fact that it's taking place here means Gracie and I had to spend long hours cleaning and that I can't even leave early. Besides, it's best to come to these family events feeling focused and sure of yourself because together the McLaughlins tend to shake one another up. You have to be ready, and today I am not. I wish I was already in my new apartment, where I could close and triple-lock the door and enjoy some peace and quiet.

Mom stops just inside the kitchen and raises her hands dramatically in the air. We look over obediently. "Well," she says, "here you are doing all this work and I found your father napping in front of the TV."

"I was watching the news," Dad says. He rubs the back of his neck with his hand. "What can I do to help?"

"Television is evil," Ryan says.

My father seems to notice Ryan for the first time. His face brightens, and he says, "I just bought your building."

"What do you mean?" Mom says. "The building Ryan lives in? When?"

Dad is smiling to himself, his arms folded over his chest. His posture is now straight, a change from a few seconds earlier. "I got the place for a song. The structure of the building is decent, but it needs a lot of work. The previous owner hasn't put a dime into it over the last twenty years."

"Vince is right," my mother says, "you are buying up all of Ramsey. Why wouldn't you tell me that you bought my own brother's building?"

"That's Dad's business, Mom," I say. "It's not personal."

"He's doing really well," Gracie says. "You should be happy for him."

"Girls," Gram says.

"Girls," my father says, shaking his head.

Mom looks appropriately squelched. Her skinny shoulders drop and I feel guilty. But the temptation to knock her down comes on so strong, it is almost impossible to resist. I can see from the way Gracie is playing with her hair, twisting and pulling it, that she feels badly, too.

There is a sudden noise in the corner of the room, a tapping sound. Ryan is patting the arms of his wheelchair. As soon as the sound begins, Gram is on her feet and moving around the table toward him. Ryan's lips have gone white from biting them.

"My building," he says.

Gram leans over him. She says, "You can stay in your apartment, Ryan, I promise. Can't he, Louis? Nothing will change. This is good news, actually. Your building will be owned by family. Louis didn't mean to surprise you like that. Everything is fine."

We all watch, frozen, as Gram soothes her son.

"Yes," Dad says, "of course you'll stay in your apartment. Sorry if there was any misunderstanding, Ryan. I'm just going to fix it up, that's all. No need for you to worry. Just a little fix-up."

"A fix-up," Ryan repeats. "I won't have to move?"

"No," Dad says.

"I promise," Gram says.

The tension in the room diminishes, just in time for the party to start.

THE FIRST hour or two of these family gatherings are always torturous. We see one another once, maybe twice a year. We are family, but we have very little in common except that we are all terrible at small talk. We search one another's eyes, trying to communicate something of who we really are while we have strained discussions about the weather, politics, our jobs, or absent family members. But today the entire McLaughlin clan is here, so we've lost one topic of conversation.

This is the first time we've had full attendance in ten years, since Papa died. While he was alive, there was no thought of missing a family gathering. It wouldn't have occurred to anyone, not even Uncle Pat. His presence removed all choice. But now, with Papa gone, family is an option, and somehow that changes the way we regard one another. At these gatherings we size one another up and glance for the nearest exit and wonder, Why are you here? Why am I here?

We have appetizers outside on the back porch. It's a nice day, but not warm enough for people to take off their coats. We find seats (the catering company left lots of folding chairs) and eat buffalo wings and Cheddar with crackers and raw vegetables with dip.

I sit with Gracie on one side of me and Angel on the other. Angel is a sad-looking woman in her early forties. As far as I know, she is sad for two reasons: one, because she is married to my uncle Johnny, who is very depressed and hardly ever speaks, and two, because she has been unable to conceive a child despite years of fertility treatments. I usually try to avoid Angel, as I find her sadness contagious. She sighs a lot.

I have barely taken a bite of a cracker before Angel leans in. What I've been dreading the most is about to begin. Ever since the moment I declared premed as my major in college, my aunts and uncles have considered me a medical expert. No matter what I say, my family refuses to give up their grossly mistaken belief that wanting to be a doctor is the exact same thing as being one.

"Lila," Angel says, her voice so soft it is almost a whisper, "I've been having these pains in my lower back. What do you think it could be?"

Theresa, seated on the other side of Angel, joins in. Her black Farrah Fawcett waves bounce in my direction as she says, "My Mary's been suffering from terrible menstrual cramps. Is that normal for someone her age?"

My whole body hurts. My aunts sound like patients, like the men and women whining at me from their hospital beds. I can't help any of them. There is nothing I can do.

"Mom." Mary is suddenly nearby, gripping one of the three crosses around her neck. "Don't talk about that, please. You're embarrassing me."

I clear my throat and give them my usual spiel. "I'm not a doctor yet. You should really ask your physician for advice." But they keep looking at me as if I have a direct line to God. I hear myself give one of Angel's sighs. "I assume you've both tried Advil?"

"Yes," Angel says.

"Morning and night," Theresa says, her hand on Mary's knee.

Meggy passes by on her way to the food. "What's the point of having a doctor in the family if you can't get free advice?"

"I'm not a doctor," I say. "I'm still a fucking student. Will you all please hear that for once?"

"Lila," my mother says, from the other side of the porch. "Your language!"

"I'm sorry," I say, but my aunts look unfazed. I expect Travis to add insult to injury and ask me about his bum knee, but he is busy talking to my cousin John.

Aunt Meggy starts to complain to the group at large about the traffic she hit driving up here. She says three times that she will have to head out early in order to be in her bed before midnight. Aunt Theresa reaches out and smoothes Mary's hair away from her face until Mary stands up and crosses to the opposite side of the porch. Angel, keeping an eye on Uncle Johnny, praises the food while taking small nibbles from a buffalo wing. Mom makes her usual joke about how she has spent hours slaving over a hot stove to make this meal. Dad doesn't say much; he hardly ever speaks at these family gatherings. He keeps his eyes on Mom to make sure she is okay, but that is his only involvement.

I notice that the porch is already a mess, particularly around Aunt Meggy and Uncle Travis. Travis has somehow managed to drop three entire rolls off his plate, and not bothered to pick any of them up. He has also lost a handful of green beans to the wooden porch floor. He is obviously more concerned with taking care of his beer can than with holding his plate steady. And Aunt Meggy keeps picking food off Aunt Theresa's plate because she is too lazy to get up and refill her own. While transferring crackers and forkfuls of cheese spread, she has also managed to drop a fair amount of food.

"Can you believe that we have to clean up after these people?" I whisper to Gracie. "I don't have time to spend a day scrubbing the damn floors. I have work to do."

Gracie just shakes her head. She seems intent on being quiet to the point of invisibility. She might as well have not shown up. She and I are usually allies at these events. We rarely leave each other's side. We roll our eyes at each other, and whisper jokes about Uncle Travis and our cousin John. We rescue each other from boring conversations, and from the moments that sometimes arise when one of our aunts or uncles asks a question that is far too personal. But today Gracie has made it clear that she will not engage. I've never maneuvered my way through one of these family events without my sister, and I can't believe she is going to make me start now without so much as an apology.

I turn my back to her and try to pay attention to the stilted group conversation. Uncle Ryan, still patting the arms of his wheelchair, tells us that Dad bought his building, but that it's all right because he will not have to move out. Uncle Johnny, during the half hour when we are going around the porch giving a sentence or two about how our job/school is going, tells us in excruciating detail about a new super-powered, mega-memoried computer he just bought.

"Mega-memory," Dina, Meggy's daughter, says, "just like Lila. A smart computer and a smarty-pants."

I smile at Dina. This is the other side of our family gathering's polite conversation—small jabs and burns. Dina is at her third high school in as many years due to disciplinary problems. She is a mean kid, but, by the unspoken rules of the family, she is allowed to cut at me and I'm not allowed to respond. The reason is that I have been more fortunate then she has by drawing Mom as a parent instead of Aunt Meggy. I was raised with money and privileges and Dina was not. So, no matter what Dina says to me, I'm supposed to take it.

To distract myself, I think about the review for my oncology rotation. I give myself thirty seconds to come up with as many different kinds of cancer as possible. Uterine, throat, colon, ovarian, esophageal, cervical, prostate, skin, pancreatic, liver, lung, breast, brain.

The rest of the family gives a forced smile to Dina's comment, and then the subject is swiftly changed. As in all awkward moments, Mom turns to Uncle Pat, who sits, tall and thin, in the corner of the porch next to Gram, and offers him more food. She doesn't seem to notice that his plate is still full from the first serving she gave him. Uncle Pat is in his third marriage, to a woman named Louise, but he showed up today alone without an explanation. Gram keeps touching his arm, and Uncle Johnny gives him a wave from the other end of the porch whenever they make eye contact. I think Uncle Pat reminds everyone of Papa, which is ironic since Papa hated Pat. But in a family of nervous, awkward, quiet people, Pat holds his quiet with a kind of peace. I don't look down on my mom for her idol worship of him. It seems understandable. When I was younger I used to fight my cousins for a seat on Uncle Pat's lap. I once gave my cousin John three silver dollars out of the silver-dollar collection in my mother's underwear drawer just so I could sit in the front seat of Uncle Pat's car when we went for ice cream.

It is Uncle Pat who initiates the next phase in the gathering, which is when the kids separate from the adults. This is a crucial phase because it is when the drinkers start to drink and the mood of the event changes, but I hate this phase. I grew up with my cousins, but we are so different now and unfamiliar with one another.

Pat says, "I thought I saw some cookies in the kitchen that still need to be decorated."

"Oh yes." Mom claps her hands. "Why doesn't everyone under thirty go into the kitchen and take care of that very important job?"

The family smirks at Gracie as she stands up, twenty-nine years old and the one who each year raises the bar for us all. It is a running joke that is not that funny. Last year it was "Why doesn't everyone under twenty-nine go and do so and so . . ." There is the sense that if only Gracie didn't keep getting older, then maybe the cousins would all still be little kids, laughing and talking and loving one another before we absorbed the rules of the McLaughlin family and shut up and grew up. During our childhood the family gatherings were very different. Papa was still alive, of course. Gram was young and energetic. Possibility was in the air for all of us. Everyone misses those lost times, in a way. And with that lame joke, each year that loss is pinned on my sister.

"So, we're being ordered around in our own house?" I say, in a half-joking tone. I don't really see the point in fighting. This is the way these evenings unfold. I can't see any other way.

"You're moving out," Gracie says. "It's not your house."

"You heard Uncle Pat," my mother says. "Off you go."

Obediently, we kids file into the kitchen, having outgrown our use to our parents. Gracie and I lead the group. Then there is Dina, wearing a too-short skirt that Gram has already commented on, along with Theresa's daughter, Mary, and her son, John.

Gracie gets the tubes of colored frosting out of the refrigerator, and I get the sprinkles and the Red Hots and the pastel Easter mini-M&M's out of the pantry. The cookies, stacked on cooling racks, are already on the table. We sit down to work.

John can't take the quiet for long. He picks up the biggest and best-looking rabbit cookie and bites its head off. "Mmmm," he says loudly. "This is some good shit, these cookies." Then he laughs with his mouth open so we can all see the chewed remains of the rabbit's head.

This is the way John has talked ever since he was twelve years old. He is nineteen now and still everything is "good shit" or "bad shit"; every sentence is prefaced by an "Oh man." Gracie and I have a running bet on whether John is stoned all the time or just stupid. I actually think he's both, but Gracie thinks he's just stupid. I once heard Gram say to herself when she thought no one was listening, that she was glad Papa had died before it was clear what kind of man his only grandson would be.

Gracie and I exchange a look now—stupid or stoned?—our first real communication of the day, as Dina says, "John, you are so repulsive!"

Mary looks at the ceiling, which is, to her, heavenward. She is fourteen and claims she wants to become a nun. I suspect it is because you can move into a nunnery when you're sixteen, and Mary just wants to get away from her family as quickly as possible.

Gracie, who seems more relaxed away from the adults, tries to make polite conversation. She says, "Uncle Ryan seems to be getting worse, don't you think?"

"Oh man, he gives me the creeps big time," John says.

"I don't know why they don't lock him up," Dina says.

"Because he's not a danger to himself or anyone else," I say.

"I wonder who pays his bills," Mary says. "I don't think Gram can afford it."

This is a question we've asked, in our cousin mini-gatherings, for years. "I bet they all chip in," Gracie says. "And his church probably helps, too."

"The shoreless lake," Dina says, squirting red frosting eyebrows onto a rabbit cookie.

"The what?"

"That's the name of his cult church, the Shoreless Lake. It's such a weird name, I could hardly forget it."

We are quiet over our cookies. I picture a shoreless lake, calm water stretching on and on, the land always receding in the distance, forever unreachable. I speed up my decorating, to try to block out the image.

"That church gives me the creeps, too, big time," John says, and then eats the cookie he just finished decorating.

We nod in agreement, and Mary's crosses jingle around her neck.

Just then there is a burst of laughter from the porch. It is intense and a little hysterical. We all recognize the sound. It means that the McLaughlins are now drunk enough, loose enough, to start telling stories from their childhood. Their stories are about outwitting baby-sitters and being rescued from the top branch of a tree by the fire department, and breaking bones falling off roofs and bloodletting battles between siblings over stolen wedding dresses and prom dates. There is nearly always some violence and the stakes are always high. My mother, Uncle Pat, Aunt Meggy, Aunt Theresa, Uncle Johnny, and even Uncle Ryan tell of a vibrant childhood and adolescence when life was lived right down to the bone.

My cousins and I used to love to hear those stories. When Gracie, John, Dina, Mary, and I were little, we would run to the room where our parents were when we heard that particular shout of laughter. We would crouch at the door, or behind a table, and listen as the stories were told, happy to picture our parents living such large lives. But at some point, as we got a little older, we began to hear the stories from a different angle, and with less pleasure. We realized that our parents and their brothers and sisters had lived those stories when they were *our* age, and that we had nothing to compare in our own lives. Our problems were normal and boring; we couldn't come up with one exciting, knee-slapping story among us. We had fewer brothers and sisters, fewer brawls, fewer secrets. Our lives were not shaped by unbreakable Catholic rules and inescapable Irish history. We began to feel small, and although we never voiced the decision, at some point we simply stopped running toward the sound of the McLaughlins' laughter. We stayed where we were, just out of earshot, and kept on doing whatever it was we had been told to do.

Tonight we bend over the cookies and focus on decorating. We pass around the different colors of frosting, try to stay within the lines of the cookies, and dot M&M's where the rabbit's nose and mouth should be.

There is still laughter rising and falling out on the porch when my father and Uncle Travis come inside for more beer. "You guys sure do take your work seriously," Dad says. He rests his hand on my shoulder as he leans over to inspect the cookies. Travis picks up the egg-shaped cookie Mary has just spent twenty minutes decorating and bites it in half.

"Mmm," he says, his mouth full. "Not bad. Not bad at all."

"Right?" John says, and laughs with a sound of relief. He pushes his chair away from the table with his long arms and stands up. He seems to be shaking off the somberness of us girl-cousins and the faraway laughter on the porch. "Oh man," he says, "I can't take all this sitting still."

"I wanted to show that cookie to Gram," Mary says, looking down at her hands. "That was my best one yet."

Uncle Travis, who is not a bad guy, just an insensitive drunk, shrugs. "Sorry, kiddo. Hey, Doc, any new ideas on my bad knee? It's killing me these days."

"You need surgery."

"Nah. I'm looking for an option that doesn't require a knife. I'm not the kind of wacko who signs up to have himself cut open, I'll tell you that much."

"No? What kind of wacko are you?"

Gracie hits me in the arm, but Uncle Travis just laughs. "You're ballsy, girl."

John laughs, too, trying to wedge himself into the banter. "Hey, funny. Listen, Uncle Travis, how about if I have a beer? Just one? Mom won't care."

My father's hand presses down harder on my shoulder. Meggy and Theresa are close, meaning that Theresa lets Meggy boss her around on a daily basis. It also means that Travis has been the one steady man in John and Mary's lives. He is almost a father to them, the emphasis on *almost*. My dad would like to step in here and tell John he can't have a beer; I can feel that through the weight of his hand, but he can't speak up because he has no right. He only sees John once or twice a year. He is a barely known uncle, and nothing more.

"Sure, John, but just one." Uncle Travis hands John a can with a wink.

This is one of those moments when we are painfully, clearly, different. Different tastes, different manners, different socioeconomic classes. Everyone in the room feels it, and is uncomfortable. It is nearly impossible to believe that we belong to the same family, until we hear Gram's voice at the door. The sound turns each of our heads, wraps us all together, puts us back into our proper places. Under the sound of her voice, we are again, simply and only, Catharine McLaughlin's children, sons and daughters-in-law, grandchildren.

"It's getting cold out there," Gram says. "Do you mind if I join you?"

AND WITH THIS, the third and final phase of the family gathering begins. Gram's children follow her into the house, and a chill has fallen over their clothes and faces. They have apparently left the childhood stories behind; perhaps one among them has already turned mean. The people who are going to get drunk are well on their way.

We uncover the cold dinner the caterers left on the dining-room table: a cooked ham, fruit salad, macaroni salad, potato salad, loaves of bread, and miniature sandwiches. We put out large paper plates, with real utensils. Papa couldn't stand to eat with a plastic fork and knife, and we still always use real utensils. With the plates loaded with food, we sit scattered around the living room and eat off our laps. I try to figure out who has been drinking too much, because that roster always changes. This time, I choose Mom first, because her cheeks are red, and she keeps looking up from her plate with a stupid grin. She gets emotional when she is drunk, and sentimental is always the first stop. My suspicion is confirmed when she crosses the room for another serving of macaroni salad and stops to squeeze Gracie's shoulder and mine.

"I just want to thank you girls for throwing such a wonderful party for the family," she whispers, just loudly enough so that everyone hears her.

Gracie and I smile and nod politely. Everyone knows we did not throw this party. We reluctantly agreed to let it take place here, and that was only because Gram asked. I just hope everyone knows that we know our true involvement and that we don't think we're any better than we are. I hope they know that I wanted this gathering to take place anywhere but here. I want that now more than ever because I have stumbled upon yet another unexpected negative. Watching the family sit where I have been living, breathe beer and wine into my air, crisscross my space, put my forks into their mouths, has made the usual identity crisis—the question of who am I this year with these people compared to who I was last year and how much do I have in common with these men and women who share my blood—even more acute. It does not help that Gracie has removed herself and left me alone. It also does not help to know that my memory will undoubtedly brand this day, and this sight, into my brain. I will not ever be able to walk into this house without thinking of this onslaught of McLaughlins and the shaky way it has made me feel. Thank God I am moving out. Thank God it is soon.

"Ryan, why aren't you eating?" Theresa asks.

Ryan is sitting in his wheelchair with his hands folded, pointedly not touching his plate. "Nobody said grace. I refuse to eat food that has not been blessed. Something terrible is bound to happen."

This stops most of us, forks in the air, mouths full.

"Goodness," Gram says, "you're right, Ryan. Please, someone say grace."

"Grace," John says, and gives an open-mouthed laugh that falls off in the middle when he realizes no one else is amused. He follows up quickly with, "Dina was smoking out front."

"She most certainly was not," Meggy says, without even looking at her daughter.

"That's right," Dina says, reeking of Marlboro Lights.

"I'll say grace," Pat says.

Everyone sits up straight. Mom points her goofy grin right at him and I watch her eyes fill with tears.

"Lord, please bless this food and bless this family. Amen."

"That's my brother, man of few words," Johnny says, and I put him on the drunk list, too. I imagine that with all the antidepressants he's on, he probably doesn't have to do much imbibing to get a buzz.

"Pat said all that needed to be said," Gram says. "Son, you do remind me of your father."

Gram spoke with a gentle air of apology, but Pat still took the comment hard. No one else would have been able to tell, but our years of family gatherings have boiled down to hours of studying one another locked in either awkward silence or awkward conversation. We all watch Pat's shoulders draw back. We know he will leave soon. The party is just about over.

Gram puts her plate down on the floor beside her foot. She has seen the sign, too. She'd better say what she has to say before her audience disperses. "While you all finish your meal, and before we eat the lovely cookies my grandchildren have made, I'd like to say a few words." She folds her hands in her lap. "I want to thank each of you for coming. It has been a few years since we've all been together as a complete group, and this gathering was important to me. I think it is important for us as a family. Since Patrick died our family has drifted—"

With the mention of Papa's name, whatever is frozen in Pat freezes a little deeper. Perched on the folding chair, he looks as if you'd have to use an ice pick to get at anything living inside him. This unnerves me, because I suddenly realize that I have this tendency in myself. I know I have looked like Pat does right now, frozen and locked away, unreachable. I know that deep in there he probably feels smug and safe. But he's wrong. He's not safe; he's dead. I don't want to look like that. I don't want to be sitting like a Popsicle on a folding chair in the middle of this family when I am fifty, completely alone, with no kids and no husbands who stick.

"Are you all right?" Gracie whispers.

I look down and see that my knees are shaking. My legs look like they want to dance. I shake my head, neither affirmative nor negative.

Gram says, "I want that drifting to stop. If I have to continue to force you all to come together like I did this time, I will. But there will come a time when I won't be here, and you'll have to gather, or disband, on your own."

"I *knew* Mom was sick," Theresa says in a shrill voice.

"You don't need to talk like this, Mother," Mom says, but whereas Theresa sounded scared, Mom sounds annoyed.

I stare at my knees. I watch them shake, and wonder what I should do to make them stop.

"I am not sick," Gram says. "But I *am* an old woman. I have been fortunate to live for as long as I have. I'm not trying to upset you children. I just need to tell you what it is that I want."

"What do you want, Mother?" Ryan looks prepared to get up out of his wheelchair and give it to her.

"I want this family to come back together. I want us to know each other, and to help each other. I think it is very important, especially now that we have a new baby on the way."

This stops my knees from dancing. I look up. I feel the ripple of wonder and curiosity pass around the room, from folding chair to folding chair. Gracie's fingernails bite into my arm.

The mood in the room changes. Everyone looks—gradually, unbelievably—hopeful. Mom's grin lurks around the corners of her mouth. Pat's eyes are blue again; there has been a slight thaw. Theresa balances herself on the edge of the couch. Dina has lost her bored smirk. I see the McLaughlins' thinking, collectively, with wonder, A new baby.

Gram goes on. "This child is a second chance for us as a family. I want to get together every holiday from now on, and maybe once a month as well. If that seems like too much, then perhaps once a season would suffice."

No one is listening to Gram. All they care about now is if she spoke the truth. She doesn't sound like herself—did the car accident knock her into senility? Who could be pregnant?

Eyes dart from face to face. I can practically hear their thoughts. Kelly is too old, it can't be her. Meggy? She is forty-six, so it is possible, but very unlikely. Theresa and Angel are only forty-one, though. If Angel is the one who is pregnant, it will be a miracle. In fact, it is common knowledge that she and Johnny have recently, finally, given up trying to have a baby.

Along the lines of this heart-pounding, eyes-darting reasoning, Theresa seems to be the most likely candidate. But Theresa is nearly single. Uncle Jack is a traveling salesman and is almost never home. No one in the family has seen him for over a year, and even Meggy is not sure when he last slept in his own bed, because Theresa lies about him. She makes up romantic dinners that never happened, and nights spent together as a family: just her, Jack, and the two kids playing Scrabble. No one, not even Meggy, has the heart to ask Mary and John to corroborate their mother's stories.

The aunts' and uncles' knowing nods turn to puzzled looks. There is no one else it could be. The new baby, the first McLaughlin born in fourteen years, seems less and less possible. They don't even think to look to the next generation. None of us are married. As far as our parents and aunts and uncles are concerned, we are still teenagers. We haven't earned adulthood. My mother and her brothers and sisters don't notice that Gracie's cheeks have flushed red and that there is sweat on her forehead and that she is holding on to me like a boat passenger who suddenly believes the ship is about to go down. They don't, even in the backs of their minds, even in their wildest thoughts, even in their least Catholic moments, think that it could possibly be one of the cousins, one of the next generation, one of the *children*.

Finally Meggy interrupts Gram, who has continued to expound on the symbolism of this new baby, and Easter, and a rebirth for the McLaughlins.

"Ma," Meggy says, "who's having a baby?"

Gracie's fingernails have now passed through my skin and my flesh and are burrowing into my very bones. I try to think of a way to help, but between my still-weak knees and my sister's hold on me, I have been pulled to the edge of the cliff with her. I feel lucky I can breathe. I just want to make it out of this room alive, away from my burning-hot sister and my frozen uncle and the rest of these strange characters who share my history and my holidays and my genes. But I know that the odds of any of us making it out of this moment unscathed are slim. This moment is going to roll this family over on its back like a helpless animal, arms and legs waving in the air.

Gram looks at Meggy as if she is slow. As if she should know the answer to this question already. As if we all should. "Why," she says, in her familiar, nuts-and-bolts voice, "it's Gracie."

Part Two

GRACIE

I stand in front of the mirror and look at my swollen belly, pushed out with five months of life, and try to picture my grandmother like this. Gram still has the same blue eyes, the same straight spine and haughty chin, but the young woman I conjure also has strong bones, smooth cheeks, and my mother or one of my aunts or uncles curled up inside of her. Gram looks happy in my mirror, confident and sure. She appears to belong to her body. There is a sense of a full life in her, so much so that it spills out beyond the lines of her skin, her eyes, her belly. I look behind her expecting to see my grandfather walk up with a question or a complaint, or to see one of her small children bump into her knees. But no one appears. My grandmother stands alone, her hands cup her stomach, her eyes meet mine.

When I try to measure up to Gram, I am left staring at my own reflection. My body looks small, and the bulge in my front ridiculous. I see only deficiencies: skin too pale, no sexuality in this body; it has been sapped away. There is not a drop of moisture, of saliva, of juice. I have spent the last two months drying out. The doctor says I haven't gained enough weight, but my hips and butt have widened until I don't recognize them as my own.

Easter night, after my family left with my mother crying, her head averted so she would not have to see me, I wanted so badly to go to the Green Trolley. It was all I could think about. Lila had left, too, and she stayed out all night. I was completely alone in the house. The quiet around me rang with the earlier silence and the looks, the question of,

Who did this to you? I heard my cousin John tell Dina that he'd heard I got around. Meggy murmured that this family became less with every generation. Pat pretended he hadn't heard anything; he just kissed Gram on the cheek and walked out of the house. Mary was praying silently on one side of the room while Ryan prayed loudly on the other. Gram appeared confused by the tumult, and then increasingly unhappy and tired as she measured everyone else's reactions against her own. Mom and Dad looked sick to their stomachs, their mouths loose as they tried to figure out what to say.

All I'd wanted was to feel a man's hands on me. I wanted lips on mine and skin that I could reach and follow and own. I wanted that kind of oblivion, the delicious kind, the powerful kind. I wanted it so badly my entire body ached. But the general announcement of my condition seemed to make that impossible. For the first time, it occurred to me that I might be physically undesirable. I had never considered the idea that being pregnant might affect my sex life. But what would a man think when a woman who had even the faintest mound to her belly came on to him? He would wonder if I was looking for a husband and father, not a lover. My body would suggest more than I wanted it to. There would be questions, concerns, emotions—nothing I had ever asked for when I stepped up to the bar and checked out the room.

I didn't go to the Green Trolley Easter night, and I haven't gone there since. I haven't had sex, or anything even approaching sex, in over two months. That is the longest I have been celibate since I was sixteen years old. I don't know what this dearth is doing to me. I feel like my only option is to wait and see. Wait and see what happens, wait and see how it all turns out. I am waiting, specifically, for someone to tell me what to do. I am hoping someone will say, *This* is how you will make everything right.

I have been keeping quiet and staying in the house. I have given myself over to the ebb and flow of everyone else's reaction to my situation. That is how I tell time now. I have lost track of hours, mealtimes, and days of the week. I am listening too hard, waiting too intently, to pay attention to those kinds of logistics. Instead, several soft, quiet days will blur together into one, into waking and eating and going through letters looking for people who are worse off than me.

I had one phone conversation with my mother about my situation, and since then she has left a few breezy "I'm on my way out the door, just checking in to make sure you're okay" messages on the answering machine when she guessed or hoped I wouldn't be home.

The one real conversation we had was very short, and as with all of my worst conversations with my mother, it twisted and poked and yanked at every nerve in my body.

She called me clearly in tears. There was a big, watery gulp before there were any words, and then she said, "Do you think this is my fault, Gracie? Is it something I did or didn't do?"

"No, Mom. This has nothing to do with you."

"Of course it does, don't say that. I didn't even know you were involved with that young man . . . Joel. Can I ask—"

"We're not together anymore, Mom. He won't be involved."

There is a note of panic in my mother's voice that makes me wonder if she has been drinking. "Oh Gracie, why didn't you tell me? I could have helped you."

I am almost certain my mother thinks I should have had an abortion. Quietly, without bothering anyone. She prides herself on being a modern woman, with all of its complications and sacrifices. But she is not modern enough to embrace my single, pregnant status. She doesn't know how to present this to her women's group. This kind of event would never take place in the wonderful mother-daughter relationship she conducts in her head. At the moment she doesn't even recognize me as her daughter.

I do feel badly. I have busted up the game my family has been playing since Lila and I hit puberty. In the game, Lila and I are polite, well-educated, achieving daughters who love and respect their parents. In exchange for presenting this front, and going to college and meeting other expected life landmarks, we have been permitted to keep our personal lives completely private. My mother never really wanted to know me, she just saw the daughter she wanted to see. She picked out a few relevant facts, that I was popular and a strong writer, for instance, and then she made up the rest. She has done the same thing with Lila. Really knowing someone is too messy and disturbing and even tedious for my mother. It doesn't mean that she doesn't love me, because she does. That's why this hurts so much now. I have behaved in a way no daughter of hers would ever behave, and that has forced her to face the reality that she does not know me. This was not pleasant for either one of us.

"I'll be fine, Mom, I promise. You don't have to worry."

There was a hard sob. "I shouldn't have worked so much when you were a child. A few of those nannies were not the best role models."

"I should go, Mom. Can we talk about this later?"

"I need to ask you one question first. I've been wondering, how did your grandmother know about this? Did you tell her?"

"No," I said. "Gram just knew. I didn't have to tell her."

"I have to go myself," my mother said. "I'm just running out the door. Do you need anything?"

"No thanks," I said. "I'm okay."

WHEN I tell Lila about this conversation, she says, "Mom always makes everything about herself."

I say, "Do you realize she's going to be a grandmother?"

Lila laughs so hard she snorts, and I laugh, too, watching my sister's face. It is no problem for me to keep laughing; I like the sound. I am so thankful that Lila didn't move out. She said something happened to her student loan situation, so that she couldn't afford her own place after all. I know she's not telling me the whole truth, but I don't care. I don't want to drive her away by asking too many questions. For the first time since she moved in we are hanging out together. We watch television. Lila flips through magazines while I read my letters. We go food shopping. She seems to not mind my company and I enjoy hers.

But Lila's schedule is more insane than ever, and she creeps in and out at odd hours. More than once, she and I have frightened each other in the hall in the middle of the night, me in my bathrobe, her in her jacket and shoes smelling of fresh air. I know that regardless of whatever else is going on, she is getting laid on a regular basis. I knew she had had sex when she came home the morning after Easter. There was a vagueness to Lila's eyes as if she were unable to focus on the chairs, the table, the room around her. I recognize that look.

At first she denied it, and then when I wouldn't let up, she admitted it was true but refused to say anything more. She said that it didn't mean anything and was going to end any minute, so there was no point in discussing it. Then she would leave the house, and I wouldn't see her until the next morning.

The phone rarely rings when I'm home alone. My father has not spoken directly to me since Easter. I'm not surprised. I know he's embarrassed and ashamed and doesn't know what to say. I don't want to speak to him for those same reasons, but I miss him.

The constants in my life right now are Gram and Grayson. If the phone does ring, it is one of them. Since our last meeting, Grayson and I have spoken about nothing but work. I haven't apologized for yelling at him. He hasn't apologized for insinuating that I can't handle having a baby on my own. Just like when I broke up with him on his answering machine, we are ignoring the issue at hand and focusing on business. Grayson requested that I come into the office three days a week instead of my usual one. He says that a professional, sterile environment will help me choose my letters and my responses with more balance and objectivity.

He gives me the office of a writer who spends most of his days covering stories in South Jersey. I sit in the gray room with no windows and center my laptop on the steel desk and arrange my letters in neat piles. Then I tuck my chair in and put both feet flat on the linoleum floor. I arrange and rearrange the correspondence. I type a few starting lines on the screen. But that is as far as I get. The lighting is too harsh in the office. The waistband of my pants cuts into my swollen stomach. My pumps are too tight. There are too many distractions. That gossiping goat Charlene pops her head in at least once a week and asks me, with the most malicious smile, how my bubbala is doing. During one visit, she hands me a white envelope.

"What's this?" I ask.

"Another letter from your adoring public. It must have gotten separated from the normal mail. Strange, isn't it?" Charlene smiles, but the curve of her lips is cold and mean. She flips her hair and then leaves without closing my office door.

I look the envelope over. It couldn't have come in with the mail. There's no stamp, and it is addressed simply to the Dear Abby Department, *Bergen Record*. I slit the envelope open with my favorite silver letter opener and pull the thin piece of paper out. The cursive writing on the page is so full of loops and flourishes that it takes a minute before I can concentrate on the words.

Dear Abby,

My boyfriend and I are deeply in love. What we have is the real thing. We are very blessed because we know that God made us for each other. We couldn't be any closer or any more committed. Unfortunately, we went through a rough patch last year, and the town tramp took advantage of the situation by seducing my true love.

When she realized he would never be able to care for her, she tried to trick him into marriage by getting pregnant. She is the worst kind of woman, a weak slut who can't keep her legs shut or hold on to a man. Dear Abby, please tell me how I can get it through this girl's dim brain that my man is off limits. She won't get a thing from him. Not his love, and not a dime.

Sincerely,
Righteous in Ramsey

I breathe out slowly and fold the letter shut. I know I shouldn't be surprised by Margaret's ferocity. I should be relieved to have this letter. I've spent the last few months on the lookout for an approaching red-head, anticipating her attack. Still, I've never received a Dear Abby let-

ter from someone I know, or from someone who knows me. My letters have always been my best escape, and my peace. Until now they
have been written only by strangers who trust me, look up to me, and
turn to me when they need to be saved. A line has been crossed, and I
feel oddly revealed by Margaret's choice to come at me in this manner.
I flip the letter over so I am looking at the blank side of the page, then
tear it into tiny bits and drop it in the garbage.

GRAYSON INSISTS that I attend the weekly staff meetings, which I
have always skipped in the past. I sit through only one, which is suffi-
ciently humiliating to keep me away in the future. The meeting falls
first thing on a Thursday morning, which is the day my column comes
out. I get my first look at the paper as Grayson's assistant hands them
out at the door of the conference room. I can tell that everyone else in
the room ran to the end of their driveway at the crack of dawn and read
their copies. When they walk in the room they toss the newspaper the
assistant hands them onto the table and take a seat. There are about
twelve people at the meeting, including the major front-page writers
and the main editors: Business, Local, National, Sports, Arts, and
Lifestyles. My boss is the Lifestyles editor, a cranky man with prostate
problems that make it difficult for him to sit. I've never had much to
do with him. When I have column problems I have always gone to
Grayson. The editor frowns every time he sees me, so I figure he's
happy enough with our arrangement. Today as he paces the length of
the room, he says, "What are you doing here?"

"I asked her to come, Bill," Grayson says from behind me. That
shuts him up. Still frowning, he takes a seat. It is interesting to see how
all these editors and writers, mostly men in their forties and fifties,
respect Grayson. I rarely see him in this kind of group setting. My personal and professional relationships with Grayson have generally taken
place one on one.

While Grayson grills the editors on the major stories in their sections, I flip through the paper to find my column. I try not to listen to

their discussion. Wars in countries I can't find on a map, car wrecks, plane crashes, abandoned children, drug busts, local zoning battles, etc., have never been anything I've gone out of my way to hear about. I ignore the news and turn right to the Lifestyles section.

Once I've located my column, I see that Grayson has done it again. He has rewritten my advice. This has been going on to a small degree since the beginning. He used to edit my writing. He would cut a sentence here or there, or rework a phrase. But over the last six months, he has begun to alter the content of my advice. He has deleted parts, and changed the very nature of what I was trying to say.

I look up at Grayson. He is pacing with great energy at the head of the room. He says, "I think the Route 17 overpass coming in two years ahead of schedule and ahead of budget is front-page material. Who disagrees? Then let's move on to the story on Christie Whitman's presidential ambitions. Quick answers please."

This week the response Grayson has changed the most radically is the one I wrote to a girl grieving over the death of her mother. The girl felt her life had fallen apart and that she didn't know who she was anymore, or what to do next.

My advice was for her to experience her sorrow from beginning to end. I suggested she keep a journal, and live one day at a time. I suggested that if she ignored her sadness, or buried it, she would just have more problems later on. I told her that once her mourning had ended naturally, she would see who she was and know what to do. Her course would unfold before her.

Out of the advice that was actually published, only the first sentence was written by me.

Dear Sad in Secaucus,

Your sorrow is completely appropriate and natural, don't let anyone tell you otherwise. But it has been several months now, and it is time to return to your life. I am sure that right under your nose there is a good friend or a relative who cares about you and knows you. Turn to that person now and let them lead you back to your life. You have

been trying to make things work on your own and that can be a mis-
take. Don't be ashamed to ask for help.

I read this advice over and over again. I try to imagine this young
girl, twelve or thirteen, sitting in her pink bedroom in her dad's house
in Secaucus, reading this advice. Seeing it for the first time this morning, just like me. Letting it seep in, trying to feel whether it is true.
Trying to feel whether it is what she needs.

I can only hope that it is. I know I have let her down. If my advice
can't make it through a run-in with Grayson's red pen, then it is not
strong enough, right enough. Things have changed; I can't deny that.
I can still feel the heat of Margaret's letter on my fingertips. Maybe I
do need somebody to check and balance what comes out of my
mouth. Besides, Grayson is the only one who seems to pay attention
to me at all, as of late. Gram is just interested in the baby, and Lila is
so often gone. I shouldn't disregard the only person who is listening to
what I have to say, even if he is forever rewriting the content.

"Gracie," Grayson says. "You with us?"

I look up from the newspaper. Grayson is staring at me from the
head of the room, and many of the editors and writers have swiveled
their chairs in my direction.

"Yes," I say.

"You read your column? Any problems or comments you want to
make?"

Bill the Lifestyles editor shifts uncomfortably in his chair. There is
a tangible feeling of resentment. I am the smallest fish in this room, and
they'd like to either throw me out the door or into the frying pan. I
don't belong here.

The business editor says, "Grayson, I think we need to take a harder
line with the Dow Jones story. I'd like your guidance on that."

"One minute, Carl. Gracie, anything?"

"No," I say. "Nothing. Thanks."

～

I AM back home in the empty house and on my way upstairs to change
when I glance out the front window and see a car sitting in the driveway. It is an old gray sedan that looks vaguely familiar. Because of the
way the afternoon sun glints off the windshield, I can't see who is sitting behind the wheel. I stand perfectly still, watching, torn between
hiding in my bedroom and walking outside to see who it is.

I am still deciding on my course of action when it is decided for
me. The driver-side door opens and Aunt Meggy gets out. Then the
passenger door opens, and I see Aunt Angel. Meggy walks around the
car and extends her hand. Angel takes it and lets Meggy help her out
of the car. I watch from the window, wondering what is going on.
Neither of my aunts has ever visited me before.

They seem to be conferring by the side of the car. Angel leans
against the door as Meggy rubs her lumpy shoulders. Suddenly, I
understand: Angel is sick, and they have stopped by looking for Lila,
looking for help. I cross the living room and swing open the front door.
But I have moved too quickly, and the sunlight hits me in the face and
turns the world into bright spots of loose color. I move my head and
struggle to focus on the two women.

"Lila's not here," I call out. "She's at the hospital."

They both turn and look at me. Meggy says, "We're not here to
see Lila."

"Isn't Aunt Angel hurt?"

Angel steps away from the car and I can see that she's been crying.
Meggy says, "She's fine. We came to see you. Aren't you going to
invite us in?"

I move so the door is left unblocked. I tell myself to calm down.
No one is injured. This is not a matter of life and death. My thoughts
reorder, and I know that if my aunts have come to see me, it must be
about the baby. They have come to tell me what an embarrassment I
am to the family.

Meggy requests a cup of tea, and Angel accepts a glass of cold
water. We sit at the kitchen table while the teakettle rattles and shivers
its way to hot.

"So," I say, looking from Angel's swollen face to Meggy's determined one. My silly hope that I might be able to keep the conversation light and pleasant fades.

"All right, Angel," Meggy says. "You wanted to talk first. Go ahead."

I am almost amused by Meggy's obvious sense of agenda, but not quite because I know that my situation is what she is headed for, and I suspect that the collision is going to hurt. I have never had much to say to Meggy. She and Lila can banter back and forth, but I don't have the quick wit or sarcasm to take part. My aunt and my mother don't get along because my mother's feelings are so easily hurt and Meggy has such a sharp tongue. Meggy cuts immediately to the point and my mother never gets there. Mom complains that her younger sister is selfish. I don't argue with my mother, but I never thought that her accusation was entirely fair, because Meggy always seems to be looking out for someone—Aunt Theresa and Aunt Angel, for instance. She took in Mary and John when Aunt Theresa became upset about Uncle Jack. And she is always harassing Johnny to be a better husband to Aunt Angel, and to stop being so absorbed in his alleged depression. Today I assume she is here on behalf of all my aunts and uncles, to tell me what a disappointment I am.

"How's your job, Gracie?" Angel says. She taps the tabletop with ragged fingernails. "I always enjoy your column. I tell everyone I know that you're my niece."

"Okay, you've lost your chance," Meggy says.

The teakettle lets out a sharp whistle, and we all jump. The noise always reminds me of Gram, and this time it reminds me that she's expecting me to visit her tonight to pick up my monthly check. I pour the hot water into Lila's favorite mug, which is covered with scientific equations. I have already set out the tea bag, milk, and sugar, so I simply hand the mug to Meggy and sit back down.

"Listen up, Gracie," Meggy says. "I'm going to start with a story that took place when I was a kid. It's something that happened all the time in the Irish community, but this is just one example."

"It happened where I grew up, too." Angel nods.

"There was a family that lived two houses down from us. They had eight or nine children, the normal amount in our neighborhood. Your mother and I used to baby-sit for them. Anyway, the oldest girl got pregnant when she was in high school. She was sent away on a trip before she started showing. When she gave birth, her mother adopted the baby and said it was the child of one of her husband's business colleagues. The teenager then came back home and finished growing up. And it all worked out. The girl went to college and got married, and her little boy was raised by his grandmother, who loved him."

A dark feeling fills my stomach, as if I have swallowed something that doesn't agree with me. I must be misunderstanding the story. This can't be headed where it seems to be. I try to keep my voice casual. "What happened when the kid found out who his real mother was?"

Meggy and Angel look at each other. "That's not the point. The child could have just as easily been raised by a cousin or by an aunt. This practice was very common at the time. It's like adoption, but within the family so everyone remains together."

My body folds over slightly, protective against the hunger in my aunts' gaze. The air in the room is so heavy I have a hard time opening my mouth. "You think I should give up my baby?"

"You're barely showing, for being five months along," Angel says softly.

"You haven't told many people, right? Your mom has mentioned that you don't have any girlfriends. And you have to admit that this is not the best time or way for you to have a baby." Meggy's voice is hard, insistent. "It might work out better if you waited."

"You're alone," Angel says, her eyes down. "I'm married. I've been ready for a baby for years. He or she would be so loved. Your uncle Johnny would be a wonderful father. Can't you see?"

"And the kid would be well provided for," Meggy adds. "How do you plan to support yourself and a child? I bet you're getting money from your grandmother, and that's fine, but how long do you want to be on the dole from her? The only other person in the family she supports completely is Ryan. How would you feel about being in that company for the long term?" She shrugs. "It would make me feel like a loser."

Angel says, "You'd get to see the baby as much as you want."

I look down and see that my hands are gripping my stomach. I move them away and start playing with my hair, twisting and pulling at it. I've been trapped in a terrible nightmare. I have spent too much time alone and started to hallucinate. This is not happening.

"Does my mother know about this?"

"Of course not," Meggy says. "I thought that if you were adult enough to get knocked up, then you were adult enough to make this decision."

"Meggy," Angel says.

"I'm keeping my child," I say. The sentence rises out of me clearly, as the only thing I do know.

"Just think about it," Meggy says, and stands up. "You'll realize that the best thing you could do for this baby would be to give it to Angel and Johnny."

Meggy takes Angel's elbow and guides her up from her chair. Angel's eyes, so sad and wanting, are fixed on my face.

"Just think about it," she echoes.

I can't seem to move, so I don't see them to the door. I hear the door click shut, the clack of their shoes on the front walk, the hum of the car engine, and then I am left alone in silence, my hands back on my stomach.

I visit Gram later that day at the agreed-upon time. I considered canceling, but knew she would be disappointed, and then I would have had to see her tomorrow. There's no point in putting Gram off.

On the way to the assisted-living center I stop at McDonald's and buy a chocolate milkshake. The shakes seem to be my only pregnancy food craving. I am on a steady diet at this point of one small and one medium shake a day. There are two McDonald's in Ramsey, so I alternate which one I go to, and whether I use the drive-through or the inside counter, so I don't see the same staff people too often.

When I enter Gram's room she is sitting where I usually find her these days, in the desk chair beside the window. I don't know why that spot appeals to her. There's not much of a view. Just some grass, a few trees, and the parking lot. It's much nicer on the loveseat, where all of her family photographs and the television are in her line of vision. I kiss her on the cheek and sit down on the loveseat.

"What's wrong?" Gram says. "What a face you have on, Gracie."

"I don't have a face on."

"If you say so. Tell me, how's Lila? I haven't seen your sister in quite a while. Tell her she owes me a visit."

"She's been really busy lately. I think Lila might have a boyfriend." I feel guilty as soon as the words are out, as I know this is something Lila wouldn't want Gram to know.

Gram gives one of her pleased nods, a quick tuck of her chin. "How nice."

We sit in silence. I study the black-and-white photographs on the wall and try not to be bothered by the fact that Gram is watching and waiting for me to break. Of course, I can't keep quiet for long.

I gesture to the photographs, the jumble of smiling or unsmiling freckled McLaughlin children. "I heard a story about a family in your old neighborhood. The oldest daughter had a baby when she was a teenager and her mother adopted the baby as her own. Did that really happen?"

"The O'Connors." Gram nods.

"Did the child ever find out who his real mother was?"

"Goodness, yes. When he was a teenager he started to get into a lot of trouble, which seemed odd, because the eight brothers and sisters ahead of him had been on the whole very good children. I believe he was caught smoking marijuana, and drove drunk several times. Wouldn't listen to his parents, who were, of course, his grandparents. In the meantime, the oldest daughter, the child's mother, had gone to college and ended up marrying her high-school sweetheart, the father of the boy. They had two or three children of their own by the time the boy started acting out. Everyone was very worried about him; he seemed headed for even bigger trouble. As a last-ditch attempt to save him, someone decided to tell him the truth. That his oldest sister was his mother, her husband was his father, and their children were his full-blooded brothers and sisters." Gram shakes her head. "That really confused the boy for a few more years, but then he finally settled down. It was quite a scandal—everyone in the neighborhood was talking about it."

"Aunt Angel came by this afternoon and asked me to give her my baby."

I keep my eyes straight ahead on the pictures, on the faces of the children. I hear Gram's sharp intake of breath. I think, Why did I say that? Why can't I keep anything from her?

"Poor Angel," Gram says after a minute. "I wonder if Johnny knew she was going to ask you."

I rush out the words. "I said I wouldn't do it."

"Of course you did. You and I will raise this child up fine. I'm going to help you."

When she says this, all the muscles in my body, which I hadn't even known were tense, relax. I realize I had been worried Gram would think Angel had a good idea. That she would agree that any mother other than me would be best for my child.

Gram purses her lips. "Meggy and Angel stopped by this afternoon to see me, and Angel barely spoke. I didn't think anything of it, though, because Meggy was running on at the mouth so, complaining about everything under the sun. I always hear her out and just hope that she's not as unhappy as she says she is."

"I think she just likes to complain." I have to fight not to smile. I feel like I have won a victory. I am so glad I came to see Gram today instead of tomorrow. I am so glad my answer to Meggy and Angel was the right one. But I am also ready to leave. This day has been long and exhausting, first fighting Grayson, then my aunts, and then waiting for Gram to weigh in with her opinion. I feel like a dishrag that has been twisted dry.

Gram says, "I admit I did think of Angel raising the baby, when I first knew you were pregnant. After all, she and Johnny have wanted a child so badly, and tried so hard."

"They should adopt," I say loudly. I don't like this turn in the conversation.

"I was taught, growing up, that if you find yourself pregnant at the wrong time for the wrong reasons, you leave home for a few months, have the baby, and give it to a family member to raise. In a way, it's a nice tradition when it doesn't go awry like with the O'Connor family. All of the children are well loved, everyone who wants a child ends up with one, and the family stays together."

"Sure, if you're prepared to pay for the years of therapy that kid's going to need when he finds out the truth. And odds are he will find out the truth, I'm sure." I don't like the sound of my voice; it is angry and rasping.

"I agree."

"You do?"

"I can't bear to see any more children in this family hurt." Gram turns her face away from me. She stares out the window. Twilight has fallen, the landscape is gray with shadows.

I lean forward in the loveseat, trying to get a good look at her. "Are you all right, Gram?"

She keeps her eyes on the window. The shadows from outside and inside meet on her profile, but her voice is normal. "I'm meeting some girls on the hall for dinner in a few minutes, and I need to get ready. I'll call you tomorrow, Gracie. Take your check out of the desk on your way out."

I cross the room, open the desk drawer, and look down on the check laid neatly on top of a pile of papers. From that distance, the thin piece of paper might be a letter, or a quick note. On the top left, under the date, is my name: Gracie Leary. On the line beneath it, written in my grandmother's neat script, is the monthly sum we agreed I would need. Below that is my grandmother's name: Catharine McLaughlin, the inevitable bottom line.

I look over my shoulder at my grandmother. She is still facing the window. I wonder what she is seeing, what she is remembering. It is clear that to her I am already gone. I fight the urge to call her name, to draw her back to me, to surprise her, to tell her something she doesn't know. But I don't have any idea where to begin, so instead I pick up the check, fold it, slide it into my pocket, and do as she has asked.

LILA

I woke up the morning after Easter changed, and changing. I felt as if some sort of dam had broken inside me and I was now being tossed around on the rapids and eddies of myself. I knew I was far beyond the point of stopping the motion; I had no choice but to give in.

Literally, I woke up that morning feeling awful. As if someone had hit me across the back of the head with a steel pipe. I ran my fingers over my scalp feeling for a bump. Finding none, I took the risk of opening my eyes. There was searing daylight, and it was then that I remembered what had happened. I remembered where I was.

"Good morning, Doc," Weber said from behind me.

I rolled over. We were lying on plaid flannel sheets. There was a poster of Lynda Carter dressed as Wonder Woman on one wall, and a poster of Bon Jovi on the other. "Oh my God," I said. There was a swollen feeling in the back of my throat. I imagined that the alcohol had burned my esophagus, leaving an inky trail from one end to the other.

I had gone to the Green Trolley after the Easter gathering, and I had drunk vodka because I had been told it tasted like nothing, and that's what I wanted to feel, nothing. The man next to me had continued to talk and talk and talk while I drank, and when I had drunk enough, I went home with him to his apartment above the hardware store on Main Street.

"I always knew we were going to get together, Doc. I just knew it. This was fate." Weber was lying on his side, his head cushioned under one bent arm. Where the sheet ended, I could see the hair on his chest and then the beginning swell of his beer belly. "I love fate," he said.

I was fishing under the covers with my hand, careful not to touch his side of the bed. "Have you seen my clothes?"

"I've known for about a year that our lives were going to become intertwined. I even told my buddies. Joel thought I was crazy, but I said no—"

"Our lives are not intertwined." I found my bra under the sheets, but no underwear. The air in the room was biting cold. I could see my jeans on the opposite side of the room. Next to them was the disgusting sight of a used condom. My jeans had fallen on the floor in a running pose, as if trying to make a getaway without me. I was not at all comfortable with the idea of walking across the room naked to get them. No one had seen me naked in a very long time. I could not, in fact, remember the last time anyone had seen me naked. The very few times I'd had sex I'd managed to keep most of my clothes on. I was almost more amazed to find that the vodka and Weber had induced me to take off every stitch of clothing, than I was to find myself in his bed.

"This was a mistake," I said. My breath made little clouds of white in the air. "I'm sorry if I misled you, but I was in a bad state last night. I wasn't myself."

"I foresaw last night, Doc, so it couldn't have been a mistake."

"I'm not a doctor. Please don't call me that." I sat up, clutching the covers to my chest. The air climbed up my spine with icy fingers. "Why the hell is it so cold in here?"

"I forgot to turn the heat on when we came in. I was distracted by the lovely lady with me. Close your eyes, Doc, and I'll get your clothes for you. I'm shy, so no peeking."

The last statement made me smile, but only for a split second, because doing that made the drumming in my head increase to double time. When I closed my eyes, the darkness was at first loose with spots of light, and then it began to revolve with the single-mindedness of a washing machine in the spin cycle. I moaned and fell back on the mattress.

I heard Weber's bare feet padding across the room toward me. "I turned the heat on, Doc. It should warm up in here in no time."

I kept my eyes closed and said, "You have to make a deal with me."

"Can't help you there. Sorry."

"Why not?"

"I don't believe in deals."

My clothes dropped into my lap, freezing and stiff, completely unwelcoming. I stared over at him. "You don't believe in deals? What kind of statement is that?"

"I don't believe in anything binding. I take life as it comes."

"Don't be ridiculous," I said. "This is simple. If we see each other out in public, we'll act as if nothing happened. We'll pretend we don't know each other. We won't tell anyone about last night. And that includes all of your stupid firehouse buddies."

Weber was next to me in the bed again, co-opting my space and using up what little warmth there was to spare. "How about if you keep your side of that deal, and I'll play it by ear?"

I heard this from beneath the sheet, while I was wriggling into my jeans. When I was dressed, I rolled off the bed. The sudden movement made me nauseous, but at least I was on my feet, looking down at him. This is the room of a teenager, I thought. A New Jersey, Bon Jovi–loving, gold jewelry–wearing teenager who has never grown up.

"Please," I said. "Please promise me you'll keep quiet."

"No can do, Doc."

"Let me guess," I said. "You don't believe in promises."

"That's right," he said, and pointed a big fat grin in my direction.

It was only when I got out of that room and that apartment that the slamming in my head abated, but the swelling in my throat had not gone down. It was difficult to swallow, and my breath caught sometimes on the way in and out. I couldn't help but think of what diseases might cause this kind of symptom. Making the list calmed me slightly. Pneumonia, strep throat, herpes, allergic reactions, esophageal obstruction, chicken pox, bronchitis, tonsillitis.

∾

I MADE my way home, ignored both the signs of sleeplessness and the curiosity in Gracie's eyes, and rushed into the bathroom. I stopped moving for only one moment, right before I stepped beneath the steaming-hot shower. I closed my eyes and was unexpectedly overwhelmed by my smell. I hadn't noticed it before, not in Weber's bed, not while I was putting on my clothes, but now it was impossible to escape—the salty, warm, grainy sex smell took over the small bathroom. I couldn't believe that the odor, spreading out in every direction, emanated from between my legs. There was something fascinating about the strength of it, and I had to force myself to duck under the stream of water and wash it away.

After I got dressed I dodged Gracie again and drove to the hospital. My favorite parking spot was free, so I pulled in and then sat in my car for a few minutes, too tired to move. I pulled down the sun visor and looked into the small rectangular mirror. I studied my face, feature by feature, categorizing the parts the same way I would the symptoms of a patient. Freckles across my nose (my mother's thin, haughty nose), chubby little-kid cheeks, thick sheets of dark brown hair hung on either side. I was not pretty, but no one in my family was pretty. I was not sweet and dreamy looking like Gracie. I was not striking looking like Mom. I didn't have Gram's innate dignity. My features had a hard, separate look to them, as if they each belonged on a different face but were fixed so firmly where they were that there was no hope of rearrangement or change.

My reflection blurred for a second and I was suddenly swamped with memories. This was another sign—as if I needed one—that I was not in complete control. I was always aware of the endless memories that filled an entire section of my brain, but I didn't experience them unless I chose to. I kept them locked away. The recollections were voluminous and mundane, but when I was tired, or feverish, or upset, or, apparently, hung over, they had the ability to take me unawares.

I remembered a screaming argument my mother and I had over a pink cardigan she'd bought for me to wear to my first day of high school. I remembered one dinner when Papa was drunk and he told me he was going to marry me and take me deep-sea fishing off the coast of Florida. I remembered winning my first horseback riding trophy and lifting it up over my head while my father took my picture.

I pulled my white coat out of the backseat and walked toward the jigsaw-shaped hospital. I had to squint to see anything past the ridiculously bright sunlight. I'd left my sunglasses somewhere. I couldn't remember where. I felt myself stagger slightly. The pounding in my head remained.

"Jesus, Lila, you look like you were run over. Are you here for work, or to check yourself in?"

It was Belinda, standing outside by one of columns, holding a cigarette.

"I didn't know you smoked," I said.

"I just started. I needed a hobby."

This struck me as very funny. I tried to laugh, but the noise went dry in my throat and made me cough instead. I said, "I drank vodka last night for the first time."

Belinda lifted her cigarette in the air as if it were a drink. "To numbers one and two in the medical school class of 2001."

"Why aren't you being as annoying as you usually are?"

Belinda gave a small smile. "I've been here for thirty-seven hours with no sleep."

"Oh." I felt as if I had gone thirty-seven hours without sleep, too. I felt not sleepy, but exhausted. I had to sit down suddenly, so I did, on the curb.

When Belinda spoke again, the competitive lilt was back in her voice. "Have you had any more thoughts on what you might do your Sub-I in? I'm thinking about vascular surgery or neurosurgery."

I tried to play along. I knew what was going on here. Belinda wanted me to declare my intent so she could follow me into that field and finally beat me there. "I'm not sure," I said. "Maybe dermatology or family medicine? I haven't decided yet."

"Bullshit. You have to do something more demanding than that, Lila, and you know it. In order to be really challenged, we both have to be some kind of surgeon. It's our responsibility."

"Responsibility to whom?"

Belinda dropped the barely smoked cigarette. It fell a few inches from where I sat. "To ourselves, silly. And to the world. We can't waste our gift. You can't be nonchalant about something so important."

I squinted up at her. Between her blond hair and the sunlight, I nearly went blind. "Enlighten me," I said. "What is our gift?"

Belinda answered seriously. "Medicine."

I rubbed at my eyes, wishing for dark and coolness. "That's very interesting. I wasn't sure. Do you have any other pearls of wisdom to drop in my lap?"

Belinda's teeth disappeared. "You know what your problem is?" she said. "You can't even carry on a simple conversation. You have no idea how to talk to people."

She walked toward the swinging door marked *Emergency,* her blond hair swishing behind her.

I reached over and picked up the cigarette she had discarded. I held it for a minute between two fingers. Then I brought it to my lips and breathed in. I coughed hard, the taste of hot gravel on my tongue.

I'd come too close to being truthful with Belinda in that exchange. I'd almost opened up to her. I could feel the words pressing on the back of my throat, creating the same swollen feeling I'd had when I left Weber's. I wasn't even sure what I would have said, which was particularly worrying. I couldn't afford any lapses of judgment.

The more Belinda knew about me, the more she had to use against me. The next thing I knew I would be telling her that I was in medical school only because of a conversation I'd had with my mother and grandmother when I was a sophomore in college.

I had come home for Christmas break, and my mother was on me about the fact that I had not yet chosen a major.

"I can't decide," I said.

Gram had been invited to dinner and had arrived an hour early. Since we were ordering food in, as usual, there was nothing to do but sit around. My mother suggested that we sit in the living room. Once we were settled, Gram in the low armchair, Mom and me in opposite loveseats, Mom decided this was an ideal time to have a discussion that was guaranteed to make me miserable. Even though Mom was annoyed at Gram for coming over early, she was obviously counting on Gram to back her up.

"What are the choices?" Gram said.

"Anthropology, literature, biology, or religion."

My mother shook her head. "That's just a list of the classes you're taking."

"No it's not. I left off water aerobics and philosophy."

"Why?" Gram asked.

"I don't like to exercise, and I don't enjoy philosophy."

"Why don't you enjoy philosophy?"

"Mother, you are veering off point. We're discussing what major the child should choose and what she wants to do with her life."

"Kelly, there's no need to make everything so deadly serious. We're just talking about Lila's major. She already knows what she's going to do with her life—Lila wants to be a lawyer like her grandfather."

"That's what I wanted when I was ten years old, Gram."

"So? You had a calling when you were young, that's all."

I could feel the heavy history behind my mother's and grandmother's gazes. My grandfather was a powerful lawyer who threw his weight around in New Jersey politics. He had been respected by nearly everyone, but most of all by his family. For all the bad talk that has come out within the family about Papa since his death, his career and his professional achievements have only been polished and embellished. I knew that one of Gram's greatest hopes was that one of the grandchildren would become a lawyer, since none of her children had. I also knew that with my top grades and studious habits, I was the best candidate.

But I wasn't about to accept that burden. I was the smart, dependable grandchild, while Gracie got to have fun and sex, John got to smoke dope, Mary got to drift in and out of religious fervors, and Dina got to be a general pain in the ass. I wasn't going to sign on for a career that would demand, by my grandfather's precedent, that I be perfect for as far into the future as I could see.

I looked down at my nail-bitten fingers and finally spat out the truth I had been holding in for years. "I don't want to be a lawyer."

There was a silence, during which I stole glances at Gram's face. I was relieved that, unlike in my imagined versions of this moment, she didn't appear to be having a stroke or a heart attack. She just looked sad.

My mother gave a sharp intake of breath and then turned her head away in a dramatic show that she was disappointed, too. I suspected that she wished she had become a lawyer, but when she was my age it hadn't been an option.

"Well," Gram said. "If you don't want to be a lawyer, you should at least choose a career that lets you use your brains. You're a smart girl, Lila. You have so much promise. Perhaps you should become a doctor. Your grandfather considered studying medicine as a young man, before he settled on the law."

"Medicine is a wonderful field," my mother said. "Very prestigious."

And that was that. I registered my college major as premed and I was on my way. I was so glad that Gram had accepted my aversion to a career in law that it never even occurred to me to turn down her second choice. All I wanted was to make something that was my own, and with medicine I could do that. I wasn't disinclined to the subject, either. I had spent my childhood reading about terrible injuries, and now I would learn how to treat the accident victims whose wounds and contusions and broken limbs I had read about in great detail. And medicine was fascinating, a great match, at least at first. It was a natural fit for my brain. But now the book-learning portion was over, and suddenly medicine felt like a horse I'd borrowed that didn't like me and was doing its damnedest to buck me off.

I thought about Gracie, and how her decision to keep the baby had thrown her life off course. She no longer went to the Green Trolley at night. My father no longer looked at her with a shine in his eyes. Gram looked at her with something akin to ownership. Gracie didn't make getting thrown off course look too good. But maybe she hadn't been thrown, maybe this change in course was meant to be.

I wasn't making sense. I could recognize that. I gave myself a minute to straighten out. I felt the vodka, clear and lethal, move through my system. I wondered if this was the smoldering remains my grandfather tasted most mornings, his brain clouded, hung over on scotch. I leaned against the column Belinda had just occupied. I knew, suddenly, that I was not going inside. I knew that I couldn't, even if I had wanted to. I was not going to school, to work, to be tested, to be tried and hanged. Not today.

I CLIMBED into my car and drove away. I didn't tell myself where to go and I didn't pay attention to where I was headed. The next time I took notice of my surroundings, I was on Main Street in Ramsey, stuck in traffic. I looked at the long row of cars in front of me. Driver after driver sat behind the steering wheel, placid, waiting, unquestioning. "What the hell is going on here!" I honked my horn. I didn't want to sit still. I wanted to drive. I wanted motion.

I looked around for some reason and noticed the curl of smoke. It hung in the air beyond the Green Trolley, above a strip shopping mall that sat perpendicular to Main Street. The curl seemed to hover above the Carvel ice cream store. Without thinking, I pulled the car over to the side of the road and parked. I left my bookbag on the passenger seat, locked the doors, and walked toward the shimmering line of smoke. This whole day seemed to be about doing the opposite of what I was supposed to do. I was supposed to be at the hospital. I was supposed to stay in the car, in the line, and wait to be allowed to move forward toward home. Instead I was out on the pavement, walking toward a fire.

I could see, from the sidewalk, that traffic had been stopped by a policeman who stood in front of the docile line of cars, his hand forcefully raised as if he were engaged in an act of great courage. His gesture was actually redundant, since a massive red fire truck was parked behind him. There was no place for the cars to go.

It was early afternoon on a Monday. These drivers and passengers didn't mind the holdup. They had no place better to be. They were housewives, elderly men, women and teenagers. They were pleased to be told what to do, to be engaged in some kind of drama. They were already happily thinking of the story they would have to tell at the dinner table that night. They felt alive, dangled between the prospect of the actual fire and their story about it. The very possibility that any kind of danger existed was exciting and tantalizing. They felt involved.

I slowed my walk in front of Mayor Carrelli's barbershop. Through the glass I could see the mayor in his neat blue barber coat that snapped up the back. He was cutting a customer's hair. It was a woman, and something familiar about her drew my eye. She was thin and sat erect in the chair. With her wet hair and the strange smile on her face, it took me a moment to recognize my mother.

It was such an odd sight, I just stared. My mother was laughing, as if the mayor had just told a great joke. The barbershop, a dim, dusty place, had to count as one of the roughest places my genteel mother had ever set foot in. What the hell was she doing in there? Why would she let the mayor cut her hair? It made no sense.

I was curious, but not enough to face my mother. I didn't want her to ask me why I wasn't at the hospital. I didn't want to hear her thoughts and feelings about Gracie's news. I didn't want to give my mother a chance to put me in the middle. I backed away slowly, a few careful steps until I was out of view of the window. When I turned I saw Joel standing on the curb. He was wearing his fireman's thick rubber jacket and boots. He had his helmet under his arm.

"Hey, Lila," he said. "You looking for your new boyfriend?"

Joel was someone I had always completely disregarded. He was my age; we had been in the same class at Ramsey High. When Gracie was dating Joel she was forever going on about how gentle he was, as though gentleness were a trait that got a person anywhere in this world. As far as I could see, being gentle didn't make a person rich, successful, or happy. For Joel, all it had gotten him was drunk. I could smell Budweiser on his breath now from a few steps away. He was one of those quiet drunks who got away with it most of the time because he was so soft-spoken and well mannered. I had no doubt that if I managed to stay on the path I was on and he managed to stay on the path he was on, I would be treating him at Valley Hospital in twenty years' time for cirrhosis.

But when he said that, I knew he was right. I had been headed toward the fire hoping to see Weber. I had promised myself that I would never see him again, and I'd held out for a mere three hours.

"I heard you got laid, Lila. I don't believe it. In fact, I said that it couldn't be true because sex is a life-affirming gesture and Lila Leary is not one to affirm life. I told Weber you wore black every day to high school and won the perfect-attendance award."

I could feel color climb the ladder of my face. It was a McLaughlin trait, the ease with which we all blushed. "Bastard," I said. "You've been drinking."

Joel smiled, his nice-boy smile. "There was a fire at Carvel. But by the time I got there all the ice cream had melted and the fire was out." He said this with great sorrow.

"You're going to be a father," I said, partly to wound him, partly to shake the truth into him and into myself. This drunken man-child who was saddened by melted ice cream was the father of my sister's baby. This truth seemed so random, and so unlikely. It was placed here like the cars lined up in traffic, like the hospital where I was supposed to be, like my parents' long marriage. It was all there, all in existence, but that didn't make it right. It didn't make it make sense.

"Not really," Joel said. "Margaret took me back. We're back together. We're in love."

"So what happened between you and Gracie doesn't mean anything?"

"Why do you always have to make everything so complicated, Lila? I always disliked that about you." He patted the pockets of his huge rubber coat, then wiped his forehead with the back of his hand. "This uniform traps heat," he said. "I'm burning up in here." Then he walked away.

∾

THAT NIGHT on the way to Weber's apartment, I tried to trace the possible path of the news Weber had told Joel. The task was dizzying and crazy-making. I knew that for the sake of my sanity I should stop, but I couldn't. I hadn't done anything gossip-worthy in my entire life; I had managed very well to keep myself to myself. Now I could see all my control, all my highly prized privacy, spinning away from me like a ball of yarn.

Joel would tell Margaret. Margaret was the assistant to Mayor Carrelli and the best friend of the *Bergen Record*'s gossip columnist. My mother apparently had her hair cut by the mayor. The mayor could tell my mother and/or my father. Joel or Weber might tell one of the bartenders at the Green Trolley, which meant the entire town would know the news of my one stupid, thoughtless misstep.

I told myself that it was no big deal and that I was overreacting. For God's sakes, Gracie's entire life was made up of one-night stands that many people knew about and few people even thought less of her for. She had screwed up her entire life, which was not what I had done. But—I couldn't help but think—I am not Gracie. I am stronger.

So in the end my common sense was unable to stop the train barreling along: This person will know, this person will know, this person will, too. In every possible direction I could see the small bomb-shaped truth headed right for the heart of my life. There seemed to be no point in stepping out of the way.

"Welcome back, Doc," Weber said when I showed up. He didn't seem surprised to see me. His bed was made and his apartment was a little neater than it had been the night before.

"We need a new deal," I said.

"I think you should just loosen up and go with the flow, Doc. It's a lot more fun."

I was worn out, shivering, hung over from my hangover. "I'm not interested in having fun. I'm not here to have fun."

"You seemed to have fun last night, Doc. Take off your coat, why don't you. There you go. Sit down. Relax."

I sat on the very edge of the bed.

"I had a really weird day," I said. "It's just twenty-four hours of insanity. I can accept that, but after tonight, the craziness will be over. Understood? I will go back to my normal life, and my normal self. We won't see each other again."

"I understand that you have control issues. I can help you with that. Loosening people up is one of my specialties." Weber was grinning at me again. A big stupid, happy grin.

"Look," I said, "I'm not here to argue with you. I'm not here to talk about my issues—"

He reached out and caught my right arm midair. I had been waving it to make my point. He held on to my wrist, and tiny shivers began to spread out from where his fingers pressed into my skin. "Of course you're not here to talk," he said. "You've got me for that."

And he did talk, and I didn't try to make him stop. His voice revved up as smoothly as a brand-new car and he was off and running. There was no chance for me to say a word. He talked about his job, about fighting fires, about the blazes he'd seen. I just stared at him while he talked about the heat on his skin, the way it felt running up stairs toward a force that wants to kill you. Weber talked all the way through our getting naked, all the way through our skin becoming slowly reacquainted—intertwined hands, then arms, then torsos pressed against each other, my breasts flattened, our legs spread, my cheek pressed against his. Still he kept talking. I stopped following what he was saying. I stopped listening and working and wondering. I just stopped, and it was a great relief. Only at the moment of orgasm, while Weber was deep inside of me, did the monologue cease for one long, shaking moment.

Then he pulled away and said, "Waka waka." The phrase sounded vaguely familiar, and when I asked what it was, he told me it was the catchphrase of Fozzy Bear on *The Muppet Show*. Waka waka.

"What does it mean?"

"I dunno, Doc, but I like the way it sounds. It sounds like I feel."

"What does that mean?"

Weber, with all his words, couldn't give me a good answer. And that drove me crazy. It still drives me crazy. Because that day, that long, weird, hung-over day, has deposited me here. And I don't like here. I'm still mired in a fog that I can no longer blame on vodka and which I do my best to blame on Weber. I went to the hospital three days that week, and four days the week after that. I can't explain why, but some mornings I show up at the hospital and I can't make myself go inside. I stand in the parking lot and argue with myself. I tell myself that I'm ruining everything, throwing away my chance to show Gram that I can be a brilliant doctor. But the internal debate is of no use. I have to turn back and drive to Weber's apartment. I don't know how to explain my behavior. I am at a loss.

At first I told my attending that I was sick. I claimed fatigue, malaise, a general sense of illness. That was not lying, it was true, is true. But now, as the days I can force myself to walk through the hospital doors grow more sporadic, I am forced to come up with a lie. I claim to have been diagnosed with mono. I actually forge a doctor's note and hand it in to the dean of the medical school. Because mononucleosis is infectious, I am officially excused from school for the next two weeks. I will be able to make up the missed rotation at some later point.

I have had to give up my new apartment before I even moved into it, as I cannot count on student loans being paid out to someone who is not behaving like a student. I now officially live with my visibly pregnant sister. We are both aimless. I spend my days at the library or driving around in my car. And to my confusion and dismay I continue to spend my nights with a man who says things to me, in the moments of what should be the greatest intimacy, that are meaningless.

CATHARINE

I walk around the corridors of the home every day for exercise. I have a route that I follow. I walk along the upper hallway, then down the stairs and along the lower hallway. If the weather's decent I also travel the main path to the parking lot and back. I've tried to get a few of the girls on the hall to join me, but they say that they're too old to exercise and that ladies shouldn't sweat and why fight the natural aging process. I tell them that is all a bunch of malarkey. I have a college degree in nutrition, and I know that as bones age they grow brittle, so it is more important than ever to exercise and strengthen the muscles around the bones. And exercise keeps the mind fresh and alert. You don't see dotty senior citizens out power-walking. I explain this to my friends, but do they listen? I remind them that I am only trying to help, and then I walk by their open doors on my daily rounds with my head held high, so I can show them the right way by example.

I think about this, my daily campaign for fitness and health, as I fall to the floor in the middle of my room. It is just after lunch, and as I stand up from the loveseat to get the remote control off the top of the television, my foot catches on something. I feel myself tip forward; my balance is lost. I reach out to grab anything that might stop my fall, but there is nothing to grab. In the next second, I am lying on my side on the floor. It happened so fast—standing, falling, fallen. My first thought from my new position on the floor is: If the girls on the hall find out about this little spill, they'll think it's my just reward after all my talk about the benefits of exercise.

I give myself a minute before I try to stand back up. The fall knocked the wind out of me, and my breath is choppy in my throat. I feel as if someone kicked a gate open in the center of my chest. There is also a dull ache in my hip, but it is my breathing and the odd sensation in my chest that concerns me more. I wait until my breath grows steady before I attempt to move. It turns out not to be much of a move. I manage to prop myself up on one elbow, and then that arm turns to rubber, and I am forced to lie down again.

I decide I will try again in a few minutes. I still don't have my strength back—that much is clear—and it is foolish to rush. After all, I have nowhere to be until dinner. So I lie there on my side, the painful hip up in the air. I tuck my arm under my head and am relatively comfortable. I look around and confirm that I have stranded myself in the only clear spot in this small room. The loveseat and the coffee table are a few feet behind me. The television is more than an arm's length beyond my head. There is nothing solid within my reach.

However, I can see plenty. The photographs on the wall above the loveseat. The waving trees through the window. I can make out only part of the view, but I know the entire scene. It is just past one o'clock, which means the two old men are reading their newspapers on the bench beneath the oak tree. The more able Alzheimer patients will be crossing the grounds on their supervised daily walk. Mrs. Malloy will be standing at the edge of the parking lot, waiting for the driver she hires to take her into town once a week. She asked me if I wanted to accompany her today, and I declined because Mrs. Malloy talks too much for my liking.

Perhaps, I think, my head cushioned on my arm, trying to breathe as lightly as possible, I should have said yes. Then I wouldn't have been sitting on the loveseat. I wouldn't have stood up for the remote. I wouldn't have settled into this room after lunch. I would have picked up my purse and met Mrs. Malloy at the end of the hall. I would be listening to her talk about her grandson the lawyer right now instead of lying here. But then I hear a car engine outside the window, and the light tap of a car door closing. So, Mrs. Malloy is gone. My chance for a different present has driven away.

I glance back by the loveseat, to see what it was my foot caught on. I want to get a look at what made me fall. It felt like a book, or a stack of magazines. But I don't see anything, at least not from this angle. Only the smooth Oriental rug that used to be my mother's. I am lying in the center of the rug now. Its weave is soft beneath my cheek. I think how odd it is that although I have lived with this rug for most of my life, I have never done anything but walk over it until now. My children used to crawl and play and watch television from this rug, but I never had time to sit down with them. And, honestly, it never would have occurred to me to sit on the floor. During that time, parents didn't play with their children like they do today. I was amazed, years later, by the ways in which my children *enjoyed* their own children. Theresa adored Mary and John from the minute they were born. She played house with Mary, and went to every one of John's football games before he quit the team. Up until Dina turned eleven or twelve and developed such a mouth on her, she and Meggy were inseparable. They even went through a period when they dressed alike. And Kelly, though maybe not as playful with her children, was the proudest parent I ever saw. It seemed as if every time Lila brought home another A, or Gracie got an article published in the school paper, Kelly called me and her brothers and sisters to let us all know.

During my time, parents were the disciplinarians. There was no playing, and enjoyment never entered the picture. There were so many children, and it was so much work to get them from infancy to adulthood. I was exhausted for fifteen straight years. I didn't mind that, though. It was my job. I got the children up and dressed and to school and church and helped with homework and broke up fights and washed endless stains out of endless shirts and pants and demanded good manners and prayers before bed and respect for their father and mother. Times were either normal and hard, or something was wrong. I preferred normal and hard. That was what I wished for. Enjoyment, or fun, never occurred to me. I just prayed to God that I would not lose any more children.

I shift my shoulder slightly against the rug. I plan to lie here for a few more minutes and gather my strength before I try to get up again.

It's better to just bear through pain. When my children came inside crying from a scraped knee, I used to tell them that complaining wouldn't help, and that if they were quiet the discomfort would eventually go away. I wasn't going to lie to them and say that life wasn't supposed to hurt. I was afraid that if I coddled them they wouldn't grow strong enough. I needed them to be strong. I always hated the sound of their tears, their weakness.

I was almost embarrassed when Pat sobbed and wailed while Patrick punished him. Didn't he know that his blubbering made his father even angrier? I knew the blows couldn't hurt that badly—Patrick would never really hurt one of his children. I also knew that Pat's sobs were for me in the next room. They were to make me feel bad. It worked, of course. Those were awful moments for me, but I also knew that if I went in there and tried to stop Patrick, things would only be worse. He would become more angry and hit harder, because I was questioning his authority. It was better for Pat if I stayed away. I couldn't help the fact that Patrick somehow tied together in his brain the birth of his oldest son and the death of his oldest daughter. He hated Pat for being born right after that death. Patrick never got over the loss of that baby girl. It was something I couldn't help. But when Pat Jr. had finally had enough and didn't want to come home the summer after his first year in boarding school, I found him a summer job through one of my father's contacts and bought him new clothes and packed his bag. I knew I wouldn't see Pat for a long time, and that he would never live in my house again, but I was glad to see him go.

I wanted life to be just normal and hard in our house. I yearned for that. And indeed, when Pat left for boarding school, the semblance of normalcy returned. Patrick joked at the dinner table. The other children laughed more. Lightness returned to the household, but I was unable to find comfort in it. I could see that it was a false lightness, an imitation of a peaceful time. I was the only one in the family who seemed to notice, so I kept the truth to myself. I pretended I was happy, too. I pretended everything was as I had wanted it to be. But by that time I had lost not only my daughter, but the twins as well. I had watched my oldest son walk away, still a boy, knowing that I had not gotten him safely from infancy to adulthood. I had lost him as well. I was losing the live ones now, too.

When Ryan's behavior started to change shortly after Pat left, when he started to say odd things, and stopped playing with the other little boys, I was not completely surprised. I had failed at holding my family together. I should have fought for Pat. I should have noticed my baby girl's symptoms earlier. I should have done something, anything, to bring my twins into the world whole and full of breath. I should have found a way to stop these cracks from forming. I should have kept everyone together, and safe.

I feel tears, which I recognize in disgust as self-pity, push at the backs of my eyes. To shake away that sensation I heave myself up on my elbow. I breathe there for a moment until my vision clears. I am fine from the waist up aside from the creaking gate door in my chest, but I can't seem to move my legs. My lap is twisted slightly under my periwinkle blue dress. Apart from the same dull ache, there is no real pain. I just can't seem to move. My legs have gone to sleep. It is growing dark in the room.

I will wait a little longer and then try again. I need to drag myself just a few feet across the floor to where the phone is. Then I can call one of my grandchildren. I could convince Gracie to slip in here, help me onto the loveseat, give me an aspirin or two, and then slip out. Lila would be a little more risky; she might insist on an unnecessary trip to the hospital. I'll make an appointment with Dr. O'Malley for tomorrow. No one here at the home needs to know that anything happened. I can just imagine the hubbub that would result if I was to be found lying on my floor by the staff. There would be whistles and sirens and a stretcher and everyone would crowd around to gawk. The girls on the hall wouldn't even try to hide their glee that it was me and not them— not yet, anyway. There would be jokes about what good my exercise routine did me. And after I had been wheeled from the building, there would be bets made on whether I would be able to come back to this room, to this building where the fittest and the most able people in the center live. There are three buildings on the grounds, each with different levels of care and support. Most people start out in my building and then move to one of the other two. The girls on the hall would wonder—still thinking, Thank God it's not me—whether I would be able to live as independently after this, whether I would still be able to take care of myself.

I hear a noise behind me and freeze so I can listen better. Someone dropped something in the hall, I reassure myself. But it's not the right kind of noise for that, and it sounds too close to be in the hall. It is unmistakably the soft, swooshing noise of my door opening. The door is behind me, so I can't see a thing. I fold my arms over my chest so that I look as together and respectable as possible. I pray that whoever is looking into the room somehow doesn't see me, and goes away.

But he or she doesn't go away and I don't hear the sound of the door closing. This infuriates me. It means some person, or even more than one person, are staring in at me lying on my side like a child curled up for a nap. They might be laughing, or jeering at the sight.

Hello, I say, sharply, to put an end to this rudeness.

Sweet Jesus, Catharine. What in the world are you doing on the floor?

Mother? I look as best I can over my shoulder and see that my mother has stepped into the room and let the door shut behind her.

She walks around to the front of me and stares down, her hands on her hips. She has on short white gloves and a gray dress with a belted waist. She also wears a gray hat with a wide brim. *Answer me, child. What are you doing on the floor?*

I shake my head and try again to raise myself up. Again, I only manage to prop up my elbow. I use all my strength to stay there, feeling that this position has a little more poise to it, a little more composure. *I fell, Mother. Will you please help me up?*

My mother shakes her head under the wide hat brim. She actually steps back from me and sits down in the armchair. *I don't think I can.*

Why not?

It's just not possible.

I sigh. I've been lying on the rug for over an hour at least and I am growing tired. I have always found talking to my mother frustrating. *Where's Father?*

He couldn't help you either.

He'd find a way, I want to say, but don't.

I am surprised to hear myself say, *Do you know that I'm having a great-grandchild?*

My mother has taken a piece of darning and a needle out of her purse. The darning looks like one of father's black dress socks. *I never even met my grandchildren,* she says. *It wasn't fair of you to keep them away from me.*

I didn't keep them away from you. My arm has grown weak again, and I am forced to lay my head back on the floor. *You lived all the way in St. Louis, and it wasn't like people flew in those days. You could have come out with Father on the train.*

You were happy I didn't come. My mother speaks matter-of-factly. *You thought I was crazy and didn't want me around your family.*

My cheek is against the carpet. I have stopped fighting my position on the floor. I feel instead as if I am sinking into the rug and the concrete floor beneath it. I am taking root, losing all possibility of escape. I think of the Ballen children, tied to the tree in the backyard. I see my mother, mending holes in hundred-year-old socks on the other side of the room. I think of Ryan. I think, *I tried to keep you from rubbing off on my children, but failed. I couldn't do it. I wasn't strong enough.*

It doesn't seem fair that you should know your great-grandchildren as well as your grandchildren when I never got to meet anybody, but then life hasn't been fair since I left Ireland.

This is one of my mother's favorite expressions, and it has always annoyed me. She left Ireland when she was twelve because people were starving there, so it doesn't even make sense. Life wasn't fair when she was *in* Ireland. But I don't let it bother me this time because of the mention of the new baby. The gate in my chest opens a little farther. My thoughts leave Ryan and I feel hope.

I don't approve of why you want this great-grandchild so badly. My mother shakes her head and the darning needles brush against each other with a *tsk-tsk* noise.

She's bitter, I think. Mother has always been bitter.

You think each time that you're going to get it right and have the perfect happy family. You think you can make up for every mistake you made and everyone you lost by getting it right this time around. Haven't you learned a thing about how the world works, Catharine? Every Irish ditty your good husband knew the lyrics to would have told you the truth. You should have listened to him once in a while. Everyone in those songs had a heavy heart. There is no such thing as love without loss. You can't make things right. Her needles move faster now, speeding up with her argument. *But then you always were stubborn. Thinking life was like a jigsaw puzzle you could put together with a few well-shaped pieces. After all, only the most stubborn of Irish women would lie in the middle of her own floor for hours and not call for the decent help that is only a few feet away. Listen to the footsteps, Catharine! There are people walking right by your door!*

I listened to Patrick, I say, trying to remember the words to "Miss Kate Finnoir" or "McNamara's Band" but coming up with nothing. *I was a good wife.*

Yes, my mother says, her head shaking again. *You were a good wife, Catharine, and now your husband is dead ten years and you still haven't a lick of sense. At your age, you ought to be plenty embarrassed. And you think I'm the crazy one.*

I am suddenly very cold. Goose bumps cover my arms and legs. *Can you throw a blanket over me, Mother?* I say. *Can you do that?*

I must have fallen asleep. I remember closing my eyes thinking that if I shut my eyes and mouth, less cold air would get inside me and I would not freeze solid curled up in the center of the floor.

The next thing I know, there is a slash of bright light across my face and shouts and Nurse Stronk is leaning over me. "Catharine!" she yells. "Catharine!"

I stare at her, wondering if she sees me right here under her rather large nose. Why does she need to shout? I look over at the armchair, but, of course, my mother is gone. The television is on, though; the noise of static fills the room and gray lines crisscross the screen. Was the television on this entire time? No, no, it wasn't. Did my mother turn on the television on her way out? Did she use it to get Nurse Stronk's attention and tattle on me? I wouldn't put it past her. I really can't trust anyone except myself.

Nurse Stronk keeps shouting. "Can you hear me, Catharine?

"Do you know where you are?

"How many fingers am I holding up?

"Do you know what day of the week it is?

"Are you hurt?"

I look past Nurse Stronk at the photographs on the wall. I find the black-and-white photograph where all of my children are smiling. They are not smiling with joy; they are smiling because Patrick, who was holding the camera, ordered them to. Again I think of the Ballen children, linked together but laughing, tied to the trunk of a massive tree. I think of my grandchildren, each of them wandering around aimless and unhappy. I try to picture one joyful smile on one face that I love, and come up with nothing. I think that maybe my mother is right, and that I am stupid to keep trying. I am stupid to think this new baby will right all past wrongs. The gate door in my chest swings wide open.

"Catharine!" Nurse Stronk bellows.

I will answer her questions so she will be quiet. Only halfway through my responses do I realize I am not speaking out loud. But still, I don't stop until I'm finished.

Can you hear me, Catharine? *Yes.*

Do you know where you are? *The Christian Home for the Elderly.*

How many fingers am I holding up? *Two.*

Do you know what day of the week it is? *Wednesday.*

Are you hurt? *Yes.*

KELLY

My heart has been heavy since I found out that my oldest daughter has ruined her life and embarrassed herself. Since hearing the news, everything has been shuffled up and dark. My life feels like a teenager's bedroom—everything a mess, in its wrong place and noisy.

My own bedroom is pristine. It has been months since Louis and I slept side by side. A situation I'd thought could only get better has gotten worse. I no longer have the energy necessary to run our marriage for the two of us. I'm having enough trouble finding a reason to get out of bed in the morning. I suppose I'm depressed.

Being around me makes Louis feel guilty, I know. I rarely see him, but strawberry frozen yogurt is in the freezer at all times. My favorite brand of pretzels is in the cabinet above the bar. The gas tank in my BMW is perpetually full. I never have to take out the recycling or bring in the mail. It is always done, everything is done, before I have the chance. I'm not sure when it happens. When I am out or asleep, I suppose. I give my husband plenty of opportunity to play phantom provider. I sleep the sleep of the drugged. Long and deep. Sleeping pills are my new best friend. And when I'm not asleep I am either at the office or in my room at the motel.

At the motel I try to pass time reading magazines. Occasionally I switch on the television, only to switch it off a moment later. I reorder the money in my wallet. I make sure the high-school photographs of Lila and Gracie are straight in their plastic covers. I file my credit cards in the order of which ones I use the most. I make sure my mobile phone is switched off. I check my To Do list in my Filofax. There are fewer items checked off these days. I have been too distracted to run the errands that need to be run. I have too many responsibilities.

Mostly what I do in the motel room is hide. I hide from phone calls from my mother and sisters. From the phone calls I am not getting from my daughters. I hide from what is left of my marriage. I know that it is only luck that Gracie or Lila or my mother hasn't realized the truth of our situation. Louis and I probably won't be able to keep it a secret much longer. Something will have to give. The elephant in the room is getting too fat to walk around, much less to pretend it isn't there. And I hide from the reality that I often find myself thinking about Vince Carrelli. I have gone back to him for two more haircuts since the first.

Initially I didn't like my new hairstyle, thought it was too short, but when a few days passed of simply showering and running my hands through my hair and not needing to use a blow dryer, I loved it. My new style is truthful and simple and right out there. What you see is what you get. And I have come to appreciate the fact that no one commented on the change. The haircut, and my time with Vince in the barbershop, is all mine.

I had one conversation with Gracie when I tried to reach out to her, to really understand her, and she pushed me away. The worst thing was that she basically stated that my mother was her confidante and the person she turned to. Also, over the last few weeks I have asked Lila to lunch several times only to hear that she is too busy. She was apologetic and very nice about it, but the message remains the same. My brothers and sisters call me only when they need something: money or advice. The gulf that lies between us is based on the fact that I have more than each of them. I have more money than Meggy and Theresa, and more family than Pat and Johnny. I don't look down on them because they have less than me, but nonetheless that reality sits between us and keeps us from being equals. And my mother . . . I admit I haven't tried to reach out to my mother. My mother is seventy-nine and I know better than to try to convince her to change her ways.

No one is prepared to deal with me as directly as Vince Carrelli. Whenever I am bored at work, or at home preparing a baked potato for myself for dinner, my hands drift to my short hair, and my mind drifts to Vince. I picture him standing in the barbershop, framed by the big window and Main Street behind it. I see his deep brown eyes, his square fingers, his uncertainty. Apart from his hands, Vince is a smaller man than Louis. He is less confident, less indomitable. I have always liked the look of Italian men. There is a warmth to them, to their eyes and to their skin, that is very different from the pallor and the fair eyes of the Irish.

You need a friend, I tell myself at the end of two hours lying on the motel bed staring at the ceiling. It's all right to need something. It's okay. You deserve this.

I pick the phone up off the bedside table and lay it on my flat stomach. I call information first and ask for the barbershop phone number. I ask the operator to connect me, and almost immediately the line begins to ring.

I hold my breath to block out the noise. What are you doing? I wonder. Who are you?

"Hello? Barbershop?" Vince says.

"Did I catch you at a bad time?" I say. "I thought you might be gone for the day. I'll call you tomorrow. Go back to whatever you were doing."

"Kelly? Is that you? No—it's not—I was just about to close up. I have a planning board meeting. With Louis. You're not calling for an appointment, are you? I told you to walk in anytime."

Foolish, I think. I am foolish. I am a fifty-six-year-old woman lying on a bed in a motel room calling a strange man. "I don't need an appointment," I say. "That's not why I called."

I hear him hesitate for a moment on the other end of the line. "Are you all right? What's wrong?"

"Everything's fine," I say. "Perfectly fine."

"You don't sound perfectly fine."

"Well," I say.

"I'm glad you called," he says.

"Are you?" I hear my voice, as hard as nails, and shudder.

"Yes, this is like a dream, Kelly—it makes me happy. Please tell me why you called."

This is not like a dream. This is nothing like a dream. This is my life, my blunder. I can only block his question. "Why did you want to talk to me?"

"This is a strange conversation," he says. "Are you sure you want to know?"

I put my hand over my eyes, as if I am approaching a car wreck and don't want to look. "Yes."

"I've wanted to tell you that I have feelings for you."

My heart threatens to leave my chest, it is beating so hard and crazily. I think that it is my good luck that women have a lower risk of heart attacks or I might have one now. I have wondered, when I thought about Vince and our meetings, if my memory exaggerated his intensity, his remarkable ability to say only what matters. But I'd remembered correctly. I had both dreaded and hoped this phone call would lead to this. I am alive in this moment. I am living.

"Let me explain," he says. "I don't want to scare you."

My body is shaking on top of the green bedspread. I think, Maybe he means gratitude, or friendship, or fondness. Those are feelings.

"I haven't been able to stop thinking about you since you came into the barbershop. I've come this close to calling you every day. I've tried to put my finger on what it was, what element of our conversation made this happen, but . . . I talk to people all the time. As a mayor, that's three-quarters of my job. And here as well, that's why people go to barbershops, so they can talk and make sure someone is listening. Men either go to bars and unload their problems on the bartender, or they talk to their barber while having a centimeter shaved off a head of hair that doesn't need cutting."

A car honks loudly outside my room. A lover is waiting for his mistress to join him. Or an angry father is trying to get the attention of a wayward teenager in the kind of trouble that only takes place in motels.

"Where are you, Kelly?" Vince asks. "What is all that noise?"

"You talk to a lot of people," I remind him. I like to hear Vince describe his life, his world. It is hard to believe he lives in the same town and the same time as I do. He makes everything sound so much simpler than I have ever found it to be.

"I don't want to make a mistake," he says. "I don't want to say too much."

"We all make mistakes."

I feel like I did when I was a little kid, standing at the edge of the high dive at the pool. The board quivering under my weight, sending chills of terror up my spine. My mother giving me a look from her lawn chair that said, *Just jump, Kelly. Don't keep everyone behind you waiting.* And Theresa or Ryan yelling from the side of the pool, "Be careful!"

"You can say whatever you want," I say.

"I've fallen in love with you." His voice wavers like a teenage boy's. "I know this is completely inappropriate. I know you're married to one of my oldest friends, who is a wonderful man. I know this means nothing to you—"

"Not nothing," I say.

"This . . . this sensation hasn't happened to me in over thirty years. At first I decided to keep my feelings to myself, to avoid you, to leave you in peace, but I'm not that strong. I told myself we could have just one more conversation, that I would tell you how I feel, and I would back away. And then you called tonight."

My cell phone rings in my purse. I forgot to turn it off when I came into the room.

"I've upset you."

I unzip my purse and pull out the ringing cell phone. I lay the real phone next to me on the bed. "Hello," I say, still a mix of quivering and blankness. Still waiting at the edge of the diving board. Still not responding.

Louis says, "Your mother just broke her hip. She's on her way to Valley Hospital."

When I turn off the power on my cell phone and Louis's voice dies away, all I can think to say to Vince is, "Can I call you back later?"

LOUIS IS waiting at the entrance to the emergency room when I arrive. He takes my coat from me, which I am carrying balled against my chest like a bag of groceries. I don't know how I drove here. I don't remember one road sign I passed or one turn I took. All I could think during the short drive was that my mother had known what I was doing and had decided to punish me.

"She fell in her room," Louis says. "Apparently she lay there without calling for help for hours. The doctors think she might have had a stroke."

"Why did they bring her to Valley instead of Hackensack Hospital?"

"That was my call," Louis says. "Valley's closer, and I thought that since it's Lila's training hospital, we might get special treatment." We walk in through the automatic doors. He says, "She's very tough, Kelly. Don't worry."

"I know she's tough. Can I see her?"

"She's with the doctor now. The nurse said the doctor would come out as soon as he was done with the examination."

"I should be with her," I say.

The waiting room is almost empty. There is a young man reading to a small girl, and an old man dozing in the corner. Louis takes my elbow and leads me to one of the neon green chairs by the door.

I say, "I thought you had a planning board meeting tonight."

He gives me a sharp look. "Listen, I'll call your brothers and sisters for you. And the girls should know."

I shake my head. "No phone calls. There's no point in the entire family sitting beside us with nothing to do."

I look at the young father reading to his daughter on the other side of the room. The little girl looks to be about six years old. She has pale hair tied up with a pink ribbon. I used to tie different-colored ribbons in my girls' hair when they were small. Blue for Lila, pink for Gracie. "She's all alone," I say, "and I don't even think she realizes what that means."

"Your mother's not alone, Kelly."

"Not my mother." I shake my head again. "Gracie. Gracie is all alone. She's doing this alone."

Louis leans forward and rests his elbows on his knees. His barrel chest and long legs seem to overwhelm the chair and all the space around it. His voice is tight. "Let's not talk about that here, okay? There's enough going on at the moment. Are you hungry or thirsty? I could run down to the cafeteria. What would you like?"

I mouth the word *nothing,* and hope that Louis will move his eyes away from my face.

"Mr. and Mrs. Leary?" A young man in blue scrubs is in front of us.

We both stand like obedient students who have been called on in class.

"Your mother broke her hip, and she bruised a few ribs. You can see her, but I gave her something for the pain, so she's groggy. She needs an operation to repair the break. Two other doctors checked her and agreed it was required. I'll schedule the surgery for tomorrow morning—the sooner the better."

"Surgery," Louis says.

"That can't be necessary," I say.

"It is necessary," the doctor says. "In over ninety percent of fractured-hip cases, surgery is the only possible course of action. Your mother isn't one of the lucky exceptions."

We are walking now, following the doctor down the hall. I am thinking that he looks awfully young with his smooth face and blond hair. Perhaps he is too young to understand the difficulties of someone as old as my mother. Perhaps he is mistaken.

He says, "We've already moved her to a room. There was no reason to keep her in emergency. She's stable. And you're in luck, because one of our best surgeons will be working on her tomorrow morning."

Why does he keep mentioning luck? Do we need luck?

The doctor is walking in front of Louis and me, and he suddenly turns his head and looks into our faces. "My name is Doug Miller, by the way. I know we've never met, but I'm friends with your daughters."

He gives us such a wide smile that I feel compelled to smile back. I notice Louis does as well. "You must know Lila from medical school," Louis says politely.

"Yes. And I dated Gracie a few years ago."

"I thought your name sounded familiar," I say, although I know I've never heard his name before.

Doug Miller keeps up his big smile as if this is some kind of reunion. As if Louis and I had the faintest idea five minutes ago that this man existed, much less that he is one more in what seems to be a long line of men Gracie has been close to. As if we're not standing together in a hospital to talk about the fact that my mother needs to be cut open.

As the three big smiles finally fade, a space spreads through the gray linoleum hallway. Space between us and the doctor, space between me and Louis, space between where we stand and the last door on the hallway, behind which my mother lies with tubes and machines attached to her. The distance seems insurmountable.

"They put these tubes in me without asking," my mother says when I enter the room alone. "Please tell them I don't like pain medication, Theresa."

"It's Kelly, Mom."

"So Theresa couldn't be bothered to come." She tosses her head like a petulant child.

"Theresa doesn't even know you're in the hospital yet."

"You can't do everything yourself, Kelly." The fog seems to lift from my mother's blue eyes for a moment. She is tiny in the hospital bed, lost in the yellow sheets. They have her propped at a funny angle on her side, I assume to take pressure off her hip. I was worried when I walked in that she would look broken, but she does not. Any damage is hidden by the bedding.

She says, "I don't want to leave my room at the home. I do not want to move into the other building. Please don't let them move me."

My mother's appearance does not match up with that of the woman I had pictured sitting in her room, manipulating my life. This frail-looking patient couldn't have known what I was doing two towns away. She probably wasn't even thinking of me when she fell to the floor. Her accident wasn't a moral message; it was simply an accident. I think that perhaps my mother is finally getting old.

"It's all right, Mother," I say, using the same soothing tone I used when my daughters were babies. "Everything's going to be all right."

Apparently that tone, as rusty as it is, works, because at that moment my mother closes her eyes and falls either to sleep or unconsciousness.

I sit with her for a minute. I watch her breath. It occurs to me that I have never seen my mother sleep. That is something you do with your children, not your parents. This state of affairs is organically wrong. My mother should not be lying, tiny and injured, in this bed before me. She should have called for help instead of lying on the floor of her room. I should not have to sit and watch her rest with her head tipped back, her mouth slightly open. My mother in her right mind, off of drugs, would never allow me to see her in this condition.

When I go back out into the hallway, I don't see Louis right away. He is standing halfway down the corridor, his arms crossed over his chest. He is staring in the direction of the nurses' station. He turns when he hears my high heels click on the linoleum floor.

"How does she seem?" he says.

"I'm going to stay with her in case she wakes up. I'll call my brothers and sisters and let them know. Will you call the girls?"

He nods. "I'll wait with you."

Anger crashes over me, so strong I have to grit my teeth. "I'd rather be alone with my mother," I say. "I'll see you at home later. Tell the girls everything is going to be fine."

Only when Louis turns the corner at the end of the hall and his broad back has disappeared from view do I calm down. I abide by the NO CELL PHONES signs on the wall and find a little booth with a bench and a pay phone inside. As I step in and close the glass door behind me, the setup reminds me of a confessional. My mother used to insist as children that we confess every Wednesday and every Sunday. She would load us all in the car in our good clothes and then line us up outside of Father Brogan's confessional stall. She would use her hand to smooth our hair into place. She would warn us that omission was as big a sin as lying, and then she would give each of us a small shove toward the velvet curtain. Inside the dark spartanlike box, on my knees with the priest's voice and, even worse, the sound of his breathing seeming to come at me from every side, I would pore over the four days since I had last confessed, trying to find any sins. I suspected that Father Brogan was bored on his side of the stall, and hoped I would come up with something good and challenging for him, a real Commandment breaker like murder or coveting your neighbor's wife. But I was a very good child, and usually the only bad acts I could think of had been committed by my brothers and sisters. Most afternoons, for lack of anything better to offer, I would end up telling on them. The priest seemed to enjoy that. He would give a soft chuckle and dismiss me after assigning one Hail Mary for tattling. He would then call back in one or more of my siblings who had already confessed that afternoon. Meggy and Johnny spent most of our childhood muttering Our Fathers and Hail Marys under their breath in penance for their sins. I wore constant bruises on my shins for turning them in.

I call Theresa, and she sobs the entire time I am on the phone with her. Finally Mary has to pick up the extension and write down the surgery time and room number.

Meggy curses and tells me how many days she has already had to take off from work this year. In a threatening tone she says she'll come up tomorrow but that she may end up getting fired for it.

Angel and Johnny get on the phone together. I imagine Johnny nodding and Angel growing tearful. Johnny used to be a volunteer paramedic, so he asks me technical questions about Mother's condition, questions I can't answer.

Ryan starts to pray into the phone the minute I tell him the news. I tell him that I will pick him up in the morning, and then hang up.

Pat says he is very busy at work right now, and that with everyone else being at the hospital, Mother won't need him. He asks me to call him after the surgery and let him know how it went.

When I hang up the phone I am exhausted. I feel like I have been awake for days on end. My eyes are dry from the sterile hospital air. I rest for a minute on the tiny bench in the booth, my forehead pressed against the metal change box on the phone. I take deep breaths, the cleansing kind that we talk about in my women's group. I breathe until I am light-headed, and then I open my purse. I take out the card I wrote the mayor's home number on. I dial, and when he answers, I say, "Meet me on Route 17 North next to the Houlihan's restaurant."

There is a silence, and then he says, "But that's the—"

"I know. Just please meet me there."

When I arrive at the Fairmount Motel he is waiting in the parking lot in his bruised-looking Honda. Chastity peers wide-eyed out of the back window. In the darkness, the dog looks alarmingly like a small child. Vince gets out of the car with his head down, wearing a baseball hat. He looks at me anxiously from under the brim.

"Don't worry," I say. "I come here to think. I rent the room from one of the women in my reading group."

"You come here to think?" He is looking at me as if I am a stranger, not the woman he confessed to love a few hours earlier. The summer air is a little cool, and I shiver in my thin blouse. Louis still has my coat. I think, Maybe this wasn't a good idea.

"Look," I say. "I've had a really hard evening. I thought maybe we could talk here."

"All right," he says.

"Are you sure?"

He tips his hat up and I can see his warm brown eyes saying, Yes.

I am suddenly so nervous I can feel my arms and legs break out in goose bumps. I walk ahead of him toward the room on the end of the strip motel, room number 111. I picture what lies ahead of me. The room simple, but clean. The bathroom with its nice deep bathtub. My novels in a neat stack on the closet shelf. My own pillows brought from home, extra firm. The room that has been filled with everything I need. I cannot believe, as I reach the door and fit the key into the lock, that I have actually invited another person inside.

LOUIS

I wake up at dawn on the den sofa, a paperback mystery folded over my chest. I tried to wait up for Kelly last night, but kept nodding off. I stand up carefully, stretching to ease the cramp in the middle of my back. I find my khakis where I left them the night before, in the den closet, folded on top of the Scrabble board. I know it is important to Kelly that our cleaning lady not know I am sleeping down here, so I have taken to doing my own laundry.

I make my way upstairs and look in on my wife. She is lying on her side, perfectly centered on her half of the king-sized bed. I can tell by her steady breathing that she is asleep. I don't wake her. She will have to get up soon enough, to make it to the hospital in time to see her mother before surgery. I miss Kelly. I miss lying beside her. When I first started sleeping downstairs, I thought it would just be for a night or two, just until I pulled myself together, until I had done enough work on the Ortizes' house to get some peace. Until I stopped having nightmares about Eddie's fall. But the nightmares haven't stopped, and I am never able to climb those stairs when it's time for sleep. Each night I try, and each night I convince myself that I'm not ready. I want to return to Kelly whole.

On my way back down the hall I catch myself tiptoeing past Gracie's and Lila's rooms, and shake my head. In the early mornings I often think all the women in my life are still in this house. I used to love being the first one up, and hearing one sleepy pair of footsteps after another pad down the stairs.

I put on a pot of coffee and check my beard with my hand. I need to shave. It is only after I've poured myself a cup that I see the note on the table, propped up against the sugar bowl. *Louis, I was with my mother nearly all night. I have set the alarm to wake up. Will you please pick up Ryan and meet me at the hospital?* The note is not signed. Kelly is too practical to sign a note that clearly could only be from her. I always sign mine. The writing looks too unfinished and impersonal without some kind of closing. I usually close with *Have a good day* or *Call me if you need anything.* Then I add, *Love, Louis.*

Today I scrawl at the bottom of her note: *There's fresh coffee. Your brother and I will see you soon. Love, Louis.* I carry my coffee up to the bathroom to shave. I look in on Kelly again before I leave. Asleep, she appears much younger than fifty-six. Her face is softer. This sleeping woman looks like the girl I married, in a way that she never does when she's awake.

It is only for her that I am willing to put up with Ryan. I generally avoid him as much as I can. And if anyone had asked me, I would have told him he couldn't come to the hospital today. After all, what good is he going to be? His inane rambling, his prayers, and his sudden cruel comments have no use. I can't help but feel that with the number of children Catharine and Patrick McLaughlin had, someone should have cut their losses somewhere along the way. I couldn't expect Catharine to do it, because how do you turn away your own child? But there is no reason for Kelly or her other siblings to deal with this sick person who refuses to take his medication or be anything but a burden to the people around him. He should be living in a home with people of his own kind. But Kelly won't listen to any negative talk about her youngest brother. She won't discuss him in any light. It is as if Ryan is a given in her life, as elemental as her arms and legs. He's not hurting himself, is all she'll say. Yes, but he's hurting you. You don't need to waste your energy on him.

I am accustomed to Kelly not listening to me, not allowing me to help her. The drive across Ramsey to his apartment building—my apartment building—calms me down. I pass a few buildings I own, and

a few others I am interested in buying. I note the decay of the building Ryan lives in as I ride the elevator up to his apartment. The elevator itself is a kind of death trap. It has the old metal gate you pull
across the opening that could easily catch fingers and toes. And the
motor makes some bad noises, accompanied with abrupt stops and
starts between floors. I am sweating by the time I reach his floor, wondering whether I should just tear this building down and sell the land.
I'd hate to have my men working here among the hidden landmines
of rotting floors and faulty electricity. I wouldn't be able to sleep at
night.

I will tear it down, I decide, as I knock on Ryan's door. I will move
in with a crane and some heavy trucks and in no time this building will
be gone. That's the only way to ensure everyone's safety. The decision
immediately makes me feel much better. It will be easier now for me
to be patient and pleasant with my brother-in-law.

"How you doing, Ryan?" I say when he opens the door. I scan the
apartment. It is disgusting. A fat white bird eyes me from on top of the
television, and an even fatter yellow one is perched on a bar in an open
cage over the couch. There are three large crucifixes that I can see at
first glance, one on each wall. The room smells like a zoo.

"Good, Louis. How are you?" Ryan straightens in his wheelchair.
Kelly says he looks up to me. I wouldn't know about that, but I do
know he makes an effort to act more normal during the rare moments
that we're alone together. The one or two times a year when I allow
that to happen, I appreciate it. "Where's Kelly?"

"She stayed with your mom at the hospital until very late last night.
So she's sleeping in a little and she'll meet us there. You ready to go?"
I back toward the door, keeping my eye on the white bird.

"I spoke to Mother around nine o'clock last night and she said Kelly
had already left." Ryan wheels after me as I head for the elevator.

I press the button and wince to hear the elevator chug into motion.
I'll dismantle the elevator the day I close on the building. "Your mother
was on some serious painkillers. She was confused. She thought Kelly
was Theresa for part of their visit."

"Oh my," Ryan says. "I've been praying for her all morning. I wish I didn't have to go to the hospital. I've known for weeks that something bad was going to happen to her, though. I've been waiting."

"Your mother's getting older. It was only a matter of time before she fell, or had a stroke, or something along those lines." I push him toward the car. I could let him wheel himself, which is what Kelly does to foster his independence, but then the whole process would take much longer. Besides, why let him think he's independent when he's not?

"A matter of time," Ryan repeats. "I guess everything is just a matter of time."

I help him into the front seat, then fold up his chair and fit it in the trunk. I make sure he's buckled in before I start up the car.

We arrive at Catharine's hospital room before anyone else. It is barely eight in the morning. I push Ryan in ahead of me, up to her bedside. Catharine looks better this morning than she did yesterday. "Your color's better," I tell her.

"It was all that medication," she says. "I insisted they hold off this morning until they have to put me under."

"You look fine, Mother," Ryan says. He is hunched forward in his chair, stretching toward Catharine. "I don't believe in hospitals, you know that. I don't feel God's presence when I'm in a hospital. Maybe the doctors were wrong. In my opinion they usually are. I bet you don't need the operation."

"I'll be outside," I say, and squeeze Catharine's hand before I leave the room. I know I won't see her again before the surgery. Soon she will be mobbed by children and grandchildren, all terrified that this fall is the beginning of the end. As far as I can tell, she has been fading, ever so slowly, since Patrick died. I don't understand why she has chosen to take so long about it. My own parents seemed to disappear in a matter of minutes. It was startling and painful for me at the time, but later I came to appreciate the fact that it was quick. There was no gray area, no ambivalence. One minute they were here, the next they were gone. They never met Kelly, much less my daughters. My mother and father have no connection to the family I have now. I rarely think of them.

I take a seat in one of the orange plastic chairs in the hallway. I pick up a magazine on auto racing someone left on the chair next to mine, but before I can even turn the page the shaky feeling comes over me. It shows up out of nowhere. I hate and dread these moments. It is how I feel whenever I think of Eddie's fall, but lately the shaky feeling has come to me on its own, with Eddie nowhere near my thoughts. I am unable to function until the sensation leaves me. It rumbles through me like an attack of nausea. All I can do is double over and pray for it to pass. Until the shakiness leaves and I feel normal again, I am in a cold, dark place where all I can think of are the terrible moments in my life. Moments that give me that same uneasy feeling.

I remember coming home early on a weekday afternoon fourteen years ago. There were no cars in the driveway, and no one responded when I called hello. But when I went upstairs to change into clean clothes, I heard noise coming from Gracie's room. I walked down the hall, trying to place the noise as music, or girls laughing. Through a crack in the door I saw my fifteen-year-old daughter standing naked by her window. I watched a boy's hand reach out and grab Gracie by the wrist. She disappeared from my view and then there were giggles, high and low. I stood frozen for what felt like an hour, and all I could see were their feet, twisted up at the end of the bed. I knew I should bust into the room and throw this kid out on his ass. I wanted to. My baby was only fifteen and this was my goddamn house. Gracie needed my protection. She needed to know that she was too young for this. But the sounds they were making were so loud, and when my feet could move I found myself headed in the opposite direction. I slammed out of the house and got into my truck and sped down the street. All I wanted to do was get away. I never told Kelly. I never talked to Gracie. I never wanted to think about it again and I did a pretty good job until just recently. I detest the inky black feeling deep in my gut that comes when I think about Gracie standing by the window, that comes when I think of Gracie now, pregnant, that comes when I think of Eddie. It's as if I'm rotting from the inside out.

LAST NIGHT when Kelly told me to leave, I wandered the halls of the hospital looking for Eddie's wife. I thought that if she was on duty, and if I could just catch a glimpse of her in her white nurse's uniform looking professional and capable and well, I would feel better. I walked from one area of the hospital to the other with a purposeful stride, knowing from experience that few people stopped me when I looked like I knew what I was doing. I scanned the nurses' stations and glanced into open rooms, but had no luck. I still don't know her maiden name. I actually looked at the mail in her mailbox one afternoon, hoping some of it would be addressed to her professional name, but every piece said Mrs. or Mr. Ortiz.

Today I feel worn out, and I'm worried about Kelly. This fall must have upset her more than she let on if she spent the night at her mother's side. Kelly is not usually one to hover. When the girls were babies, she always insisted we let them cry themselves out. That was awful for me, as there was no sound worse than Gracie or Lila screaming, but Kelly was so convinced it was best for the girls that she wouldn't let the crying bother her. It is as if my wife is able to convince herself when and what to feel. That's how I know her mother's broken hip has gotten to her. Sitting by a sleeping woman's bedside isn't Kelly's way. That kind of behavior has no practical effect, and she is always practical. I blame myself. I know I have been disappointing her on every level lately. She wants to talk about Gracie being pregnant, and I don't. It's as simple as that. I am not mad at Gracie. She is an adult and she has made a choice and I have to respect that. I'm glad I don't see as much of Joel as I used to, since Vince is no longer assigning him to spy on me. But other than that, I have no feelings on the subject. I just know that I don't want to talk about it.

The door to Catharine's room opens, and I look up. Ryan is wheeling toward me. "The nurses asked me to leave," he says. "I was saying prayers with Mother and they asked me to leave."

"They probably need to prep her," I say, not sure exactly what that means but knowing I have heard the term "prep her" on medical television shows.

"Right," he says. He gets the same crease between his eyebrows that Kelly does when she is worried. "I wish I trusted doctors."

I nod, because at least that wish makes sense.

"Hi, Dad," Lila says, rounding the corner. She comes at me and gives me a hug with so much speed and strength that I am suddenly nostalgic for when I was young. There were times in my twenties, before I got married, when I felt as powerful and fresh and full of purpose as my youngest daughter looks. I smile down at her.

Lila slides out of my arms, and then I see Gracie. I try to control my look of surprise but fail miserably. I have not seen her since Easter. And yes, I know that I knew she was pregnant, but I was not expecting to see Gracie with a new body. Her belly is swollen. She looks like any pregnant woman walking down the street. Even her face is wider. She has curves everywhere. She looks nothing like the little girl who used to follow me around every weekend and inspire me to come up with stupid jokes just so I could hear her laugh. She doesn't even resemble the fifteen-year-old girl I saw through the sliver of an open door. She looks like a stranger.

I pat her awkwardly on the arm. It seems as if a hug might hurt her.

"Gram's going to be all right, right?" Gracie doesn't meet my eyes.

"The nurses won't let you in to see her," Ryan says.

I don't know where to look. I hope that we won't have to stand out here and make small talk for long. I can't think of a damn thing to say.

The door to Catharine's room opens again and we all turn. A tall nurse stands in the doorway, caught in the early-morning sunlight. A jolt runs through me and I think, Thank you. It is Eddie Ortiz's wife. I've found her.

A cough strangles deep in my throat, and Lila slaps me on the back. "You okay, dad?"

Gracie says to the nurse, "How is my grandmother?"

Eddie's wife looks like everything I had hoped for: professional and capable and well in her white nurse's uniform. Her long black hair is tucked up under her cap. I lean forward to get a look at the name tag pinned to her uniform.

Her voice is soft but firm when she addresses Gracie. "I'm Noreen Ballen. We're about to take your grandmother down to surgery. She's groggy, but you can spend a minute with her if you like."

Lila, Gracie, and Ryan head through the open door. Past them, I glimpse Catharine, small and pale laid out against her pillow. The drugs seem to have taken away even the glimmer of her usual strength. She barely turns her head in the direction of her grandchildren.

"Will you be with her in the surgery?" I ask. I keep my eyes down and speak in a low voice. I don't want Eddie's wife to notice me, but I want to keep her here, near me, for just a few more moments. I don't want to let her get away.

"No, I'm not a surgical nurse." There is an abrupt silence. I keep my head down, even though I know Nurse Ballen has recognized me. "Mr. Leary?" she says, in a different voice. "My goodness, hello."

"Hello," I say, like an idiot.

"Are you . . . are you related to Mrs. McLaughlin?"

"She's my mother-in-law."

The woman standing before me looks dazed. "I was part of the prep team," she says. "You can be sure she's in fine hands. Dr. Slotkin is an excellent surgeon. And Mrs. McLaughlin seems to be very strong and alert for a woman her age."

"I don't know what her family will do without her," I say.

She tilts her head to the side. I think, Eddie must miss the way she tilts her head. He must miss the way she stands, so straight up and down. He must miss the freckles on the backs of her hands.

"I've wanted to apologize," she says, "for falling apart in front of you at the funeral." Her face sags and then pulls back together. It is a horrible moment when her grief shows.

I should have walked away when I saw her walk out of Catharine's room. It was cruel of me to stand here and think I could have a conversation with her. The sight of me has brought up what must be the most painful memory of her life. My goal over the last six months has been to alleviate this woman's troubles, not add to them. I wonder if there is anything I can say to fix this.

"I'm sorry," she says, her voice different. "I didn't expect to see you here. I wasn't prepared . . ."

"Don't apologize," I say quickly. "You just go on with your work." I gesture toward the nurses' station down the hall. "I'm going to read a magazine. Gracie and Lila will be out any minute. If we have any questions about Catharine, we'll ask another nurse. Really. Please."

"Don't say that," she says. "It's just a surprise, that's all. Eddie thought so highly of you. And the flowers you sent. Goodness, I should have thanked you long ago."

"No," I say, horrified. She can't thank me for watching her husband fall off a roof. I won't let her. I will change the subject. I will keep talking. I say, "I almost thought it wasn't you, because of the name tag."

She touches the name tag without looking down. "I use my maiden name professionally. I always have. It helps me," she says, after a pause, "to have a different persona at work. I don't think about Eddie as much here."

"Of course, sure."

"When I'm at home he's everywhere I look."

He's everywhere for me, too, I want to say, but don't.

"Louis." It's Kelly's voice. I turn and see her walking down the hall. She has her car keys in her hand and her hair is slightly messed. I see that the sight of me talking to a nurse frightens her. "Am I too late? Have they already taken her in?"

"No," Nurse Ballen says, her professional half-smile back on, her eyes growing calm and distant. "You still have time."

WHEN MEGGY, Theresa, Angel, Mary, and Dina arrive, all bursting out of one cramped Toyota as if they have been at one another's throats the entire drive and are now ready to take on someone new, I make my escape. Catharine will be in surgery for at least another hour, and with her two sisters and sister-in-law and nieces and daughters there, Kelly won't need me. I kiss her good-bye on the cheek. She still smells like she does when she first wakes up, rumpled and like soap.

"You smell nice," I tell her.

She shakes her head so abruptly that her nose hits my chin. I pull back, rubbing where contact was made.

"I took a shower last night," she says, sounding angry. "I told you I overslept."

"You look fine," I say.

"I don't care if I look fine. We're in a hospital."

"It's a very common operation, Kelly. Your mother will be one hundred percent in no time."

"I know." She looks at Meggy, Theresa, Dina, and Mary in the chairs across the hall. Mary has a set of rosary beads she keeps fingering. Dina is wearing a ripped T-shirt that has LIFE IS A PARTY! written across it. Angel is on the other side of the hall with her hand pressed against Gracie's stomach. Lila paces around them all.

Kelly suddenly looks down. "I don't want to be here, Louis. Did you notice what Gracie's wearing?"

"Should I give her money to buy some clothes?"

"My father's cardigan. Don't you remember? It was his favorite. My mother must have given it to her. Why would my mother give that to her? Why would she wear it?"

"Probably because none of her own clothes fit her."

"I shouldn't even try to talk to you," she says. "You don't want to be here for me. You're faking it and I'm faking it, too. I'm too tired to pretend, Louis."

"I'm not faking anything," I say. I've become used to the way things are between Kelly and me, and I feel only a little guilty. After all, I'm not faking. That's the wrong word. "But I do need to check on my men. I'll come right back."

"I don't want you to pretend to care," she says. "We're past that. Just leave."

Because I can't bear to look at Gracie for another minute, I do as she asks. I take the most direct route out of the building. Once outside, in the hot, sticky July morning, I concentrate on swallowing the fresh air. As far as I'm concerned, what you breathe inside a hospital is not real air. It is sickness and medicine and air conditioning and ammonia. It is the unholiest combination of molecules and chemicals that can be found anytime, anyplace. Both of my parents died in the hospital, wrapped in tubes and plugged into machines. I spent days sitting beside their adjustable beds, first with my father and then with my mother, drinking lukewarm coffee. I rode in the ambulance with Eddie Ortiz, although he had died long before we reached the emergency room. I hate hospitals.

"Hey, Mr. Leary," a voice says. I rub my hand over my eyes. My legs have taken me out into the vast parking lot, but I am nowhere near my car. A heavy young man sitting on the hood of a pickup truck is talking to me.

"Hello," I say. The boy looks vaguely familiar.

"I dropped off your daughter," he says. "I'm waiting to see how long she lasts in there. I bet her she wouldn't stay very long. These kinds of family emergencies can be real stressful, you know."

I stare at him. I wonder if exiting the air-conditioned hospital into this humid summer day has done something to me. My head aches. "You dropped off Gracie?"

He shakes his crew-cut head. "Lila."

"Oh." Now Lila has a boyfriend?

"I'm Weber James. Sorry about that—I should have introduced myself right off. It's just that I feel like I've met you already. You look like Lila."

I am placing him now. "You're a fireman?"

"One of the full-timers."

"I've seen you around with Joel Shane."

"Yeah. He's a friend. You probably saw me with him at the Municipal Building. When I'm bored I go with him on the mayor's espionage missions."

Something about the way he offers this information bothers me. In fact, everything about this boy sitting on the hood of a pickup truck in front of the hospital as if he is tailgating at a ball game bothers me. What does Lila see in him? Who are my daughters?

"Lila's a medical student," I hear myself say. "She spends half of her time in the hospital. Why would you think she'd have to leave after twenty minutes?" I force a smile, trying to lighten my tone. "It just seems like you might be wasting your time out here."

Weber swings his legs to the side and, with a surprisingly graceful motion, jumps to the ground. "She doesn't have very good attendance at school these days," he says. "So she's not crazy to spend time in this place. I'm betting she'll show up soon."

I scan the parking lot for my car and find it, dull under the late-morning sun, several rows away. This boy doesn't know what he's talking about. "I need to get going," I say. "Nice to meet you, Weber."

"Hey," he says. "I might have said something I shouldn't have. I have a hard time keeping track of what Lila's official story is about school. I might have blown it big time. Can you just pretend I never said anything?"

I am already a few steps away. I have to turn to hear him. My head is killing me. "No problem."

"Thanks, man. I owe you one." Weber's face cracks into a smile, and I see in it the joy and the youth I saw in Lila's face earlier. I nod in the boy's direction, and then weave my way across the hot asphalt.

I HAVE no intention of leaving the parking lot right away, which makes the presence of Weber even more irritating. I can't very well sit in my parked car while he sits on the roof of his truck a few yards away. I don't know him, but I am pretty sure he would see that as an invitation to come over and continue to chat. To avoid that possibility, I turn on my engine. I pull slowly out of the parking space. As I take the car out of reverse, I see Lila. She slams out of the hospital door and pauses, just like I did, to breathe. Then she heads across the parking lot, book bag swinging from her shoulder, toward Weber. My only consolation, as I pull away, is that she does not look happy to see him.

I drive around to the other side of the hospital and into the portion of the parking lot that is reserved for the medical staff. I easily locate Eddie's big white Cadillac. I drive past it and find a parking space near the hospital exit. I turn off the engine but leave the radio on, and settle in to wait. I heard Nurse Ballen tell another nurse that she was off at noon, which is a half hour from now.

I listen to the local news on the radio. The anchor lists the road closings in the county, the sites of major construction, the governor's ambivalence toward the expensive renaissance of the city of Newark. I think about how Newark, just ten years ago, was more frightening to drive through than the worst sections of Manhattan. It was dirty and run-down and full of gangs. Every day at major intersections in broad daylight cars would be hijacked, people shot, drugs sold. I would never let my girls go anywhere near Newark. But now, thanks to a new arts center and new businesses and talk of a hockey stadium, and lots of money, Newark is becoming a golden place. Full of hope and promise. It is amazing to me that in my lifetime I have seen the rebirth of a city. Anything can happen, and sometimes anything does. It makes me think about what I can do for Kelly. Perhaps I will bring an ice cream back to the hospital with me this afternoon. A triple-header of her favorite flavor, pralines 'n' cream. She is bound to forget to eat, with all the commotion of her family. The idea of handing her the white bag with a cup of ice cream inside pleases me. I can practically see her smile.

When Eddie's wife leaves the hospital, she is not wearing her uniform. She has on gray slacks and a short-sleeved blouse. Her hair is down. She carries a large purse, as most mothers of young children do. I have seen her, on other days, pull amazing things out of that purse. A sandwich for her son, a doll for her daughter, an entire newspaper or an apple or a fat novel for herself. Now she takes a pair of sunglasses out of the purse and slides into the white Cadillac. She drives out of the parking lot, and I follow her.

My men used to make fun of Eddie because of his car. They called it the pimp mobile. Eddie called it a classic. When I got pulled into the teasing, I would only say that I'd never understood why anyone would buy a white car. Like white carpet, a white car shows dirt too easily. There is no way to hide or diminish its bumps and scrapes, and it's hell to keep clean. Eddie washed the damn car twice a week, though, and it was always gleaming. It is clear that his wife no longer abides by that practice. The white has grown grimy, and there is dirt streaked across the windows. I am two cars behind her, and the glimpses of dirt bother me. We approach a car wash, and I think, Turn in, turn in. But she drives right by. We hit a traffic light and I watch to make sure her reflexes are good. I know she must be tired after the night shift, but she doesn't show it. She's a good, solid driver.

I worry that I upset her this morning more than she showed. I have seen a comment from Catharine or one of the girls set Kelly off for days. I know how sensitive women are. And Kelly has never suffered a loss like Nurse Ballen has. She has not felt that kind of pain. I hate the idea that I might have sent her back there, reeling toward an abyss. I know from what I've seen that this woman is very strong, but still, everyone has a breaking point.

As we turn onto her street, it occurs to me that I now think of her as Nurse Ballen, not Eddie's wife or Mrs. Ortiz. She has a new name to me. Noreen Ballen. She pulls into her driveway and I slow down, pretending to be interested in a house a few down from hers. She gets out and kicks the car door shut with her heel, adding another scuff mark to the white paint. She follows the short walkway from the drive-way to the front door. There are weeds poking through the cement, and the lawn needs to be cut again. I make a mental note to send over one of my guys with a lawn mower when she is at work. Now she looks tired to me. Her blouse has come untucked in the back. There is a thin stain of sweat on the fabric between her shoulder blades. It is half past noon, which means she can sleep for only two hours before her kids are dismissed from school. She stands at the front door for a minute, the key idle in her hand, before she lets herself into the house. She crosses the threshold with her head down.

I can feel, sitting behind the wheel of my truck, the effort it takes Nurse Ballen to go inside. To walk into the loss, the memories, the grief, the life that no longer exists. I can feel all of that. It washes over me, so heavy and viscous I can hardly breathe. I shake my head, trying to shove the sensation away. I am angry for a moment that I have to feel this for a woman who is essentially a stranger. But then the anger is gone, too exhausting to hold on to. I watch the shades in her bedroom window clatter down like rain out of the sky, and then turn back toward the hospital.

GRACIE

I have not gone to work this week. I have not read any letters. I have not turned on my laptop. I have not returned Grayson's phone calls. What I have been doing is sitting at home in my bathrobe when it is not visiting hours and sitting beside Gram's bed at the hospital when it is visiting hours. Nurse Ballen says Gram is doing very well, but it doesn't seem that way to me. She is going through the motions, and doing what she is told, but she's not really there. She is quiet and she avoids my eyes and she sleeps much more than I would have thought possible. She seems like a totally different person, like an old lady who has taken over my gram's body. Some of this behavior is the drugs, I know, because Gram says things to me, particularly in the first forty-eight hours after the operation, that are inexplicable and strange.

"My mother turned on the television."

Even though I want to reason with her and draw her back to me, I don't want to argue with everything she says the way Mom and Aunt Meggy do. "Maybe there was something your mother wanted to see."

"No. She did it to get me in trouble. She did it because she knew I didn't want her to. She is always doing that to me."

"Doing what?"

"Saying things I don't want her to." Then, suddenly, Gram is asleep again. Breath slides steadily in and out from between her parched lips.

Aunt Meggy complains that the hospital staff is abusing Gram because they force her back on her feet only one day after her operation. A rehab nurse comes in with a walker, practically lifts Gram out of bed, and insists she walk into the center of the room and then back to the bed. Even with the drugs, Gram's face is drawn and her green eyes watery as she takes one shuffling step after another.

"You've just cut her open with a knife and rearranged her bones," Meggy says. "She's old and hurt. Can't you give her a few days of rest, for God's sake? Is there someone with a brain around here that I can talk to?"

Standing behind Meggy in the corner, watching Gram's eyes swim with tears, I agree.

Meggy sees me nodding, and says, "Shut up, Gracie." Even though Angel seems to have forgiven me for refusing to give her my baby—she has been nothing but sweet, asking after the pregnancy, acting as if my situation is a positive one—Meggy has not been so kind. Nor has she given up the cause. She has made it clear that as far as she is concerned, my child will, by some means, go to my aunt and uncle.

Nurse Ballen enters the room then, and Meggy turns her eyes away from my big stomach. Nurse Ballen explains that it is critical to get Gram moving as soon as possible so that she doesn't lose any of her strength, flexibility, or capacity to walk. She explains that if Gram stays immobile now, the odds of her recovery will be cut in half. She says that this is a critical and dangerous moment in Gram's health, and that if we can all point her in the direction of her pre-fall self, she will have a better chance of reaching that goal.

Nurse Ballen's talk seems to make Meggy feel better. At least she leaves the room and stops yelling. I am left alone with Gram, who is back in her bed now, eyes closed. But Nurse Ballen has made me feel worse. To me she seems to be saying that Gram is lost, and all we can do is force her to stand up and force her to eat and hope that she comes back to us. I need more assurance than that. I need more than just hope. I need Gram.

I sit by her bedside through every visiting hour for the five days that she's in the hospital. At the end of the week she will be moved to a rehab hospital, where she will stay for two weeks before she returns to the assisted-living center. I read to her from magazines, then baby books, anything I think might get a response from her. I even try, toward the end of the week, to read some of my letters and answers to her. Ordinarily, hearing an expert opinion on feeding or bathing an infant would get some kind of rise out of Gram, who does not believe in expert opinions. And any mention of my column, or the letters from my readers, brings a snort of disgust. But I get nothing from her now. If she's awake when I enter the room, she says hello, and she says good-bye when I leave. Other than that, she sleeps or looks out the window. The view is nothing to look at. The tops of a few trees green with leaves. A sliver of sky.

I tell Gram that the baby has started kicking, and that some days I think she is on the verge of breaking through the wall of my uterus. When I'm sure Gram is sleeping, I tell her that this kicking makes me feel even more alone. It makes me feel that my body is just a big, ever-growing shell, and that the only life in it is concentrated in this baby. I also tell Gram that each morning I give the baby a little pep talk about focusing all her energy on growing different organs and limbs. I rec-ommend to the baby that she grow up to be stronger than me. To be more open and accessible than Lila. To be less difficult than my mother. To be more communicative than my father. To be a person who knows herself completely, like Gram.

I tell Gram that I worry over this baby, a little more every day. The worry grows with the size of my belly. I think of Gram's missing chil-dren, the twins and the little girl, and I know I could never survive that kind of loss. I can't help but notice Meggy eyeing me every day at the hospital. The worry grows until it is the size of a full-grown person sit-ting beside me. How will I manage to hold on to anything, how can I hold on to this tiny future person?

Lila says, "Gracie, you smell. Will you please go home and take a shower?"

My mother says, "Your grandmother doesn't need you here every single minute. You'll feel better if you change out of those clothes. How about if I take you girls out to dinner?"

Meggy makes whispered comments to Angel that I am meant to

hear. "Gracie is losing it. She sits there in Daddy's sweater and mutters under her breath. She acts more and more like Ryan every day, don't you think? Does she look like she has the makings of a good mother to you?"

I try to ignore them. Meggy is wrong. They are all wrong. What they don't understand is that I will be fine as soon as Gram is better. When she is herself, I will cease to worry. When she is herself, I can go back to being myself. The problem is, after a few days at Gram's bedside, I cannot for the life of me recall who that was. Which makes me worry for the baby, too.

When I return home one afternoon, there is another message on the machine from Grayson. "You need to do your work." An annoyed pause. "You need to call me."

GRAM SHOWS signs of life the day before she is to be moved to the rehab hospital. She notices the nurses gathering her things, and my mother filling out paperwork. She says, "Kelly."

My mother crosses the room to her bedside. "What is it, Mother?"

My father and I, the only other people in the room, pay close attention. The hazy quality to Gram's voice is gone. She sounds like herself.

"Promise me I won't have to move into the other building at the old-age home. I don't want to leave my room."

My mother leans over Gram and speaks in a slow voice. "You're not going anywhere for a few more weeks, Mother. You're going to the rehab hospital first. We have to get you comfortable on your feet, moving around. The doctor says you'll be back to doing the fox-trot and running up the stairs really soon."

"Don't waste my time," Gram says. "I know all that. After this other hospital, I want to go back to my room. It's very important to me. I want you to promise me that you'll make that happen."

"Mother, you need to be in a safe and supportive environment. It's possible that you'll need more care from now on, and the other building has more advanced medical care available. I want you to be realistic about that possibility. I am not going to make false promises. We'll just have to wait and see what kind of progress you make."

When my mother finishes talking, Gram turns her face away and closes her eyes.

"Did you hear me, Mother? You shouldn't be concerned. No matter what room you have, we'll decorate it however you like. We'll hang the pictures in the exact same formation on the walls, if that makes you feel better."

Gram has slipped away again, to sleep or to unconsciousness. She does not answer.

LATER THAT afternoon, in the hall, I say to my mother, "You should have told Gram that she could go home to her room."

My mother has trouble making eye contact with me, which has been the case since Easter. She looks over my shoulder, or down at her hands. She likes to rotate her left hand while she talks, making the diamond on her engagement ring flash under the lights.

"Your grandmother is failing," she says. "It's my job as her oldest child to take care of her. I can't give in to her whims, Gracie. I have to do what is right."

The ring flashes, and the fact that my mother won't look at me makes me feel a little nuts. I have so few conversations these days. I am so often alone. I say, "You're not really the oldest child."

"What?"

Now I feel mean, and guilty. "You had an older sister, didn't you?"

I can feel my mother's eyes on me, poring over my dirty hair, my ill-fitting clothes. She says, "Why would you talk about that? You've always let yourself get caught up in those old stories. What's past is past. I don't see the point. What is the point?"

Maybe she's right. Maybe I don't put enough stock in the present, in what is real. The most recent phone message from Grayson said, "Snap out of it, Gracie. It's time to get back to living your life."

But I can't really agree with the narrow vision my mother and

Grayson fix on the world. The past and the present are each important. They share equal weight, don't they? That's why it is so hard to make decisions. There is always so much to consider. I say, "They're not just stories, Mother. They're our family's history."

She blinks a few times rapidly. "I have been the oldest, the one my parents depended on, forever. And now that my mother is sick, I have to make choices for her. Do you think Pat is going to step up to the plate? Or Meggy? No. That doesn't mean I like playing this role, Gracie, and it doesn't mean it's fair. Life is not fair. But I am a person who takes my responsibilities seriously."

This is a dig at my pregnancy. Any person who takes her responsibilities seriously would not let herself become a single parent. My mother is telling me that she would have done it differently, better. Hell, she did do it better, at least in her own mind.

I wish that Lila were here, so we could share a look and roll our eyes. She has barely shown up at the hospital. We spend a lot of time together at home, though, each in our pajamas. I don't ask her why she stopped going to school, and I don't ask her about Weber. I know about him because I ran into him one afternoon at the supermarket and he told me that he was hot and heavy with my sister. I think she's crazy to get involved with that jerk, but I keep my opinion to myself. I have been keeping everything to myself lately.

I take a deep breath and say, "Well then, as the head of the family you must know that Meggy and Angel came to my house a few weeks ago and asked me to give my baby to Angel and Johnny to raise."

The look on my mother's face confirms that she didn't know anything about it. She clasps her hands, and the diamond ring is covered. "They wouldn't have—"

"They did. They told me a story about a family on your street growing up. They told me that handing off your baby is part of Irish heritage, part of how Irish families take care of each other."

My mother shakes her head slowly, as if a hinge in her neck has suddenly gone loose. "They wouldn't dare . . . I should go in and check on your grandmother."

I think, Everyone wants to get away from me.

"I have an idea how you can make that promise to Catharine," my father says.

We both turn. Coming toward us in khaki pants and denim shirt, my father appears even bigger than usual. He looks over my head at my mother. I feel myself dwindle into invisibility.

My mother says, "I thought you were going back to work."

"I know how we can help your mother."

"I don't appreciate everyone attacking me," my mother says, her voice on the edge of hysterical. "I am doing the best I can for my mother. I don't need to be second-guessed."

"No one is attacking you."

She gestures with her hands, palms upturned. "Then why do I feel like I'm being attacked?"

"Please," my father says, "just listen for one minute. I know you're exhausted, and I'm trying to help."

My mother stares at him. I can see that she is seething.

My father smiles and crosses his arms over his chest. "I think we should hire a private nurse to sit with your mother every day at the home. I spoke to the director there, and as long as your mother's not seriously ill and we provide outside medical care, she can stay in her current room. They have no problem with that as long as she doesn't require any medical apparatus like oxygen or an IV, which she doesn't. After all, what she really needs is an aide who will keep an eye on her, and make it easier for her as she readjusts to her old life."

My mother nods, thinking. "Well, we could talk to some agencies and do some interviewing. It's not a bad idea, Louis. It might work. Let's just see how my mother does at the rehab hospital and play it by ear."

"Sure," he says, "but I actually already spoke to someone about the job."

Her eyes widen. "Why on earth would you do that?"

"She's a wonderful nurse, and she already has a relationship with your mother, and it turns out she's looking for a more regular sched-ule that will allow her to be home with her kids."

My mother looks at my father as if he's nuts.

"Who?" I say. "Nurse Ballen?"

He nods. "I just spoke to her, Kelly. Nothing is definite. I knew I had to talk to you first."

"She's my mother, Louis. I should hope you would talk to me first. For God's sake."

I walk away from their voices, into Gram's room. She is lying on her back, eyes closed, skin ashy. I close the door, but I can still hear the rise and fall of my mother speaking, the steady murmur from my father.

"Gram," I say, "I have great news. It looks like you'll be able to stay in your room at the home. Mom and Dad are working it out now. You'll be able to go back to your old life. Everything will be exactly the same as before. Just like you wanted."

There is no response from the old woman, the stranger, lying on the bed.

"Gram," I say, a little louder.

"Visiting hours are over," a nurse says, from somewhere behind me.

WHEN I arrive home Lila is there. I'm surprised, pulling into the driveway through the twilight, to see a light in the kitchen window. She usually spends the evenings at Weber's place. When I walk through the back door I find Lila sitting at the table flipping through the newspaper, drinking peppermint tea. I can smell the peppermint from across the room.

I put my purse down on the counter and try to order the thoughts that have rattled through my head these last few days in the hospital. There is so much I want to talk to her about. I try to think of what to say first. I want to tell my sister that I have pictured her, us, in the future. I've seen her as an adult with wrinkles at the corners of her eyes and a streak of gray in her hair. I've seen her playing games with my baby on the kitchen's linoleum floor. I've seen the two of us growing older, side by side. Finding ways to make use of each other, to depend on each other.

I am wondering if she will laugh, or maybe say something mean, when Lila speaks.

"Your advice this week is really odd," she says, rattling the newspaper with both hands. "It's incredibly practical and you answer three letters from guys, which isn't like you. This advice to the man who really wants to work on his car at night but doesn't want to hurt his wife's feelings cracked me up." Lila smiles down at the paper.

"Oh God." I had forgotten it was Thursday. Column day. "I didn't write that," I say. "I was too upset, what with Gram . . . Grayson must have written it to cover for me. Let me see."

Lila pulls out the Lifestyles section and hands it to me. "There's another message from him on the machine. Editor Boy is a little obsessive compulsive."

"Oh God, oh God." I sink down into a chair. "He must be furious."

"Who cares," Lila says. "You care too much about what other people think."

Oh sure, I want to say. *You care so little about what other people think that you can't even tell your sister that you're sleeping with a beer-swilling fire-fighter?* I know now that I'm not going to tell her about my glimpse into our mutual future. We would both think I was crazy. "He's my boss, Lila. I'm paid to care what Grayson thinks."

I skim the column. Grayson is a news writer and his sentences are short and to the point, very different from my more conversational style of writing. His advice is much more specific than mine usually is. He tells the man who is more in love with his car than his wife to bring home flowers and candy on the nights he plans to spend working in the garage. He tells a mother whose teenage son doesn't want to talk to her to make a list of topics she would like to discuss and to give her son a copy, too. Then they're to set a meeting time and neither mother nor son is allowed to leave the table until all topics have been touched on. Grayson tells a man who feels that his receding hairline is diminishing his chances with women to wear more hats and try to walk with more of a confident swagger.

I lay the paper down on the table. "He gave them hopeless advice," I say. "I'm going to get hate letters. The teenage son is going to laugh in his mother's face. The guy with the car is in huge trouble if he tries to buy his wife off with chocolates. And the man with the receding hairline needs to know that women don't care about that kind of thing. That's not why he's alone." I put my hands over my face.

"You're right," Lila says. "I wouldn't have thought about it like that, but that makes sense."

With my eyes closed behind my fingers, all I see are shadows and darkness. "I miss my good advice. I miss having the knack for it. I miss drinking cold beer. I miss everything," I say. "I miss having sex. I really miss having sex. You're so lucky that you get to have sex."

I hear Lila push her chair back. "So go pick some guy up. What's stopping you?"

"Have you looked at me lately?" I take my hands away from my eyes and the kitchen is bathed with neon spots and bright light. After a minute, I say, "Have you not been visiting Gram because you don't want to see people from medical school?"

"I stop by every day, just not during visiting hours. I know my way around the rules there. I'm not scared of them."

"I didn't say you were."

She shakes her head. "I'm due back to school next week. My sick leave is up."

"At least you're having sex on a regular basis," I say. "The world is magical when you're having sex, isn't it?"

"No."

"Maybe you're doing it wrong."

"You're delusional." Lila looks at me with tired eyes. "You always have been. There's no such thing as magic."

AFTER LILA leaves for Weber's, I heat up a frozen dinner and eat all of it plus two bananas and half of a McDonald's chocolate shake I had forgotten was in the refrigerator. Then I put my cardigan back on and sit outside on the front steps. I keep forgetting it is summertime. Every time I leave the house, or the hospital, I brace myself for a cold wind

and am surprised to find myself sweating in the humidity. New Jersey
is brutal in the summer. The high temperatures make the pavement
steam. The density of the air makes it difficult to breathe. The heat
slows your mind, and people rush from one air-conditioned space to
another. From car to house to business to mall.

With the baby heavy in front of me, I sweat more than I ever have.
My sweat is smellier now, too. I don't smell like the person I used to
be before this pregnancy. My body emits a salty, earthy odor that I don't
recognize. Several times I have walked into a room and thought, What
is that smell? only to realize that it's me. There are other changes in my
body that I didn't expect. A moss of pale hair has grown across the
stretched skin of my belly. And not only have my breasts grown enor-
mous, but the nipples are the width of one of my fingers and stained a
deep wine color. They are amazing and a complete departure from the
breasts I used to have. I go for days on end without looking at myself
naked in the mirror because the sight is so alarming.

A car slows in front of the house and then turns into the driveway.
I can tell from the sound of the engine that it's not Lila's car. It is hard
for me to see through the darkness, and I am immediately nervous.
Maybe it's Meggy, sensing my vulnerability and circling in for another
attack. I would like to declare this house a no-visiting zone. The last
welcome unexpected guest we had was Gram, and she gave up her
driver's license months ago. Since then, everyone who has shown up
has wanted something.

The car door slams and I see a man walking across the lawn.

I stand up. "Hello?" I say. "Who's there?"

"It's me," he says.

I sit back down on the step. "You couldn't wait to yell at me until
tomorrow?"

"You aren't returning my calls, so I decided to take action."

I had been feeling guilty about skipping work, but now that I'm
looking at Grayson, I'm nothing but annoyed. "You know," I say, "you
could have skipped the column this week altogether, or run an old column, or a 'best of' compilation. You didn't have to do the work yourself."

He doesn't even have a chance to respond before I start to cry. This pisses me off even more. I hate for anyone to see me cry. I don't cry the way a girl is supposed to; my tears are a messy, choking affair. My face gets red and puffy and my nose makes noises. Grayson, Mr. Unemotional, is the last person I want to cry in front of. He doesn't even have the common decency to look away while my eyes and my nose run. He stares at me through the whole thing.

"Gracie," he says, loudly, as though I can't hear him because of the tears, as though I can't hear him because my life has risen up around me in a shape I can't recognize. "Gracie, I didn't come here to talk about your column."

"My grandmother fell," I say.

"I came here to talk about getting married. Just hear me out before you object, all right? If you think about it, it makes sense for us to get married. The way I look at it, we can help each other. You need someone who understands you, Gracie. You get yourself so lost, and you have so little confidence in who you are. You need someone who knows what you want. And you know that you need financial help. When we last discussed this—"

"*We* did not discuss this." A deep exhaustion presses me down into the cement step.

"Fine. When I—"

"I don't want to discuss this, Grayson."

He shakes his head, shakes my objections off. "When the subject last came up, you couldn't have known what it would take to bring a baby into the world. You must have a better idea now of how much support is necessary. Who are you going to get that from, if not from me? It doesn't sound like the father of the child, or even your beloved gram, is going to be able to provide for you both."

My voice is very quiet. "No."

"No, what?"

"I'm not going to marry someone who feels more pity for me than anything else, Grayson. I've made it this far, haven't I? My family thinks I'm a slut, and maybe I am. What is it they say, you reap what you sow? I deserve this. I deserve to be alone with this. I am not your responsibility."

"This isn't just about you, Gracie. I've been doing a lot of thinking. I'm thirty-three years old, and I've never been in love. I've come to believe"—he hesitates—"that I'm unable to fall in love. I'm not hardwired for it. I'm too analytical, too inhibited. There is some part of me that can't let go in the way that's necessary to feel that depth of emotion." Grayson kicks at the cement walkway. "But I still want to experience life. I want to have a family. I want to experience marriage. The problem is, I don't know that many, or even one, woman who would be willing to marry me on my terms. After all, I make a good living, but I'm not a millionaire. I work all the time. I don't have anything else to offer. A decent paycheck and no chance at true love isn't much of a deal."

I can hear that Grayson is telling the truth. His wiry runner's body is bent toward me, willing me to hear him. I shake my head in amazement. "But you're saying that deal is good enough for me?"

I wonder how this could happen, that as Gram turns away from me, Grayson steps forward. The father of my first baby, the one I threw away, is offering to play father to my second. Is this how it's supposed to be? Am I supposed to take help no matter who's offering it and no matter what form it arrives in?

"I care about you, Gracie, as much as I care about anyone. I would even say that I love you. And I can say that with some truth, because, unlike most people, I've pushed my way past the front door in your life. When we stopped sleeping together, I made sure we became friends."

"You don't even like me half the time." I wipe my cheeks dry with my hands. "You don't approve of the way I make decisions. You don't approve of *this baby*."

"I have nothing against the baby, Gracie. I will love the baby, I'm sure. I want to be its father. That's part of my proposal. We have a lot to offer each other. I can steady you, and keep you on an even keel. I can help you make decisions. And you and the baby can give me a life I would have no access to otherwise. We'll be meeting each other halfway. I see a lot of positives."

I lean back against the step. My back aches and I have to pee. The baby is sitting on top of my bladder. "I don't think so, Grayson. I think we both deserve better."

"This *is* better," he says. "And I can convince you of that."

"This is not some editorial for you to push your opinion at people. You're talking about our lives."

He nods. "Just let me ask you one critical question. One question, all right?"

"All right."

"Do you know who you are, Gracie?"

I stare up at him, my insides suddenly as silent and glassy as a lake at midnight. Past and future tears clog up my throat. The McLaughlin in me seals my lips. All I can do is stare. He knows my answer. He knows exactly what he is doing.

Grayson speaks slowly now. He gives weight to each word, closing in for the kill. "*I* know who you are, Gracie. And I promise that as your husband I will teach you." He pauses. "Don't you think it's important for your baby to have a mother who knows herself?"

The baby. This frees my tongue. This gives me the only possible answer. The sound is almost a cry as it breaks out of my throat.

"Yes," I say. "Yes."

LILA

Gracie thinks I spend all of my time outside of the house with Weber, but that's not completely true. I spend a lot of that time in the library, fighting the urge to see Weber. With no schoolwork to do, I have taken to writing letters. I sit in my favorite carrel on the third floor of the library. I write a few letters a week, then tear them up and throw them in the trash. It's a new experience for me. I let go on the page, barely paying attention to what I write. When I've finished a letter, I feel cleaned out, lighter, better, at least for a few minutes.

Dear Abby,

The boy that I sleep with asked me what I believe in and I couldn't answer him. Why does everyone need something to believe in? Really, I don't see why faith is so necessary. He believes in fires and beer and New Jersey, for God's sakes. As if those are things to build your life on.

I know what I don't believe in, though. Isn't that something? I don't believe in God. I don't believe in destiny. I think that life is made up of random events. I don't think there is a point to any individual's existence. You aren't put on this earth for any one reason. And I don't believe in soul mates. People are drawn together due to pheromones and physical attraction and they choose whether to do the work to stay together or not. I don't believe in couples staying together for the kids.

My list of what I don't believe in has been growing lately. Almost exponentially. I could go on for pages. My sleep is filled with making these kinds of lists. What the hell is wrong with me?

There is suddenly a hand on my shoulder, a heavy patting I recognize, which never fails to annoy me. Weber wakes me up in the morning, or sometimes in the middle of the night, by patting the palm of his hand against my shoulder. I don't know if it is the repetition of the gesture that annoys me, or the gesture itself. Weber always seems to be coming up from behind, startling me.

"What are you doing here?" This is my one hiding place. My one escape. How dare he find me here?

He seems to read my mind. "I've always known this is where you go. It's not like you're well hidden. Your car's right outside."

"Why were you looking for me?"

"I wanted to talk to you."

"And it couldn't wait?" I have my arm over the letter I have been writing. I am furious that he thinks it is okay to disturb me here. I have been successfully hiding in libraries since I was a child. Everyone else in my life—my mother, father, sister, even Gram—knows better than to bother me in my libraries.

"I've met everyone in your family now," he says.

I stare at him, still so angry I can barely absorb what he is saying.

"I went to visit your grandmother today. She was the last one."

I can only repeat his words. "The last one?"

"Well, I already knew your lovely sister, so she doesn't count. But now I've spoken to each of the others, your mom, dad, and grandmother. I introduced myself. It's been really interesting. Educational, even. Seeing the different parts of Lila Leary scattered around her family."

I remember at the last moment where I am, and manage to strangle my voice into a whisper. "Why would you do that? Are you insane? Who did you introduce yourself as?"

"Your face is turning all splotchy," he says.

"Can we leave here, please?" I say. "Right now?"

Weber shrugs. He is draped over the study carrel behind me, perfectly relaxed. He is wearing an old pair of blue shorts and a Bruce Springsteen T-shirt. He has a vast T-shirt collection centered around New Jersey bands. There is an intricate value system to his collection that he explained to me one afternoon. The performers are ranked by the quality of each of their albums: Bon Jovi is at the top, then Bruce Springsteen, then the Fountains of Wayne and someone named Slapstreet Johnny, and then a series of local bands I've never heard of. As a means of protecting his collection, Weber wears the most valued T-shirts only once a month so they don't wear out. The *Born in the USA* T-shirt he is wearing now is one of his favorites.

"Sure thing," he says. "I have the afternoon off. Where do you want to go?"

I stand up, careful to block my letter from his sight until after I have closed the notebook and stuffed the letter in my pocket. I walk past him, down the stairs. He follows, and we travel down two more floors, then through the newspaper section, past the mimeograph machines, and out the front door.

In the hot, sticky summer air, he says, "My vote is Dairy Queen."

I am still working on what he said, on what that means. I say, "You talked to my mother?"

"I didn't have to go see her, actually. I ran into both her and your father. I only had to specifically visit your grandmother. I bumped into your mother on Main Street last week. I helped her out, actually. She tripped and her bag went flying. I helped her gather everything up while we talked."

I have trouble picturing this. I have never seen my mother trip. She is always perfectly composed, pulled together, even-gaited. And the idea of her crouched over a hot sidewalk picking up keys and lipsticks and papers and personal items while chatting with Weber . . . is too much.

"She talked awfully fast. I think she was afraid, at first, that I was going to tell her I was yet another guy Gracie had been schtupping. When I said I was a friend of yours, she looked relieved."

"That's what you told her? That you're a friend of mine?"

"I may have said boyfriend. I don't remember my exact phrasing. As soon as we got past that introduction, she acted like we'd been friends forever. She can be very charming, can't she?"

"I don't know."

"Sure you do. You can't claim to know everything in every book you've ever read, and not know that your own mother is charming."

"Are you trying to ruin my life?"

Weber scratches his stomach, right across Bruce's guitar. "I wanted to meet your family, Lila, and I knew you weren't going to introduce me to them."

"You never even asked me to!"

"If I had, would you have said yes?"

"No!" I am practically yelling.

"I'm sweating," he says. "Can we please continue discussing your paranoia at Dairy Queen?"

"I'm not paranoid," I say, allowing him to lighten the tone slightly. I head toward his truck. "All of my concerns are totally valid."

"Well, my favorite person was your grandmother," he says. "She is totally cool."

We are in the truck now, and the blast of air conditioning stands the hairs on my arms on end. I look over at Weber, and his beer belly and his T-shirt, and the way he says "totally cool" depresses me. I can't believe I let him have sex with me. I can't believe I enjoy it.

"I think your grandmother and I were meant to know each other," he says. "I felt that so strongly when I was with her in her room. It's just one more reason that you and I needed to cross paths."

"I can't stand it when you talk like that," I say. "You know I can't stand it when you talk like that."

He gives me a look meant to show that he has endless compassion for my ignorance. "Lila, just because you're a little lost right now is no reason to attack my belief system."

"I'm attacking you, you bastard, not the bullshit you believe in. You raided my life without my permission."

"Well, your grandmother and I talked about all that bullshit and more. Life, love, relationships, you name it. She told me that I reminded her of the best of both of her parents." Weber nods, and taps his thumb against the steering wheel. "You know what? I've only met her once, but I think I love your grandmother." He nods again. "I do. I love her."

I feel something flicker in my chest. I think, Am I jealous? I shake it off. I shake all of it off, because how can I respond to his loving my grandmother after spending fifteen minutes with her? How can I respond to the absurd way he talks? All I can do is brush past the fluff and look for the facts.

"So," I say, "you have essentially told my entire family that we're involved."

We pull into the Dairy Queen parking lot, and Weber screeches into the only remaining parking space. The place is packed with kids and parents and teenagers. It appears that half of Ramsey has decided to go out for ice cream at the same time.

"We need to approach this situation seriously," Weber says, scanning the crowded scene. "You find two seats at a picnic table, and I'll order. You want the usual?"

I nod, and climb out of the truck. Ordinarily I would never allow myself to be seen with him in such a busy public place, but that doesn't seem to matter anymore. Everyone important knows. Everyone is free to judge me, or ask questions, or laugh behind my back. My effort to keep myself apart, to keep up the facade of perfection, is failing in every part of my life.

I find a seat at the end of a picnic bench and then look at him, standing fourth in line at the ice cream window. He jiggles on the balls of his feet, his hands in his pockets. I wonder what the hell I am doing. I accuse Gracie of being self-destructive by bringing a child into the world when she barely has the judgment to pick out her own clothes in the morning, but am I any better? I am taking myself apart brick by brick instead of using my sister's method and running myself over with a steamroller.

I check to make sure Weber is lodged firmly in line, and then pull the letter out of my pocket. I wrote it less than an hour earlier, and the words still catch in my throat. I have no pen, but in my head I add, *Things are only getting worse.* I smooth my hand over the piece of paper, pressing it flat against the wooden table. I study my handwriting. I wait to feel the peace that writing these letters sometimes gives me.

Instead I am distracted by the sound of someone directly behind me crying. A woman is sniffling into a handkerchief, not making even the slightest effort to muffle the noise. I tell myself that this is my own fault. If I had been paying closer attention when looking for a seat, I never would have sat down next to a crier. I would have steered in the direction of some happy family whose hands were sticky from melting ice cream cones. Some cluster of people I could ignore, and who would ignore me. But now I have a dilemma. Do I pretend I don't hear this woman sob, or do I turn around and say something? She is sitting beside me on a picnic bench. As a doctor in training, I should want to help a person in trouble. It may even be my responsibility. During a white-coat ceremony on the first day of medical school, we all took an oath to that effect. The oath said something about devoting ourselves to the service of mankind both day and night, when it's convenient and when it's not. I didn't pay attention to the exact content of the words when I repeated them, because the oath seemed too ridiculous to take seriously. How could I promise to do *anything* for the rest of my life?

The woman gives an extra-large sob, a watery noise that makes me think of a goldfish named Crocodile that Gracie and I had as a pet when we were children. All day long Crocodile would race around his small bowl, making waves lap against the rim of the bowl. Gracie and I laughed and clapped at his speed, not realizing at the time that Crocodile wasn't playing or showing off, but desperately trying to find an escape from his too-small bowl. He did finally make his way out. Two years after we won him at a school fair, we found him lying on his side on top of Gracie's bureau one morning, a few inches from the bowl. He was stiff and dry and cold. Crocodile was our first and last pet. Dad was too traumatized by Gracie's days of crying after

Crocodile's death to even think of bringing another pet into the house, and besides, Mom was allergic to cats and dogs and any other animal that might make a mess of the carpets.

I don't think it's polite, or appropriate, to cry in public. It's a pathetic attempt to grab attention from a group of strangers. And besides, if a person does choose to cry in public, Dairy Queen is the last place that he or she should choose. Dairy Queen is an ice cream store; it is meant to be a happy place. It's filled with children and families and couples who simply want to consume too much cholesterol and too many calories in the bright summer air without feeling bad about anything. And this woman, sobbing and whimpering, is obviously out to make everyone around her feel bad.

I look down at my letter and mouth the words "Dear Abby."

Then I hear Weber's voice behind me. "Are you all right? Miss? Are you hurt? My girlfriend's a doctor—"

"No doctors," the woman says through her tears.

"She's right here. It's no problem," Weber says. "Babe?"

I hate it when he calls me babe. How dare he do this to me? I turn around slowly. For the hundredth time I am convinced that it is time to finally end things with Weber. There is only the matter of how and when to do it. Should I just walk away now, without a word or a look? Or should I wait to lower the boom until he's driven me back to the library for my car? Or—and this option makes me feel morally terrible and warm between my legs at the same time—should I go back to his place and fuck him one more time before I end things?

"I'm not a doctor," I whisper, looking at Weber across the bent figure of the woman. I tell him with my eyes that he has really messed up. I can see that he doesn't understand why. My expression takes him by surprise, and I enjoy a feeling of triumph. He looks ridiculous, crouching beside the picnic table with an ice cream cone in each hand. I reach out and take the chocolate cone.

The woman rises up slowly between us. Her long hair pulls back off her face, and when I catch sight of her profile, I grow dizzy. She looks at Weber.

She says, "My life is not turning out the way it's supposed to."

He shrugs, as if that isn't an odd and presumptuous thing for one stranger to say to another. "How do you know how your life was supposed to turn out? Would you like an ice cream?" He holds out the vanilla cone.

This brings the tears on again, but more quietly this time. She cannot wipe them away fast enough. "I already had three banana splits," she says. "I can feel my hips growing wider."

"I ate six cones once on a dare," Weber says. He takes a lick of the vanilla ice cream, and I focus on hating the sight of his big fat pink tongue. He is the one who continually gets me into these situations. First I am faced with the fact that he's been having conversations about God knows what with my family, and now this. Now her.

"I failed an exam," she says, "and this important man at work doesn't like me. I don't know why, I've tried everything—asking questions, being helpful, staying late and coming in early—but he just doesn't like me. It's so big there, and I get lost, and it's too hard to focus on what's supposed to be . . . oh, I don't know. For hours this morning I hated myself. And I'm so tired." She cries into balled-up fists.

"You just need some sleep," Weber says, in his calm voice. "You hit the nail on the head right there. Look, I'm a fireman, and I know that adrenaline can only take you so far. The mind needs rest. Go home and chill out. I promise that you'll have better perspective tomorrow."

"A fireman," she says. "That sounds nice. So simple." She peers up and seems to take in the sight of Weber for the first time. "You look like a fireman," she says, as if that's a compliment.

Weber puffs up at this. He gives a big grin.

You idiot, I think. You haven't put out anything bigger than an oven fire in three years.

I study the girl's face, wrinkled and wet. I know Weber's lame advice to rest won't work. I feel sick deep inside. I hear myself say, "Don't listen to him."

They both turn to me. I watch Belinda's expression freeze and then harden. "Lila," she says.

"Maybe it's supposed to be really hard," I say. "Maybe it's not supposed to be fun or fulfilling. Maybe it's called work because it is."

I am standing now, a few steps from the picnic bench. "Lila," Weber says. "What are you doing?"

What I'm doing is remembering standing with my grandmother in the hospital after her car accident. She held my hand, and her skin was fine, and papery-soft. I can feel this, her hand pressed to mine.

"Do you even go to school anymore?" Belinda asks. "Someone said you were sick. Why haven't you returned my calls?"

"You two know each other?" Weber asks.

My grandmother leaned toward me at the hospital and said, "Who said becoming a doctor was going to be easy?" She had known. She had been telling me not that I was a quitter, but that I needed to do what was hard. That I needed to push forward.

I am careful not to look at Weber. I focus on Belinda. I focus on staying frozen inside. I say, "You should get ahold of yourself. You're a mess."

Belinda seems to make an effort. Her shoulders tighten. She stops crying. Her face is shiny with moisture. "You were sitting there this whole time?" she asks. There is a choking noise in her throat. "You were sitting there laughing at me?"

I can feel a hard smile form on my face. I know that my expression is just going to fuel her suspicion, but I can't help it.

"You're hateful," she says. "Really hateful."

"I'll be back at the hospital tomorrow," I say.

I am smiling because I've finally figured it out. This moment has been a gift. Belinda, my enemy, has given me a gift. I have been expecting too much from my work. It is supposed to be hard and challenging and exhausting. I can't expect it to be more, to mean more.

"Lila," Weber says. He is looking at me with his mouth slightly open. He has never seen the real me before. And it is just as well, because I am back on track now. I am returning to my old life, a life Weber James doesn't fit into. I know, with total certainty, that my time of weakness is over.

"We go to school together," I say, in the same cold voice. "Belinda and I are classmates."

"Classmates," Belinda says, "but not equals. I'm sure Lila has told you that she's number one?" She is in her purse now, punching her hand around the inside. She pulls out a compact mirror and opens it. She pats the skin under her eyes and then clicks the mirror shut. "Not that I care. I have to stop competing. My therapist told me that I need to stop competing. I'm destroying myself."

Belinda stands up. She loops her purse over her shoulder. She addresses Weber. "Thank you for your concern. I'm going to use the restroom now."

She walks away, her posture straight beneath her wrinkled, tucked-in T-shirt and shorts. Her sandals bang small clouds of dust around her ankles. I look down, and see that the chocolate ice cream cone has melted, running in brown stripes across my hand, down my arm, and splattering across my shorts.

I pick my letter up from the picnic table and use it to wipe the ice cream off my skin. The brown liquid covers the writing completely and my arm is left sticky but dry. I ball up the useless sheet of paper and throw it into the garbage.

"What the hell was that?" Weber says.

"I'm sorry, Weber, but we're over. I mean it this time."

He stares at me as if I've spoken in a foreign language he doesn't recognize.

"I'm sorry I've been indecisive with you in the past. It was unfair of me to say I didn't want to be with you and then show up at your door two hours later."

"I understood that," Weber says. "You were fighting yourself, Doc. You really wanted to be with me—"

I interrupt him. "I'm done fighting myself. I don't enjoy it. I don't want it anymore. I don't want you."

The words sound cruel under the hot summer sun, but I tell myself that it is the sound of honesty. It is the sound of freedom.

"I don't recognize you right now," Weber says. "Your face is cold and scrunched up."

"This is what I really look like."

"I see," Weber says. And I can see from his expression that he does. He sees me, and he turns away.

AFTER WEBER drops me off at the library, I get in my car and drive home. I make a beeline from the car to the shower. I feel exhausted and gritty with dirt. Gracie is waiting in my room when I come out of the bathroom dripping wet in a towel.

"For Christ's sake," I say. "Will you get out of here?"

She is sitting on my bed Indian style. She is wearing Papa's cardigan for what must be the tenth day in a row. She is not handling Gram's hospitalization well. She says, "I have to ask you for a favor."

I am not comfortable. Gracie and I are not the kind of sisters who walk around in our underwear and borrow each other's clothes. We grew up in a house where everyone got dressed behind his or her closed bedroom door, and we live in that kind of house now. "Can we do this later?" I say. "I have to call the hospital, so I need to get dressed. I've made my decision. I'm going back to school. I'm going to be a doctor."

Gracie just stares at me, caught up in her own dreamy world. There's no way she could understand needing to be somewhere, or job responsibilities, since she has stopped going to her job and is not expected to show up at any particular place.

"Lila, will you please be my Lamaze coach?"

I grip the towel around me and study her face. "Are you joking?"

Her pale face has no humor in it. "Please? There's no one else I can ask. Really. There's no one else I'd feel comfortable letting . . . They said that I had to choose someone by this week in case I went into early labor. I know you don't want to and you don't approve and all of that, but . . ."

I suddenly remember driving my sister, then painfully thin and sallow-cheeked, to the clinic for her abortion. I remember sitting in the waiting room and flipping through *Seventeen* magazine. I remember thinking that it was odd that I was there since I was still a virgin. It was a freezing-cold January morning, and I had to half-carry Gracie down the icy walkway when it was over. When we got to the car her shoulders shook for a moment, but no tears followed. She gazed straight ahead through the windshield on the way home, not bothering to take off her mittens or unzip her coat in the heated car.

"I need someone in there with me," Gracie says. "I can't do this alone."

I try to think of other possible coaches, and come up with nothing. Mom is unthinkable in a delivery room. Joel is not an option, as Margaret would show up with a shotgun. Gram is too sick to be of any help. But Gram would be there in some capacity, if she could. She would do anything possible to ensure that Gracie and the baby were all right.

I feel strong under the weight of my decision to return to school. I will make Gram happy and proud. I will be number one in my class again, no matter how many annoying patients I have to deal with. I will simply do what is hard from now on, whenever there is a choice.

"Fine," I say. "I'll do it."

"Really? Oh, thank you so much. I'll owe you for the rest of my life." Gracie is up off the bed and coming toward me as if for a hug. But she veers away at the last minute and heads for the door. "I know you have to get dressed. The next class is on Wednesday evening, but I'll remind you later. I can meet you at the hospital." She stops in the doorway. "You're my favorite sister," she says, and is gone.

I smile at that, a saying from our childhood. You're my favorite sister, she would say. I'm your only sister, I would say in return.

I stay seated on the bed for a minute, wrapped in my towel. I stare down at my hands, at my thick fingers. They look powerful. I am still looking at my hands when the strange noise starts on the other side of the room. It is garbled and staticky, and sounds like a radio. I cross the room toward the noise. It's coming from my purse. I unzip the zipper and the noise grows louder, more urgent. It's Weber's radio. I remember now that he put it in my purse at Dairy Queen so he wouldn't have to carry it.

"Full alert, big one, 1244 Finch Way. Electrical, apartment complex, 1244 Finch Way." The radio spits out the information, gives a long static-filled gasp, and then repeats.

I listen for a minute, running the numbers through my head, and then throw the radio on my bed. "Gracie," I yell. "Ryan's building is on fire!"

A few minutes later we are in the car, headed across town. When we are a mile or two from the building, we begin to hear the sirens. Wailing and keening to one another. I pull over to the curb to let one fire truck pass, then continue driving.

"Should we call Mom?" Gracie asks. She is in the passenger seat, the seat belt stretched across her big belly. Her hair looks dirty.

"I don't know," I say. "I don't know what the etiquette is in this kind of situation."

"Don't joke, Lila." Gracie is holding on to her seat belt with both hands. "Uncle Ryan could be dead."

I don't like that she's said that out loud, but I can't argue the point.

We make it onto the block and park seconds before long blue police barriers cut off access. The street and the lawn in front of Uncle Ryan's building are a mess. There are three police cars, two with sirens going, and one mammoth fire truck parked at an odd angle against the curb. Firemen are running a giant hose across the lawn, yelling in some unidentifiable code. The air smells like smoke, and Gracie starts coughing as soon as we are out of the car. The lawn is crowded with the tenants of the building who have made it out. A cluster of elderly men and women stare at the fire, looking dazed. Some are wearing bathrobes and slippers. One old woman with curlers in her hair is yelling at a policeman, shaking what looks like a bar of soap.

The fire has consumed the center of the white brick building and is moving slowly outward. We are twenty-five yards away from the building, but I can feel the ovenlike heat against my skin. The fire has a deep hum to it, punctuated by crackles that sound like the breaking of bones.

Gracie hurries ahead. She grabs the arm of a police officer. "Have you seen a man in a wheelchair?" she asks. He shakes his head.

"Do you see Weber?" I ask her.

"Oh God. Look." She points upward.

At first I don't see what she is pointing at, and then I do. It is the window to Uncle Ryan's living room. The window is half open, and three huge yellow birds are sitting on the sill. Their beaks open and close, but we can't hear their squawks above the fire and the sirens and the people shouting around us.

I take Gracie's arm, or maybe she takes mine. I'm not sure. We stand still in the middle of the lawn. We keep our eyes on the fat, panicked birds.

"Why don't they fly away?" I ask. "How can they just sit there? They're going to be cooked."

Gracie is gripping my arm so tightly, I have pins and needles in my shoulder. "They don't want to leave Uncle Ryan," she says. "They love him. I can't watch this."

"They'll be fine," I say.

"Stop saying that." She lets go of my arm and turns away, her attention caught by something else. "Joel!"

I turn, too, and see Joel a few feet behind us. He is wearing his uniform, the huge flame-retardant jacket and hat, but he is the only fireman on the scene who's not in motion. He is leaning against a parked car. "Have you seen our uncle Ryan?" Gracie asks. "Why are you just standing there? Are you hurt?"

"He's drunk." I suddenly want to cry. "Look at him, Gracie. He's shit-faced."

"Oh," Gracie says. She sees it now, too. Joel's face is red, his eyes bleary. "Oh!" Gracie says again, loudly, as if she is angry. "You should stop this, Joel—it's ridiculous. Please tell us about Ryan. Do you know anything?"

Joel's cheeks grow even redder. His pupils swim in bloodshot sockets. He looks as close to falling apart as I feel.

"Oh jeez," Gracie says.

"You're so huge," Joel says. "The baby is in there . . . Jesus." He shakes his head, which seems to sober him enough to speak semicoherently. "I saw your dad by the trees." He points to the side of the lawn that is lined with apple trees.

"Dad? You're sure?"

We don't wait for an answer. We both turn and run in the direc-

tion he points. Gracie holds her stomach as she runs. The air smells like
a summer bonfire now. I can smell grass burning. My sense of smell is
suddenly very acute, very strong. But the scene's volume has dropped
down, the frenzy I am running past and through is muffled, until I see
my father. He is standing under one of the apple trees. He has one hand
on a wheelchair. Uncle Ryan's wheelchair. Uncle Ryan is sitting in the
chair, unburned, unharmed, alive.

The volume comes back up, and I realize I have been holding my
breath. I breathe.

Ryan is crying hysterically. "Their wings are clipped," he says
when he sees Gracie and me. "They can't fly. Louis saved me but he
wouldn't save them. They can't fly. What's going to happen to us?"

"You girls are okay?" my father asks.

"Yes," Gracie says. I nod.

We had both touched Dad as soon as we reached him, to make sure
this was real. I put my hand against his shoulder for a second. Gracie
hugged his free arm, an awkward gesture that made him revert to his
businesslike behavior.

"Good." He studies the building. "I think they got everyone out.
That elevator was a death trap. I knew what must have happened as
soon as the police called. But I didn't have a chance to start renovating
yet. I just signed the papers last week. Now I'll have to gut the building. You girls are sure you're okay?"

"Nothing is okay," Ryan says. "Please, they need help."

"It's too dangerous for anyone to go in there, Uncle Ryan," Gracie
says.

"You're just going to let them die?"

"Shush," Gracie says. "You have to calm down. This isn't good for
you."

"Good for me? I don't cares what's good for me!" A vein pumps
across Ryan's forehead.

I look at my father. "You saved him?" I don't really mean it as a
question. I know he did. As soon as Gracie and I saw Dad, we both
knew it was safe. That everything would be okay. That's what my father
does, he makes things okay. He takes care of people.

Dad puts his hand on my shoulder. We stand in a clump under the apple tree and watch the building burn. Uncle Ryan weeps through open fingers, keeping watch on his birds. They are still perched on the windowsill. We can see flames rise up behind the birds; the fire is inside the apartment now.

The smallest of the three birds hops up and down, and then, in one heartbreaking moment, jumps off the ledge. He spreads his puny wings and drops like a stone.

"What's going to happen to us?" Uncle Ryan cries.

His eyes are shut now, which is good, because the little bird has started something. The fattest bird now takes a hop toward the edge. He doesn't even bother to spread his wings, but falls three stories to the ground. The final bird, bright yellow and big-eyed, tumbles after him just as the curtains in Uncle Ryan's apartment explode in flames.

"Oh my God," Gracie says.

"I should call your mother," Dad says, and takes his cell phone out of his pocket.

I look away. I look at the sky, then at my sneakers, then across the lawn toward the street and rows of untouched, perfect-looking homes and, to the far right, the playing fields of Finch Park. In this direction, if you discount the running firemen and newly homeless people, everything looks okay. Untouched. Safe.

"Everyone step off the lawn, please." A policeman waves his arms at us to move back. "All pedestrians off the grass. Step back, it's for your own safety. Step back. That's right. There you go."

Dad wheels Uncle Ryan toward the street, and Gracie and I follow. Just before I reach the road, I turn back for a last look, and that's when I see him. Weber is walking away from the burning building, his face and his uniform covered with soot and dirt. He has an axe in his hand. He sees me at the same moment, and he grins. His teeth are a shock of whiteness. I hadn't thought that Weber could be hurt, but still, I am deeply relieved at the sight of him.

I watch him walk toward me. I watch his face with the same clarity I'd had running across the lawn toward Uncle Ryan and my father.

Weber looks so happy. I have seen him happy before, but this is different. Something in him, beyond the dirt, is shining.

When he reaches me he talks fast, like a little boy. "This is our
biggest fire in years. It was amazing, Lila. Fucking amazing. We got
everyone out. It was awesome in there! We played chess with the fire
and we fucking won." He touches my arm. "Your uncle's okay, right?
I saw your dad take him out."

"Yes," I say. Weber is looking toward the fire, which is slowing
now. It seems to be under control.

"You love this," I say. "Don't you."

"Fuck yes," Weber says. "I love it."

In that moment, with what's left of Uncle Ryan's building still
smoldering and his three birds dead on the ground and Gracie waiting
by the car holding her round stomach, I am again changed, and changing. I am filled up by what I have seen. By the expression on Weber's
face. By his notion of love. There is no room left inside me for anything else; my former decisions are fighting for ground, wanting for
traction.

I fight, too. I try to stop myself. I try to be rational. For God's sake,
this is no time to crumble. And why am I crumbling, because of a
handsome fireman? How pathetic can I be? After all, I had just figured
everything out. I knew what I was doing. I was going to return to battle with Belinda. I was going to rent my own apartment and lock
myself inside with my books. I was going to work hard at the hospital—but now I can't help but stop myself.

Why would I be working hard? And for what? For Gram? That
isn't enough of a reason. Life isn't supposed to be hard. Fuck that.
Gram's wrong. I'll end up like Uncle Pat, sitting like a Popsicle on the
edge of a folding chair, feeling nothing. And Gram wouldn't want that.
I picture Weber's face, bright with happiness. The three birds tumble,
one after another, past the closed windows of the apartment building.
A man shouts into a cell phone a few feet away from me. He is telling
someone that he's all right. I know, with total conviction, that I want
to feel what Weber was feeling while he fought the fire.

"Why are you breathing like that? Lila? Slow down," Weber says. "This air is no good for you."

My mind is spinning from point to point, truth to truth. I have not been wrong all my life; I haven't been weak. I don't love medicine the way Weber loves his work. And I should, if I'm going to keep on doing it. I don't know what would make me light up the way he is lit up now. I haven't found my thing, my passion, but I want to. I want to search for what makes me happy and then work hard. I want what is shining out of Weber's face. I will not go back to medical school. I will drop out officially. It is over.

"If you're okay, I've got to go," Weber says. "I guess I'll see you around."

His voice is cool. The adrenaline has dropped away. I look at him, confused. It takes a second for me to remember that a few hours earlier I hurt him badly. I remember dimly, as if through a long camera lens, the scene I made at Dairy Queen.

The anger and the ice are no longer resolute—they're melting. I almost laugh at myself. I am falling apart into someone Lila Leary wouldn't talk to, much less inhabit. I might as well be Belinda, sobbing over a banana split, or Gracie, waiting in the car, talking to her unborn child.

Weber is looking at me with mild expectation. I can't speak; I don't think I can string words into a sentence. A massive metal ladder passes to one side of us, rung after rung. There is a tired-looking fireman carrying each distant end.

I smile at Weber, trying to communicate something. But he's turned away. He's watching the men prop the massive ladder against the side of the building with the least damage. I am warm and whirling from head to toe, and I crane for another glimpse at the look on Weber's face. I want another glimpse of my future. But it's too late. With a short wave over his shoulder, he's headed back toward the fire.

NOREEN BALLEN

I spend most of my day sitting on a hard-backed chair next to Mrs. McLaughlin's bed. She has been home from the rehab hospital for three days, but the move exhausted her. She works with the physical therapist downstairs in the morning, and then in the afternoon she and I take a short walk around the grounds. For the moment, I leave it at that. As she gets her strength back, I will ask for more from her.

I suspect that the sleep she has gotten over the last seventy-two hours is the first good rest she has allowed herself in weeks. At Valley Hospital, she would ask me to wake her up if I saw one of her children approaching because she wanted to be conscious during their visits. She was afraid they would try to move her to the nursing facility while she slept.

From what I saw, her children were not much of a threat. Even Kelly, the oldest, was too flustered to initiate such a drastic step. All of Mrs. McLaughlin's children are worried about her. I can see that they are in for a terrible shock when they finally realize that Catharine McLaughlin is dying. She fought so hard to come back to this room because it was home, because she wants to die at home. I have seen old men and women make this decision before, and I have watched them fade until they've carried out their wish.

When I brought Mrs. McLaughlin here from the rehab facility, the first thing she told me was the meaning behind every piece in the room. The single bed with the wooden frame was her marriage bed. Her husband had slept in an identical bed to her right. The classics on the bookshelf had been her father's. The huge ashtray on the coffee table shaped like a golf course with a golfer poised on the edge with his club raised had belonged to her husband. The pictures on the walls were of her children. The half-knitted blanket on the couch was something she had been working on for her first great-grandchild.

WHILE SHE SLEEPS, I read the newspaper, or look at the photographs on the walls. I try to entertain her various guests until she wakes. After years in the hospital with erratic shifts and unpredictable days, this is the easiest and best-paid job I've ever had. If I hadn't stopped believing in God after Eddie's accident, I would have sworn this had fallen straight from heaven. Instead, I add this job to my running list of things that have happened over the last nine months that I think must have been organized by Eddie. For instance, the gutters on the roof somehow remain clear of leaves, the contractor shows up at my door at the perfect moment and offers a low estimate to repaint the house, the lawn stays neat in spite of the fact that I never once cut it, and Eddie's old white car never breaks down.

I used to be a very committed Catholic, and for me giving thanks to God is the hardest habit to shake. Now I get around that by thanking my husband when good things fall into my lap. It is a way for me to feel close to Eddie, and to feel that our lives are still intertwined. And it is easy for me to believe that Eddie sent Louis to offer me this job. The timing of his offer was perfect, since I needed the extra money and the regular hours. Eddie Jr. really wants to go to baseball camp for the month of August, and now I will be able to send him. Jessie, as always, wants everything she lays her eyes on: dolls, clothes, a brand-new bicycle, a computer. I am thinking of giving in about the computer, as both kids could use it for school.

When I first ran into Louis Leary in the hospital, it was a shock. I had not thought of Louis since the funeral, although Eddie had spoken of him all the time. Eddie had thought very highly of his boss, and hoped to perhaps partner with him someday. The few times I'd met

Louis I had been uncomfortable with him. He was so big physically that I felt towered over, even though I am also quite tall. And I could never figure out what was appropriate conversation to make with my husband's employer. But then at the funeral, having not shed a single tear since the accident, I had for some reason fallen apart at the sight of Louis. To my great embarrassment, I had sobbed all over his nice shirt, drenching the sleeve. I hadn't been able to stop crying, even after his wife led him away.

When I saw Louis at the hospital, I remembered the sensation at the funeral when something inside me cracked and broke loose. I had wanted to walk away from him then; I had wanted my shift to be over. I wanted to sleep. I wanted to hug my kids. I wanted to cry with all my might, but those feelings quickly passed. I was almost used to them sweeping over me. Regularly, whenever I think I am getting better, stronger, missing Eddie will kick me in the gut. When the sensation is gone I am left worn and emptied out.

I arrived at this job and into this room with Mrs. McLaughlin, exhausted but grateful. I watch her sound sleep with jealousy. I watch her chest rise and fall and hope that this job is a gift from my husband. I hope he is still watching out for me and trying to meet my needs. I sit by her bedside until the feeling deepens into a kind of prayer.

When her family visits and she's awake, I try to disappear into the background, but as Mrs. McLaughlin lives in a small room, that is sometimes difficult. The most frequent visitor is poor Gracie. I know she's in her late twenties, but she always looks so young and lost when she shows up at the door. And the way she looks at her grandmother— my goodness. It's as if the tiny woman lying on the bed is powerful enough to raise the sun into the sky.

When Gracie finds out that I have two young children, she starts asking questions about childbirth. She seems to know astoundingly little for a woman well into her seventh month of pregnancy. I get the feeling even when she asks the questions that she is not ready for the answers. She is speaking to me because her grandmother is too tired to give her any attention. Her eyes are a mixture of fear and vacancy while we talk.

I tell her, "You should get an epidural when you can't bear the pain anymore. There's no reason to be a martyr. You'll be able to enjoy the birth of your child much more if you've had some relief."

"Gram says the McLaughlin women give birth easily." Gracie glances at the bed, where Mrs. McLaughlin is lying asleep. "But then Gram doesn't feel pain like normal people."

"What do you mean?"

"She's lost three children and a husband." Gracie sighs. "She's unbelievably strong."

Three children. I look over at the woman on the bed. I think of Jessie's toothy smile and Eddie Jr.'s curls. I wonder if there isn't a limit to how much pain can be borne.

Gracie says, "I know that you lost your husband, because he was one of my father's men, and I'm sorry."

He was *my* man. "Thank you."

She gazes downward and seems to notice her round belly. She says, "Which part of the birth hurts the most?"

I pull myself upright in the hard-backed chair. *Be professional, Noreen.* "It all hurts," I say. "But when the doctor puts your baby into your arms for the first time, it will be worth it. You'll be filled with so much love, you won't believe it. The feeling is different, and more, than you've ever had with any man. You'll want to change the world so it's a better place for your baby to live in. You'll feel like your heart is going to explode."

"Really?" Gracie says, looking doubtful.

"Really."

Each time Gracie leaves at the end of a visit, she does an odd thing. She opens up the top drawer to Mrs. McLaughlin's desk, peers inside without touching anything, and then shuts the drawer without a word.

ALL THE family members I met in the hospital visit here, too. Louis and Kelly come separately. Mrs. McLaughlin's other two daughters and daughter-in-law drive up from South Jersey together and eat turkey sandwiches in the room while Mrs. McLaughlin rests. Her other grandchildren come as well. A young girl named Mary prays out loud over Mrs. McLaughlin's bed until her cousin Dina tells her to shut up. Mary keeps praying then, her lips moving without a sound. The only grandson, John, stays close to the door, a hazy look in his eyes that tells me he is stoned. Kelly brings Ryan for a visit, an event that seems to make Catharine, Kelly, and Ryan very anxious. Mrs. McLaughlin's oldest son, the one who never showed up at the hospital, calls twice a week.

After a nursing career during which I was always working in a different department, on a different floor, surrounded by different kinds of illness and doctors of different specialties, it is odd to sit still in this room and get to know this one woman and this one family. It was always my choice to move about in the hospital. Most nurses with my seniority had long since chosen a department to work in. Those who like old people pick geriatrics. The tough ones choose oncology, or worse, pediatric oncology. Those who wanted to do less hand-holding and more medicine became skilled surgical nurses. Many of my colleagues returned to school to earn advanced nursing qualifications in their field of choice so that they could become indispensable to the patients and the doctors they are devoted to.

I, on the other hand, never wanted to settle down. I liked the change and the movement as I switched from one part of the hospital to the other. I didn't want to get too friendly with anyone, or become too essential in one place. I wanted to feel that I belonged only at home. Only there did I want to feel the pull of loyalty. I had my family: my husband and son and daughter, and then, for the past nine months, I have had my son and my daughter. Long before I came to Valley Hospital I had narrowed my heart so that there was room only for them. Still, I was an excellent nurse, liked by everyone, and the medical staff came to appreciate the fact that I was happy to be assigned anywhere in the hospital that nursing was needed.

Even now, this job is a temporary change. I will return to the hospital when Mrs. McLaughlin no longer needs me. I have taken a leave of absence from my position at Valley; I have not quit. I remind myself that this, too, will end.

Lila says, "I would think this job would be boring as hell for you." She is standing by the window, looking out. Mrs. McLaughlin is asleep.

"No," I say. "I read the paper or my book when she sleeps. I have two young children, so this is a nice rest actually. And I enjoy doing all kinds of nursing work. I never wanted to be anything other than a nurse, since I was a small girl." This makes me think of Jessie, and I wonder what she will grow up to be. At the age of six, she said she wanted to be a princess. I always saw myself in a white uniform helping people, and my daughter saw herself in pink tulle giving orders to her subjects. How could this child have come from my body?

"I didn't want to be a doctor," I add, because Lila looks like she is about to ask me another question, and this is the answer to the usual one. People assume that every nurse is yearning to become a doctor. I was never interested in taking on the great weight of knowledge every doctor must have. I prefer to help people more simply, and attend to their comfort. Comfort is a much underrated commodity in general, and it means everything to the sick.

Lila seems less nervous in the room than her relatives, perhaps because she's in medical school and is more comfortable around illness. She looks the most like her grandmother, and I tell her so. She smiles with what looks like a combination of pleasure and suspicion.

"No one's ever said that to me."

"Maybe I can see it because I'm an outsider. There's no doubt, though, that you resemble her. Your face is the same shape, and your eyes."

Lila touches the curtain, which looks like it is made of lace doilies. "Can I ask you a question?"

I wonder why answering questions and making conversation seem to be the real work I do in this job, while Catharine McLaughlin peacefully rests. "Of course."

"Has a boy named Weber been here to visit my grandmother?"

"Not while I've been here," I say. "If you want, I can find out if he's stopped by during the evenings."

"No," Lila says.

"I like him," Mrs. McLaughlin says.

We both turn. She is sitting up in bed, her hands folded in her lap. She looks perfectly awake, as if she weren't just lying down, her face to the wall.

"I wouldn't have liked him if we'd met thirty years ago, or maybe even ten. But I like him very much now. I don't want you to be as much of an idiot as everyone else in this family, Lila. When it comes to matters of the heart, every single person in this family is hopeless."

I look from grandmother to granddaughter. Lila's face appears bruised by Mrs. McLaughlin's words, and I can tell from years of nursing experience that Lila is not getting enough rest these days, either.

"He doesn't like me anymore," Lila says.

"That's a pity," Mrs. McLaughlin says.

The old woman doesn't look surprised or even sympathetic when she says that, and I find myself thinking, not for the first time, Boy, she's a hard one.

AFTER TWO WEEKS, I am ready to climb the walls. Mrs. McLaughlin is slightly better, and I have revised my initial diagnosis. Not changed, but revised. I still believe that she has decided to die, but that it is not going to happen any day soon. There is something she is waiting for that is making her linger between recovery and death. She is fighting just hard enough to hold on, and no harder. She still sleeps a lot, but when awake she is more alert. Sometimes, though, she fakes unconsciousness when her family visits. One afternoon, after Theresa has left the room, I call her on this.

She gives a sheepish smile, like a child who has been caught stealing cookies from the jar. "I don't have the strength to reassure Theresa that she is all right and I'm all right and that the world isn't about to end. She worries too much. I prefer to lie still and listen to her talk to you."

"You faked it with Gracie yesterday, too, didn't you."

Another smile. "Only for a little while. Besides, she talks to you more honestly about the baby than she'll talk to me. I like to listen. Do you think she's taking care of the baby all right? I wonder if she's eating well. Kids these days eat all kinds of junk."

I say, "Gracie seems a little uneasy." Then I stop, and fold my hands in my lap.

Mrs. McLaughlin gives me an annoyed look, then turns slowly to see who has arrived.

Louis is standing in the doorway. "Should I leave?" he says, in a joking tone. "I learned a long time ago that a man shouldn't interrupt two women talking."

"You're right," Mrs. McLaughlin says. "Why are you visiting me so often?"

Louis crosses his arms and rocks back and forth on the balls of his feet. He looks like a massive tree in danger of tipping over. "We've been worried about you," he says.

Mrs. McLaughlin makes a disapproving noise in the back of her throat. "That's not why you keep coming here. I don't know what you're up to, but I suppose it's none of my business." With that, she rolls over onto her side and closes her eyes.

I am tempted to cross the room and tickle or shake her until she can't help but stop pretending unconsciousness. Louis is my least favorite visitor. He is so clearly uncomfortable when he is here that he makes me uncomfortable. A few times I have set him to work fixing a broken window shade or adjusting the dresser's loose leg. Those are the least painful visits, but today nothing in the room is broken and we are left circling each other. I adjust the blankets at the end of the bed and straighten the magazines on the coffee table.

As always, Louis doesn't sit down. He gets that pent-up look on his face as if there is something he badly wants to say but he can't find the words. I know that he wants to talk about Eddie. His expression is just an exaggerated version of all the looks I have gotten over the last several months from people who find out that my husband died. Their faces strain with pity and sympathy and the inarticulate desire to offer a comfort they know does not exist. There is something else to Louis's expression, too, that I can't put my finger on.

I make polite conversation because I can't stand the silence. The ache in his face goes right to my heart, and I can't help but remember that Louis was the one with Eddie when he died, not me. I remember waiting at the door of the emergency room when the stretcher was unloaded. I knew the moment I saw my husband that he was already gone. Any nurse worth her salt can tell if a patient's dead from across the room. We check pulses and breathing just to make certain, to offer proof to the family. But I can tell with one look when a person's soul has left the body. In the weeks right after Eddie died, before I shed Catholicism and tried to look at life in a more balanced way, it used to bother me terribly that I wasn't with my husband in his last moments. I should have been with Eddie when he died; he shouldn't have died with his boss and a bunch of paramedics.

After I ask Louis how Kelly is and how the business is and how long he thinks this heat wave can last, I want to ask him to leave. I want to tell him that all this daily conversation with his daughters and his wife and his sisters-in-law is enough of a struggle. I want to tell him I have not talked this much in years, and then only with my husband, not with a group of strangers. I want to tell him that the break he started in me at the funeral has opened up again, and that when I drive home at the end of the day, I have to hold carefully to the wheel so that I don't start to cry over how sweet the summer air smells, or a memory of making love, or the knowledge that I want to have more children. I want to tell Louis Leary that I can barely take what is going on inside of me. I do not have any room left to hold on to his feelings about the loss of my husband. I think at some point my stony face convinces Louis, at least for this afternoon, and he leaves.

LOUIS REMINDS me of Eddie, but the rest of the McLaughlins pull my heart in an unexpected direction. It is their eyes, which, except in Lila, are blue or green down to the last person. In their eyes, I am reminded of my own family. My own parents, and my own brothers and sisters. I am reminded that I look more like these strangers than I do my brown-skinned children. And even if I had been able to ignore the McLaughlins' pale skin and light eyes filing past me every day, I would have been unable to avoid making the connection between my heritage and theirs because Mrs. McLaughlin won't let me. As she says regularly to Kelly and Louis, she allowed me to be hired only because I am Irish.

"I wouldn't let any other kind of person sit in my bedroom while I sleep, I can tell you that."

"Mother, keep your voice down. That's a racist thing to say."

"No, it's not. I like every other race perfectly well. But I want my own with me while I'm sick in bed."

This appraisal of my value is startling because I never think of myself as Irish anymore. My own children have beautiful brown eyes, just like their father. I look at their dark skin and never think of my own pallor. Fifteen years ago I gave myself over to my husband, and to our family. I am one with them, and I am nothing apart from them. I made that choice when I fell in love with Eddie. I was nineteen years old at the time, and in my first year on full scholarship at Bergen County Nursing College. I was working two part-time jobs after classes, so I didn't have many friends. Eddie was a few years older than I was. He had moved to New Jersey from Mexico with a cousin the year before and they were part of the construction team working on the building where most of my classes were held. I noticed him the first day of the semester. He was sitting on the school steps during a break, reading a book.

I had never had a real boyfriend before, and despite the influence of all my loud brothers and sisters, I was very shy. But something crazy came over me when I saw this young man. He seemed to be clearly outlined in a sea of blurry white nursing students. I walked up to him as bold as day and offered him the cold can of soda I had just gotten out of the soda machine. He looked at me as if I was crazy, which I was, and said, "No thank you." But the next afternoon I did the same thing, and wasn't discouraged when he said "No thank you" again. I figured out his work schedule, so that I was always there when he was getting off work for the day or just for a break. He was terribly polite, and I gave him no choice but to talk to me. I made him laugh, even though I had never thought of myself as even remotely funny. I heard bright, witty remarks come out of my mouth that I couldn't believe were my own. The craziness stayed with me, and it didn't take me long to realize it was love.

When I told my mother the wonderful news, she went hard and cold. I was the last of her thirteen children. She was exhausted, and no longer open to new ideas. "If you marry a spic," she said, "you won't be welcome in this house anymore."

Of course I married him, and my heart narrowed and grew at the same time, and I stopped thinking of myself as Irish. I kept my maiden name professionally, but everywhere else I was Noreen Ortiz. I cut all ties with my mother and my brothers and sisters. When Eddie died and the pain seemed too great to bear alone, I thought of reaching out to my family. But my mother was dead by then, and my siblings scattered. What had once been a big noisy family seemed to have completely disappeared, pulled up by the roots. So I bore the pain alone and concentrated on my children and returned to work and was too tired to entertain any more sentimental thoughts.

But now Mrs. McLaughlin seems intent on reminding me of my family. My past and my history are one of the few subjects she is interested in.

"Where did you grow up?" she asks one morning.

"Paterson. Just about twenty miles from here."

"My husband grew up in Paterson. Did your parents tell you Irish stories?"

It is raining outside, so we are trapped in her room. At least I am trapped. Mrs. McLaughlin looks perfectly comfortable on the loveseat. Her cheeks have good color today. But I want badly to move around, to throw open the window and door, to let in the wind and rain. I have grown claustrophobic lately.

Mrs. McLaughlin clears her throat to get my attention.

"Yes, of course," I say. "My father told us stories when I was very young. He talked about leprechauns and fairies. All his favorite jokes started with a priest and a leprechaun walking into a bar. He had what seemed like a hundred variations on the same joke."

She says, "What made him stop?"

"What do you mean?"

"You said he told the stories when you were very young."

"Oh. He was an alcoholic. He left my mother by the time I was six. He came and went after that, until he passed away when I was a teenager."

"My husband was a dreamer, too."

"A dreamer?"

"He sometimes drank too much." Mrs. McLaughlin nods. "You and I have a lot in common."

I turn and look at her, tiny and old, content to sit still while I pace the room like a caged animal. My period had already started when I woke up this morning, and I am bleeding heavily. I can feel the blood flow out of my body. Mrs. McLaughlin is so pale she appears bloodless. It has probably been forty years since her last menstruation. "You think so?" I say, to be polite.

She gives me a measured look. "We've both lost too much," she says. "More than our share."

THAT AFTERNOON Mrs. McLaughlin takes a longer nap than usual. I stand by her bed at four o'clock, trying to decide whether to wake her. The sky has cleared, and I don't want her to miss out on her walk. She needs the exercise. I can tell, looking down on her, that she has not regained the weight she lost during her hospital stay. She makes no impression on the mattress. She lies on top of it with no impact, no pressure. She weighs perhaps eighty-five pounds, which is the weight of my eleven-year-old daughter. Mrs. McLaughlin is stronger and more independent now, but when she first came home from the rehab hospital, I had to lift her in and out of the bathtub. She was a bundle of papery skin and light bones in my arms. An old woman's body is one of loss. Loss of sensuality and suppleness, loss of muscle and bone mass, loss of color. Everything is fading away. You can catch glimpses of the woman who was once there, but no more.

Mrs. McLaughlin opens her eyes suddenly and stares up at me.

I try to smile soothingly so she's not startled by the fact that I am standing over her. I say, "It's time for our afternoon walk. You should get up now."

She stays perfectly still, her hands folded on her ribs. "I just saw your brothers and sisters," she says. "I was trying to pick out your voice, but there was so much noise, and you were too little to speak loudly enough for me to hear you. You were just a baby."

I put my hand under her shoulders and help raise her to the sitting position. It is common for older people to have vivid dreams, and to confuse their experiences asleep and awake. It suddenly occurs to me, though, my hands on this old woman, that if my mother were still alive, she would be close to Catharine McLaughlin's age. My older brothers and sisters would be the age of her children, my nieces and nephews the age of Gracie and Lila.

I say, "Mrs. Ronning had her TV on too loud again. The noise must have disturbed you. I'll go next door and speak to her when we get back. Come on now, up you go. Would you like to use the bathroom?"

Mrs. McLaughlin shakes her head no. She slides her legs over the side of the bed. When she is standing, I hold on to her elbow to help her balance, and she slides on her shoes. I hang her cardigan around her shoulders. I hold a hand mirror up to show her that her white curls look just as crisp and neat as before her nap. Together, my hand still under her elbow, we head out of the room. We navigate the stairs slowly, and I use my shoulder to push open the outside door.

Only when we are out in the sunlight and freshly cleaned air, do I feel myself relax for the first time that day. I tip my head back and feel the sun warm on my face. Then I remember my duty, and look down at Mrs. McLaughlin. She is squinting against the light, an expression of sleep and confusion still on her face. Perhaps I rushed her out of her nap because of my own eagerness to get out of that room.

"We'll take it slow now," I say. "Just to the parking lot and back."

"I never saw the children in my dreams before," she says in a groggy voice. "I'm usually awake. I see them around the big tree outside my window. They've always left me alone when I sleep."

"Did you dream about your children?" I ask. "Kelly and Meggy and Ryan?" I add the specifics to try to bring her back to reality. We are taking slow steps down the path. I think now that it was a mistake to bring her outside before she was truly awake. Most falls take place when older people are tired and distracted, unable to concentrate on each step. Mrs. McLaughlin's recovery from surgery is too recent to be jeopardized by a fall. I should have known better. I am rarely this careless.

"No," she says. "I saw you, and your brothers and sisters."

I stop walking and look at her with real concern. I have never known her, since she went off the strong pain medications, to become altered. "Maybe we should turn back," I say. "It's not as nice out as I thought it was."

"No," she says, and shakes her head. With the gesture, some of the fog seems to clear from her eyes. "I have to explain this to you. I knew, when I opened my eyes and saw you standing there, that it was time to tell you."

We are at the top of a small incline in the center of the path. Mrs. McLaughlin turns around, so she is looking back toward the Christian Home for the Elderly. I am already thinking of calling her doctor upon our return to her room. It can't hurt for her to have a checkup. Perhaps she has a blocked artery to her brain. It is a common problem with the aged, and easily fixed.

I put my hand on her arm. "Let's head back, shall we?"

She says, "My husband gave me visions when he died. I've had the chance to see my mother and my father, and the children I lost. I've spent time with them. I see them more and more frequently now."

She speaks so quietly, I have to strain to hear her. But the slight hot wind has died down, and I catch each word. There is no one else in sight, and I have the odd sensation that Mrs. McLaughlin and I are alone in our own bubble of space at the top of this hill. I think of my husband, and his boss, Louis, and this job. I wonder if these connections have been there all along, and if it is only now, months after the loss of Eddie, that my heart is open enough to see them. Is life made up of strands that link us all?

"That must be nice," I say.

"My twins were just babies when I lost them. They were . . . still-born." *Stillborn* seems to have been lodged deep in her throat—it creaks out. "But I will see them again in this life. I'll see them in Gracie's baby." Her face lights. "And my little girl will be there, too."

I know how to listen well. It is an important part of nursing, an important part of providing comfort. I bend my head toward Mrs. McLaughlin and let her go on.

"I was afraid to tell anyone about the visions for a long time. I was afraid they'd lock me up. Look what's happened to my poor Ryan. My children can be unreasonable. But when I realized who you were, I knew it was all right for me to tell you."

"No one's going to lock you up," I say in my best calming tone.

"I knew you looked familiar," she says. "It still took me a while to place you. Of course, there is the name, but you look like your brothers and sisters."

The summer air sneaks under the sleeves of my nurse's uniform and gives me a chill. I don't know why in that moment I begin to take her seriously. I don't know why I no longer believe she is confused. I say, "You know my brothers and sisters? How?"

She is gazing at me, her head tipped to the side. Her blue eyes on my blue eyes. "You were the baby," she says. "Patrick and I knew your mother, poor Mrs. Ballen. We brought her a casserole, or maybe it was a pie. But you were the baby outside my window, tied to the tree with your brothers and sisters. Noreen Ballen. Baby Ballen."

I cannot look away from her eyes as she says my name. I don't understand what is happening. I know I should, and I am searching . . . and then suddenly I remember. When I was very young, that was how my mother kept track of all thirteen of us. My mom was alone and afraid that one or more of us would run off and get in trouble. To keep control she would tie us to a big tree in the center of our backyard while she cooked and cleaned inside the house. My brothers and sisters and I developed games that we could play with one another around the trunk of the tree. We tried to forget how embarrassing it was when someone stopped by and saw us there, or when Mom didn't hear one of us calling and calling that we had to go to the bathroom. And how the neighborhood stray dog would run around and around us, just out of reach, taunting with loud barks because he was free and we weren't.

I speak carefully, wondering how it is possible that my past lies in this old woman. In this stranger. "You saw my family in a vision?"

"Your oldest brother and sister want me to set them free. They wave their arms at me, pleading." Mrs. McLaughlin's eyes darken, then grow light again. I wonder if she is seeing them now. I feel a pang beneath my ribs.

"Maybe your brother and sister sent you to me," she says. "Maybe they think I can set *you* free."

I put my free hand on the waist of my white uniform where the material gathers into a neat seam. I am too shaken to speak, but I feel the nurse, the professional in me, summon words. "We should keep walking."

"I don't know how to do it, though," Mrs. McLaughlin says. "I can't seem to help my own children. I couldn't keep them safe and alive. I wasn't there for Ryan. I can't make the ones I have left be happy. I don't know why I'm being expected to help a stranger."

"You don't have to worry about me," I say, in a voice I don't recognize. "I'm not your responsibility. I can take care of myself."

But suddenly I am not sure that I can. I am not certain at all. I can feel the soft cloth wrapped around my waist leading to the rough bark of the tree. I hear the sound of constant laughter flowing like a river over my head as I crawl beneath the feet of my brothers and sisters. I hear Eddie's musical voice, Jessie giggling, Eddie Jr. snorting like he does when a joke is so funny that he can't stand it.

The old woman shakes her head. "This is not about responsibility. I've been given the chance to fix things before I die. I never thought I would get tired, but I'm tired now. It might end before I'm ready, if I'm not careful. I have to focus."

My temper surges up from behind the wall of grief I carry around every single day. This old woman is saying that my life is beyond my control, and that I am here to facilitate her needs, her visions. "I want to be clear," I say. "My brothers and sisters didn't send me here. This job was a gift from my husband. Eddie knew that I needed the money. My children need things from me that I haven't been able to afford to give them."

Mrs. McLaughlin and I regard each other for a full minute, dueling dead husbands and children and brothers and sisters waiting in the background. Her gaze is full of belief, unbreakable.

I back down first. I look away. This is ridiculous. This woman is senile and I have to be the reasonable adult here. I need to hold on to the facts. "I haven't seen my family for years," I say. "We gave each other up."

Mrs. McLaughlin shrugs at that. She dismisses the restraints of practicality and time and distance as flimsy obstacles. Without me, she heads back toward the building. She centers her walker carefully in front of her with each step. I wait a moment, then hurry to meet her stride.

KELLY

I cannot believe the speed at which change is happening. Life whipped around again when my husband pulled into the driveway with my younger brother and his wheelchair in the backseat of his truck and the news that Ryan's home had burned down. Louis had saved Ryan's life. He carried my brother out of the burning building in his arms. I can't really express what this means to me. It is the image I am left with now when I fall asleep at night.

I was not home the afternoon that Louis and Ryan pulled into the driveway. I was at the motel, with Vince.

While Ryan's home burned, Vince and I were talking. We are usually talking. In the same way that when I met Louis as a young woman I was almost mute, since I got to know Vincent Carrelli I have hardly shut up. I tell him about my memory. I tell him about my daughters. I tell him the strangest things about myself, things I have never told anyone, like the fact that I love circuses. That I am drawn to them, reading books on the subject, watching documentaries, dragging my small daughters to Barnum & Bailey in New York every year despite the fact that Gracie cried over the caged animals and Lila asked endless questions concerning the safety of the acrobats. The circus seemed to bring out worry and dread in my daughters, while the sight of women flying through the air and men sticking their heads inside lions' mouths made me feel exhilarated and free.

I say to Vince, "I think Louis is having an affair with my mother's nurse."

We are in the motel room, which I now think of as our room. The curtains are drawn and only the lamp beside the bed is lit. I am wearing a long dress with buttons down the front. Most of the buttons are unfastened, and I am lying in Vince's arms. His hand is cupping my bare left breast.

I feel Vince's arm stiffen beneath me, and realize that I have probably said too much. For all our talking, we rarely mention Louis. We talk about Cynthia often, but then, Cynthia is dead.

"You should leave him. He doesn't deserve you." Vince speaks quickly, as if relieved to say the words he has been holding in for weeks.

"You said to me months ago that it was inconceivable for Louis to have an affair, that he was too good a man."

"I have a different viewpoint now."

"It doesn't matter. I'm not going to talk about the future with you," I say, and roll away from him on the bed. I button up my dress. That is my rule: We don't talk or think about the future while in this room. We live only in the moment.

He looks after me in dismay. "Come back here, sweetheart."

He calls me that, sweetheart. He also calls me darling. I have never liked these kinds of endearments. I broke Louis from using them early in our relationship. I never called my children by pet names, either. Those terms seem demeaning and belittling. I think a person should be allowed the dignity of being known by his or her proper name. But somehow, oddly, I don't mind sweetheart and darling coming from Vincent's mouth.

"We don't have to talk about anything you don't want to," he says. "What I mean is that Louis *is* a good man, but I have a better sense of the gray areas now. Not everything is so black and white, morally speaking."

"Isn't that convenient for us," I say.

There is a muffled bark from the bathroom, where Chastity is sleeping. Vince refuses to leave her at home or at the Municipal Building. It makes me a little uncomfortable having the dog at the motel with us, but she's blind and deaf and stays in the bathroom, so I can't really complain. The poor animal is on her last legs.

I touch my lips with my finger. They are puffy from kissing. "Do you think Louis is a better person than I am?"

"Of course not! You're the most amazing woman I have ever known."

There is a pause and I remain motionless on the far side of the bed. My dress is back in place. I have on nude stockings and off-white heels. It occurs to me that in the rigid position I am lying in, arms crossed, legs straight, that I might as well be standing upright in the middle of the room. There is no release and no relaxation in my position, nothing that suggests I am on a bed.

I think, I never relax, and that thought strikes me as so full of truth that I am shocked. Is it true that I am incapable of relaxing? Well, if I can let go at all, the closest I have come has been in this room, with Vince.

"Maybe you should talk to your daughters if you're upset about Louis," he says. "You're right, this isn't a conversation we should have. It's not a comfortable fit for either one of us."

"Talk to my daughters? About their father?" I give him a look that says he is crazy. It's obvious that he doesn't have children of his own, but I don't say that out loud. During the endless, extraordinary conversation we had the first time we came to this room, Vince told me that his childlessness is his greatest regret. Cynthia had eight miscarriages before they stopped trying. Eight tiny deaths.

"I love you," he says. This is often how Vincent opens or ends a conversation. He says the phrase as if it is an apology, and an answer, all on its own. This always amazes me. It opens me right up. He reaches his hand out toward me.

I unfold my arms and take his hand. I kiss the side of his pinky finger. I let him pull me back toward him. My body loosens. He starts to undo the buttons on my dress, but his thick fingers are too slow, and I finish the job. I slip off my heels and wriggle out of panty hose. We have sex quickly, silently, meeting each other with a rush of need. We fumble over each other's bodies. I suck in my stomach, and try to stay out of the lamplight. Our lovemaking is always the same: fast and quiet, tinged with shame. He is excessively grateful when it's over.

"Thank you," he says. "Thank you. You're so beautiful, so wonderful."

I struggle back into my clothes. I can't believe this is me, I think, while I revisit the buttons on my dress. This can't be real. To ground myself, I picture my daughters. In my head they are still teenagers, Lila dark-haired and sturdy, Gracie pale and smiling. Their arms are wrapped around each other's waist. I love them so much that I never know what to say. Everything I try comes out wrong.

"I would have bet any amount of money that I would never break one of the Commandments," I say. "I would have bet millions. With no hesitation."

Vince has heard this line of guilt-ridden exposition before. He has learned it is best not to respond. "How about an omelet?" he says.

He feeds me nearly every time we meet. There is only a mini-refrigerator and one electric burner in the room, yet he manages to make wonderful pastas and even fish with vegetables. I am rarely hungry when I'm with him, but I love the smells that fill the room while he cooks. I lie on the bed and watch him shake sauté pans and test noodles for doneness. When the food is ready Vince puts some in a small bowl and brings it to Chastity in the bathroom. She whimpers with pleasure while she eats.

Louis has cooked for me regularly over the years. He prepares dishes he thinks I will like, and while he cooks he glances over his shoulder with an Am I doing all right? expression on his face. There is so much expectation in the meals Louis prepares that the food tastes heavy and I turn nasty. He will never stop hoping that one single meal is going to make me happy. I will never forgive him for thinking it could be that simple. I wonder if I should leave Louis before he leaves me. Would he really leave me?

Vince has never even asked what foods I like. He cooks for the pleasure of it, and because he loves to eat. I watch him crack eggs out of their shells with one hand. He takes a wire whisk out of a side compartment in his bag. He leans over the pan and inhales deeply. "Garlic," he says. "Is there anything better than garlic?"

"Shopping. My convertible. Summer evenings." I sit up. "After we eat, I should go. I told Louis I'd be back soon."

The enthusiasm leaves Vince's voice. "Where did you tell him you were going?"

"To the library, and to the office. But I've hardly been home this week, so I shouldn't be too late." I stop. I want to believe that what Vince and I are doing is decent and right and pure. We are comforting each other, knowing each other. This experience is unlike anything I've ever felt, and I deserve it. But the Catholicism that I grew up with, that I raised my children with, that we have all since abandoned except for Louis, always rears its ugly head when it smells guilt. I find myself asking God to keep Louis and the girls from finding out. I ask God to give me a little more time in this room with Vince. I ask God to look out for my mother and make her well.

"I hate it when you leave," Vince says. "I'm sorry to say it, but I'm jealous of your life. You have so much to go to—your daughters, your mother, Louis. I have only my empty house."

"My life is useless," I say. "The only real living I do is in this room."

"You still have something to work with," Vince says, his back to me. I see a flash of yellow as he slides the omelet from the hot pan onto the cutting board he brought with him. Using a spatula, he divides the omelet and puts one half on one plate, one half on another.

"Utensils," he says, and I obediently move to his side to pull two forks off of the drying rack above the tiny sink. I stay there, my upper arm touching his upper arm while he grinds fresh pepper over the plates. I feel, where our bodies touch, his short, choppy breath as he works. Cooking is the most exercise he ever gets. I have chided him that he should start jogging and lose thirty pounds for his health, but in this moment I wonder if my hours spent on the treadmill in the basement have been misspent. Maybe Vince knows what he is doing. Maybe by this time in my life I should have found some activity that I love, whether it makes me sweat or not.

Vince finishes by scooping up chopped tomatoes with his hands and sprinkling them over the eggs. Bright red against soft yellow. He shakes the tomato juice and seeds off of his big hands. "Well?" he says, smiling down at the plates.

I hand him a fork. The warm, delicious, fragrant smell fills the room. I am suddenly starving. We start to eat immediately, standing there by the sink. My mouth full with steaming eggs, I manage to say, "Delicious."

I DRIVE home quickly, the top down on the convertible. Even though I'm exceeding the speed limit, I take the long way so I don't have to drive on Main Street. I visited Vince's barbershop, but that was before I really knew him. I will avoid the sight of it from now on. I like to think of Vince in our room at the motel and nowhere else. The man I know and have feelings for does not match up with that crummy barbershop. When I think of Vince cutting hair and taking cash out of men's hands, I am embarrassed for him. I am simply embarrassed. It is not appropriate work for a man of his caliber, or for a man who is in love with me.

I pull into the driveway nervous, though I don't know why. I have been gone for two hours longer than I said I would, but I don't expect Louis to have noticed. And frankly, I don't care if he does. I have stopped pretending. I live my life the way I like, without worrying over appearances. I am done fighting for or with my husband.

It is now the middle of Saturday afternoon and the sun slants over our big house. Louis's truck is not in the driveway, which means he has remembered to put it in the garage like I asked. I press a button and the convertible top motors up into position. I spray on extra perfume to cover any scent Vince may have left. I check my face in the rearview mirror, but for what? I still look the same: green eyes, well-shaped eyebrows, tiny lines leaking from the corners of my eyes and mouth.

When I let myself into the house I hear the phone ringing. I rush into the kitchen and pick up the receiver before Louis has a chance to. What if it is Vince? He isn't supposed to call here, but when I left him he said he didn't think he could bear missing me. What if he couldn't bear it and had to call?

I almost whisper into the phone. "Hello."

"Kelly, it's me." It's Meggy's voice. My relief lasts only a split second. I don't want to talk to her.

"Where have you been? Mom and I have been trying to reach you for two hours—your cell phone was off."

"I've been busy." I've been avoiding Meggy ever since Gracie told me about my sister's attempt to take her child from her. I am not sure what to say to Meggy. I am too angry to address it. "What do you want? I've been out all afternoon and I have things to do here."

"I want information—I called the hospital but they wouldn't tell me anything. The idiots in charge there called Mom and got her all worked up about what happened. Have you spoken to Louis? Do you know how he is?"

I shake my head. Meggy is talking too fast. "What are you talking about? Do I know how who is?"

Meggy's voice clamps down. "You don't know? No, of course you don't. I was an idiot to think you'd know what was going on in your own family. Jesus, Kelly. Your husband saved Ryan from his burning apartment building this afternoon. Apparently Gracie and Lila were there too."

My heart flips in my chest. "The girls? How bad . . . Are they all right?"

"They're fine. They weren't involved. Look, you need to get your ass over to the hospital so you can make sure everything's okay and call Mom. She's freaking out."

The fear that has been making my chest burn turns into anger. "You know, keeping Mom happy and well shouldn't be my job alone. You could come up here once in a while, you know." Out of the corner of my eye I spot a folded piece of paper on the kitchen table and grab for it. It's one of Louis's notes.

Meggy heaves a dramatic sigh into my ear. "You know I have a lot on my plate. I was up there for the surgery, and then when she moved back into her room. Has Pat even called Mother? Don't try to make *me* feel guilty."

"Oh, thank God," I say. "Louis left a note saying Ryan is fine. He's just taking him to the hospital for a checkup. Thank God."

"Thank God."

There's a silence, then Meggy says, "We're going to have to put him in a home."

I shake my head. "No," I say. But I was thinking the same thought. Mom can't support him anymore. None of us are willing or able to. The reality sits and sinks between us. We have been looking out for Ryan our entire lives.

"Kelly," Meggy says. "Do you think Mom is dying?"

I stand up and breathe out the word at the same time. "No. Jesus, Meggy."

"Okay." I can hear her relief.

I don't know why I lash out then; maybe it's just to get back to a kind of conversation that's less disturbing, more familiar, more comfortable. I say, "When I see Mother later on today, or maybe when I visit her tomorrow, I'll tell her you were concerned. I'm sure she'll appreciate that you thought to call."

"Oh, please. Don't give me the Saint Kelly act. I asked the nurse about visitors, and she said Louis is there more often than you are. You're no more the perfect daughter than I am."

Something black seethes up inside me. "Look, I don't care if you never visit Mom again. I don't care what you do, but you'd better stay away from my children."

There is a pause, and I think, I've got you now.

But Meggy sounds casual, not intimidated, when she speaks. "Oh, so you finally heard. I was wondering if Gracie would tell you about our chat."

"Of course she told me." I hold on to the back of the chair with my hand. "Of course she did. You need to leave her alone."

"Like you do?"

Her words ring in my ear. Meggy and I have never gotten along. At the age of three she started speaking and immediately rubbed me the wrong way. She was and is relentless and bossy. She was able to mold the others, even Pat, to her will, but never me. Several times when we were young, even though she is five years my junior, we came to blows. I can imagine her now standing in her ugly orange kitchen, which hasn't seen a fresh coat of paint or a new appliance since the seventies. She needs to have the split ends trimmed on her long, flat hair. She is tapping one badly shod foot on the linoleum floor. Tap, talk, tap, talk.

"Maybe if Gracie had more support from her parents, she wouldn't need my help, but she does. Have you even noticed what a complete mess she is? She's fallen apart since Mother fell, and she wasn't that stable to begin with. Angel would be a better mother to that baby, and that's a fact."

"That baby," I say, almost choking, "is my grandchild."

"Technically," Meggy says. "Technically. But you're a practical woman, Kelly. Think about what's best for your daughter. Mother is getting too weak to pull all the strings in this family like she used to. We're going to have to start looking out for each other, or we're going to drift apart when she dies. I've been thinking about this."

I hear myself say, "How can you bear to?"

"I'm strong," she says. "I know how to get in people's faces. Daddy told me that when I was fourteen, and he was right. It's my gift. I think we all need to play our strengths now. I can see that this family is in a crisis, even if no one else can. And I am trying to do something about it."

I pace across the kitchen, my forward motion stopped only by the pull of the telephone cord. I know that no matter how this conversation ends I will be upset for days. Only another McLaughlin can get to me like this. Untruths are mixed with truths in such a dizzying combination that the two can't be disentangled, and I am left straining and shattered at the end of the phone cord.

"I have been taking care of this family single-handedly since Daddy died," I tell her. "*I* am the one Mother calls when she needs something. *I* have been the one to make sure Ryan is all right, that his needs are met. *I* am the one who lent you money so your daughter could go to a better school. Don't tell me that *I* have to do something for this family. I gave up taking care of myself years ago to take care of all of you."

I pant for breath, caught up in the power of having given so much. Having been so much.

Meggy makes a disparaging noise in the back of her throat. "You just don't get it, do you?"

I cannot believe that after all I have said she can still condescend to me. I make my voice icy cold. "What don't I get?"

"This is a different kind of crisis, Kelly. You can't solve this one with money or carefully placed phone calls. Our family is about to change shape in a big way. I for one don't want to wake up a year from now and find Mother gone and none of us in touch and Gracie and her child on welfare. And you know that could all happen if we don't do something."

I am worn out. It is an effort to hold on to the phone. "You worry about your daughter, and I'll worry about mine."

"I am so deeply into Dina's business that she tells me at least once a week that she hates me."

The corners of my mouth lift into a smile. "Neither of my girls has ever said anything like that to me. We have a civilized relationship."

"Is that what you call it?" Meggy asks. "Congratulations, then. Good for you."

WHEN I hang up the phone I grab my purse and run for the door. I will meet Louis and Ryan at the hospital. I will show up, even if it's late. I will call my girls tonight. I will check in on Gracie. I will spend less time at the motel, and more time at home. I know that despite what I said to Meggy, it has been Louis who has been looking out for the McLaughlins lately, not me. He took my mother to the hospital after her fender bender, and he is at the hospital with my brother now. He carried Ryan, his least favorite member of my family, out of a burning building. I can picture that scene as vividly as if I were there. I see it, and I know what I should have known all along. That Louis is as much a member of my family as I am. His ties are not just to me, they trail across my heart to every person I love.

My sister's words keep running through my head like ticker tape at the stock exchange. I know that I will remember every syllable Meggy said along with the cadence of her voice and the feel of the phone cord under my hand. I will never be able to forget, despite my best efforts. *This family is in crisis.* All I can do now is lower the top on my car and drive a little too fast so the wind whooshes in my ears and takes the place of any and all thoughts.

Halfway to the hospital, I stop at a traffic light and notice a bouquet of rainbow-colored balloons tied to a white mailbox. Over the front door of the house there is a banner that reads, HAPPY BIRTHDAY JIMMY. I look at the balloons, and when the light turns green and I drive away, an idea pops into my head. A brilliant idea.

I will throw Gracie a baby shower.

It is the perfect solution. This baby is coming. If Meggy made me realize anything, it's that. Steps need to be taken. Throwing a baby shower is something mothers do for their daughters everywhere and across time. My mother threw me a shower when I was pregnant with Gracie. It is a wonderful tradition, and I can't believe that I didn't think of it sooner. Lila and I will clean Gracie up and remove the cardigan and invite my mother and sisters over. They will give her the gifts and the advice that she and the baby will need. Meggy will see firsthand that Gracie is fine, that the baby will be fine, and that I am taking care of everything as usual.

LOUIS

It is much easier for me to do favors for Eddie's wife now, because I know her work schedule. In the middle of a Wednesday morning, confident that she is two towns away sitting at my mother-in-law's bed- side and that her children are in summer camp, I park my truck directly in front of her house. I get out and check the gutters personally. I stroll around to the back of the house, my hands in my pockets, and note that the outside stairs down into the cellar need repair. I see through the kitchen window that the room's wallpaper is beginning to give around the edges. Of course, I trust my guys, who have been cutting the lawn and making small repairs under my instructions, but I feel better now that I have a chance to see things through myself. It was difficult to get a real sense of the situation from the inside of my truck, across the street.

At this point I have taken care of most of the minor adjustments necessary to the outside of the house. But now that I have gained prox- imity and can see through the windows, I want the chance to give the inside a good once-over. I worry about the internal stairs to the base- ment, a feature that is often poorly built in this level of home. Hanging light fixtures should be checked for stability. The overall wiring should be investigated because faulty wiring can lead to electrical fires. I won- der, as I circle the house, if there is a way for me to gain access to the interior without Nurse Ballen knowing.

Late one morning, I am standing on the edge of the lawn won- dering just that when a yellow school bus filled with campers pulls up.

I am surprised at the sight of the bus, as camp does not normally end for several hours. I try to think if it is a holiday, but can't recall the date. I watch a tall, skinny girl with dark braids run down the bus steps first, followed by a smaller boy wearing a bright yellow backpack. I know that this is my cue to walk past them, get inside my truck and drive away, but I find I can't move. Given the chance, I would like a closer look at the children's faces. I'm not sure what I'm looking for until they have crossed the street—the girl walks, the little boy skips, his backpack bouncing above his shoulders. They are at the mailbox, only a few feet away, before they notice me. The girl stops short, and the little boy bumps into her.

"Hey," he says. "Watch where you're going."

"Who are you?" the girl says.

She looks up at me with Eddie's eyes, deep brown and intelligent.

"Not supposed to talk to strangers," the little boy whispers. I can hear the lisp of missing front teeth.

"Don't worry," I say. "I know your mother. She's doing some nursing work for me."

"You're sick?" the little girl asks.

I keep my hands by my sides. I want to look as unintimidating as possible. "No, not me. Your mom is helping my wife's mother."

"Kids at camp are sick," the boy says. "They have mice, so we got to go home."

"Lice," the girl says.

The boy's face suddenly lightens and opens into a wide smile—it is Eddie's smile. He wriggles out of his backpack and lets it fall to the ground. "Uh-oh," he says.

There is something crawling out of the bag. It is dark and thin and moving fast.

"Step back," I say, and gesture at the children. The dark shape is moving so quickly that it is hard to keep in my sight. It snakes among the straps of the backpack. I think I hear it hiss.

"Careful," I warn, because I can sense the little boy stepping forward and I have the animal in my sights.

"Don't!" the little boy cries.

He dives to the ground right before I am about to bring my foot down. The boy comes back up with what I see now is a brown, scaly lizard cupped in his hands. Above the boy's fingers the lizard recriminates me with beady eyes.

"You're not supposed to bring that disgusting thing to camp," the girl says.

I feel sweaty and shaken. I have almost killed the children's pet.

"Poor Fred," the little boy says into the cup of his hand.

The girl picks up her brother's backpack. "We have to go," she says. She marches off across the lawn, toward the neighbor's house. Her brother follows her, murmuring words of comfort to the reptile. I notice an older woman standing in the doorway of the house next door, holding the door open for Nurse Ballen's children.

I turn away slowly. I use the handkerchief in my back pocket to wipe my forehead. I saw what I wanted to see. Two healthy and happy children. Eddie's smile and Eddie's eyes. But still, I should have left when I saw the school bus arrive. Why didn't I? Things almost took a very unpleasant turn. I shouldn't have gone near her children; I almost blew everything.

A FEW miles have passed before I remember where I'm headed. But then it comes to me: I have to get a haircut. I have been avoiding this for weeks. Except when shaving, I don't look in the mirror. My appearance is not high on my list of priorities. But this morning Kelly told me I was beginning to look half-gorilla, half-man. So I head toward Main Street, and Vince's barbershop.

Vince has been cutting my hair since he opened the shop fifteen years ago. I went there on opening day, to support him. I still remember sitting in the squeaky new barber chair eating one of the cannolis Cynthia had made for the occasion. I can see red balloons and Vince's grinning face—thinner then—in the mirror. I have referred a lot of business his way over the years. I thought, and still think, that the shop was a great idea for Vince. By nature he is a talker, not a doer, and the barbershop gives him a captive audience. On the weekends he has a steady stream of young boys and their fathers, and on the weekdays he has his regulars, a group of down-and-out guys with nowhere else to spend their time, many of whom Vince and I went to school with. Besides, the mayoral salary is a pittance, and the barbershop helps him make ends meet.

I park in front of the barbershop, which could use a fresh coat of paint and a touch-up to its sign. I've heard rumors that over the past few weeks Vince has taken to disappearing from work for hours at a time. He's been standing up regular customers and generally neglecting the upkeep of the shop. I can see that now, looking through the slightly dirty front window at the mayor of Ramsey clipping his scissors above the head of a customer. I have to wonder if he's drinking again. If we're going to go through that tired pattern of me offering help and his refusing it and then apologizing later.

The little bells tied to the barbershop's door ring as I push it open.

Vince turns, his face full of surprise, even though I am fairly sure he saw me approaching through the window. "Louis," he says. "Long time no see. How are you?"

The air in the shop is stale and musty and I suddenly want to be back outside again. I stay by the door. "Look, if the wait is going to be long, I can come back. I have work to do."

"No, no. Don't leave. I'm done with George here."

Obligingly, George stands up out of the chair. "Hey, Louis," he says.

"George," I say. George is a salesclerk at the Ramsey Outdoor store. I've known him for twenty years, but we've never said more to each other than hello and good-bye. George is a man of few words. True to form, he hands Vince a ten-dollar bill, and leaves. The bells on the door ring out his absence.

Vince and I face each other for an awkward moment. We haven't spoken since the night he asked me to drop by his office and then told me he thought I needed a friend. He said that if I needed a shoulder

ANN NAPOLITANO

to cry on, he was more than happy to offer his. Or that he could get a referral for me for a good shrink.

I walk around him and sit down. The vinyl squeaks under my weight.

"That was terrible news about the fire," Vince says. "Thank God your brother-in-law was okay. It was Ramsey's worst blaze in four years."

"I would have thought you'd have shown up at the scene, too. Didn't the chief radio you?" I am talking just for something to say. I don't want to talk about the fire.

"Forgot my radio that day," Vince says. "Gosh, you do need a trim. How long has it been?"

"Two months, probably."

Vince *tsks tsks* over my head. He is comfortable in barber mode. Vince sprays my hair with a water bottle, and a damp mist falls over my face.

"So, how are you?"

"Great. Couldn't be better. How about you?"

"Fine."

"Good."

"How's Kelly?"

"She's great, too," I say.

He clips at the back of my hair and I can feel the metal brush my scalp. "You guys are happy?"

I give a small smile. Vince is crazy to try to get me to talk about my emotions again, but I have to credit him for perseverance. I say, "I've had Cynthia on my mind lately."

The scissors swish over my head, and I think I see Vince's hand shake.

"Why's that?" he says.

"I spent a lot of time at Valley when Kelly's mom was in for her surgery, and it made me remember visiting Cynthia there. I liked our one-sided conversations. She was the only person, outside of my mother, who ever spoke Italian to me."

Vince's hand trembles. I can see it plain as day in the mirror. I pull away and turn in the chair to face him. "Vince, I'm sorry that I have to ask this, but are you drinking again?"

There is a frozen moment where we both stare at each other. Then Vince holds up his hands, as if I have him at gunpoint. "Drinking? No, I swear. I'm not."

I turn back around and meet his eyes in the mirror. I decide to believe him. "I'm sorry, then, maybe I shouldn't have brought up Cynthia."

"Don't say that," he says. "I like to talk about her. I feel like almost everyone has forgotten about her now, except for me."

"You should try to find someone new to care about."

"I wouldn't want to find just anybody," he says. "Wouldn't you rather be alone than be in a loveless relationship?"

I see something in his eyes and say in real surprise, "Do you have a girlfriend, Vince?"

"No," he says. "No. I'm still alone."

But Vince speaks in an oddly gleeful tone. Actually, the combination of the depressing words and the way he says them seems to have a kind of strangling effect. He looks almost crazed as he moves from one side of my head to the other holding a black comb and scissors.

I close my eyes and try to block Vince out of my thoughts. I think about Nurse Ballen's house instead, and how I might get inside. I wonder if I should try to make friends with the baby-sitter next door. She probably has a key to the house, and maybe I could persuade her to let me borrow it. I have to get inside somehow. That shaky, cold feeling has been coming over me more and more frequently since the fire at Ryan's building. I don't know why, but I realize now that the only way to stop it is to work on Nurse Ballen's house. To help her and her kids have a better life.

Vince picks the electric razor up off of his tray and runs it, buzzing, around the side of my head. "You and I have known each other since we were seven years old," he says. "You realize that?"

"Sounds right," I say.

"Now that my parents are gone, and Cynthia, there's no one alive I've known longer than you."

I sigh. I want to get out of this chair. I've had enough. "You okay, Vince?"

"Yeah, I'm fine. I just think that's something, don't you? That's history. I mean, I know a lot of guys, and I'm friendly with them, but we're not friends. You reached out to me after Cynthia passed. You can't deny history."

"Are you about done here?" I ask. "I've got a building site I need to check on."

"Almost," he says, squinting at my head as if searching for remaining flaws. "Okay, finished."

I stand up and my whole body aches, as if I have been sitting in that chair for hours, not just ten minutes. I am not making anyone happy. Not myself, not Nurse Ballen, not Kelly. I am not man enough to be Kelly's husband. I wonder if the best way to honor her would be to let her go. Perhaps I should be alone, like Vince. I could leave Kelly everything—the real estate, the cars, the money. I would just leave.

"The cut is on the house," he says, which is what he's said every time he's cut my hair for the last fifteen years. He swells out his chest as if he is offering me an amazing gift, when, in reality, I have brought in nearly half of his customers, so it is only good business to make my cuts complimentary.

"Thanks." I clap him on the shoulder and say, "Take care."

As I pull open the door the phone on the counter rings. Vince falls on it before the first peal ends. He hunches over the phone, his voice a soft whisper. I shake my head in amazement. This sweet, hapless man whom I, too, have known longer than anyone else in my life, does have a girlfriend. I wonder, as I walk into the humid air, what kind of woman would have him.

I PASS the burnt remains of Ryan's building on the way to the site. I will rebuild as soon as possible. I can't wait to break ground. The original structure is more than half gone, the remains blackened and gnawed. The scene brings on the cold feeling in my gut. I knew the building was dangerous; I should have acted sooner. I see Eddie Ortiz standing on the edge of the caved-in roof, and look away. No one died this time, I tell myself. No one died.

An old friend of mine on the town council runs one of the best residential psychiatric-care facilities in New Jersey. I called him the night of the fire, and Ryan had a room the next day. Ryan's been a nervous wreck since he moved in, which is understandable. The guy lost his home, after all. But all he talks about is those damn birds. They don't allow pets in the center, so he will have to find a way to get over the loss. At least now he'll have proper care, someone to make him take his medications, and some structure to his days. Kelly cried after we left Ryan at the facility, but I know it's for the best. He's safe there.

I spend a few hours at the site. I eat a sandwich with my men and use my cell phone to work on a pending real-estate deal. I walk through the site with the foreman. This is a pro bono one-week job to fix up the recreation center at Finch Park. It is not a big job and there is no structural damage to the building, which limits the danger to my men. When the girls were young they played soccer and softball on the town teams in this park. Kelly and I used to cheer them on from the sidelines. I was happy to do the favor for the town, and besides, it falls under the heading of what goes around comes around. I will get this favor back many times over from the local planning and zoning commissions. The next time I want to bend one of the absurdly outdated zoning laws or build an addition that is over scale, my renovation of the rec center will be remembered.

When I'm ready to leave it's late afternoon. I walk across the field to my truck, skirting the edge of the town's summer day camp. It is arts-and-crafts time. Little boys and girls are seated at picnic tables, heads bent over sheets of brightly colored construction paper. Fat crayons and what look like the cardboard centers of toilet paper rolls are piled in the middle of the tables. None of the children's legs are long enough for their feet to touch the ground.

I sit in my truck and watch the children before I turn on the engine. It has been a long, odd day, and I am tired. I watch the children's legs—some chubby, some rail-thin—swing above the grass. I think of Eddie's children, and the replication of his smile and his eyes. I replay my meeting with them, and imagine that this time I know that the movement in the book bag is nothing more than the little boy's favorite pet. I bend down and loop the lizard gently over my finger, which makes the girl smile and the little boy send out his infectious laugh. The three of us stand in a circle and the lizard seems happy to sit on my hand. The girl and boy talk to me about their day and about all of their worries and concerns. They don't stop talking until the woman next door calls for them. Then we wave good-bye to one another, with the boy and girl continuing to wave as I walk toward my truck.

I watch the campers' legs swing at the picnic tables as they draw shapes on the construction paper and then color them in. Children's art turns reality upside down and sideways. It's filled with purple grass and orange clouds and green people. I want to reimagine my daughters' childhoods like I did the scene on Noreen Ballen's front lawn. This time I won't let Lila and Gracie grow up alone in their rooms and I won't walk away when I see disturbing things through half-opened doors. This time I will go in and grab the punk boy by the arm and throw him out of my house. I will let Gracie know that she is worth more than what he saw in her.

But this rewrite is not as easy to believe in as my encounter with Noreen's little boy and girl. I have failed in too many moments with Gracie and Lila over too many years. I gave them too much room, too much freedom. I think that probably we all had too much freedom, the two girls and Kelly and me. Maybe Catharine was right, and we should have gone to church every Sunday and eaten together as a family every night and listened for clues to the kind of women the girls were growing into while they said prayers before bed. But we didn't do any of that and now there is no firm ground beneath our feet and it is too late to take stock in any new rules. You cannot discipline grown children. You cannot change the tone of a marriage after thirty years.

～

I TAKE my boots off and leave them by the back door so I don't track in any dirt. I find Kelly in the living room, curled up on the couch with a tall stack of magazines on her lap. The central air is going full blast; the hairs on my arms stand up at the sudden change of temperature.

She looks up at me and says, "I made our reservation for Saturday night."

"Our reservation?"

"At La Manga's."

Of course. I had forgotten. Well, not exactly forgotten—more like pushed out of my mind. Our thirty-first anniversary is this weekend. We used to celebrate that night by having dinner at the location of our first date, a tiny Italian restaurant in the West Village. But we let that tradition lapse quite some time ago. We used the same set of excuses the first year or two: We were too busy, it was such a hassle to get into the city, etc. But I don't think we even mentioned our anniversary to each other last year. I look at my wife, hoping for a clue to what is happening here. She's been behaving differently in the last few weeks. She is more emotional, and more often home.

I say, "I thought you might want to skip this year."

Kelly hesitates, then rushes forward. "We have to go on Saturday night, because I'm throwing Gracie's baby shower on Sunday. I've been going through these baby magazines all afternoon. I really want it to be something. Martha Stewart's ideas are the only ones with any class, but the execution is almost impossible. I've never done this before—I'm too young to have a daughter who's having a child."

I shake my head. I was thinking a few hours earlier that the only choice was to end our marriage. I'm not sure now whether I'm agreeing to a last dinner, or a celebratory date. "Saturday night is fine."

"The shower has to be this weekend, you see. After all, time is running out. Gracie's due in three weeks. She could give birth any time now."

I sit down in the armchair by the door, a big leather chair that used to belong to Kelly's father. No one ever sits in this chair. It is on the fringes of the room, outside of any direct line of conversation. I always feel my lack as a man when I sit in this chair. It seems to demand a pipe and a glass of scotch from its visitor. Kelly's dad was not a happy person, but he was indisputably a man in a hard-living way I've never tried to achieve.

"Your hair looks better," Kelly says. "You look human again. You went to Vince?"

I hope that my wife knows what she's doing. I have seen this determined look on her face before. She has the ability to make a decision and then inflate her emotions like a bicycle tire until they back up the decision with no wiggle room. The problem is that if her emotions are false, there is still a hole in the tire and the air will eventually seep out.

All I can do is show up on Saturday night and pull out her chair. I will chink glasses and hold her hand. I'll hope that she has found an answer, a solution that I haven't yet been able to see. I will speak loudly that night, and try not to listen for the hiss of escaping air.

Kelly seems to read something in my expression. "Are you going to keep sleeping in the den, Louis?" She sounds curious. "I know you," she says. "You're sleeping there to protect me, or to help me somehow. I want you to know that you're not helping me by doing that."

Her words, though quiet, boom between the four walls of the room. I find myself thinking that where we are headed in this moment is going to be messy, more complicated, unpredictable. I put my hands on my knees. I grip the joints through the denim of my jeans, through the pounds of muscle, tendons, ligaments, and fat. "I'm not sleeping well," I say. "I've been having nightmares. I might kick you."

"I'll kick you back," Kelly says.

"Okay," I say.

"Okay, then," she says, and turns back to the baby magazines.

GRACIE

I wake up at five-thirty in the morning. I haven't slept past dawn since the seventh month. I am so uncomfortable at night tossing and turning and getting up to pee every hour that when the first light slides under my window shade I crawl out of bed. While I make my way downstairs I remember how difficult it was for my father to wake me up in the morning when I was a teenager. I used to be a gifted sleeper. I could sleep anytime, anywhere, but as a teen I was at the height of my powers. I could go to bed at ten at night and sleep until one o'clock the next day. It drove my parents, overachievers that they are, absolutely crazy. I don't think my father has ever slept past eight in the morning in his life. Lila was always halfway to the nearest library by breakfast time, which was something my parents could get behind, but I was another story.

On the weekends my father would stomp up and down the hall outside my door and call out loudly to my mother, who had long ago delegated the task of worrying over my degenerate sleep habits to him. For some reason my father wasn't comfortable leaving the house until he had me in an upright position, so inevitably somewhere between ten and eleven o'clock in a fit of frustration he would burst into my room and yell something like, "What do you think you're doing, young lady?" My father is a big man, and he rarely yells. When he does the noise is not only surprising but capable of making a bed shake. I know, because between the ages of fourteen and eighteen I often went from dead sleep to a near heart attack in the course of a few seconds when my father woke me up.

In the kitchen I take flour out of the cupboard, and then cane sugar, confectioners' sugar, vanilla extract, vegetable oil, and baking powder. I find eggs, milk, and butter in the refrigerator. I work slowly, first with the ceiling light on, and then, as the sun rises further, with the light off. I stop in the middle of mixing to make myself a piece of toast with butter and strawberry jam. I need to eat every couple hours now or I get dizzy. After I've eaten I pull out the blender and mix the ingredients I've measured. I have to stand a good distance from the counter because of my belly.

I've realized from trial and error how important it is for me to do some kind of activity during these early-morning hours before anyone else is up. This is dangerous thinking time, because if I let myself go in bad directions, then by seven o'clock I will be so upset and depressed that I end up back in bed for the rest of the day. In order to make sure I do eventually take a shower and change out of my bathrobe or Papa's sweater, I have to tread carefully from five-thirty to seven in the morning. I can't let my thoughts fly all over the place—there is plenty of time for that later when I am in the car or visiting Gram, when I am well embedded in the flow of the day.

I am sitting at the kitchen table icing the three individual layers of the cake when Lila finally comes downstairs. She is wearing the plain shorts and T-shirt she calls pajamas. I started a pot of coffee for her a half hour ago; she pours a cup and sits across from me.

"Smells like childhood in here," she says.

"Not ours. I don't remember ever coming home to the smell of a cake baking. I made this from a cookbook I bought at a yard sale last month. Do you think the baby can smell this?"

"I doubt it." Lila rubs at her eyes. "Today's the big day," she says. "You must be excited."

I smile. "It's hard to contain myself."

"I should hope so. Mom had me folding napkins in the shape of diapers yesterday afternoon. You now owe me so much that even if you focus your energy only on that for the rest of your life, you will never be able to repay me."

"I know this is Mom we're talking about," I say, pushing the knife, fat with white icing, across the top of the top layer of the cake. "But still I don't understand why, if this shower isn't supposed to be a surprise and she's throwing it, she hasn't mentioned it to me. She could have left a message on the machine if she didn't want to talk to me. I feel like she's actually throwing the shower for someone else, and I'm going to be embarrassed when I waddle in and see another pregnant girl there holding the presents."

"Pregnant woman, you mean."

I fight the urge to plunge the knife into the cake, cut out a massive piece, and cram it into my mouth. "Whatever."

"Well, I can assure you that I wouldn't have folded napkins into the shape of diapers for anyone else."

"Mmm. Are you going to tell Mom and Dad you dropped out of school? Because I'd appreciate it if you made the announcement during the shower, to take the attention off of me."

"Not going to happen," Lila says calmly. "Speaking of occupations, you haven't been going into work much lately."

I concentrate on spreading the icing evenly. "Grayson's been away at a conference, so I'm working from home. He's back now, though. I invited him to the shower. Hey"—I point the knife at her—"why don't you invite Weber?"

"I did."

"Really?"

Lila gives a strange smile. "Actually, I sent the invitation with the return address as the Christian Home for the Elderly so he would think Gram was inviting him. He loves Gram."

I nod in approval. The stakes are being raised all around me. My malaise has been slowly lifting over the past few days. I climb out of bed every morning with a little more energy and a little less fear. Even though I don't know what exactly to do, I am now ready to take action. This change is due at least partly to the fact that my body is humming with greater motion beneath me. The baby kicks and squirms and tumbles through the days and nights. I have sudden

cramps and backaches and hot flashes. I can feel this baby warming up
to take the final leap and join the world. The least I can do is try to
keep up.

As USUAL, I arrive early at the hospital. Lila and I planned to meet
by the vending machine outside the emergency area. From there it is
only a quick elevator ride and a short walk to the room where the
birthing classes are held. This is our third class. During the first class
we watched an utterly horrific movie showing a birth in far too much
detail. The second class was a lecture on the importance of nutrition
and vitamins while pregnant. The third class is supposed to concern
breathing.

Of course, it was the first class, and more specifically the film, that
has stayed with me. I remember the pregnant woman writhing on the
bed, huge and swollen and screaming for help from the seemingly anes-
thetized doctors and nurses around her. Then the camera moves in for
a close-up on the woman's vagina, which also looks angry, red and gap-
ing, stretched well beyond reasonable limits by this baby whose head is
clearly far too big to make its way out of the available exit. It looks,
frankly, like a tragedy waiting to happen, death to both mother and
child. But then, miraculously, the baby's head pushes through the hole,
and his body wriggles free after him. The doctor holds the limp red
thing and suctions out its mouth and nose, at which time the baby starts
screaming for help from the numb doctors and nurses and the
exhausted, deflated woman collapsed on the bed with her legs spread-
eagle.

I lean against the vending machine, look down at my swollen
stomach, and shudder. I cannot believe how soon this baby is coming.
I don't even own a crib yet. I don't have any of the necessary items.
This is due partly to the fact that I have only gotten one check from
Gram over the last three months and I can't afford to buy furniture.
Grayson has offered money, but somehow in my gut it doesn't seem
right to take it from him. I'm sure I will change my mind and get off

that high horse soon. But money is only part of it. I haven't gone into the baby stores because I didn't really believe until recently that this choice to stay pregnant and not have another abortion was anything other than that. It was a moral choice, a character-building choice. Wasn't that enough? Do I actually have to deal with *having* a baby as well?

I step back and look at what the vending machine has to offer. It is filled with foods that are terrible for both mother and child: Doritos, Lay's potato chips, Snickers, Oreos, Skittles, Whoppers, Milk Duds. It seems peculiar that they plant candy and soda machines all over a hospital, a place that is supposed to promote and fight for good health. I fish coins out of my purse and select the Oreos. I press the buttons and watch the package fall off its shelf to the basin at the bottom. It takes me a while to bend down and then come back up again with the cookies in hand, and it is only then that I notice someone watching me in the reflection of the shiny vending machine. The outline doesn't look like Lila, so I turn quickly around.

I see only the back of the person, who is now near the other end of the long hall. His head is down and he is moving fast, but there is no mistaking who it is. I recognize Joel's tight kicklike walk, and his shaggy brown hair. He is wearing a blue blazer and khakis instead of his usual uniform of jeans and a T-shirt. I wonder if I should call after him and tell him that he can look at my stomach openly if he wants to. He doesn't have to sneak up on me from behind and then run away. But I realize that it's Margaret he's scared of, not me. Joel wouldn't want Margaret to find out from one of her many gossip connections that he was seen talking to his ex-girlfriend, who is pregnant with his child. That wouldn't bode well for me, either. God only knows the kind of Dear Abby letter I would get from Margaret after that. The letter would probably arrive, à la *The Godfather,* with the bleeding head of a horse.

Joel disappears through a set of swinging doors. Stranded in the center of the hallway looking at a place where the father of my child used to be, holding a pack of Oreos, feeling the weight of every one of the thirty-eight pounds I have gained, I suddenly feel very alone.

Lila is late, sneaking into the hospital in a baggy sweatshirt and baseball hat. We grab the first elevator and then run down the hallway, me holding my stomach, but we're still late for class. We take seats on the floor because that's where everyone else is. The teacher comes over and fusses with us until we are in the correct position. I sit between Lila's legs. The teacher tips me backward until I am lying against Lila, my head beneath her chin. My legs are bent at the knees. The teacher's adjustments are so quick that when she walks away it is a shock to find ourselves in this state. I can feel my sister's breasts push into my back. Her thighs wrap around me. Her breath is hot against my ear. It occurs to me that this is physically the closest I have been to another human being since the last time I had sex.

"I can't believe I am fucking doing this," Lila says.

Lila's warm breath on my ear and her saying "fucking" and the fact that my legs are spread and that I haven't had sex or even touched anyone in six months makes me start to giggle. The noise is a bit hysterical and high-pitched and sounds like my mother's laugh when she is with her brothers and sisters. The giggling tickles me from the inside out, and the tickling keeps me going.

"Gracie," Lila says.

I look up and see the teacher, a plump woman well past childbearing years, glaring at me, and all of the couples in the class, collapsed on the floor in similar positions to Lila and me, watching. There are seven other couples, and each one is made up of a pregnant woman and a male coach. They are looking at me, wedged between my sister's thighs, as if they are considering calling a family services agency and having my baby removed from my immoral, negligent care before he or she is even born.

"Sorry," I mutter to the room at large.

"Now, class," the teacher says. "Let's get to work on that breathing. The breath is the key to a beautiful childbirth experience. I want both mommies and coaches to follow along. This is the breath that I want you to practice at home, and whenever you feel stressed and achy. This will be the foundation of your labor; this is what will save you from the pain. Come on now, here we go, it's two short breaths in and one long release breath out. Hee-hee-hoo. Hee-hee-hoo."

"Hee-hee-hoo," the class says.

"Hee-hee-hoo," Lila says into my ear.

The baby gives me a mighty kick in the stomach then, which seems like a clear message that I am in trouble. This strikes me as rather obnoxious, because I didn't need the air knocked out of me to learn that. I have no time to recover because the teacher is still looking doubtfully in my direction as if she has the number for the Department of Youth and Family Services on speed dial. I struggle through the pain for a breath. My first effort is more of a wheeze than anything else. I am trying to follow along and not stand out from the group, who are deep-breathing as though their lives depend on it. But as hard as I try and as deep down in my lungs as I reach, there is no force to my breath. There is no conviction, no strength, no faith that this is going to save me from anything. "Hee-hee-hoo."

AFTER CLASS I am tempted to go home, change back into my pajamas, and climb into bed. But there is a party later, and I have vowed to take action and not spend all my time in the house, so instead I stop home just long enough to pick up the white iced cake and then continue on to my parents'. I drive slowly these days because I don't feel entirely confident sitting as far away from the steering wheel as my belly demands. I can't reach well enough to wrap my hands around the wheel, only the tops of my fingers.

I think of Gram giving up driving, and wonder if this is how she felt before she handed over her keys, just barely in control. The thought of Gram makes my back ache and I have to work to stay upright and in contact with the wheel. You'll see her this afternoon, I tell myself. She is the reason you didn't fight the idea of this ridiculous shower. This will mean something to Gram. She will want to give the baby a gift. It might be money.

I pull into my parents' driveway and park behind my mother's convertible. I get out of the car and then lean back in for the home-made cake. When I am upright with my purse looped around my elbow and the cake balanced on my palms, I notice how humid and sticky the day is. The sky is overcast and after two minutes I feel sweat run down my back between my shoulder blades. I am not dressed for the party yet, thank goodness. I am wearing shorts and a huge T-shirt. I have set aside my one maternity sundress for the event. It is light blue and clean, so I figure it should make my mother happy and keep Meggy quiet and kill Angel's last hopes. Not that I should be scared of them anymore. For God's sake, I am getting married. I will be giving this child a mother and a father, and that is all I need in order to fight my family off, right?

I walk around to the back of the house with cautious steps, wondering how to break the news to my mother. Remember Grayson? He's one of my ex-boyfriends who you did know about, remember? Well, he's asked me to marry him and I've said yes.

I think she will be happy. This is good, solid, presentable news that she can share with her women's group and her family. I think this should go all right. I open the back door and then pause to kick off my flip-flops. I leave them on the tile floor next to my mother's favorite sandals and a pair of my father's shoes that I've never seen before. I place the cake on the kitchen counter and then, out of habit, look in their refrigerator. There is not much normal food to pick at, because the space is filled with plastic catering platters filled with crudités and bite-size sandwiches and three different kinds of cookies. I grab a bottle of water off the door of the refrigerator and walk into the hall. I am just about to call out my mother's name when I see movement and a flash of color from the corner of my eye. I unscrew the water bottle as I look into the living room. I expect to see my mother walking toward me, or to see her reading in one of the chairs. I take a deep breath, and tell myself that I can have an adult conversation with her. I can do this.

But what I see is my mother standing in the middle of the living room pressed up against a man who is not my father. This man is shorter than my father, and he is overweight with dark slicked-back hair. My mother's hands are on the nape of this man's neck; she has her fingers in his hair. As I watch, she lifts her face off his chest. It is my mother, but she looks different than I have ever seen her. She has a changed, softened face. She is crying, her cheeks are wet, and then she is kissing this man. Her lips are pressed against his. His hands are moving around the small of her back. I know kisses, and this is the unhurried, soft kind that leads straight to the nearest bed.

My heart is beating so hard I can hear it in my ears. I am afraid the couple in the living room can hear it, too. I feel wetness on my stomach and notice that I have spilled half of the water bottle on myself and the floor. There is a dark spot on the beige carpet in front of my feet. I take a few tiptoed steps backward, until I am safely in the kitchen. I stand there in the half-dark for a full minute. I am shaking, and I wonder what I should do.

No answers come, except that I have to leave. I am certain that if my mother knew I saw her, she would never forgive me. I know that in this moment, as well as I know anything. I reach into my purse and pull out the Happy Anniversary card I bought to go with the cake. Still shaking, I pick up the cake and drop it and the card into the garbage bin under the sink. The white icing sticks and slides down the side of the plastic bag. The cake folds in half slowly and deliberately before it comes to rest on top of coffee grounds and a milk container.

I look down at the cake for a minute, amazed that I have done this. I think this may be the most aggressive thing I have ever done, after deciding to keep this baby. The sight makes the crazy giggles start up in my stomach again. I clamp my hand over my mouth, tiptoe to the door, and gather up my flip-flops. Barefoot, I leave the house. But when I turn to close the door behind me, I lose my balance. I reach my hand out to keep myself from falling, and, caught under the full weight of my body, the door slams shut. The noise is amazingly loud. It seems to boom through the entire neighborhood. The giggles rise up through me then, like bubbles swimming for the surface, and I let go.

Hugging my flip-flops to my chest, choking on laughter, I run awkwardly down the back steps, across the top of the back lawn, and down the burning-hot driveway. It occurs to me as I huff and puff and snort, my heart pounding so hard I have to worry about whether this is bad for the baby, that this is the second time I have run today, after months of near complete inactivity. I may well be headed toward a heart attack, or something worse I don't yet know the name of. With all the grace of a St. Bernard, I hurl myself into the car, turn on the engine, and reverse until I am on the street. I don't allow myself to look back as I drive away, because I can't bear to see my mother and Mayor Carrelli staring out at me from the living-room window.

FOR TWENTY minutes I drive up and down the streets in my parents' neighborhood. The giggles have died away and left me weak but focused. I repeatedly pass the access roads that lead to their block. At first I am not aware of what I'm doing. I'm busy getting my breath and heart under control. I concentrate on the idea that there is someone else in my body and that I have to be cautious for her. My fingers keep sweating, which seems odd. I wipe them off on my T-shirt and return them to the wheel. I study each car that passes. When I am able to think clearly, I know that I am looking for my father. I am watching for his pickup truck. I need to keep him from turning onto his street, into his driveway. I need to stop him at all costs. I decide that if I see my father I will honk and wave and gesture for him to follow me. I don't know where I will take him, but I can figure that out when the time comes. I have no doubt that he would follow. He would follow Lila or me anywhere. He would think I needed him and he would never disappoint me.

But on one of my swings past my parents' street, I see a familiar-looking beat-up Honda paused at the entrance as if deciding whether to turn left or right. It is the mayor's car. I recognize it because sometimes Joel had to drive it on one of his spying missions or to bring it to the shop. I can see the shape of the mayor's dog in the backseat. I didn't see the car near my parents' house while I was there; the mayor must have parked it down the street. Perhaps—now that anything was possible—he and my mother meet like this every afternoon. Maybe part of the thrill for them is getting away with it in the middle of the day, in my mother's own home, where her husband or her kids could—and finally one did—walk in at any moment.

I drive faster, so the mayor doesn't recognize me. I see only the blur of his dark hair and white face, his stomach pressed against the steering wheel. I don't circle back this time. My mother's lover is gone. There is nothing I can protect my father from now. I keep going, pointed toward home.

When I get there, Lila is still in the oversized sweatshirt and baseball hat, as though she is trying to hide from someone in her own house. She is in the kitchen making iced tea. She points toward the TV room.

"I know," I say, "I saw his car." I watch her for a minute, stirring tea and lemon and honey in the big crystal pitcher Gram gave us when she moved into the assisted-living center. She adds the ice cubes last. I am waiting to see if I am going to tell her what I just saw at Mom and Dad's house. But nothing comes out of my mouth. I can't even begin to think of the words it would take to explain.

I say, "I wasn't able to talk to Mom."

"That's the problem with Mom," she says. "Nobody can."

I watch Lila mix the tea with a big wooden spoon for another moment, then go into the TV room. Grayson is sitting on the couch holding the remote. The TV is not on. I know he was eavesdropping, listening to Lila and me talk, trying to gather information.

"Now's not a good time," I say. "I have to get ready."

He looks me over with stunned eyes. "Look how big you are," he says.

"Thanks a lot." I know I look disgusting. I have sweated through my T-shirt in places. My hair has gone flat; it is sticking to my neck.

"I'm not leaving," he says. "You invited me to the shower on my answering machine. You haven't returned my calls since I got back from Seattle."

"What is there to say back to an invitation?"

"We have to talk, Gracie, and not in front of your entire family. We need to make plans."

When he says that, I have the image of a seat belt being fastened. I hear the final click as metal hits metal. I feel tired, and sit down in the nearest chair.

"Do you need something?" Grayson asks. He leans forward, still holding the remote control. "Some water? You look pale."

"I could have this baby at any time," I tell him, but really I am telling myself. I just realized it today for the first time, during birthing class, while driving, in the hallway watching my mother kiss Mayor Carrelli, lowering myself heavily into this chair. Time is moving by so fast, spinning me, flipping me along like a leaf on an empty sidewalk. I need to put my foot down. "We should get married soon," I say. "Maybe this week."

"This week? All right . . . sure. We can go down to the county courthouse." Grayson gathers himself. He is not used to me meeting him anywhere near halfway. I wonder what he will say when I tell him I've been sending out my résumé in an effort to get more freelance writing work, to supplement my *Bergen Record* income. I've even been looking over the journal I've kept while pregnant, wondering whether it might be publishable. I think it might be. I think it might be of interest to other young women.

"I can take care of the license," he says. "I know someone in the department. We'll just show up at the courthouse and do this and then you'll move in with me. We can invite family to the ceremony, or not. But you're right, it needs to be done. It's important that we get married before our baby is born."

He sees the look I give him. "We're getting married, so it is our baby, Gracie. I will be the baby's father. You know very well that Joel has no interest in being involved."

"I never asked him," I say. "Did you?"

He looks down at his hands, and I realize that he did. I should have known. Grayson is thorough; he does his research. He probably felt Joel out before he proposed to me the second time. It is a strange thought.

I rarely think of Joel; I don't want him in my life. But still, it is a different thing altogether to know that he told Grayson he wanted nothing to do with us, the baby and me.

"Gracie?"

"There's one more thing," I say. "We'll live here. I don't want to move."

He takes off his glasses and then puts them back on, something I have seen him do during meetings when he is caught off guard. "You want me to move in with you and your sister? I have a great apartment overlooking the Hudson River and the city. We can have our privacy. There's a second bedroom for the baby."

"Maybe later," I say. "I want to bring my baby home to my house."

"Have you discussed this with your sister?"

I shake my head. "No."

Grayson studies me. I know he doesn't understand what is going on in my head and that that excites him. He enjoys the challenge. I know that I have already done the worst thing I can do to him by shutting him out these past few weeks. Nothing I say to him can be as bad as the silence, the absence of information. "So, this week?" he says. "We're really going to do it?"

His words sound odd to my ears, because there is no question. This is simply the right decision, the safe decision, the only decision. This is my leap forward. The baby thumps hard in my belly. "Yes," I say. "This week."

Then, our conversation over, something resolved, I go upstairs. I strip off my clothes and stand under a stream of cold water in the shower. I just stand there at first, eyes shut. My mind flicks past the image of my mother and the mayor kissing, then the sight of me sleeping beside Grayson, then the scary video of a birth I saw at the hospital. None of the images are upsetting; I feel instead as if I'm watching someone else's life. The pictures fall away as suddenly as they appeared, and all that is left is the cold water against my skin. The patter of drops, the coolness, the wet.

Then, slowly, my hands start moving. It takes a moment for me to realize what I'm doing. My hands have set out to cover the extensive groundwork of my body. Starting first with the face, then moving to the neck, the shoulders, the breasts, then lingering over the swollen belly. No inch of skin is left untouched. It takes a long time. My fingers stroking, memorizing, documenting, greeting, accepting.

LILA

I arrive at my parents' house an hour before the party, as instructed. I am wearing a sundress, because my mother asked me to. She wanted me to show up early so I could help with last minute setup, but as with all gatherings hosted by my mother, there is nothing to do. She is so organized and prepared that everything has been taken care of. During every Christmas afternoon in my life, while other families raced around the kitchen, passing pots and pans and checking the roast, wondering if they would be ready in time for their guests, my family was silently lounging in our party clothes, flipping through magazines and newspapers and waiting for the doorbell to ring.

The party platters were dropped off this morning by the caterers, and the flowers have been set out. I folded the napkins decoratively yesterday, and my father bought pastel-colored balloons. There is a cake in the shape of a rattle in the downstairs refrigerator. My mother is upstairs taking a shower and my father has disappeared.

I wander through the house. I want to keep moving. I am nervous, with all of the symptoms: butterflies in my stomach, mild diarrhea, dry mouth. I went to the registrar's office this week and filled out the three forms necessary to drop out of medical school. The head registrar, a square-faced woman in her forties, seemed very happy to tell me that I am the only student in the last decade to drop out at the beginning of the fourth year. It seems that the students in their fine institution who have made it as far as I did—three-quarters of the way—usually manage to hang in there.

I e-mailed Belinda, because it seemed right to let her know that her arch nemesis had left the picture, making her number one by default. I can't deny that that bothers me, a little. I enjoyed kicking Belinda's ass. I'll need to find a new hobby, a new punching bag. I'll also need to find a job. The registrar has alerted the Office of Student Loans that I am no longer in school, and so I will need to begin paying off my debt. I have no idea what I am going to do.

Lately, I haven't done much. I've watched TV, eaten a lot of Cheddar-flavored Goldfish crackers, and sat on the back porch in the sun. I've put on big, shapeless clothes and a hat and gone to birthing classes with Gracie. Those moments in the hospital, incognito, sitting with my legs wrapped around my sister listening to the detailed description—a horror story really—of what it feels like to give birth, have been like an out-of-body experience. How did I end up there? What made me think I could coach Gracie through this? How could I possibly be of any help?

Whenever I am in my car I go out of my way to drive down Main Street. I pass the hardware store at a slow crawl and look up at Weber's apartment. During the daytime it is difficult for me to tell if he's home because the sun is so bright that he has to be standing directly in front of his window for me to be sure. I can check to see if his truck is parked in back, and sometimes I do, but that isn't a foolproof method of detection. Weber often walks to the firehouse, plus he has this ridiculous habit of lending his truck to anyone who asks to borrow it.

At night it is easier. I just have to look for a light in the window. I have to hope he is in there alone. I know he might not be. After all, he picked me up at the Green Trolley and brought me home even though he disliked me at the time. Now he dislikes me again, so why wouldn't he bring home a new girl? Is he saying "Waka waka" into someone else's ear? I know that he hates sleeping alone. When he wakes up in the middle of the night, he automatically starts talking, and he likes to have someone there to listen.

I have wondered, sitting in my car parked on the side of Main Street, if seeing me for who I really was depressed Weber. I wondered if he cared enough to feel that intensely about me. I can't be sure that I made that much of an impact on him. Weber is so sure and complete in himself, with his crazy ideas and his beliefs and his enjoyment of life. I think that to him I was just company, sex, and a sparring partner. He grew more sure of himself, more pleased with himself, less needful of anyone else, in the face of my relative cynicism.

Besides, there's another reason he could not possibly have cared as much as it turned out I did. The trick is that I don't have a choice. Since the fire, I have cared more every minute. There is no escaping my memory, and now I know that I was right all those years to avoid anything verging on a relationship, to push the boys away before there was even a chance of one getting close. Because now, with Weber, I remember word for word every conversation we had. I remember everywhere we went, every street we drove down. I remember each time we made love and how the sheets rubbed against my skin and how warm or cold the air was. I remember exactly how it felt when he touched me here, and there, and the goose bumps it gave me when he kissed me in that place. I remember the light in his face after the fire. Every second, every moment is tattooed into my brain.

I need to restart my life and try to experience it this time around. I need to figure out what makes my face light up, and then try to make money doing it. The catch is that I am not good at the here and now. I tried to get out of my car and walk up to Weber's apartment and approach him, but I couldn't. It took me two weeks to come up with the idea of sending him the shower invitation with Gram's return address. I can only hope there aren't disastrous results.

I TRAIL through my parents' house wishing there was something for me to do. Something to keep me occupied until Weber either does or does not show up. I spot a crumpled-up napkin under the kitchen table and make a dive for it. I squeeze it in the palm of my hand while I cross the room. I smile at myself, because this level of excitement over this small a task is pathetic. I stop by the garbage pail and drop the napkin into the bag. Even the garbage bins are empty in this house.

"Mom?" I yell. I heard the shower water turn off a few minutes earlier.

"Yes?" Her voice comes from upstairs at the far end of the hall. "Is someone here already? It's too early!"

"No one's here. Is there anything I can do to help get ready?"

"To help?" Her voice is closer now. She appears in the kitchen doorway. She is wearing a polka-dot sundress with a belted waist. It's a dress I haven't seen before. It looks like a dress from a past era. Occasionally, like now, the sight of my mother is a surprise. I forget that she is in her fifties. I can see the blueprint for her face as an old woman etched in the lines around her eyes and mouth. Someday it will be my responsibility to take care of her in the same way she is now taking care of Gram.

She glances over the kitchen. She looks distracted. "There must be something you can do. Why not take out the cheese platter, so the cheese can soften."

I go to the refrigerator and take out the plastic catering tray. I take off the lid and place it on the counter. Then my mother and I are left staring at each other again. I can't think of anything safe to talk about. I have no intention of telling her about medical school today. I won't drop that bombshell until I have a new life plan to present at the same time.

"Where's Dad?"

"Buying ice at the supermarket." Mom gives a small half-smile and says, "Do you know what today is?"

It is August 2, which is her and my father's wedding anniversary, but I'm sure she isn't referring to that. My parents haven't done much to acknowledge or celebrate their anniversary the last few years, and from the way I've seen them treat each other lately, I doubt this is the year they'd choose to draw attention to the event. My mother is probably thinking of something corny, like it is the first day in our family's relationship with the new baby. She has been on a sappy streak since she told me about this shower and asked me to help. She has tears in her eyes right now.

She says, "It's your father's and my anniversary."

"Happy Anniversary," I say. I wait to see if there's more.

She sighs heavily, as if I am trying her patience. "I want today to go really well. Can you please help me make *that* happen?"

That's what I want, too. "Sure," I say. "I'll try."

GRAM AND Nurse Ballen arrive first. It is strange to see Gram make her way across the lawn with a walker. It is slow, unsteady work, and Nurse Ballen keeps her hand on the small of Gram's back. It occurs to me that this is part of what I didn't like about medicine. I don't want to put my hand on a stranger's back. I don't want to ease a patient through a slow recovery or a slow descent. I am not interested in slow, period.

I watch the sluggish course of Gram and her nurse with something that feels like regret in the pit of my stomach. "Go help them," my mother hisses. We are both standing awkwardly at the door. Gram has not been here since before her fall, since she was well and able to walk briskly on her own. This is a new sight for us.

"They don't need my help," I say, and go back in the house. I am sure Gram doesn't want my mother and me watching as she maneuvers the three front steps.

I kiss Gram on the cheek once she is safely inside. "What's up with you?" I say.

She smiles at my informal speech, as I knew she would. Then she looks me over. I haven't been to see her for a few weeks. She nods at my sundress, then turns her attention to my face. Her eyes scour mine. This is the kind of attention Gram used to show me on a regular basis, before she became preoccupied, first with Gracie's baby and then with her own health after her fall. It makes me realize how much I have missed being truly seen.

I am not surprised when her response to the once-over is to ask, "How's school?"

"School's school," I say.

"And your classes at the hospital with Gracie?"

"Good."

"Good."

"I miss being in the hospital on a daily basis," Nurse Ballen says. "The hustle and bustle."

Gram nods in Nurse Ballen's direction. She says, "You'll be back there soon enough."

Her tone is light, and strangely intimate, as if she and this nurse already have inside jokes and shared inferences. Could Gram possibly be joking about her death? All of this seems unlikely, as Gram isn't a joker and it's not like her to take the time to get to know someone outside of the family. Even within the family, she has her favorites, her own hierarchy of those deserving attention.

As if she hears my thoughts, Gram says, "I'm so glad you are doing this for your sister, Lila. She's always needed more help than you."

I know I made it look that way. But it wasn't true. It isn't true.

My mother's voice rings out from the kitchen. "Lila, did you ask everyone what they would like to drink? Tell them we have wine, lemonade, iced tea, Crystal Light, and sodas."

I look at Gram and Nurse Ballen. Gram is seated in the big armchair that used to be Papa's. Nurse Ballen and I are both standing. I say, "We have wine, lemonade, iced tea, Crystal Light, and sodas."

They both request lemonade, and I head into the kitchen. By the time I walk back out, Meggy and Angel are here. Then, a moment later, Theresa and Mary pull up. I watch each of the women bend down over the sides of the old armchair and kiss Gram. My aunts have dark circles under their eyes and the look of women who only had time to blow-dry part of their hair that morning. I walk to and from the window and watch the street outside.

Meggy says, "Dina was sorry she couldn't make it today."

Mary arranges herself into a cross-legged position on the couch and then gives an uncharacteristic laugh. "Yeah, she'd rather be here than in Sunday double detention."

I look my cousin over. There is something different about her appearance, but it takes me a minute to pick out what it is. She is only wearing one tiny cross instead of her usual three heavy ones. I wonder if Mary is lightening up.

Theresa says, "Has anyone talked to Ryan today? We should stop in and visit him on the way home."

"That place is crawling with weirdos," Meggy says. "There was an old man who introduced himself as Dr. Kevorkian when I visited. It's not somewhere I want to spend a lot of time."

"Your brother is getting help there," Gram says. "He's making friends, which is something he never had, not even as a little boy. The Lord works in mysterious ways."

This shuts everyone up. I swipe a carrot stick through the onion dip and stick it in my mouth. I watch Mary untangle herself from her cross-legged position on the couch. She puts a cracker, some cheese, and a few olives on a napkin and then curls back up in her corner.

My mother calls out from the kitchen, "Gracie should be here any minute."

Meggy says, "You let her drive here by herself? Shouldn't someone have picked her up? It's not exactly safe to be behind the wheel in your ninth month."

"That's true," Angel says. "The belly is too close to the steering wheel at that stage."

Theresa says, "Jack never let me drive when I was pregnant. He forbade it."

"Sure, when he was home," Meggy says. "But what about when he was out God knows where doing God knows what and you had to get to the supermarket?"

"Careful with the name of the Lord," Gram says.

"Don't say those things in front of Mary," Theresa says.

"Mary is old enough to hear the truth."

Mary looks as if she might have something to say for herself, but my mother cuts her off. Her voice is a combination of flustered and defensive. "Gracie is twenty-nine years old. I can't forbid her to do anything. What do you expect me to do, be her chauffeur?"

She looks at Meggy nervously, as if she half-expects the answer to be yes.

"Don't worry," I say. "Gracie's not coming here alone. Grayson's with her, so he'll probably drive."

There is a muffled hum in the room as the women absorb this piece of news.

"Were men invited to the shower?"

"Is Gracie dating?"

"Someone other than the baby's father?"

I almost speak up to explain that Grayson is simply Gracie's boss and friend. But there seems to be little point in jumping in. I need to save my energy, and Gracie can handle the aunts' questions when she gets here. I no longer doubt that she can. Gram is wrong; my sister does not need my help. She is stronger than she looks.

"Stuffed mushrooms?" A heavy platter is balanced on my mother's hands. She glares at me. I am not being what she considers helpful.

"I hope this baby comes soon," Gram says. She is sitting in the corner, but her presence there has made it the center of the group. Except for Mary, we are clustered around Gram, some standing, some sitting. Nurse Ballen is standing beside her chair. She seems vaguely uncomfortable. She has the look of someone who is trying to pretend that she is not in the room, and certainly not listening. She emanates: *I am on duty, and nothing more.*

"Noreen, won't you please sit down?" my mother says.

"I'm fine, thank you. I sit all day. It's nice to be on my feet."

I press my fingers against the pane of glass. I watch my father pull into the driveway in his truck. I watch Grayson's black sedan parallel-park into the space between my aunts' cars at the curb. I watch Grayson hold on to Gracie's elbow as she and her round stomach bob slowly across the lawn.

The windowpane, which was at first cold to my touch, grows warm. Just before I take my hand away, my sister looks up, sees me, and waves. She thinks I am at the window for her, to greet her, to perpetuate her belief that she is the center of every story. She is a little selfish in that way. My story fits only in the margin, scrawled in poor handwriting around the typewritten, spell-checked account of her life. Mine is thrown together at the last minute, secured with tape and spit, while hers is as real and substantial as the hard, round belly she holds in front of her. She will soon have a child, but she has a job and a lot of support; I am a dropout struggling to get back together with someone I used to sleep with. I can't believe it, but I am actually jealous of Gracie.

Gram says, "It didn't used to be like this. There was a much smaller gap between generations. Women had more children, and they had them younger. Families didn't have to wait so long between babies. It's the waiting time that's hard. You lose your hope, and you lose sight of the point, when there are no young ones." Gram's purse sits on her lap, and she rests her glass of lemonade on the leather bag. I can see a ring of wetness beginning to form on the fabric. In the past Gram never would have done something so untidy and careless. The bag will be ruined.

She says, "A family needs the old, the young, and the infants. When you only have two out of the three, it doesn't work." Gram nods at the cluster of daughters around her. "I know some of you girls have been fighting over this baby. We all have. But we don't need to fight. You'll see when the child is born."

Gracie walks in then, with Grayson behind her. My sister is wearing a light blue maternity dress, and her hair is up in a ponytail. She looks like a pale young girl who has swallowed a basketball.

Everyone regards her. Mom puts the tray of stuffed mushrooms down on the coffee table so quickly, I wonder if she's afraid she might drop it. I hear my father come in through the back door and take off his boots and place them on the tile floor.

"Sweet Jesus," Meggy says. "That baby looks ready to come out."

"I think we're getting there," Gracie says. Her voice is shy. She has been mostly alone or with me for the latter part of her pregnancy. I'm sure she is startled by the attention, and is unsure whether it's friendly. I want to tell her that I've been charting the swing of moods and that I think the combination of Gram's speech and her appearance have softened all of the McLaughlin women to the core. For the moment, anyway.

Mom sounds practically giddy when she says, "I read about a few shower games in a magazine, and we're all going to start a pool on when we think the baby will be born. Hold on one minute, and I'll go get the pieces of paper where you each have to write your guess for the date, time of birth, sex, and weight."

"How much is the pot?" Meggy asks, but my mother is already gone.

"Grayson," Theresa says in a polite, let's-dig-for-dirt voice, "are you Gracie's birth coach?"

"Yes," Grayson says.

"Um, no," Gracie says quickly.

"It's probably the birth father," Angel says in a low voice to Meggy, but everyone hears her.

"Lila is the coach," Gracie says with an apologetic look at the man standing next to her. "I asked Lila weeks ago."

"Really?" Mom is back in the room, her hands filled with pieces of white paper.

"Isn't that lovely?" Gram says.

Confusion clouds Grayson's face. He turns to Gracie. "I should be the coach. I can't be your husband waiting outside in the hall with the rest of your family. I need to be in the delivery room."

The air leaves the room then, as effectively as if Grayson had used the last bit up. My aunts gape like fish. My mother says, "Your husband?"

"You're *marrying* him?" I say. I can't believe what I've heard. I can't believe I'm finding out something this big at the same time as Mom.

Meggy says, "Isn't this interesting."

Mary gives her second laugh of the afternoon, then claps her hands over her mouth.

Gram says, "Gracie?"

Gracie gives Grayson a look that makes it clear that the timing of the announcement did not go according to plan. At least not according to her plan.

"We're getting married," Gracie says in a reluctant voice.

"On Thursday, at the Hackensack courthouse. You're all invited." Grayson is as pale as Gracie now. He's not used to surprises. He likes to be prepared. I wonder how well he is going to fare making a life with my sister.

My father appears at the doorway to the living room then, clearly having heard this last part. His appearance is so sudden that he frightens Nurse Ballen, who visibly flinches.

My mother looks as if she's afraid she's going to drop the pieces of paper. She grips them so hard, I see her knuckles turn white. But she is the first to speak. Her voice tilts toward excited and gets faster as she goes along. "You're going to be married," she says. "What a surprise! Grayson, you're the editor of the *Bergen Record,* aren't you? Louis, you knew Grayson's father. Remember?"

"Yes," my father says. "I remember." He looks stunned in a bad way, as if he has now had one more shock than he could take.

"Why are you doing this?" Gram asks, her searching eyes turned on Gracie. "Are you in love?"

The room is quiet, but still I am sure that I am the only one who hears another vehicle pull to a stop out front. I edge around the group, hoping to escape without my mother's notice, without anyone's notice. I hear my sister, caught by Gram the same way I was earlier, choose to lie as well. "Yes," she says. "Well . . . why else would we be getting married?"

"You don't have to do this. I told you I would take care of everything." Gram's voice sounds weak and is lost beneath the noise of my aunts, who have finally found their tongues.

"You were such a quiet girl growing up," Meggy says. "Who knew you would provide this family with such excitement. A baby and a wedding to someone other than the baby's father, all in one year. Well done."

Theresa nods, seeming to agree in all seriousness with Meggy's sar-
castic comments.

"Oh Gracie, you should let your husband be your birth coach."
There are tears in Angel's eyes. I wonder if they are from sadness,
because she has now lost any chance of raising this baby. "That would
be such a perfect opportunity for him to bond with the newborn."

My mother gives Meggy a look. "A wedding should put all of your
ridiculousness to rest." She is as high as a kite, envisioning endings that
make sense to her, that she can work with. "Maybe you should have a
proper wedding, Gracie, in a church? Why have a rushed ceremony at
the courthouse? We could plan a wonderful wedding."

This is the last thing I hear as I make it undetected out of the room,
down the front hall, and out the door just in time to stop Weber from
ringing the bell.

HE IS standing on the front step with his hand raised. He takes a step
backward when I appear, and makes room for me on the top step.

"Hi," he says.

"Hi." We are standing very close together and I can smell him. He
always smells like a sandy beach, like salt water and waves. He is wearing a sports coat and a tie. I have only seen him in jeans and one of his
many T-shirts, or his fireman's uniform. Today he looks like a boy
dressed up as a man. Even his crew cut appears neatly combed. He has
a wrapped present under his arm.

"I've never been to a baby shower before," he says. "I didn't know
what to wear."

I am pleased that my voice sounds fairly normal. "I wasn't sure
you'd come."

"I thought it would be bad karma to turn down an invitation from
your grandmother."

"Oh." It occurs to me that maybe I should have worried about bad
karma when I asked him to come here with a lie. The least I can do at
this point is be honest. I have nothing to lose. Weber can't even bear

to look at me. He is here because of my grandmother. Never underestimate the power of Gram.

"I sent the invitation," I say. "I put my grandmother's return address on it because I didn't think you'd come if you knew it was from me. Are you dating anyone?" The last question slips out, a surprise that makes my face burn.

"No." Weber looks at me now. He seems to be blushing as well. "Why did you want me here, Lila?"

"So we could talk." I think, Be more specific. "So I could apologize."

"You could have called. I thought you might, a few weeks ago."

This stops me. I should have called him. Of course. I'm an idiot. He was waiting for me to call.

The only response I can think to make is: "I dropped out of medical school because of you."

Weber stares at me as if I've lost my mind. "You did what? Why would you do that?"

"It wasn't all because of you . . . it's just that you made me realize . . ." I stop. I can't put into words the emotions that led me from seeing his face at the fire to making things official at the registrar's office. I have no idea where to even start.

"Lila, you said that you didn't care about me." Sweat appears on Weber's forehead almost as soon as he finishes wiping it away. I have the crazy urge to lean in closer and lick the beads of salty water away with my tongue. I want to taste him, to have that taste inside me while we talk.

"I meant it at the time," I say. "I wish you'd kept ignoring me."

"I ignored you at first because I thought you were putting on an act. I could tell you were scared. And I believed we'd been drawn together so that I could show you how good it could be." Weber gives me a sharp look. "See, you can't stand my talking like that, saying that we were drawn together, even now!"

"That's not true," I say, trying to keep my face perfectly composed. "I might agree with you, you might have been right."

"Might have? That's wishy-washy language."

"Are you calling me a liar?"

"I'm trying to tell you why it doesn't matter. Because that day at Dairy Queen I knew that you were talking to me. I mean, you were talking through that girl to me. You were telling me, in a different way, that you really didn't want anyone around you. And I believed you. You were so furious that I had to believe you."

I can feel my brain rushing around, grabbing bits of ideas. "So, you're saying that you were wrong all along? We weren't meant to be together? Your karma and destiny and all that lied to you? You can't believe that."

He seems unbelievably calm. "People have to work to meet their destiny, Lila. I think one of us just didn't work hard enough, that's all."

"But I dropped out of school!"

"So? That has nothing to do with me."

"Yes, it does."

"How?"

I shake my head. How can he expect me to answer these kinds of questions? These kinds of questions are impossible. I say, "You should see the women inside, my mother and my sister and my cousin and my aunts. You think I'm crazy, but they're the crazy ones. I'm sane in comparison to them."

Weber looks everywhere but at me. He looks at the sky and he looks at his shoes and he looks at the present in his hands. His voice sounds as if it's coming from far away. "Maybe we should go in. I can say hello to your grandmother and then I can leave. I know Gracie doesn't want me there. I just remind her of Joel."

I don't want him to go in the house until I've said the right thing. I have to keep trying until I figure out what that is. I say, "I wasn't try-ing to say anything to you through Belinda. I was just being a bitch. I can be a bitch sometimes."

"I didn't know what kind of gift to bring," he says, his eyes on the wrapped box. "I never bought a present for a baby before."

I stop trying then because he has stopped me. He tells me without saying a word that there is nothing else to say in this moment on the front steps of my parents' house. I have exhausted the opportunity. So I step aside and let Weber walk into the blast of air conditioning. Then I follow, the skirt of my sundress in my hands because I need something to hold on to. But as I walk into the cool air toward the women in my family, I feel a strange, surprising hope beat against my ribs. I have the sense that I am walking toward my strength, toward my saving grace. The feeling is inexplicable, but still it feels like the most real thing I have come across in weeks.

I hope, I wish, I think, that somehow these women—my grandmother, my mother, my sister, my cousin, my aunts—will be able to say to this boy what I have not. Will be able to fix what I have broken. Will make clear everything I have convoluted with my memory and my coldness. I hope, wish, think—with no logical reason for doing so, with no precedent to rely on—that they will help me make everything all right.

NOREEN BALLEN

Shortly after Lila and a young man with a crew cut walk into the room, I tap Mrs. McLaughlin on the shoulder to let her know I am going to step outside. It is still a few minutes before I expect my kids, but I am uncomfortable in this close room with the McLaughlin family. In their paleness and their freckles and their fair eyes I see my own family, but these people behave differently than mine ever did. The conversation is stilted, and there are long silences, and everyone looks either upset or worried. I do not belong here; I do not understand the sharp way they speak to one another, and they deserve their privacy.

To draw less attention to myself, I leave through the kitchen. I loop my purse over my shoulder and look over the plastic catering trays balanced on the kitchen counters. There are tight balls of cellophane scattered about. There is the smell of prepared food and the zap of the microwave in the air-conditioned air. When I swing open the back door, I am hit by the heat of the day. It is August in New Jersey, which means hot, sticky weather that makes walking even a few steps a chore. "This air is like molasses," my mother used to say during the Augusts while I was growing up, when there were too many children and not enough space and no air conditioning.

I take off my cardigan as I walk around to the front of the house. I stop under the dogwood blossom tree and breathe in the pink perfumed scent. I don't turn my attention to the street yet, as I have never known Betty Larchmont to be early. I hate to have my neighbor watch the children on a Saturday, as the few hours after camp each day are more than enough, but I felt I had to accompany Mrs. McLaughlin to this party. I was concerned by how excited she had been all week. Her excitement was high-pitched like a child's. She worked feverishly to finish the blanket for the baby, and each afternoon called her daughters to make sure they were coming to the shower. I think she's become aware that there are a limited number of family gatherings left to her.

I wanted to be on hand today to keep her from overtiring herself. She argued with me at first. She said she wasn't interested in paying me for a Saturday and that she didn't want to show up at Kelly's house with a nurse. She said she didn't need the help. But I have found that the best way to deal with her is to not argue back, but to just go ahead and do what I need to do. That was why I forced my way into the bathroom with her upon her return from the hospital, so I could help her wash herself. That is how I get her, at least once in a while, to stop faking sleep. I talk to her softly and ask her questions about her children and her husband and her past until her eyes open and she responds.

And today, that is how I got here, on the front lawn of Kelly and Louis's large house, looking for my neighbor's car and my children's faces. Tonight is my daughter's first sleepover, so I asked Betty to stop here on the way to Jessie's friend's house. A few months ago I would have told Jessie there was no way she could go to the sleepover, and particularly not if I wasn't home to help her pack and drive her there myself. But I am trying to be more open now. I am trying to let go of some of my need for control. I'm doing this not for myself—it is too painful for that—but for my children. Shortly after Mrs. McLaughlin told me about her dream of my brothers and sisters and the massive oak tree in our backyard, Eddie Jr. came home from camp and asked me if he could invite a boy he'd met over to play. It wasn't the request that struck me, but the look on Eddie's little face while he asked. He seemed afraid of me, and of what my response might be. I remember staring back at him in disbelief. Had I caused this? Had I said no every time my children wanted to leave our house or bring someone into it?

The truth was, I had, ever since my husband died.

I hadn't been aware that I was limiting Jessie's and Eddie's lives by keeping them close to me. I just knew that I needed them in my sight. I needed to know where they were at all times. I needed to call their names and see their faces turn toward me. I chose not to go to the hospital staff picnic this year for the same reason. I did not want to lose my children in a cluster of six- and nine-year-olds in a potato-sack race. I did not want to sit on a blanket and compare notes with other mothers. I wanted my children with me inside the walls of the house my husband had renovated over the course of countless weekends. I wanted Jessie and Eddie Jr. seated at the kitchen table where their father had drunk his black coffee every morning. I wanted them tucked into their twin beds in the small, neat bedrooms across the hall from each other. I wanted to be able to hear them breathe from where I lay down the hall on my half of the big bed. If either of my children had a bad dream in the middle of the night, I was at their side in an instant.

But the look on my son's face was a shock. It made me realize that I had gone too far. So now I am trying to do things differently. I am trying to make changes, and, as Jessie says, loosen up. But it is hard, and as I stand in the center of the lawn, my eyes on the road, I have to remind myself not to cry when my daughter bounds out of the car full of excitement because she gets to sleep across town from her mother and little brother for one night. And sure enough, this little girl whom I know so well, who has her father's quick, face-lighting grin, jumps out of the station wagon as soon as Betty pulls to the curb.

"Mommy, I almost forgot to pack my pajamas! Can you believe it?" she says, headed for me. Then she stops, distracted by the house in the background. "Wow, this place is huge."

"Which pajamas did you pack?" I say.

Jessie purses her lips, thinking. I can see in her face the teenager she will too soon become. "The blue ones with the pink seam."

"You don't look like you're working," Eddie Jr. says from behind his sister. He is unhappy because he wants to go to a sleepover, too. Or, at the very least, he does not want to be left all alone with Mrs. Larchmont on a Saturday.

"Mrs. McLaughlin, the woman I take care of, is inside," I say. "I just came out here for a few minutes to see you two. But I won't be late, Mr. Bean. You and I will have dinner together, just you and me. It'll be our date night."

He smiles, a slower version of his sister's.

"We have to go now, Mom," Jessie says. "I don't want to be late."

"You're not going to be late, I promise. I just want another minute or two of your time. Can you spare that, please?"

Jessie is bouncing on her toes now. "Mother, why? Are you trying to torture me?"

"Hey!" Eddie points behind me.

"Please don't do that, it's rude." Eddie is forever pointing at something, no matter how many times I scold him. His arm seems to shoot up from his side without his noticing. His favorite things to point at are large machines like bulldozers, eighteen-wheelers, and fire trucks. I don't let him roll the car windows down when I'm driving because I'm afraid his arm will shoot out and be hit by the passing eighteen-wheeler that has caught his excitement.

"But it's the man that almost hurt my lizard. Remember, when I told you about that?"

I turn around now and Jessie does, too. I see Louis standing at the base of the front steps, looking confused to see all of us standing on his lawn.

I wave to Louis and say in a low voice, "Eddie, that's someone from Mrs. McLaughlin's family. You've never met him. Don't point."

"No, Mom, that is the guy," Jessie says. "He was on our front lawn the day camp ended early because of the lice." She automatically touches her long black hair, which she has insisted I check nightly since the outbreak at camp. Contracting lice and then having to cut off her hair is her worst fear. "You never believe us."

But suddenly I do believe her. I watch Louis walk toward us. I hear Jessie say, "That is the guy." Something I have known for a while is rising to the surface.

He has almost reached us now, an awkward smile on his face. His hands are in his pockets. "Hello there," he says.

"Hello," I say, in a polite voice a little harder than my own.

Louis flicks his gaze from the ground to my face. He looks to Eddie. "We had a little run-in with a lizard, didn't we?"

Eddie giggles behind his hand.

Of course it was Louis. I realize now that I knew it all along. The facts come at me in a rush. He is the one who arranged for the lawn to be cut. For my car to be serviced. The gutters to be cleaned. He arranged for me to have the cushy job with his mother-in-law.

"I happened to be in the neighborhood that afternoon, and wanted to see if you needed any work done on your house." Louis's face brightens slightly. "I'd like to check inside and make sure your wiring is all right. Would you be comfortable with that?"

I hadn't looked closely enough to see the truth because I hadn't wanted to. I'd let myself be distracted. I grew attached to Mrs. McLaughlin, I believed in her stories and dreams. I even called information and gathered the phone numbers of a few of my brothers and sisters. The numbers are written on a piece of pink construction paper and taped to my refrigerator.

"That won't be necessary," I say. "Jessie, you don't want to be late for your sleepover. Betty," I call to the woman standing at the curb, "will you please take the children?"

"Don't yell at him, Mom," Jessie says, with her best imitation of teenaged weariness. "He was nice. He didn't do anything."

"I'm not going to yell at anyone," I say. "Eddie, I will see you soon. Jessie, call me later tonight please."

She looks horrified. "In front of all my friends? Please Mom, no, I can't."

"Then I will call you. Go on now."

Eddie kisses me and gives me one of his neck-strangling hugs that I love so much. Jessie presses her lips to my cheek so quickly, we barely make contact. Betty loads the children into the car and drives away.

I am left alone with Louis Leary. All I can think when I look at him is that he was the one who was with my husband when he died. I feel surprisingly calm. "Did you fix the railing on the front steps too?" I ask. "Is that why it doesn't wriggle anymore?"

"Um, yes," he says. "I didn't want you or the kids to fall. And I would like the chance to check the wiring inside the house. If you'll just let me know when it's convenient for me to stop by . . ."

"I don't want you to stop by."

"Oh." Louis looks uncomfortable. He glances at my face. "You're not going to quit, are you? Catharine needs you."

An idea occurs to me. "She didn't know, did she? Does Mrs. McLaughlin know why you hired me? And that you were snooping around my house?"

"No! I wasn't . . . She has no idea. Nobody knew, except for me. It was all me. And I never meant to invade your privacy. It was just a little exterior work. I thought that it must be difficult raising two children on your own. And I owe—Eddie meant a lot to me." Louis takes his hands out of his pockets. They are huge and callused from years outside in all weather on building sites. "I needed to help."

I raise my voice slightly, to make sure this man hears me. I can't believe he is making me say this. "You don't *need* to do anything. You don't have to help us. You're not responsible for my husband's death."

Louis's face freezes for a second, then he turns his head away.

My calm is beginning to break apart. I feel myself splitting into large pieces, like a volcano exploding from deep within. I wanted it to be Eddie. I wanted, magically, impossibly, for my husband to be the one caring for my family. I know Louis meant well. But he watched my husband—my heart—die and then dragged his ill mother-in-law and the rest of his family with him into what remained of my life. Then Mrs. McLaughlin made me believe that I should open myself up again. That I should relax my grip on my children and my husband. And I let myself be changed by these people. It is too late to stop that. I have been changed.

I watch, as if from the other side of this big lawn, as I split open, all the different pieces of my self afloat in boiling lava. I don't know what the answers are. Jessie is probably in her friend's bedroom by now doing things I don't allow her to do in her own room, like jump on the bed and listen to music too loud. Eddie is probably knee deep in an ice cream sundae at Dairy Queen because Betty has no sense of nutrition and reveres junk food as if it were a religion. I grasp for something to say. I talk to hear my own voice, to make sure I am still here.

"You don't think you're in love with me, do you?"

"No," Louis says, looking pained. "I love my wife."

I hug my cardigan to my chest. "Then, thank you." The words are hard to say. They are powerful words. "I won't quit, but you don't need to help me anymore. I don't want you near my house or my children unless I'm there. Okay? Do we have a deal?"

I look from his face down to my hands. I need to see the shape of my fingers and my wedding ring. The ring is a simple circle of gold Eddie put on my left hand in a church ten years ago, which I have taken off only during the late months of each of my pregnancies when my fingers swelled so badly that the ring no longer fit. I flex my fingers now. These are hands that mother, and hands that nurse. My hands have always been strong and capable. They have never let me down. They look unfamiliar to me now, though. There are new lines around the knuckles, and a rash of freckles I never noticed before.

"It's a deal," Louis says.

I remember standing beside Mrs. McLaughlin at the window in her room. She seemed to be mesmerized by something outside. I watched her and wondered if she were seeing my brothers and sisters, my childhood outside, tied to a massive oak tree. I wondered if she was right—that it was her job to set me free. I wondered, watching her old face pointed toward daylight, if I would know when that moment took place.

Perhaps being free feels like flying. Or, like I fear, it is the most terrifying thing that can happen to a person, because all of a sudden anything is possible. When my mother used to untie us at the end of an afternoon, my brothers and sisters and I would hesitate, staying close to the tree trunk for a long moment before bolting in every direction. We wanted badly to be untied, but there was safety in that rope looping us together, in that solid tree firmly rooted in our yard. We couldn't lose one another or ourselves then, whether we were playing games or singing songs or just kicking at one another and the tree and the air. There was security in the noise of our thirteen separate voices hoarse from calling out and reminding the world we were still there, still waiting.

Louis has his eyes on my face, wanting me to make everything okay. I am wondering if this is how he looks at his wife—as if it is her responsibility to make miracles happen—and if this is why she is so rarely in the same room with Louis, when the front door of the house clatters open.

It is Meggy, her voice jumbled with necessity, her long arm waving in our direction. "We need help. Come on!" she says, and then disappears back inside. There is a moment's pause while Louis and I stare at Meggy, then at the space where she used to be. Then I am running toward the house. Meggy's voice, with that familiar life or death urgency that has threaded its way through my professional career, shimmers in my ears. The hot air seems to part before me, allowing me to run faster than I ever thought possible. I have left Mrs. McLaughlin for too long. I have momentarily lost sight of my duty. I am in danger of letting everyone down, but still, with the August afternoon buzzing around and through me, I know that it is within my power to make it right. I run like I have watched my daughter Jessie run: my body weightless, my focus absolute. Aware only of the pumping of my arms, the complete efficiency of my body and the fact that with each step my feet barely touch the ground.

CATHARINE

I watch Lila slink into the room behind that nice boy who came to visit me in the hospital. Neither of them looks happy. When I scan the room, that is the case across the board. My daughters and daughter-in-law and little Mary are busy writing dates and times and other numbers on the white scraps of paper Kelly handed out. They are bent over and serious.

But there is something else in the room as well, something besides serious. I can't put my finger on what it is. It has to do with the way Gracie has her hands wrapped around her stomach, and the way Lila is looking at Weber, and the way Kelly is racing around, her cheeks flushed. There is something going on between these women that I don't know about. I am no longer up to date on my grandchildren's lives. They are living at a distance from me for the first time since I can remember. I realize this all at once, watching their faces. How could I have let this happen?

"Do you need help with that?" Noreen says into my ear.

I look down at my blank white sheet. "No," I say. "I just think this is stupid."

Heads rise up. I notice that several of my daughters have gray hairs mixed with brown.

I agree, I hear a voice say, from across the room. I follow the sound with my eyes and see my mother sitting on the couch next to Theresa. She is wearing white gloves and the same gray dress with a belted waist that she wore the day that I fell. I have not seen her since then. I am

298

not happy to see her now. I am still angry with her for turning on my television and luring nosy Nurse Stronk into the room.

But the sight of her is also a disappointment, because I have been hoping that the next parent to visit me would be my father. I have been missing him lately. My father was always so clear and organized. Lately I have been dipping in and out of confusion, and I want to look into my father's blue eyes. I want for his clarity. He always made me feel calm and purposeful. My mother just confuses me further.

If I ignore her, she might go away. I turn toward Weber and say, "It's so nice to see you again. Come sit here by me."

He smiles and Lila smiles, too. She trails two steps behind, and when he sits down on the ottoman beside my chair, she stands beside him in the spot Noreen vacated when she went outside to see her children. I would like to meet Noreen's children, after hearing so much about them. In a few minutes perhaps I will slip outside and do just that.

"I met you in the street," Kelly says to Weber, a confused look on her face.

Lila says, "This is my . . . boyfriend, Weber."

"You don't know your daughter's boyfriend?" Meggy says.

"I ran into him outside the barbershop."

Gracie leans forward sharply in her chair, almost knocking Grayson's hand off her shoulder. "Outside of the barbershop?"

"Yes," Kelly says. She looks as if she's spun from confusion to something much worse, something more uncomfortable.

"What were you doing at the barbershop, Mom?" Gracie's strange voice seems to immobilize Kelly. I watch the mother and daughter face each other. This is torturous, because I don't know who, or how, to help. I have never known Gracie to speak up like this. For her, this is the equivalent of a direct attack.

At first it doesn't seem as if Kelly is going to respond. The entire room waits. "It's no longer relevant," Kelly says, and turns to Weber. "Can I take the present from you? We have a pile of them on the table."

Weber hands over the wrapped present he has been holding on his lap. Kelly walks the box with great purpose over to the dining-room table. I can almost see a line of anger, of something, run across the room between Kelly and Gracie. Between my oldest living daughter and her oldest daughter. The line lengthens, and crackles with electricity with each step Kelly takes.

"What is going on here?" I say. "For heaven's sake, can't we even show a little politeness to a guest?"

There is another murmur from the women in the room. "Sorry . . . nice to meet you, Weber . . . Would you like an iced tea? Didn't know Lila had a boyfriend . . . Full of surprises."

So, these are your children, my mother says. I cannot be sure from across the room, but I think there are tears in her eyes.

These are my daughters, I say, wishing that they would behave more appropriately. Didn't I tell them from the time they were young: Be on your best behavior while at a party? I remind my mother that I also have three sons. Johnny, Pat, and Ryan.

My mother nods. *Ryan is the crippled boy who almost died in the fire. The one who reminds you of me.*

I cannot answer this. I concentrate on Gracie. The baby is coming so soon. It will be any day now. I don't have long to wait.

"Mother," Kelly says. "Everyone has filled out their slips of paper. We're waiting on you."

"I want to know what we win if we're right about the size and due date," Meggy says. "I hope you put up some decent money for the pot."

"I was thinking more along the lines of a gag gift." Kelly sounds tired. "Are you done, Mother?"

"That's bogus," Meggy says.

I hope that my mother doesn't notice Meggy and Kelly's endless bickering. I know I shouldn't care, but I want her to think well of my children. What I have made is in this room. This is my life's work. This is what I have left and this is what I will leave behind.

"Gram doesn't have to play the game if she doesn't want to," Gracie says. "Let her do what she wants, Mom."

"It's your party," Kelly says. "I just thought it would be fun. I'm sorry if it was wrong to try to create some fun."

"Are you angry at *me*?" Gracie says to Kelly. Grayson's hand has not left Gracie's shoulder since she sat down, but he seems speechless. I reflect that the women in our family often render the men quiet. Especially since my husband died. All balance is lost.

Beside my chair I hear Weber whisper to Lila, "Is your family always like this?"

I cannot hear her answer. I hope she is shaking her head. I hope that she tells him that we are not like this. That when Patrick was alive nothing like this would have happened. There was order to our family then, and small children running around filling the rooms with laughter. It is only in the past few years, when perhaps I was not as firm as I should have been, that things have come to this. I hope Lila tells Weber that when the baby comes, when the laughter of children fills our rooms again, everything will settle down. This family will be whole and we will find our way back to solid ground.

Something in Kelly's face crumples. "No," she says. "I was saying good-bye when you saw me this afternoon, all right? I was trying to say good-bye."

"Outside the barbershop?" Theresa asks politely, trying to clear things up for everyone.

"All right," Gracie says. "All right. Don't cry."

Kelly gives a single sob, which she masks as a cough into her cupped hands.

I wait for Meggy or Lila to jump in and attack Kelly for trying to conduct a private conversation in front of everyone. But neither of them says a word. Lila is standing so close to Weber, she might as well be touching him, and Meggy has found a seat on the arm of the couch beside my mother. Both women appear almost sedate.

"Gracie," Angel says in a bright voice. "What do you think the sex is going to be? Do you have a feeling either way?"

"I keep picturing a girl," Gracie says. "I saw her once."

I am pleased that no one in the room laughs or even smiles at this.

What used to annoy me now gives me pleasure. I am glad that my children listened when Patrick told them stories about leprechauns and lovelorn boys and people who knew hunger and want. He told those stories instead of ones about his own poor childhood. He rarely mentioned his parents, or his brother. But I think for him—and I am understanding this now, too late—everything, all of his experiences, his disappointments, and his faith, was in the stories he told. Our children heard Patrick's stories and absorbed them. Perhaps, I think, looking around the room, these gray-streaked versions of my children have even had their own visions from time to time. Perhaps they have lives and hearts I don't know about. The idea gives me hope.

My husband has been in my dreams lately. He is holding my little girl on his lap, or hugging the twins against his shirtfront. He looks very uncomfortable sitting on the small couch in my room at the assisted-living center. The little girl tries to wiggle off his lap and run to me, but Patrick won't let go. He holds on to her arms until I can see the pressure of his thumbs against her skin, until she cries out. *Gentle,* I say, *please be gentle.* Her face is too pink, as if she is preparing for the fever that is to come and take her away from Patrick and me for good. I think that perhaps Patrick feels the heat of her skin and that is why he is holding so fast. He doesn't want to let her go.

"Are you all right, Gram?" Lila asks.

"Of course," I say, and hand over my white slip of paper to Kelly.

"Do you have to be so difficult, Mother?" Kelly says. "You didn't write anything down."

I feel the hot touch of my feverish girl. Patrick is forcing her on me, making me see that I couldn't change what happened, that no matter what, she was still going to die. I push her away, I push him away. I push the truth away while at the same time feeling it settle into my skin like the finest, the most inescapable dust. I breathe it into my lungs. I am covered with it.

"I'm an old woman," I say, "leave me alone."

Kelly gives me a hard look over the bowl she has filled with everyone's guesses for the baby.

"You're not old," Theresa says.

"Gram," Mary says, her first words in at least a half hour.

Now you've upset them, my mother says, from beside Theresa.

She is right. My children and grandchildren are looking at me with expressions of discomfort on their faces. But they know I am old. They know I won't be with them forever. How can this hurt them?

People don't like to hear the truth, Mother says. *It's unkind.*

But they need to be strong, I say. Stronger than this, anyway. How will they ever find happiness, ever move forward in their lives, if they aren't strong enough to hear that their mother is old? I scan the faces in the room. How can they need me this much? My baby daughter cries now from a room in the back of the house, and Patrick walks past me holding the twins. I want to make my way out of this room. I want to breathe in the hot summer air. I want to leave them all behind, but at the same time I know that I can't move.

"Would you like more iced tea?" Lila says.

"I think she's getting tired," I hear Angel say in a hushed voice. "Where's that nurse?"

"I'm going to open the gift you brought the baby first, Gram," Gracie says.

I can feel my grandchildren and children wanting, vying for my attention like a pull on my sleeve. There is laughter outside the window, and I know that if I cross the room, I will see the Ballen children tied to a massive oak tree in the center of the yard. I glance beside me, to make sure that Noreen is still there, grown, safe, and free. But she's disappeared. Lila is in her place. I forget where Noreen's gone, although I know she told me. It will come to me in a minute.

"You sure you're okay?" Lila asks.

My mother says, *Why are they all so careful of you, Catharine? They seem frightened of you. What did you do to them over the years?* She shakes her head. *I should have been allowed to see my grandchildren when they were small. You thought you could control everything, and make happy endings all on your own. You taught your children that that was what was expected of them. How could you do that? They thought they had to make their own lives right with no help or good luck or charity, and that if anything went wrong, it was their own fault. Look at all the guilty faces in this room. For heaven's sakes. They all think they've failed you, and just plain failed life.*

I wanted to teach my children to be strong. I wanted them to take care of themselves. I didn't want them to hurt. I didn't want them to die.

She says, *You didn't want them to act crazy like me.*

I feel weak deep inside of my body. Did everything have to get so clear, so honest, at the end of my life? Now, when there is nothing I can do about it? Now, when it's too late?

It's never too late, my mother says. She has one hand on Theresa's shoulder and the other is stroking Meggy's knee. *I got the chance to see my grandchildren, didn't I? Anything is possible.*

I remember who I'm talking to. I should not be listening to my mother. I shouldn't let what she says matter. I say, *You used to have conversations with dead people in our hotel suite. You hid in the hall closet during thunderstorms. You behaved so inappropriately that Father couldn't bring you to business dinners.*

You're the one behaving inappropriately, my mother says. *You've been looking forward to this party all week. You had a hard time falling asleep last night because you were so excited. You should be talking to Gracie and your daughters right now, not to me. Take care of them.*

You're right, I say. She is right about that much. I should concentrate on the present and stop listening for the cries of children who are grown or dead for fifty years. I turn to Gracie, who is unwrapping the gift that I made and that Noreen wrapped in bright blue paper. It is a two-part gift, and she unwraps the small box first.

It is a framed picture of Gracie and Lila as girls. They have their arms around each other's shoulders. Gracie is smiling, Lila is not, but they look linked together, two Irish faces, bodies entwined, fitted like two pieces that belong in the same puzzle.

Gracie smiles in the same soft, polite manner she has in the picture, as if she doesn't know what to make of this. "Thank you, Gram," she says. "It's sweet."

"I remember that afternoon," Lila says. "We had just finished fighting over the last cupcake. I threw up right after the picture was taken."

Kelly says, "I remember that day, too. You were both a piece of work. No sooner was I done being angry at one of you than the other would act up." She laughs, and sets down a tray of cookies on the coffee table. It's her first moment of stillness all afternoon.

You see, my mother says to me, *you are doing something now. It's not too late. You're showing them what to do, what to hold on to. Catharine, you're not as hard or as useless as you think you are.*

The room feels lighter now. Meggy hasn't said anything negative in at least ten minutes. The boy with the crew cut sitting by my knee has turned Lila into a kitten. Mary is leaning against her mother on the couch, allowing Theresa rare contact. Gracie is ripping open the second present, the larger box. It is the baby blanket that I knitted out of the softest yarn I could find. Gracie holds it up for everyone to see and then drapes it over her belly, as if to warm the baby inside her.

"I didn't know you could knit, Mother," Kelly says. "It's lovely."

"I taught myself," I say.

"Gram, I love it. It's perfect," Gracie says, and then she starts to cry.

She cries into the blanket first, and then into Grayson's handkerchief, and then into a sheet of paper towel someone gets from the kitchen. Her pale cheeks are wet in no time. She cries as if she'll never stop. At first everyone just stares at her, and then at the floor and the ceiling and one another, trying to give her some privacy. I can see that this is something that she needs to do, so I just leave her be, but I can see how much her tears upset the others in the room.

The McLaughlins are not big criers, but when one of us is moved to cry, it is done alone, the noise muffled into a pillow. The way Gracie is crying, unabashedly, tears pouring down her cheeks, her breath caught in sobs, is completely unfamiliar. It bothers me at first, too, I have to admit. She should pull herself together at least until the party is over, but she doesn't seem to be even trying to find control. She has completely let go and forgotten we are here. I can't tell for certain what kind of tears she is shedding. She appears to shift from almost laughing to sobbing so hard, I worry that it is bad for the baby.

"Gentle," I say, "gentle."

Grayson still has his hand on her shoulder, and Kelly crosses the room and rubs Gracie's back in the smooth circles a mother uses to comfort an upset child. Gracie doesn't seem to notice.

"Do you want to go outside for some air?" Grayson says.

"Is she all right?" Meggy says.

"The baby," Angel says.

Gracie doesn't seem to hear anything. She does not respond. Her eyes are shut and she rocks back and forth slightly. Her cheeks are shiny and the tears keep falling.

It occurs to me then that this is how I should have cried when I lost my baby girl, and again when I lost the twins. I should have released my tears instead of holding them in. I shouldn't have been embarrassed or worried over appearing weak. I should have given my children, my babies, that much. And besides, as the tears go on, Gracie does not look weak to me. She looks honest. There is something of my mother and my first child in her eyes, and I can see the unborn child that she already loves there, too. In that moment I can see everything, everyone, the entire McLaughlin family, shining out of her tear-stained face.

"Oh dear," Angel says. She looks next to my chair, and I notice that that is the direction Meggy is looking in, too. And Theresa. And even my mother. They are all looking at Lila, their eyes beseeching. Asking for something.

"What?" Lila says. "What do you think I can do?"

"Go see if she's all right," Meggy says in a low voice.

Lila shrugs, but she walks over to Gracie. She crouches down in front of her and puts her hands on her sister's knees. "Are you in pain?" she asks. "Has labor started? Gracie, open your eyes. Look at me."

The two girls are still in that position for a long time. Lila almost on her knees, her hands on her sister, her eyes on her face. Gracie leaning toward her. I think of the framed picture that now lies on the floor by Gracie's feet. I glance over at the couch to make sure my mother is still here, to make sure she is still within arm's reach of my daughters.

In the same calm voice, Lila says, "Tell me where the pain is, Gracie. Tell me you're all right."

Gracie half-opens her eyes, like someone reluctantly waking from a deep sleep. She says, in a voice so soft it is almost a whisper, which seems meant only for Lila's ears but which everyone present hears: "I think our baby is coming."

After an intake of breath, the entire room erupts in pandemonium. Meggy makes a beeline for the front door. Angel starts weeping. Kelly runs into the kitchen, whether to boil water or use the phone I don't know. Mary moves to the far side of the room, where she stands with her back to the wall. Grayson keeps saying, "Are you sure? It's too soon." Weber offers to use his beeper or cell phone or some special fireman's device to call the paramedics. When no one answers him, he pulls a black box out of his pocket and speaks into it. He speaks in what must be code, because it sounds like he repeats over and over, "I love you, I love you."

Lila stays on the floor in front of Gracie. Together the two girls start breathing oddly, in rhythm with each other. They sound like the old-time train Patrick and I took from St. Louis to New York after our wedding. The huge black train puffed and chanted as it climbed over hills, straining each time as if it would never make the top. The two girls, my grandaughters, chant, their young voices clear, "Hee hee hoo. Hee hee hoo."

Noreen comes in and almost falls on me, her cheeks flushed and her eyes shining. At first I think she is there because she has something important to say. She has the look of a woman who has made a discovery. But then she pulls her stethoscope out of her purse and presses it to my chest. It is a full minute before I can make her understand that I am fine and that Gracie is the one who needs attention.

I don't tell Noreen that I am terribly tired and unsure whether I can stand of my own accord. I want her to leave me be, and besides, those things don't matter in this moment. In this moment I am seated in a miraculous room that is singing with the voices of the people I love. My babies cry out to greet the next infant, the one that will grab hold of life and this family and turn everything around. My husband is standing in the doorway beside Louis, both men helpless with relief.

Noreen is now giving orders, and kindly allowing everyone something to do. Mary calls the hospital. Angel is in charge of Gracie's purse. Meggy makes sure there are no appliances left on in the kitchen. Kelly finds a blanket in an upstairs closet so her daughter doesn't have to lie under an itchy hospital-issued one.

My oldest child, my poor girl, gives a sharp cry of thirst from the back room. The twins seem to have disappeared, knowing that I will see them in a few short hours in the newborn's dewy face. Lila and Gracie continue to breathe together, the only still figures amid all the chaos. I catch my mother's eye across the room, and I wink. I have never winked before in my life, because it is not a ladylike thing to do. But there's a first time for everything. For everyone. Besides, I want to reach across the space between my mother and me with some kind of gesture. If I were able, I would weave my way to the other side of the room and take her hand. The boundaries, the squabbles, and the resentments have dropped away. Time has dropped away. I am lucky enough to recognize this for what it is: one of those perfect, full-to-bursting moments you wait a lifetime for, when it all comes together.

About the Author

Ann Napolitano is a graduate of Connecticut College, and received her MFA from New York University, where she studied with Paule Marshall and Dani Shapiro. She lives in New York City.